KNIGHTS
OF THE
BORROWED DARK
THE FOREVER COURT

Books by Dave Rudden

Knights of the Borrowed Dark

The Forever Court

DAVE RUDDEN

Random House New York

 Published in the United States by
Random House Children's Books, a division of
Penguin Random House LLC, New York. Originally published
in hardcover by Penguin Books Ltd., a division of
Penguin Random House LLC, London, in 2017.

Visit us on the Web! randomhousekids.com

Educators and librarians, for a variety of teaching tools,
visit us at RHTeachersLibrarians.com

Library of Congress Cataloging-in-Publication Data
is available upon request.

ISBN 978-0-553-52301-0 (trade)—ISBN 978-0-553-52302-7 (lib. bdg.)—
ISBN 978-0-553-52303-4 (ebook)

Printed in the United States of America
10 9 8 7 6 5 4 3 2 1
First American Edition

To Graham Tugwell, Deirdre Sullivan, and Sarah Maria Griff—

Doomsburies, yo.

Fire was our first magic and our first science,
and we have harnessed it hardly at all.

Nick Harkaway, *The Gone-Away World*

People think that stories are shaped by people.
In fact, it's the other way around.

Terry Pratchett, *Witches Abroad*

TABLE OF CONTENTS

THE WORDS OF THE CROITS:

SHE LOVED.

SHE STOLE.

AND WE KNEW FIRE.

PROLOGUE

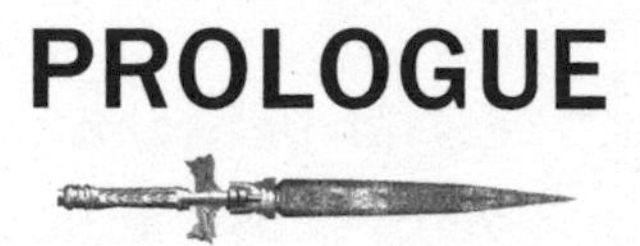

FAVORED

THE DAY DAWNED AS gray as gossamer, and Uriel fought his sister on their grandmother's grave.

The mausoleum was the largest on the hill—stone and gold and dark electrum, slick and sharp and spired. Much like the old woman herself, if Grandfather's stories were to be believed, and Uriel believed everything that came out of Grandfather's mouth.

Cold lines and jagged edges—the Family values of the Croits.

Blade found blade in shrieks and hums of steel. Bare feet kicked dew from the ice-smooth marble. Uriel nearly slipped, catching a spire with one hand and whipping his sword at Ambrel with the other.

She dodged. Of course. Uriel was stronger but Ambrel quicker, and so far he had hit nothing but the sound of her laughter. His elbows and knuckles ached where they had banged against the mausoleum's crown of stone spines, but he was laughing with her. He couldn't help it.

"You're never," he said between parries, "going to forgive me for my growth spurt, are you?"

"It's *our* growth spurt," she called. "You stole it."

She leapt into the maze of graves below.

Uriel pursued his sister through the Garden of the Waiting—a city of the dead. No two tombs were the same. The necropolis was a mismatched assortment of pale towers and low-peaked vaults, ancient dolmens and weather-bruised sarcophagi, linked only by the ever-present crest of a crow perched upon a skeletal hand.

There was a saying from Outside—*the past is another country*—but here the centuries were packed close as cousins, the history of the Croits rendered in statue and stone. Some of the paths between the graves were as wide as city avenues—borders of trimmed grass, peonies winking in the dirt. Along others, the statues had advanced, reaching out to their brothers and sisters across the way, coming together in a tangle of limbs and blank white faces.

Memorial plaques dusted the ground, the dandruff of the deceased. Uriel didn't spare them a glance. He knew all their names already.

Was that movement? He picked his way through a

thicket of great-aunts, pausing for a moment on the shoulders of

EUTHALIA CROIT

~ DIED IN BATTLE ~

to get his bearings.

To another family, using the resting places of one's ancestors as a training ground might be considered disrespectful. *Irrelevant,* Uriel thought. That was the point of being a Croit: what *other* families felt didn't matter. The only reason Uriel even bothered imagining others' feelings at all was because Grandfather said that it was useful to think like your enemy, and that's what other people were. Not because they had *done* anything—*doing* things to Croits was, historically, quite violently discouraged—but because they weren't Family; they weren't Favored. It was as simple as that.

Uriel swung down from Euthalia, giving her a fond pat on the knee. He was sure she'd be happy to know she was contributing to his training. Croit blood was in short supply, after all. You didn't get to stop serving the Family just because you were dead.

Bar the cawing of fat gray crows, the necropolis was silent. Uriel gave one a nod as he passed, touching the embroidered bird on his shirt for luck.

If he were Ambrel—which wasn't a stretch to

imagine: there was and always had been a mere half second between the beat of their hearts—he'd be moving slowly, carefully, his pale skin and graying hair hiding him among the statues, the natural camouflage of a Croit.

There. A hint. A flicker of motion. A limb moving where it shouldn't.

Uriel prowled after it, his own limbs soundless, his breathing stilled. The approving glances of dead relatives followed him as he hunted, his ambush already planned.

There was a curve ahead, where the Middle Ages lapped up against the Renaissance. Uriel had always liked this district of the Garden—history was his favorite subject, and the sculptors had included every war wound. Armor hung in tatters, each strand of leather and link of chain lovingly rendered in stone. Uriel had spent hours in the archives of the Weeping Gallery, matching stories to scars.

It was a good place for an ambush, but, moreover, it would annoy Ambrel *terribly* to be brought down in his favorite spot, especially after she'd chosen the Garden as their battleground.

With siblings, it was the little things.

The figure ahead had paused. If Uriel had been silent before, now he was a ghost. He barely disturbed the air as he crept to the top of one of the mausoleums—

—and geckoed along its roof. He did not raise his head, for fear the weight of his gaze would alert her.

He tensed, blade trembling a hair's breadth above the marble, and lunged.

Nothing.

Uriel landed with a graceful roll that was appreciated by absolutely nobody. He spun in a circle, blade raised to block an attack that didn't come.

Well, this is embarrassing.

And, just like that, his sword was gone, smashed from fingers already turning numb. He opened his mouth to yelp and a fist filled it, the world exploding to streaky darkness. It was almost a relief to hit the ground.

Uriel spat grass. "Grandfather."

A man of angles, sparse and strange, with a bloom of iron on his cheek, Grandfather looked like he had been carved from the heart of a glacier, his skin colorless and tight on his skull. At times, Uriel expected to see the light shining through him, yet at others the old man was the most solid thing in the world, as dense and heavy as a neutron star.

His right hand flexed with a creak of sinews. His left sleeve hung empty by his side.

"What did you do wrong?"

It was a common question for the old man to ask.

"Focused too closely on the target," Uriel responded immediately, pushing himself to his knees. "And excluded the thought that I might become a target myself."

Nothing in his expression betrayed the fact that Ambrel was inching up behind Grandfather. Not a muscle. Not an eyelash. His eyes were Grandfather's eyes: cool, calm, and the color of glass.

"We must all be ready to die when the time comes, Uriel," Grandfather growled. "But we are Croits." He said the name with the hard pride the sharp syllable demanded. Ambrel's blade glittered behind him.

"Our blood is rarer than the purest diamond, the finest gold. Sacrifice is expected. But only when—"

Ambrel struck, a perfect thrust, and Grandfather stepped around it as if they were two parts of the same machine. Her momentum carried her into his elbow with a *crack*, but as she slumped back, dazed, she caught Uriel's dropped sword with her foot, flicking it up to slap into her brother's palm. He came to his feet with a snarl.

Grandfather held up his hand.

Uriel halted his lunge immediately, flipping his blade round in a salute. Ambrel queasily mirrored it from the ground.

"When She wills it," they said in unison, completing Grandfather's phrase.

It always sounded more impressive coming from him, though, thought Uriel. The head of the Family had a voice like a saw bisecting a coffin lid. Uriel's was still in that unpredictably squeaky phase that made him reluctant to use it at all.

"Good," Grandfather responded. "It's time."

Two hearts skipped the same beat, half a second apart.

THE ANCESTRAL HOME OF the Croits was called Eloquence, and it was a ruin. The island on which it stood was only a few kilometers across, split in two by an ax-wound of a valley, sheer and bare and brutal, as if someone had tried to murder the world and this was where the blade had fallen. Straggly, desiccated trees halfheartedly dotted its flanks. The air smelled of dust and the distant sea, and it was so cold that the weak sunlight felt like ice water on Uriel's skin. This wasn't the kind of landscape that was content to be photographed by tourists or painted by nice men with beards. This was the kind of landscape that made poets fall in love with it and then drove them steadily mad.

And within it lay the corpse of a castle.

Eloquence had once clung to the western cliff, all needle towers and battlements, its insectile silhouette dominating the sky. But that had been a very long time ago. The castle had fallen, and the fall had not been kind. Its former perch was nothing but a swath of shattered stone, and the castle itself lay in crushed folds a hundred meters below.

It must have been like an iceberg calving, Uriel thought as he and his sister left the Garden of the Waiting and picked their way up the slope to Eloquence. He imagined that centuries-ago fall: a great groan shaking the air, stone separating from stone, the shock of looking out of the window and seeing the whole world move *up*.

Ambrel flashed him a nervous grin. He felt it too—the same mixture of dread and excitement that had driven them out to fight in the sleepless dawn. This was the day. This was *their* day. Everything they had learned, everything they had been, their every heartbeat—

It had all come to this.

Slowly, carefully, they entered Eloquence. The impact against the valley floor had violently reordered the fortress, like a body dropped from a height. Once-wide hallways had been forced into new shapes; chambers had collapsed while others opened; floors turned to ceilings, ceilings turned to floors. And everywhere the wires—taut and gleaming, crisscrossing every path, dividing the gloom into strict geometric shapes. Some were blunt braids. Others were pin-thin and razor-sharp.

It had been their black embrace that had held the castle together on its semi-fatal plunge, the way ivy bound a wall even as it strangled it, and, despite the centuries, not a single one had slackened or sagged.

Specks of dust peppered the air. Some drifted against the wires and cut themselves in half.

Down and down the three Croits went, through the departed glory of the Hall of Receiving, between the splintered pillars of the Majesty Seat. Everywhere, the Crow and the Claw could be seen. Eloquence twisted the sound of their steps into overlapping echoes until it was an effort to separate their own footsteps from the multitude of ghostly feet trailing them.

Had any other Croit been making this journey, their path would have been lined with Family in silent support. The insult washed over Uriel without purchase. He had everyone he needed right here.

And, ahead, the door. *Her* door. Grandfather disappeared through it without a word and, just for a moment, Uriel and Ambrel hesitated. This was where the light gave out. Soon, if all went well, the twins would no longer need it.

Their final descent was completed in darkness so total that Uriel's eyes felt like they had been filled with oil, but he and Ambrel had practiced this walk. Slipping between the unseen wires felt as natural as breathing: an arm crooked here, a leg angled there. Once, though, Uriel felt a brush on his cheekbone and knew that he had lost a layer of skin. But that was only right. No one had descended without shedding blood since Grandfather was a boy. There was always a price to pay.

Finally, the feel of the air changed. Uriel could

sense space around him where before there had been the close press of wire and stone. *The Shrine*. Ambrel was beside him, Grandfather somewhere ahead, and above—

Her.

Suspended. Silent. Gigantic. There wasn't a single photon of light in the chamber for Uriel to see by, but he felt Her presence all the same, displacing the darkness with Her grandeur. His eyes *ached* trying to pierce the gloom, but nothing of Her shape was given to him.

As is proper. They would see Her when they were Favored. *If* they were Favored. For a moment, Uriel felt a decidedly un-Croit-like thrill of fear.

"Kneel," Grandfather commanded.

The twins did so.

"Long ago," Grandfather intoned, "we were given a duty. A calling. And now here you kneel, where the first of us knelt, ready to know whether that calling will be yours. Whether you are Favored. Whether you are *Croits*. The Redemptress looks upon you and, if you are worthy, the world will tremble with the fire She bestows.

"Have each of you chosen the shape that fire will take?"

Ambrel answered first. "My Prayer will be a song, Grandfather. My voice, Her inferno."

"Good," Grandfather said. "And Uriel?"

His mind flew back to long mornings of meditation,

of holding a shape in his mind until he saw it behind his eyelids, until it filled his dreams. The Redemptress gave much, but asked equal in return, and the necropolis was full of those who had been unworthy.

Faith was fire in the blood of a Croit.

"It will be a sword, Grandfather." *And so will I.*

"Our forefather told us that She will return." Grandfather's voice was full of dark promise. "She will lead us in the War That Will Come. The Adversary will appear, and we will smite him down, and in return . . ."

Sweat was rising on Uriel's cheeks. A feeling that was at once part of him and something distant squeezed his head in a vise of pain. He pressed his palms flat against the stone floor to steady himself, and felt Ambrel's little finger find his own, barely touching.

What if we're not—

A worse thought came.

What if Ambrel is, and I'm—

No. He refused to even entertain the thought. They had lived their whole lives a half second apart. There could be no division now.

In return we will be saved.

His heart was hammering so loudly it felt like the whole chamber shook. Grandfather was still speaking, but for the first time in his life Uriel didn't heed him. Agony striped the blackness in his head. His breath came shallow and shaky, and as Ambrel's finger trembled against his, Uriel wanted to shout with relief.

It was starting, and it felt like destiny.

Light spilled from Uriel, rich and gold as honey, hot and searing as a star. Two stars. His twin sister's hair rose as crackling fire, the air twisting with unbearable heat. It cried for release, but Uriel tamed it, as a Croit was meant to do.

Because they were special.

The darkness around them had fled. No, not just fled: it was no longer there. *I will never fear darkness again,* Uriel thought, blood dripping down his skinned cheek. Grandfather was revealed before them, grim and towering. However, as tall as the old man was, he was dwarfed by what loomed behind—its rictus grin, its gaps and gleams.

The glory of Her, Uriel thought. *The terror.*

Their Redemptress.

Grandfather favored the twins with a rare, triumphant smile.

"Happy birthday."

1

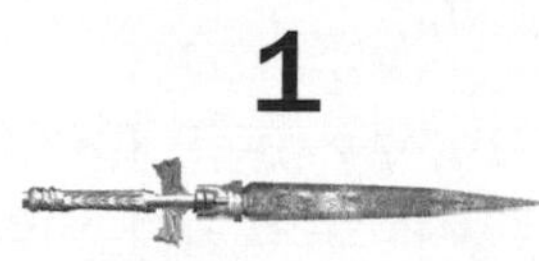

PAPER CUTS

DENIZEN HARDWICK LOVED BOOKSHOPS.

It was a new romance for him. There simply hadn't been any near the orphanage in which he'd grown up. Then again, Denizen hadn't been a dramatically rich orphan, just a regular no-parents orphan, so it wasn't like he could have bought anything anyway. But now Denizen lived in a city, with bookshops on every corner, and you couldn't get him out of them with a crowbar.

Whether a great sprawling emporium or a tiny tucked-away burrow that only opened for half an hour on wet Tuesdays in March, there was a magic to bookshops. A quiet sort of magic, which wasn't Denizen's area, but a magic nonetheless.

And he'd never seen one as beautiful as this.

Oak shelves gleamed caramel with varnish, filling the air with the faintest scent of forests. The shop's actual dimensions were a mystery: antique furniture colluding artistically to carve up the quiet, turning each aisle into a clandestine affair between customer and book.

Outside, the sun was half hidden in cloud, but somehow in here it was rich and golden—the sunlight of Narnia, of Lórien, of Faerûn and Hyboria and Klatch.

It's almost too perfect, Denizen thought. Charts on the walls and overstuffed, mismatched armchairs lent the place a reassuring feel of clutter and age. There was even a globe on the counter, as wide as Denizen's shoulders, tattooed with the curves and jags of the world.

Denizen let the door close behind him gently. A little silver bell chimed—the tonal equivalent of a polite cough.

The owner's head rose at the sound. He fitted the decor perfectly, as if the bookshop had grown up around him like the shell of a hermit crab. Tweed-clad—*of course tweed-clad,* Denizen thought—with tawny curls bobbing down round the dome of his liver-spotted scalp, the man was the *epitome* of a bookseller. There could never have been any other profession for a man like this, except maybe were-owl.

His voice was the scrape of a finger down a page.

"May I help you?"

Denizen scrubbed a hand through his shaggy red hair. Encouraged by the coming summer, new freckles were pushing from the paleness of his skin like seeds, the darkest of them a single inkblot on his lower lip. He peered warily from the turned-up collar of a too-big coat.

Wariness wasn't unusual for Denizen Hardwick. It was how he'd looked at the world his entire life, as though he knew there was a blow coming, but not from whom or where. It had been a strange few months, however, and they had left their mark in peculiar and indefinable ways. Denizen still looked like he was expecting a blow, but now there was the distinct impression he might hit you back.

He stared at the bookseller with sharp gray eyes.

"I like your shop," Denizen said. He really did—though, for all his admiration of each carefully chosen detail, his gaze kept drifting to the brightly colored flyers taped to the door, their cheap ink smudged from being passed through too many hands. "It's quiet."

"Yes, most days," the old man said, "but I get by."

"I get quiet days at work too," Denizen said, glancing down at the wrinkled cover of a detective novel, "but . . . I think this is going to be a loud one."

The bookseller's smile became confused. "I'm sorry?"

Denizen chose his words carefully, anger pulsing a tight band round his temples. That had been happening more and more recently. Normally, he could lose himself for hours in a bookshop . . . but lately that peace had been eluding him.

He kept thinking—*fragile*. He kept thinking—*flammable*.

"I'm just supposed to be doing recon," he said. "Watch. Observe. That kind of thing."

His eyes never left the bookseller, but the captions from the flyers swam in his head.

MISSING!

HAVE YOU SEEN OUR . . .

HELP

It was the last that stung him the most. A picture, a phone number, and a one-word plea.

The old man's smile remained, but his thin lips had drawn back, retreating from his teeth. His pupils glimmered blackly.

"It took a while to be certain," Denizen continued conversationally. "Taking photos. Staking out the shop. Even went through your trash, not that you have any. That was another clue. People always forget the little things. And so do you, I guess."

One of the ceiling lightbulbs flickered. Neither the bookseller nor Denizen looked at it. The tweed grain of the old man's suit shifted, like muscles under skin. A single curl fell from his mottled scalp, a comma white and surprised.

"My orders are to let *her* deal with you," Denizen continued. "But I can't. Not after . . ."

Blackness in the bookseller's eyes. A twist of fire in Denizen's throat.

After what? the old man whispered, his voice the fluttering of dry, dead wings.

"You put their pictures up on your door."

The Tenebrous attacked.

The old man's face came apart in a howl of paper and dust. Human teeth clattered to the floor, forced out by fangs more akin to those of an eel—serrated, back-hooked barbs. Limbs popped, shadows rushing free to clot the gaps. The lightbulb sizzled as the Tenebrous bounded across the bookshop floor, reality twitching uneasily in its wake.

"Now!" Denizen shouted.

Simon Hayes shimmered into view on his left, hands ablaze. The eel-in-tweed tried to twist in midair, but the tall boy snarled and a dart of fire folded the creature in half.

It flew across the shop, smashing through a shelf in a flurry of books. Smoke rose from its flanks, but the flame vanished as quickly as it had appeared. A single spark spiraled downward to hiss harmlessly against the floor.

Denizen sighed with relief. The power that roiled beneath his skin was many things, but *subtle* wasn't one of them. Ravening beasts from the dark end of forever

Denizen could handle—sort of—but he would never be party to the burning of a book.

"Good job," Denizen said, turning to his friend. "Very controlled. And you're getting really good at bending light. I completely lost track of you."

"I know," Simon said, grinning wryly. "You nearly caught me in the door."

"Oh, sorry," Denizen said, "I got—"

His next words were lost to a rising purr of wind. Books were eviscerated of pages; the flyers on the door beat helplessly at their tape before ripping free as well.

"—distracted," he finished.

The bookseller's skin dangled in folds from a shape now gaunt and towering. One hand still hung human at the end of its arm, the other a bulging claw of paper and bone. The heavy cabinet it lifted must have weighed more than Simon and Denizen together, but the beast flung it one-handed all the same.

It was exactly what Denizen had been waiting for.

Holding back when the Tenebrous attacked had been a struggle. If he were being honest, it was a struggle from the moment he opened his eyes in the morning to the moment he closed them at night, and then that same struggle haunted his dreams.

It felt very good to cut loose.

A shield of fused air blinked into existence for just long enough to catch the edge of the cabinet in midair, spinning it harmlessly sideways. It came apart against the wall, neatly reducing the antique globe to a collection of antique shards.

Oh dear. It had been a really nice globe.

Paper flexed and tore as the Tenebrous drew itself to its full height. The bulb above them finally cracked, its light bleeding to grays and blues as if lenses were being swept across it, as though filtered through the nictitating eyelid of a snake.

"Well, go on, then," Simon hissed out of the corner of his mouth. The unglow of the bulb had washed all the color out of his skin.

"What?" Denizen hissed back.

"You do it. You're better."

"Wait, hang on—"

The beast bolted for the door, skittering low and using the bookshelves as cover. Denizen hesitated—like an idiot, he hesitated—and when the Tenebrous ripped the back door from its hinges and flung it at him, all Denizen could do was duck.

A hideous smirk distended the creature's face.

Readers, it hissed with absolute scorn, and then shrieked as a comet cored it from behind.

Abigail Falx had been raised to be thorough. She never took her eyes from the eel-of-tweed, light spilling from her fingers to pin the Tenebrous down—consuming every page that spun from its flailing coils, every drifting mote of dust. Layer after layer sloughed away until there was nothing left but a sketch of darkness curled against the floor.

Soon there wasn't even that.

A smudge of soot marred Abigail's dark cheek as the inferno faded from her eyes. She swept it away with a finger of iron.

"You two," she said pleasantly, "are idiots."

2

A Question of Half Steps

It turned out to be a popular opinion.

"Reckless," snapped Denizen's mother, "absolutely reckless. What were you thinking?"

She waved a connecting rod in the air as she spoke. At least Denizen thought it was a connecting rod. It might have been a camshaft. Or a piston. Or something . . . else.

For the garrison of a secret, mystical Order of Knights, Seraphim Row had quite a modern garage. Tools hung on the walls; engine components sat in tidy lines on the floor. Denizen might have inquired as to what some of them were, but Vivian Hardwick had been fiercely protective of her car *before* it had been ravaged by a pack of marauding Tenebrous, and now she barely let anyone near it at all.

"You were just supposed to locate the beast," she

said, wiping black grease from her black iron hands, "*not* confront it yourselves."

Denizen stared at his toes and knew without looking that Simon was doing the same. It wasn't the first time they had stood in an office together and been told that their behavior was unacceptable, though back in Crosscaper Orphanage there had been far less risk of dismemberment.

Abigail, he was sure, would be staring straight ahead, but that was because Abigail was Abigail. She had been raised in garrisons just like this one, and while Denizen and Simon had been trying to liberate sweets from the orphanage kitchen, she had been learning how to disassemble a crossbow. Leather *creaked* as she flexed her gloved fingers. Abigail wasn't used to disobeying orders, especially ones from a war hero.

Vivian Hardwick was . . . intimidating. She towered over them, even Simon—a lean, rangy woman with steel-gray hair and a stare that could etch glass. Her skin was threaded with scars, the map of a hard and violent life, and her movements thrummed with coiled tension—as if, at any moment, her long limbs would unfold into precise and unstoppable violence.

"I'm waiting for a strategy," she said flatly. "A *reason*."

Vivian was a Malleus, a Knight Superior of the Order of the Borrowed Dark, and she had been fighting Tenebrous since before Denizen was born. He and the others were just Neophytes, trainees, and, like everything else in their lives at the moment, this was a test.

"Darcie identified the Tenebrous," Denizen began. "John-of-Sorts—it favors replacing people, insinuating itself into a community to feed off their mistrust and paranoia."

Animals made sense. Plants made sense. Humans made sense, if you just looked at them from a biological point of view and ignored all the messy, individualistic fluff that went on inside their heads. Tenebrous came from outside this reality, and so were under no such obligation. The Knights of the Borrowed Dark knew very little about what they were capable of, and what they did know they had paid for in iron and blood.

Denizen had paid his fair share too. He had firsthand experience of the Tenebrae, the pitch-black otherworld from which the Tenebrous came. He'd felt their very presence distort reality like a stone flung in a pond, their every move a message: *We do not belong here.*

And he knew they were flammable. As far as most Knights were concerned, this was all you needed to know.

"We found out people had stopped going to the bookshop," Simon said without looking up. "There had been hardly any customers in the last two weeks, and those who had gone in left looking . . . scared."

"Local teenagers confirmed strange vibes," Abigail added promptly, pushing a strand of black hair back from her ear. They'd been quite happy to chat with her—she was charming and friendly, and she possessed the ferocious beauty of a hawk. "They wouldn't go near the shop."

Some Tenebrous hunted. Others laid traps. But no matter how good a Tenebrous's disguise was, unconsciously, people still picked up that something was awry. A wrongness around the eyes. A joint that twisted instead of bent. Some trace of the monster beneath.

"So you charged in?" Vivian asked darkly, but Simon shook his head.

"We made sure. *I* made sure. I bent light to make myself invisible and scouted the house behind the shop. There was food rotting in the cupboards. Mail piling up in the hall. And in the basement . . ."

"It had taken children," Denizen said suddenly. "They were in cages, but it hadn't hurt them—yet."

He risked a quick glance upward. Vivian was staring right at him.

"I didn't go into the bookshop to attack," Denizen lied. "I went in to scout, with Simon invisible as support. Abigail was covering the back. The Tenebrous knew what I was as soon as I got in the door. All we did was defend ourselves."

Maybe it wasn't a lie. Maybe the best defense *was* a good offense. All Denizen knew for sure was that it was the first time he'd ever enjoyed the smell of burning paper.

Vivian nodded. "The children?"

"We set them free. They were too scared to even look at us. They're not going to identify us."

A thread of softness entered the Malleus's voice. "And the bookseller?"

Denizen shook his head. Abigail looked away.

The silence lasted until Vivian cleared her throat. "Well. I still believe you behaved recklessly, but it does seem you had reason to act. Your strategy was solid and none of you were hurt." She frowned. "I do not condone disobeying a direct order but . . . I am glad that you're all unharmed."

Relief threatened to slump Denizen's shoulders, but he squared them straight.

"One last thing," said Vivian.

They waited.

"Did you rehearse this?"

"No!" they exclaimed together, and Vivian's eyebrows rose.

"I see. All right. You can go."

The Neophytes turned to leave, but Vivian's voice called out: "Denizen—a moment?"

Simon threw him a sympathetic look before he disappeared through the door, and then Denizen and his mother were alone.

Until quite recently, Denizen had believed himself to be an orphan. In his defense, there had been quite a lot of supporting evidence. He'd been raised in an orphanage, for one thing. You didn't just grow up in an orphanage if you weren't an orphan—it was like an exclusive and depressing club—and so Denizen had always believed himself alone in the world. Everyone around him had been alone too, though, and that had given him a miserable sort of peace.

Six months ago, all that had changed. His thirteenth birthday had brought with it a gift for volatile magic. He'd learned of the existence of the Tenebrae, a world a shadow's width beneath our own, and the Knights of the Borrowed Dark—the secret organization that held the line between. Most terribly, he had learned that this secret war had cost his father his life when Denizen was just two years old, driving his mother into a mad crusade of grief and revenge.

It had been a busy few weeks for revelations.

Vivian swept a hand over the newly restored hood of her car. "*What* you did made a sort of sense, considering the situation," she said. "But it's the *why* that concerns me."

Somewhere deep in Denizen's chest, power woke in curling tendrils of heat. The Tenebrae. It was the foremost weapon of a Knight, a seething inferno lodged just below the heart. Maybe it was that proximity that made it treat emotion like fuel. The first time Denizen had channeled its power, he had been so *angry*, and Vivian had encouraged that rage, provoking him to fling it at her in fire. He still wondered why she had done that, instead of any number of gentler ways.

"I think you wanted a fight," Vivian continued. "I think you wanted to give the power inside you, the . . . the anger, a way out."

Denizen had been brought up on a diet of fantasy books, so he'd always imagined *evil* as the flip side to good—dark, brooding, a little romantic. He'd been wrong. When a pack of rogue Tenebrous named the Clockwork Three had invaded his life, he had been surprised at their sheer pettiness.

They'd schemed to provoke the Tenebrae's ruler by kidnapping his daughter Mercy, framing the Order for it, and starting a war between the worlds—but the Three had spent just as much time and effort smashing windows, or eating lightbulbs, or scaring children. It was all about misery for them, not some great purpose or to convert the world to their cause. They just liked hurting things.

It was why they had killed Denizen's father, all those years ago.

"I'm not angry," Denizen said. This lie came more easily. It was one he'd been telling himself a lot. "I did what needed to be done. That's all."

Fire thrashed in the pit of his stomach. There had always been an eagerness to the power, but in the last few months that eagerness had grown teeth. Maybe it was the same for all Knights, but Denizen's education had been . . . different.

"Your ability with the Cants is far more advanced than your training should allow. That's dangerous. Whatever Mercy did to you—"

"She helped me," Denizen said, more sharply than he intended. "We never would have survived without her."

Desperate times call for desperate measures, wasn't that the phrase? And times had been extremely desperate six months ago. The chaos of the Three's attack and the imminent wrath of the Endless King had left the Order scattered, Vivian wounded, and Denizen alone—an untutored Neophyte yet to master a single Cant, the eldritch words used to channel the Tenebrae's power. Without the Cants, using that power was an act of sheer willpower for a Knight—one that more often than not resulted in said Knight being scraped off the walls.

And then Mercy had . . . *spoken* to him. The Cants had originally come from her father, apparently—there was another revelation for the pile—and she had breathed an unparalleled understanding of them into Denizen so they both could survive.

"Mercy made me fluent," Denizen said, forcing calmness into his voice. "It would have taken me years to learn them all. I know them now. I can *feel* them in my head."

Every hour. Every minute. *I can feel them.* A bead

of sweat ran down Denizen's forehead. He fought the urge to brush it away.

"I know," Vivian interrupted. "I know. But you have to be careful. Most Knights only learn as many Cants as they need, because with knowledge comes desire. The fire wants to be used. Power carries—"

"A Cost," Denizen said. It had once been small, just a crushed bud of dark metal in his left palm, but six months of Cants and battle had made that flower bloom. Now it spread over both palms, lapping at the veins of his wrists as if aching to spill over. "I know."

"I'm not talking about that," Vivian said tiredly. "There are . . . other prices a Knight can pay." She turned the car part over and over in her hands. She'd been obsessed with restoring everything damaged by the Clockwork Three, as if killing them hadn't been enough and she wanted to erase any trace of their existence.

It was one of the few things about his mother that Denizen really understood.

"I just want you to be careful," she said.

"I know."

Denizen's cheeks were burning, but whether it was from anger, embarrassment, or his power he didn't know. The irritating and unglamorous side effect to being a Knight: drawing deep on the power made light spill from their every pore, a halo of warrior intent . . . that manifested most of the time as a low-level blush.

He awkwardly shrugged in the direction of the door. "Can I . . . ?"

Vivian gave a single, silent nod. The scrape of a scouring pad followed Denizen as he disappeared into the candlelit dark of Seraphim Row, and her words echoed in his head.

I just want you to be careful.

Power crackled and hissed within him. It felt like it disagreed.

3

Little Boxes

Seraphim Row loomed over every other building on the street like the tumbledown bones of a giant. Gargoyles keened silently from its roof, baring long stone fangs. At first glance, they were terrifying—asymmetrical tangles of claws and wings, the worst parts of serpents crossed with nightmares of birds. Only close inspection would reveal that each gargoyle was not roaring but cowering, limbs bent as if to ward off a blow.

This was a place, the unseen message went, of which monsters should be afraid.

Simon and the others had gone outside to try to soak up the last of the evening's sunlight, and Denizen found them lounging in the back garden, dappled in the patchwork shadows of trees.

He took a seat beside Darcie and she nudged him with a shoulder. "I'm glad you're OK. All of you."

"Thanks," he said, flashing her a halfhearted smile.

"You idiots," she added reprovingly. Darcie Wright had a very good reproving voice—clipped and precise. It didn't hurt that at sixteen years old she was the smartest person in the room—*any* room—and when she spoke, even Vivian Hardwick listened.

"Well, that's everybody," Simon said, and Denizen grinned. "Are we idiots because we got distracted or for going off assignment in the first place?"

"Pick one," she said. "I don't approve of needless danger."

"Sorry," Denizen said, and meant it. Away from Vivian's searching gaze, some of his anger had leaked away.

Abigail was looking at him with her arms folded.

"What?"

"Did you talk?" Abigail pressed. "How did it go?"

"Fine," Denizen said. "Or—I don't know. Terrible. Something."

"Well, you've covered all the bases there."

"Simon," Darcie said. "Be nice." Dark glasses did little to hide her mock-serious expression, her mass of black curls bouncing as she turned to Denizen. "But did you talk?"

Denizen threw up his hands.

"We talked. We didn't *talk* talk. We never *talk* talk. We don't have anything to *talk* talk about."

"'Course not," Simon said. "I mean, she's only the estranged mother who left you in an orphanage eleven years ago to pursue a suicidal revenge mission. Why would you need to talk about that?"

Had anyone else summed up the great, tragic, and extremely melodramatic story of the Hardwick family in one sentence, Denizen might have been annoyed. Simon had earned the right to flippancy, though, because so much of Denizen's story was also his own. He had been in the orphanage every lonely night of Denizen's life, just one bed across. He had shared the same violent awakening of Tenebraic power on his thirteenth birthday. In fact, pretty much the only part of the whole debacle Simon hadn't also experienced was having one of his parents mysteriously reappear.

Denizen was very glad Simon was here at Seraphim Row. It made it seem slightly more like home. A lot more than having his mother there did, which was basically the entire problem.

Vivian and Denizen didn't talk, in general. Well . . . they talked about training, the correct usage of Cants, or the right direction to run a whetstone down a blade. They had once had an extremely long conversation about the appropriate amount of grout for retiling the bathroom after the Tenebraic assault.

What they hadn't talked about was why, after the Clockwork Three had murdered Denizen's father eleven years ago, his mother had chosen to seek revenge instead of being . . . well . . . his mother.

"We talked about what we always talk about,"

Denizen said, shoulders hunching as if he were trying to fold into himself and disappear. "She's afraid that having all the Cants in my head is going to have some . . . ill effect. She wants to talk about *restraint*. Which I totally understand. It's her area of expertise."

That came out a little harsher than he'd expected, but Denizen didn't care. "It took a very-nearly-apocalypse for her to open up to me last time about my father, and now that the world *isn't* in grave peril she's clammed up again."

"You could try bringing it up with her," Darcie said gently. "Meet her halfway?"

"But *why should I*?" Denizen said hotly. "Why can't she talk to me? She spent years running away from me and now I'm just supposed to what—forgive and forget? Even *thinking* about it makes my head want to explode. And she keeps bringing up Mercy and staring at me like I'm a time bomb. Like there's something *wrong* with me just because I . . ."

Denizen's lip tingled where lightning had once touched it. He hastily cleared his throat.

"Just because I was helped by a Tenebrous." He sighed. "Look, I can talk to you guys about it, that's . . . that's *easy*. You all understand."

He looked around at the expressions on their faces.

"You do understand, right?"

Abigail held up a hand. "Well . . . No. You're right. We do what has to be done."

Simon shrugged. "I'm generally in favor of not-apocalypses."

Darcie frowned. "I want to understand," she said gently. "But are you all right? Because you told us what happened with Mercy, but we haven't discussed it. Not really."

The Cants shifted uneasily in Denizen's head. It took the barest thought to set them off, like birds spooked from a wire. And when they moved, spiraling round his head, making it hard to concentrate or think . . . sometimes he saw a *pattern,* the way a language can almost be heard in the crackling of flame.

It took him a moment to realize he hadn't answered Darcie's question. "I'm fine. I am. And, besides, I needed her help. It was the only way to survive."

"I know," Darcie said quietly. "I'm sure Mercy did what it had to do."

Her choice of pronoun wasn't lost on Denizen, and so he turtled behind a noncommittal phrase.

"I'm sure everything will sort itself out in the end."

"Things aren't just going to sort themselves out with Vivian, Denizen," said Abigail, turning gracefully on a bare heel. "If she can't start the conversation, you should. Honestly, lay it all out on the table—"

"I can't *lay things out on the table*. The table would collapse," Denizen said, with a bit more acid than he had intended, and then sighed. "Sorry. I will. When I'm ready."

He knew his friends were right. He just wasn't particularly good at opening up about his feelings. It wasn't a skill that had been very useful up until now. Eleven years of believing his parents to be dead had left Denizen with a fairly straightforward coping strategy:

Avoid feeling anything. Box it up. Shove it somewhere deep, unlabeled and unmarked, in the vaults of your head.

He could feel those boxes there now—stack upon stack—teetering at the slightest breath.

Pull one out and they might all come crashing down.

When Denizen's father had been killed by the Three, Vivian had gone looking for vengeance, fully believing that she would die in the attempt. Had she not proven herself tenaciously unkillable, Denizen would never have known her at all.

How did you even start to process that?

No. It was far easier to ignore emotion, push it away, run from it, or feed it to the flames. And the worst thing of all was the question in his head—

Was that what Vivian was doing too?

4

Redemptress

Uriel wondered sometimes what life would be like without certainty.

For every Favored Croit, there were a dozen un-Favored. Unblessed by fire, they were the ones who dealt with provisioning Eloquence and managing all Outside concerns—watched over, of course, by Grandfather. Then, obviously, there were *other* people—mundane irrelevances, swarming over the world like ants. Grandfather spoke of them with disgust, when he acknowledged them at all.

To Uriel, their existence was hearsay. Only the Favored could walk this sacred ground. And yet . . . Uriel had always *wondered.*

What was it like not being a Croit?

How did you know what you wanted to be? How did you find your purpose? Did you just randomly *pick* things to do? How did you know if you were right or not?

Insanity.

The Croits were certain because the Croits were chosen, and Uriel thanked the Redemptress that his life was not left to such wanton chance.

"Tell me the story," Grandfather said, his voice echoing round the Shrine.

"It's not a story," Uriel and Ambrel said together, and he could feel the fire thrashing inside her, just as he knew she could feel his.

"Then tell me the Truth."

The warriors filling the Shrine wore armor, not that it had done them much good. Every one of them had perished here, eyes wide with fear and hate. Uriel's practiced eye made out myriad different styles of armor and weapons—this was not an army but an attack of individuals, bound together by a single cause. They had only two characteristics in common: first, not one had faced death with anything less than fury.

Second, they were all made of iron.

The Truth.

Uriel began, just as they had practiced. "There was a man. A great man. The First Croit. He walked the world, and darkness was no barrier to his sight."

"Darkness was no barrier to his sight," Grandfather and Ambrel repeated, hands ghosting over their eyes.

Though there was no light in the Shrine, Uriel now saw perfectly, every detail outlined in cold silver.

The Luster. Thank you, my Redemptress.

Ambrel stepped over a woman in her death throes, eyes wide behind the grille of her helm. A man's hands were raised as if shaping something in the air, mouth open in a vicious snarl.

"He heard a voice," his sister continued, weaving through the statues, "a darkness in the shape of a girl." A radiant smile lit her features. "They fell in love."

It seemed like such a small thing. Such a tiny word, to be so important, and so when Uriel thought of love, of *that* love, he thought of the Favor in his chest—the incandescent heat of it. It longed to be used, to spill out and light the dark, but Uriel tamped it down, using the words that Grandfather had taught him.

It is not mine to use.

It is Hers.

Eloquence swarmed with wires, but it was *here* that they came together, an elegant snarl of serrated black. Round and round they built, winding and twining until they formed a wide skirt, then the slimness of a waist.

The Redemptress of the Croits—a sculpture of a thousand filaments, splaying to form limbs and chest and head. A goddess in wire frame.

She was beautiful.

Not beautiful in the way a human could be beautiful. No, this was a sparse and terrible kind of beauty, a beauty like that of the island, the kind of beauty that wanted you dead.

"They fell in love," Grandfather repeated, and there was a strange new sadness in his voice. Uriel had never considered it before, but the tremor in Grandfather's words made Uriel consider just how lonely the old man's life must be. It had been so long since Grandmother had died.

"She wore the light of a world as a bridal veil." Grandfather's right hand clasped the gaping sleeve of his left. "And the fire of that Favor bloomed in his chest."

It was a simple catechism. Easy to remember, as these things should be. The words all Croits knew.

SHE LOVED.
SHE STOLE.
AND WE KNEW FIRE.

All their certainty came from here.

Ambrel's hand found Uriel's. Her voice was low. Reverent.

"She's perfect. Isn't She?"

Wires split and wove to create the suggestion of cheeks, eye sockets, and a cruelly imperious nose.

Her hair trailed down the skeletal jag of Her spine, or maybe became Her spine—with the black on black, it was hard to tell. In places, Uriel could see through the gaps of Her, and in others She was opaque.

Filaments poured from Her body in jagged cascades, binding the statues' limbs, throttling, slashing, and pinning, like a thousand sword blades all wielded at once.

Uriel's heart ached with it. This was his Family's history—*his* history, right in front of him. Uriel knew *mundane* people had their own beliefs—beliefs born of uncertainty, of fear, of hope. *Idiots*. How could you believe something you couldn't see?

His goddess was right in front of his eyes. *She* was Truth. Compared to Her, it was Uriel who felt unreal, a flimsy paper lantern barely containing Her flame.

"Now tell me of the Adversary."

Grandfather was already in the center of the chamber, having weaved his way in between the frozen warriors like they weren't there.

They weren't statues. Uriel would have known that even if there wasn't now a spot of black iron in his own palm. Statues didn't have the same painfully frozen vitality these metal warriors had. Statues didn't have eyelashes.

Uriel's voice didn't shake. More than Eloquence itself, this tale was the architecture of their childhood. "The Adversary came for them in a hundred iron bodies, their hearts hard and cold. They hated the love She had for the First Croit, and the battle was so great it shook Eloquence from its perch, tumbling it to the valley below. And, wounded gravely, our Redemptress sank into a deep, dark sleep."

Their eyes were so angry. So afraid.

"We failed Her that day. We survived when She fell. And from then on we were cursed to wear the iron of the Adversary. Our Transgression. Until, as the First Croit promised . . ."

"She rises again," Ambrel finished. "And forgives us our sins."

"That is why we serve Her," Grandfather said quietly. "Our fire must be a Prayer to Her because only She can save us from the iron. Only She can save us from ourselves."

Uriel's hand hurt from where Ambrel was clutching it. He turned, and she was *crying*, tears spilling down her cheeks. It was very disconcerting to see his twin smiling and sobbing at the same time, but that was nothing compared to the horror he felt at the thought of her lost to the iron, just one more statue in the dark.

The Redemptress's hatred of the Adversary radiated from Her, even in stillness, and Uriel vowed to carry that hate with him wherever he went. For his sister, so that one day she might be saved.

A single wire arced across the chamber, scribing jagged words on one wall. The language was ancient and outdated, but Uriel's training pierced history the way his eyes pierced the dark.

Her last message to her Family.

I LOVE Y

Tears were welling in Uriel's eyes now.

I love you too.

He was certain of it.

5

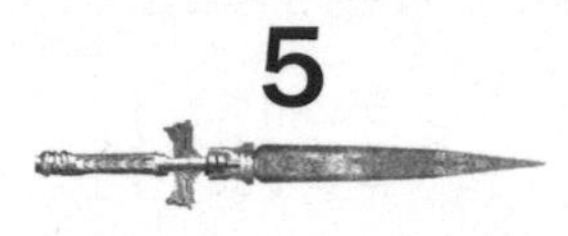

Two Wars and a Promise

They fought by candlelight.

Denizen had learned many hard lessons under the grim eaves of Seraphim Row, but first and foremost was this: Knights of the Borrowed Dark didn't march into battle flinging Cants like bad-tempered firework displays. Cants were used sparingly, as last resorts and dirty tricks, spoken only when you had no other choice. The first rule of Knighthood: you only have so much skin to give.

"Oh, sorry, are you all right?"

Unfortunately, some lessons were easier to learn than others.

"Yes," he mumbled into the floor. "Just give me a minute."

He hadn't even seen Darcie's foot move. Why did people have to have so many *limbs*?

Fire snapped and growled in his heart, and Denizen imagined it licking away the blossoming aches. It helped a little, though he'd be sporting bruises tomorrow. *More* bruises, he corrected himself. His back was a palette of green and yellow and healing brown. At first, he'd sort of enjoyed waking up as a barrel of pain every morning. It felt like an achievement, each twinge a stepping-stone on the path to being a Knight.

That had lasted a month. Now they were just bruises.

Simon and Abigail waited their turn on a couch in the corner, draped in gold and black by the shifting light of candles. But for the occasional comment on technique, Vivian could have been just one more portrait on the walls. Mallei from centuries past—hard-eyed men and women in battered steel armor, the grim and honored dead.

Denizen tried to ignore them. It was a tough crowd to please.

"Will we go again?" he asked, wincing slightly as his limbs creaked him upright.

"That's the spirit," Darcie said, smiling. "You are getting better. It just takes time."

As the *Lux Precognitae* of Seraphim Row, Darcie was so keenly attuned to the barrier between worlds that she could sense the ripples of a Breach before Tenebrous spilled out. It made her far too valuable to risk in real combat, but Darcie had made a point of undergoing training as arduous as any front-line Knight.

Denizen liked sparring with her. Her encouraging manner took some of the metaphorical sting out of being flipped onto hard surfaces. Besides, he thought, trying not to grin at Simon's hopeless-looking expression—he could have been sparring with Abigail.

"How much time, exactly?" the taller boy called. It was taking Denizen an inordinately long time to get the hang of hand-to-hand combat, but Simon was even worse. His arms and legs were so long that by the time he'd convinced all of them to move at the same time, Abigail had him on the ground.

"Training replaces instinct," Abigail said. "Soon your reaction to a punch won't be *Oh no, someone's punching me*. You'll just grab their hand and—"

She made a complicated series of violent gestures. Denizen's eyes started to water.

"Oh good," Simon said weakly.

Thinking *Oh no, someone's punching me* wasn't Denizen's problem, though he had to admit it was a very Denizen thought to have. That was no longer his instinct at all. The Cants had been jarred from their slumber by repeated impacts of head against floor and were offering far more . . . effective solutions.

Scintilla Scythe, barely there at all, just enough to bisect Darcie . . .

The flames in his chest were flickering red and raw.

Simon is weak; gather him up in Eulice's Ram and break him against the wall. . . .

Vivian was staring at him as she always did during these sessions, as if waiting for something within him to snap.

She would be difficult, maximum force required, but what was Cost beside the thrill of fire?

"Denizen?"

Denizen carefully folded up the smoldering hunger in his chest. It wasn't that it had anything against Darcie, Abigail, or Simon. It just sought escape, any escape, and saw very little distinction between *training partner* and *foe*, and even less between *surrounding area* and *fuel*.

He let out a shaky breath, focusing on Darcie's voice.

". . . like any skill," she continued, slipping back into a fighting stance, "it takes time and practice. Your body is learning, even if you don't feel you are."

Denizen nodded. That would all be fine if it were just Darcie he was fighting, but with the fire in his heart, he felt locked in two wars—one far more dangerous than the other.

"Ready?" Darcie asked.

Deep breath. Denizen gave his mother one last sidelong glance and then slammed great walls of willpower between him and the furnace of his magic, winding up his training and his determination and the pain in his back until he *thrummed* with readiness.

He was a Neophyte. He was a weapon. He was thoroughly sick of the taste of floor mats.

"OK," he said. "Go."

There was a knock on the door.

Darcie hit the floor in a tangle of limbs and a *whoosh* of expelled breath.

"Touché," she said, wincing, and then broke out into a bright smile. "See, Denizen? Training replaces . . ."

She trailed off when she saw Denizen wasn't even looking at her. He was staring at the great oak doors.

"Did you hear that?"

Someone had knocked. At the *door*.

As a rule, the aura of Seraphim Row did not encourage visitors. Footballs kicked into its backyard stayed there, abandoned to the vines. Salespeople didn't approach the place, or if they did, their remains were never found. There had been only three visitors to Seraphim Row in all the time Denizen had lived there, and the building still carried the scars.

Vivian was already striding toward the door, hammer in hand. Abigail had produced a pair of her ever-present knives—sharp little wands of steel. In any other house, and at any other time, Denizen might have considered this an overreaction . . . but they were Knights.

Everyone *was* out to get them.

The knock came again—three short raps, as if the person knocking were unsure whether they even wanted to be heard. A glance from the Malleus split the Neophytes up to find their angles, spreading out to avoid catching her in the crossfire. A small part of Denizen was pleased. *At least some of the training is sticking.*

Vivian's hand closed on the door handle and turned. Denizen tensed.

"Jack!"

An unbidden grin flashed across Denizen's features. Darcie stepped forward too, clasping her hands together.

Fuller Jack filled the doorway like a bald eclipse.

"How are ye all?"

Jack had been Seraphim Row's blacksmith—a massive man with a beard like a gorse thicket and iron hands scarred from a lifetime at the forge. His face had the blunt lines of a statue carved by someone with more enthusiasm than skill, iron sweeping across it in black tides, but Jack had been one of the first to welcome Denizen to the Order, and that iron softened when he smiled.

Then his eyes flicked to Vivian, and his smile faltered.

"Vivian."

"Fuller."

Vivian had on what Denizen thought of as her Malleus face—jaw set, eyes blank. There were shields on the wall with more human warmth and expression.

Jack had on a fair approximation of a Malleus face himself. It didn't suit him.

He ran a hand across the new scars on his scalp and sighed. "It's good to see you. All of you."

"It's good to see you too, Jack," Darcie said. She was the one who'd been in the most contact with him, ever since . . .

Seraphim Row had not always been so empty. Corinne D'Aubigny, one of the most dangerous people Denizen had ever met, had lived and loved and fought here before meeting her death against the Three. The Frenchwoman had stalked these corridors like a tiger—vicious and vital, a warrior to the bone.

Denizen missed her.

He'd never heard either of them say the word, but love had radiated from Jack and D'Aubigny like heat from a furnace. He had been the maker, the smith, and she had wielded the blades that he had forged.

And then she died, and he left.

Denizen had never lost anybody close to him before, which was strange, considering so much of his life had been dictated by loss. It had been the bedrock of his existence: already there, already real. His parents had always been gone. It wasn't a process; it was a truth.

Crosscaper hadn't helped—grief was as much a part of the orphanage as the air or the dust. There were always new arrivals. Parents were such fragile things. There had even been a poster on the wall of the infirmary detailing the various stages of mourning, not that it was needed. All you had to do was look down any corridor: denial, anger, bargaining, depression, and somewhere, finally, acceptance.

For Denizen, those losses were people he had never met or seen. But what the Three had done was different. Now he knew both sides. People who had walked around, talked, joked, and loved, now just . . . didn't. Grief wasn't a thing of the past. It was a knife that swept into your life and divided it into two sides—the part where you loved something and the part where you missed it.

Cold October sunlight. The crackle of flame in a plastic cup.

I'll show you real magic.

Denizen swallowed past a lump in his throat. D'Aubigny wasn't the only person they'd lost that night.

"I'm glad you are well," Vivian said quietly. Jack shrugged.

The Neophytes exchanged glances. Jack had left a few weeks after D'Aubigny's funeral, headed to parts unknown. This was the first time he'd returned to Seraphim Row. Was there a chance he was coming back?

The big man sighed. "You won't like this, Vivian, so I'm just going to go ahead and say it. The Palatine is coming."

Vivian scowled. "Why?"

Somehow Denizen wasn't surprised Vivian didn't seem to care for the leader of the Order. He was more surprised when he discovered things she *did* like.

"A message has arrived from the Tenebrae." Jack sounded like he couldn't believe the words he was saying. "Not a threat, or a demand, or a declaration of war. A message. An offer from the Court of the Endless King himself."

Vivian had gone very still.

"What . . . what did he say?"

"Well, that's the thing," Jack said, his gaze turning to Denizen. "The message isn't from the King. It's from his daughter."

6

The Beginning and End of Stars

"It's a trick," Vivian said flatly. "A trap. A plot of some kind."

The warm, acrid smell of coffee filled the kitchen. Jack took a long swig from his cup and set it back down.

"Well, it was a nightmare receiving the letter," he said, "so, when the Palatine did get it, he thought it best to actually read the thing. Mercy and the Forever Court wish to thank the Order for their part in her rescue. For avoiding a *potentially damaging conflict*. Her words, not mine. And . . ."

Denizen felt the blush starting, inexorable as a sunrise.

"She wants to thank one of us in particular."

Six months ago, Denizen Hardwick had saved the world.

He hadn't meant to. It had sort of happened by accident while he was trying to stay alive and he hadn't really thought about it until it was over and, when the adrenaline had worn off, he'd gotten a migraine and had to lie down.

But yes. World-saving. It was a very large thing to have done, and he could only comprehend it in little segments or the headache would come back. It hadn't even resulted in glory or praise or any of the other things normally associated with saving the world. No medals, no ceremony—he hadn't even been thanked, and it wasn't like he could go and put it on his CV.

That was fine with Denizen. He'd had the panicked notion that after scrambling for their lives against the first stirrings of a Tenebraic invasion, the Order mightn't have been best pleased with the very stressed thirteen-year-old who'd solved the whole thing when their backs were turned.

The Order. Denizen had *known* there were other Knights outside Seraphim Row, but it was one thing meeting Jack and D'Aubigny and Darcie, and another facing the grim strangers who had taken Grey away, leaving Darcie sobbing into Denizen's shoulder.

The Three had enthralled Grey, forcing him to cage Mercy and divide Vivian's cadre, giving them the chance to attack Seraphim Row and kill D'Aubigny, leaving Jack gravely wounded and broken by grief.

A further source of food for the Three.

Denizen *wanted* to be ignored, in the aftermath. It hadn't seemed fair that he had emerged unscathed.

Besides, it wasn't like he could explain how, when *real* Knights had fallen, he had somehow survived, as the only honest answer was: *I have no idea.*

"Anyone could have done it," he said in a small voice. "Really."

"That's as may be," Jack said sympathetically, "but we've never received a message like this before. Everyone's running around like chickens with their heads cut off, trying to figure out what we should do. Before all this, we didn't even know the Endless King *had* a daughter. Now we find out he does, and she's offering thanks, and her handwriting is pretty good. It's a lot to take in."

"It," Vivian repeated coldly, "is a trap."

Raw limbs of mist and storm, lightning climbing the distance between their lips. A creature of light rather than darkness, a smile luminescent and ever-changing . . .

Denizen's cheeks burned.

"The Malleus has a point," Darcie said. She was taking notes, because Darcie always took notes. "The Endless King, the Forever Court . . . these are human names for inhuman things. They might speak our language or mimic our forms, but only to hunt us. How can we be sure what they really want?"

The Knights only knew the barest fraction about the Tenebrae, but what *was* known was that somewhere in that sea of pitch there was a King, and a Court that served him. They were the oldest and most terrible of the Tenebrous—dread nobles shrouded in the worst of stories, if they appeared at all.

That was the problem. Stories needed survivors to tell them, and the Knights' records had a bad habit of cutting out whenever the Court came into play.

And Mercy had never appeared in those records at all.

"Denizen?"

Denizen was jerked out of his reverie by Simon poking him in the side. "What?"

Simon gave him a searching look.

"You've gone all red."

Yes. That was the other thing. He could almost hear Mercy's voice.

We will see each other again, Denizen Hardwick.

Denizen had assumed that was the kind of thing magical glowing girls said all the time, to promote an air of mystery. He hadn't realized it was something she was going to go and organize. Then again, he didn't have a lot of experience with girls, ethereal princesses in particular, and perhaps the best prophecies were the ones you organized yourself.

"Look," Jack said. "We can't afford to ignore it. Or risk offending her. The meeting is going to be held in Dublin in a few weeks. The Palatine is coming personally, along with representatives from the Order and our allies abroad."

"And Edifice Greaves chose you as a messenger?" Vivian said the name like a curse.

Jack didn't seem fazed. "Yes. He's been in contact a good bit since . . . that night. About Grey, for instance. And other things. I came early to prepare the venue, and he thought it best if I dropped in to give you the news in person."

"They're not coming here," Vivian said sharply. "We've only just—"

Jack lifted a massive hand. "Not here. In Retreat. It's a secure location."

Vivian looked disgusted. "Monstrous place."

"Then it suits its purpose." Frustration was evident in Jack's tone. "Look, Vivian. None of us need this. And I understand you've been through enough. We all have."

Now it was Vivian's turn to look away.

"But *this has never happened before*. I don't know what it means. Greaves doesn't know what it means. But we owe it to the world to find out."

Denizen swallowed. He wanted to see Mercy again. The thought did something to his insides that had nothing to do with the Tenebrae and everything to do with the taste of lightning on his lips.

But this wasn't about him and Mercy. Denizen had learned enough in the last few months to know that events didn't just *happen* one by one, neatly and politely. This was the opening salvo to a barrage.

The last time he had seen Mercy, Denizen had had to save the world.

He really hoped he wasn't going to have to do it again.

AFTERWARD, DENIZEN AND SIMON got chips. It was a little anticlimactic.

That wasn't a complaint, exactly. Anticlimaxes were usually better than the alternative. Life in Seraphim Row had a very inconsistent quality to it. One moment you might be fighting for your life against impossible odds, and the next you'd be doing the dishes. Maybe that was why Knights were constantly on edge—you never knew whether the next five minutes would contain soul-crushing horror or chips with garlic sauce.

Everyone had gone to do *something,* leaving Denizen and Simon alone in the kitchen. Like everywhere in Seraphim Row, the room bore the scars of the Three—two of the ovens had been removed, leaving pale patches on the slashed wallpaper, and most of the trestle tables had been smashed to kindling. It made the kitchen seem emptier than ever.

Abigail was calling her parents. They were in Honduras, Denizen thought. Or Haiti. They weren't in the Palatine's inner circle, but she wanted to check if they were coming anyway.

Darcie had retreated to the library to research the Court. Jack and Vivian had disappeared somewhere to talk about *adult* things, or Knight things, or both. Vivian had been the only Knight in Seraphim Row since the Three had attacked. Sometimes Denizen wondered if she was lonely.

Frown No. 8—I Am Missing Something Important Here, Which Is Unfair Because It Concerns Me—creased his brow for a moment. *Why am I not in that conversation?* Surely he was just as involved as they were? No, his mother would tell him when she was ready. *Or,* he thought sourly, *she'll tell me when she has absolutely no choice.*

Fine, then. He could wait. He didn't want to talk to her either. Right now he was going to sit here and eat chips and have a think.

"What's she like?" Simon asked, examining a chip before popping it delicately into his mouth.

Denizen knew the Cants back to front. He *knew* there was absolutely no way another Knight—especially a Neophyte—could read your mind. It was just a coincidence that Simon asked that question.

In that tone. With that raised eyebrow.

"Who?" Denizen asked, knowing full well who the *who* was, but very much wanting another few seconds in which to answer.

"Mercy. The Endless King's daughter." Simon shot Denizen a sidelong glance. "What's she like?"

His first thought had been of stars.

Underneath Crosscaper, beneath several floors of

bad dreams and beige wallpaper, Denizen had made his way through fear and doubt and a pitch-black basement only to find a star waiting for him.

No—*not a star*. Denizen was a stickler for accuracy, even in his complimentary metaphors. Stars changed, but that process took hundreds of millions of years, so long that the only thing that could observe the process begin and end was the star itself. Mercy had changed with every heartbeat—a writhing skein of light and girl.

There weren't words for what she was. *Incandescent. Terrifying. Beautiful.* They were just human noises in the end. You might have been able to describe her with Cants, but only if you didn't mind breaking the world apart.

"She's . . . nice."

"Nice?"

Denizen thought furiously. He'd never speculated about the size of his vocabulary, but suddenly it seemed depressingly small.

"Yes. Um. Nice."

"Oh," Simon said after a moment. "Well, that's . . . good."

The next few minutes were filled with the industrious sound of chips being eaten. Denizen ate all of his, even the inexplicably green chip that somehow always ended up in his bag. *Why is there always a green chip?* He focused on keeping his mouth full, but there were only so many chips in his bag.

Denizen knew that. Simon knew that.

It was just a matter of time.

"What kind of . . . nice?"

Denizen began to seriously consider the fact that his best friend might be evil.

"Hmm?" he said, busying himself with folding the grease-stained paper.

"Mercy," Simon said. "What sort of nice is she?"

He was innocently scraping the last of the garlic sauce out of its tiny plastic cup, his expression calm and torturously disinterested.

"What do you mean?"

"Oh, you know," Simon said airily, "is she . . . funny-nice? Scary-nice? Bit-weird-nice? There's different types, you know."

Are there? Denizen shut the thought down. He already categorized his frowns. That was bad enough.

"Mercy wants to talk to you, Den," Simon continued. "Anything you can tell us about her could be vital. The Order didn't even know she *existed*. You're the closest thing to an expert we have. You must be pretty freaked."

"*Yeeeess,*" said Denizen. "I mean, I suppose."

"Especially because you fancy her," Simon said, and then burst out laughing.

Denizen went scarlet. Blazing bright red. Visible-from-space vermilion. His fingers tingled as every available drop of blood abandoned the rest of his body, turning his face an unhealthy shade of puce. *Nothing should ever be puce,* Denizen thought before his mental faculties overheated entirely.

It took a long time for Simon to stop. There was guffawing, chuckling, a brief detour into cackling, and then finally a sort of dry creak.

"Ahem," Simon said when the wheezing had finally dissipated. "Sorry. *Ack.*"

Frown No. 9—You Are Making Fun of Me. Denizen wasn't fond of that frown. It only narrowly missed out on being a glare. Simon recognized the look and stopped.

"How long have you . . . Is it very obvious?"

"I've had an inkling ever since Crosscaper," Simon said. "The way you talked about her. Or didn't talk about her. Like you weren't sure you knew what to say and didn't want to get it wrong. And the look on your face when her name comes up . . ."

"Ah," Denizen said, cringing slightly. "Right."

"No, look," Simon said. "I'm not judging you. I've just never known you to like anybody before. Ever. And the first time you do it's the inhuman princess of a shadow dimension. I don't even know if I'm surprised or not."

"I've liked people—" Denizen began, and then stopped. He hadn't really. He'd grown up with everyone of his own age in Crosscaper. They were as close as cousins. And, if anyone else had shown up in the orphanage at the right age and at the right time, well . . . you'd have to be soulless to see that as an opportunity to date.

And he didn't fancy Mercy. He didn't know *how* he felt about her at all. Fancying someone was supposed to feel good, wasn't it? That was the point, surely? That was *biology*. If fancying people felt bad, they'd presumably stop doing it.

Fancying was the wrong word. It was a ridiculous word. It wouldn't be the right word even if Mercy were human. Denizen just . . . thought about Mercy all the time. There were dreams where he was in the dark and she wove trails of light in the distance—an unreachable firefly glow. He'd analyzed every single word she had ever said to him, over and over again, sometimes to look for hidden meanings and other times simply to remember that summer-thunderstorm voice. They'd only met once, but somehow she'd invaded his head and set up permanent shop.

But that wasn't *fancying* someone. Was it?

And now she was coming back into his life. Into everyone's lives, actually, and she was bringing a pack of the most ancient and deadly Tenebrous in history with her.

All in all, it wasn't an amazing basis for a second date.

"What am I going to do?" he asked. "The Palatine is involved now"—Denizen had no idea what the leader of the Order was like, but he was imagining Vivian in a bigger hat—"and the Forever Court. *The Forever Court.* What am I supposed to do? Make conversation? Maybe if it was just Mercy it'd be—"

He cleared his throat.

"Well, maybe remember that, then," Simon said gently. "There's a lot riding on this. Maybe don't . . . get feelings all over it. You know, in case we end up with an apocalypse."

He had a point. The Endless King had been fully prepared to attack this world when he thought the Order had taken his daughter. They'd been lucky to survive.

Sadness made its cold way through Denizen's chest. Not everyone had been so lucky.

"You're right," he said. "I'll just keep thinking about the imminent threat of death. That'll keep me on the straight and narrow. Perfect."

"Exactly."

There was a pause.

"I can't believe you fancy her."

"Shut up."

7

In the Absence of an Adversary

Uriel stared out into the Garden of the Waiting. A thousand marble eyes stared back.

They gleamed in the noonday sun—a host clad in white stone, an army forever denied its War. Not that most of them hadn't died violently anyway. It was a given, in a world constructed of *us* and *them*. There were always going to be far more of *them* than *us*.

Uriel looked down from his perch on a low tomb—

EREBUS CROIT

~ DIED IN FIRE ~

—to where Ambrel stood with one leg behind her head, arms held out for balance, her slim sword at her feet.

"Dare I ask who they'll send?"

Without wobbling, Ambrel bent and picked up her sword. "Guess."

Uriel thought for a moment. "Tabitha. Definitely Tabitha. She was saying . . . things at dinner again. And she's been dying to test her Prayer against mine. Don't know who else." He sniffed. "That's fine. Makes it an actual challenge."

Ambrel gave her brother the ghost of a smirk. She had the same Croit wanness and graying hair, but, where his eyes were almost colorless, hers were the bright green-white of a smashed emerald.

"Meredel? No . . . you sprained his wrist last week."

"Sprained?" Uriel said with mock-indignation. "I'm not an amateur. If you're going to do something, sister, do it right."

"Broken?"

"In two places."

"Nice."

Uriel didn't bear his cousin any malice. Meredel was Family. They all were. The second the Redemptress woke, every Croit would march toward their destiny in lockstep. But this was training, and training was supposed to hurt.

Tabitha was another matter, but any reason she had to hate them should have been excised on their thirteenth birthday, when they had been shown to be Favored. Then again, Croits weren't very good at letting go of the past. That was sort of the point.

"What are you going to ask for?" Ambrel said. "If you manage to cross the Garden?"

"Haven't thought about it."

"What do you mean you haven't thought about it? Grandfather said if we cross, we get something from Outside. I've been thinking about what I'd get for *ages*."

Uriel shrugged. "I don't know. A book, maybe? There's a couple of new ones Grandfather just approved. What would you ask for?"

Ambrel *hmmed* as she slid her blade once more into its scabbard. "I would ask for . . . hair dye."

Uriel frowned. "What?"

She quirked a gray eyebrow. "Apparently, Outside girls dye their hair different colors. Blue. Green. Purple. Can you imagine?"

He couldn't, as it happened. "What for?"

"Haven't a clue," she said. "But doesn't it sound grand?"

Uriel leapt to the grass, mentally running over their chosen route. It was two kilometers straight across as Eloquence's murder of crows flew, but, where they had the advantage of altitude and freedom, Uriel and Ambrel would be zigzagging through fifteen centuries of dead relatives. He wondered who they'd cheer for if they could.

"Hair dye it is, then," he said.

Now it was her turn to frown. "Don't be rusted, Uriel. Two kilometers. Start thinking of something good."

"Sister . . . are you sure you want to do this?"

She grinned. "Stop asking me that and run."

He obeyed. There was a direct path through the necropolis, but *direct* was expected, and so the twins dodged between mausoleums, temples, and shrines, freezing and running and freezing again.

Two steps forward, one step back. Dolmens scaled, pyramids slid down, statues and shadows used as cover. Marble shapes loomed round every corner, and only training and reflexes stopped Uriel from drawing his Prayer and slicing them to pieces. This was a test of restraint as much as anything. Grandfather would be checking the Transgression in their palms when it was over.

A third of the way across and . . . nothing. No opposition. Uriel had to resist the urge to bolt, trusting their quickness to carry them the rest of the way. He could see the same impatience in Ambrel's movements too—no longer carefully checking intersections but just running, and Uriel racing to keep up. He wanted to call out to her, but sound traveled too well in these avenues of the dead. Sprinting beside her, he tried to catch her eye—

Just as Cousin Magnus tried to take it out.

His Prayer was as ugly as the rest of him: a dirty gold lattice that spat sparks as it whipped at Ambrel's head. Only its scorched-air whine gave Uriel warning. He grabbed his sister by the hand and *yanked*, and the two went down in a tumble.

The world rang with the gravel of Magnus's laughter.

Ambrel was first to rise, gripping the cold marble ankle of

ALANYA CROIT

~ ASSASSINATED ~

and, to her credit, she didn't lash out. Light danced beneath her skin, turning her eyes into spotlights, her other hand hot on Uriel's wrist—but she didn't strike. They turned, back to back, but Magnus was nowhere to be seen among the white marble shoulders of hunching tombs.

Typical, Uriel thought. He knew each of his Family like the back of Ambrel's hand. Not just their Prayer—the shape their fire took—but their strategies, strengths, and weaknesses. Magnus was a coward. He favored the kind of fight where his opponent didn't know it was a fight at all.

A shared glance was all they needed. Ambrel went high, Uriel went low, and, where he had previously been careful, now he was sloppy, sword loose in his hand, his face flushed and panicked. Magnus had scared him, obviously. He was weak. He may as well have had a target painted on his—

Cousin Barstrel, on the right, forgoing Favor to simply lunge at Uriel with grasping, spade-like hands. He made it three steps before Ambrel flung herself from above to wrap her legs round his neck like a bola whip. Barstrel's huge eyes got huger, he reared—and Uriel's terrified scramble became a cobra strike.

Thank Her for that, Uriel thought, as the older man's lanky form folded. Running like an idiot was actually a lot more strenuous than doing it properly.

They loped on.

Uriel usually felt at home among his Family's dead. They were inspiring. Their lives, their scars, even the delicately painted coils of black on their skin—a constant reminder that only through serving the Redemptress could a Croit be saved. Now, though, the cold stone faces had taken on the feel of enemy territory.

Eight hundred meters to go.

Statue after statue after statue. Uriel's vision blurred with names and deaths.

ABADIU CROIT

~ DIED IN BATTLE ~

His eyes flicked back and forth, hunting movement.

WULFSTAN CROIT

~ DIED IN GLORY ~

Fingers flexing on the hilt of his sword.

"Wait," he whispered. Ambrel gave him a sharp

glance. There was something—some detail he had registered but not understood. He turned back to

ISKOR CROIT

~ DIED IN SHAME ~

and took in the hunched posture, the wringing hands. They had all learned about Iskor, his cowardice, the rust in his heart, and the black on his skin.

It *moved*. The painted Transgressions on Iskor's statue began to coil upward, the dark rising like wires hungrily seeking—

Tabitha.

If you took a winter sunset and packed it into a few short seconds, made what should be beautiful into an assault, that was the Prayer of Tabitha Croit. The twins turned in unison to see the tombs, the grass, and the summer sunlight simply disappear, swallowed by an avalanche of black.

Ambrel's hand found Uriel's half a second before it hit.

It was as if the day had never existed. Uriel *knew* he hadn't moved. They still stood at the same intersection under the same sun, but he could no longer see his hand in front of his face. Sound was muffled, fractured. Bright curlicues of nothing burst against his eyelids as he blinked, but it didn't make a difference.

Of course it didn't. Real darkness had no hold on a

Favored Croit. That was from where their Redemptress had come, and She had polished it to a Luster so they could see. This darkness had a mind behind it, and that meant it could be beaten.

The Favor came quickly. It always came quickly, but Uriel was trained not to take that as a sign of approval. It *wanted* to be used, and there was only one shape it could flow into, a shape he'd spent years building in his mind.

Uriel took a deep breath, squeezed Ambrel's hand, and pulled a sword of fire from the devotion in his heart.

The darkness didn't like that—swarming back to reveal a circle of grass and daylight—before Tabitha redoubled her unseen assault. Uriel's tiny sphere of respite caved in beneath the black, and he was blind; blind as he'd been that first time he had walked into the Shrine beneath Eloquence.

He had been afraid then. He wasn't afraid now.

Uriel charged, blade a roaring line of fire in the air. It was searing in his hand, but soon the pinch of cooling iron made the pain a distant thing. He swept it in a circle, and grinned as he heard someone curse. The blade sliced and sliced again, cutting the darkness to sections, to ribbons, to shards.

Iron Transgression was creeping across his skin, and for that Uriel would pay Penance, but he knew it must be racing across Tabitha's as well. Maintaining this globe of night was far more draining than a simple sword.

Think of all that sin, Auntie, and break.

Tabitha broke.

Uriel threw himself through falling curtains of night—and there she was, perched on a dolmen, wide silver eyes blinking in the sudden sun.

Ambrel recovered first and charged, but she hadn't taken two steps before Magnus's lattice drove her to her knees.

She shrieked into the dirt. Uriel raised his sword, but a trailing frond of gold struck him so hard across the face he saw stars. His grip on the Favor vanished, searing his mind as it went. By the time his vision cleared, sickly yellow bonds had snared him as well.

Tabitha Croit was taller than Grandfather, and while she did not possess his air of terrible grandeur, she made up for it in sheer bulk. Her arms were monstrous with muscle, her every movement a terrible, audible flex of sinew. A waterfall of gray hair swept down to hide the beads of iron pushing through her cheek.

Magnus was dwarfed beside her, rodent face crunched in concentration. Lassoing gold was fused round Uriel's fingers. He could feel the heat of it, like a pot of boiling water lifted with a towel.

What would happen if I—

No. Even if he summoned his sword, he wouldn't have been able to hold it.

Another loop wrapped round the lower half of Ambrel's face, blocking the song of flame Uriel *knew* would be building in her throat. They'd both wear burns tomorrow. Anger pulsed through him and he tensed, gathering his feet underneath himself to leap.

Ambrel gave a tiny shake of her head.

"And I always thought Uriel was the smarter one," Tabitha murmured. Magnus chuckled by her side, a little too late to convince Uriel he actually found her funny. Magnus always had been a suck-up. "Maybe you should listen to her this time, boy."

The leash of light tugged at Uriel and he staggered. It didn't stop his sneer. "Barstrel still unconscious?"

"I think you misunderstand who is doing the gloating here, nephew," Tabitha said, her smile disappearing. "You didn't make it. Didn't even get close. And that was with *her* cheating." Her eyes burned gold. "You were *supposed* to be hunting him with us."

Ambrel shrugged. Uriel couldn't see her mouth, but he was sure she was smiling. Tabitha hated being disobeyed, or ignored, or anything that wasn't groveling respect.

"I don't know why I'm surprised," Tabitha hissed. "Of course you'd stick together. Who else would trust you, knowing what your parents did?"

Uriel rolled his eyes a half second before Ambrel did. *This again.* Uriel could never understand why Tabitha thought the actions of strangers would shame them. UnFavored did what they did for whatever reasons unFavored had for doing things.

It's nothing to do with us.

"Maybe it would have been better if your parents had succeeded in hiding you from Grandfather," Tabitha purred. "Then we wouldn't have to put up with this unseemly loyalty to each other, instead of to the Family and the cause. You could have grown up Outside. In the suburbs, with nice sweaters and a little dog, far away from us. Far away from Her."

Ambrel's hands had curled into fists. Uriel's teeth were clenched. Every Croit child belonged to the Family. Uriel and Ambrel's parents—or, rather, the strangers who forfeited their right to that title—had tried to conceal the twins' birth from Grandfather so they . . . well, Uriel didn't know. He had no idea why they had done what they did or what they hoped to get out of it.

He was just tired of having to pay for it.

"We *are* worthy, Aunt," Uriel snapped. "Our thirteenth birthday proved that. We are as Favored as you."

"Please," Tabitha said. "Look at you. Bound and trussed. Neither of you are strong enough for what the Redemptress demands. You're just half a person each." She smirked. "*Worthy.*"

Ambrel snarled something through her bonds. Uriel's eyes widened.

Tabitha frowned. "What did she say?"

Then let us show you.

And Uriel's sword burst from Ambrel's hands.

He couldn't tell who looked more surprised—Tabitha scrambling backward, Magnus reeling in agony as the golden blade slashed his leash to ribbons, or Ambrel herself.

Holding a sword was a familiar feeling for any Croit, though, and training took over. Ambrel leapt to her feet and spun the blade in a flaming figure eight.

Magnus bolted. Tabitha stayed only long enough to stammer, "I'm . . . I'm *telling*!" before turning on her heel and running after him.

The flaming sword came apart with a sigh of sparks. Uriel and Ambrel both stared at the place where it had been.

"Uh . . ." Ambrel was opening and closing her hand, the skin shiny pink where the sword had lain.

You get used to it eventually, Uriel wanted to say, but the words wouldn't come.

"How did you . . . do that?" he said finally. The Prayer of a Croit was a sacred thing. You devised one, or chose one an ancestor had made, and the rest of your life was spent practicing it, studying it, learning how to channel Her fire into a usable form.

"I was there for all of it," Ambrel said distantly. "All your preparation—I helped you choose it, remember? You've told me a hundred times what it feels like, the pattern you imagine. I just . . . I just *thought* it into shape."

She was right. Uriel had watched her do her lung exercises, her meditations. He knew the channels of her Favor almost as well as she did.

"Grandfather didn't . . . say we weren't supposed to try each other's Prayers," Uriel said, with the yawning sort of horror he always felt when he realized the old man was going to be angry. "He didn't *say* that."

No. He hadn't. He hadn't said anything about it at all, which is why every Croit had thought it impossible.

Did Grandfather not . . . know? Had he been *wrong*?

"Sister," said Uriel. "What does this mean?"

Ambrel was still staring morosely at her hands. "It means I'm probably not going to get my hair dye."

8

VERY EDIFICE GREAVES

DUBLIN WAS A CITY of secrets.

It was what Denizen liked about it. He'd loved maps as a kid, how cities seemed to make *sense*—neat grids of buildings and streets, geometric and solvable. Places where you could know where you were.

Dublin, however, was a liar of a city. It hid its enormity from you—tucked it into alleyways, veiled its true proportions in skirts of stone and lamplight. Dublin would trick you into thinking you'd figured out a new shortcut and then reveal a whole town hiding between you and your destination, like a folding paper puzzle.

Maybe it was a bit early to have a favorite city. The one constant in the life of a Knight—besides horrible danger—was travel. London, New York, Sofia, Moscow—there was a good chance Denizen would get to bleed over all of them.

But Dublin would always be his first crush.

Palatine Edifice Greaves was arriving today, and so Denizen and the others had walked from Seraphim Row in the gray haze of dawn, winding through the brash color of the shopping streets and the hidden green of Mountjoy Square.

Eventually, they reached the red, shade-dappled brick of Upper Drumcondra Road. Trees rustled in the day's first breeze, casting traceries of shadow across the white stone building nestled demurely between the grim gray of two Georgian houses. A small sign peeked out from behind a fall of ivy, discreetly informing you that the building was the Goshawk Hotel and that it would like you to come in.

A line of smaller text asked you first to wipe your feet.

"Fancy place," Simon said, staring down at his hastily polished shoes.

"Oh, absolutely," said Darcie. "Fascinating venue. It has politely excluded itself from every hotel award in Europe."

"Why?" asked Abigail.

"So other people can win," Darcie replied.

"Right," Simon said. "So . . . very fancy." He sounded a little nervous. They'd scrubbed up as well as they could, but the clothes Vivian provided were more functional than showy. Besides, Simon was so gangly that it was his limbs more than his clothes that made him look untidy.

"I've never heard of it," Abigail, the most traveled of them all, said.

"Well," Vivian said. "They consider advertising . . . impolite."

"You don't sound like you approve," Denizen said, giving her a sidelong glance.

Vivian scowled. "No. It's just . . . it's *very Edifice Greaves.*"

They made their way up the steps, where a charcoal-suited concierge swept the door open with a flick of his gloved hand.

Beyond was the kind of opulence that made Denizen intensely aware at a molecular level of his each and every flaw. Black and silver couches lurked in every corner like comfy jaguars, lit by discreet lamps. Pale vines had been seduced into growing up the walls, filling the room with a cold and sweet perfume.

He spoke in a whisper. It was the kind of room that bred them.

"What do you mean, *very Edifice Greaves*?"

Vivian wore a sharp black suit, scars pink against the pale of her cheek. With her granite eyes and dark expression, she looked like an undertaker, possibly one willing to drum up her own business. Her hammer was in a duffel bag on her back, but her hand was tapping unconsciously against her thigh where it would normally hang. Denizen wasn't sure she was even aware she was doing it.

It was strange seeing her out in public, surrounded by and interacting with other people. The sunlight had seemed to wash her out, making her at once ghostly and far more permanent than the world outside—something separate and distinct.

"We could have at least lodged them in Seraphim Row," she explained, scanning the room with a warrior's practiced eye. Denizen had been under her tutelage long enough to know she was clocking exits, blind spots, and choke points where she could direct the flow of enemies toward her. "A far more defensible location."

She ran her hand down a cushion and sniffed. "But something like this has never happened before, and the Palatine wants it to be an *event*."

Abigail glanced around with a fair approximation of Vivian's disdainful expression. "Wasteful."

Denizen and Simon shot each other wry glances. Abigail hadn't ended up in Seraphim Row by accident. She'd requested to be sent there because of a respect for Vivian that bordered on hero worship.

"Oh, I'd imagine he paid for this himself," Vivian said. "He wouldn't like to be accused of misappropriating Order funds. He'll dress it up as just a nice thing he wanted to do for people who'll soon be risking their lives."

An amused frown flitted across Denizen's face. It was quite a new one, but he'd found himself using it more and more. No. 26—My Mother Is Pretty Much a

Lunatic. Only Vivian Hardwick could make the words *a nice thing he wanted to do for people* sound like dentistry with a rusty nail.

A porter materialized beside Vivian, so close the Malleus flinched. His prepackaged smile faltered as she turned toward him, inexorable as a guillotine.

"May I . . ." He swallowed, his voice coming out a lot smaller than he intended. "May I take your bag?"

"No," Vivian said flatly, and then cocked her head in thought. "But would you like a tip anyway?"

The man's smile returned, twice as wide.

Vivian leaned into his face.

"Don't ever sneak up on me again."

The man went white and vanished. Denizen couldn't be sure—he never was around Vivian—but for a second he could have sworn a smile lurked at the corners of her mouth.

She may have been doing the porter a favor, Denizen thought, looking around the Goshawk's foyer. The residents might have seemed normal—reading papers, drinking tea, chatting—but if you knew what to look for . . .

There. A woman with half her head shaved, the bright coil of a dragon tattoo on her cheek. She seemed engrossed in the magazine she was reading, but her eyes had tracked Denizen and the others from the moment they entered.

There. A whipcord-slender Asian man examining

one of the paintings on the wall, a thin plastic tube in his hand. It looked like something an art student would carry to protect rolled-up drawings . . . but it was also the perfect size for a duelist's sword.

The Cost was the easiest way to pick out a Knight, but it was by no means the only one. You looked for the wariness. The focused calm. The grace that came from a life lived between claws and fire.

There were ten—no, twelve—Knights scattered around the room. Denizen followed Vivian to a corner couch—back against the wall, naturally—but there was someone already there.

Jack stood out against the opulence of the Goshawk like a bear on a catwalk, shirt straining against his muscles. A paperback sat on his lap and Denizen resisted the automatic urge to cock his head and see what he was reading.

"Lads," Jack said.

Vivian nodded. There was an underlying tension there, but neither one of them seemed willing to acknowledge it. It made Denizen wonder why Greaves had chosen Jack as his messenger. Did he not know? Or . . . *maybe that's why he sent him in the first place.*

Denizen was starting to put together a mental picture of Edifice Greaves, and he had the creeping suspicion he didn't like it. On the other hand—as the doors of the Goshawk slid open to admit a sharp slant of summer sun—Greaves did know how to make an entrance.

The Palatine of the Order of the Borrowed Dark stalked through the doors like a warship cleaving the open sea. A close-cropped black beard cupped his chin and lips, half a shade darker than his skin, his smile a stripe of sunlight in the Goshawk's artful gloom. He was tall but not toweringly so, handsome but not distractingly so, and the sleeves of his expensive shirt were rolled up, as if he were more used to working with his hands than dressing well.

And yet something moved with him, a cloud of confidence and easy mastery that made even the normal residents hush and stare. The hammer strapped to his back had been wrapped in black silk, but Denizen recognized it all the same. Somehow it irked him.

Five Knights followed—the Palatine's personal bodyguard. Violent storms in slick attire, each scanning the foyer with flat, cold eyes.

Greaves swept toward the white marble counter dominating one wall. Without so much as a gesture, Knights rose from their seats one by one. The girl with the shaved head tossed aside her magazine. Jack pushed himself to his feet with a hand like an oar. From every dark and secret recess of the foyer, men and women with black gloves and dark expressions appeared, falling into Greaves's orbit like comets cold and sharp.

Denizen joined them. He couldn't help himself.

We have to go sign in, he thought. *That's all it is.*

The receptionist was a young woman with complicated hair. Her bright smile faltered as Greaves pressed both hands down on the counter, staring her dead in the eye.

"Hello," he said, in a voice as warm and deep as a subway tunnel, "we're librarians."

Her eyes went very wide.

"Oh," she said, before—in a magic that had nothing to do with the Tenebrae but everything to do with the Goshawk—she was replaced by a manager, who took in the lupine circus before him as if it happened every day.

"Good morning, sir," he said with an unctuous smile. "Can I—"

"Guild of Esoteric Librarians," Greaves said slowly, drawing out each word. "We've booked rooms. A lot of rooms. Page under your right hand, thirty-three lines down."

He hadn't seemed to look down at all, but it took the manager three long seconds to find it.

"Ah! Mr. Greaves. Your rooms are ready. I shall just—"

"You do that," Greaves said, already turning away. There was something very familiar in his smile. "Hello, Vivian."

"Showy," Vivian remarked coolly. "Palatine."

"This is the Goshawk," Greaves responded simply. "They don't gossip. And if they did, what would they say? We're librarians."

Vivian sniffed, but Greaves had already moved on, clasping Abigail's hand in his two. "You must be Abigail Falx."

One eye on Vivian, Abigail grudgingly let her hand be shaken.

"I had the pleasure of training with your mother years ago in Iran," he said. "I think I still have the bruises."

A smile quirked Abigail's lip before she straightened it. "Oh," she said. "Cool."

He shook Darcie's hand next, inclining his head in something that wasn't quite a bow. "Madame *Lux*." He turned to Simon. "You know we were getting book requests from our central archives from Darcie at, what, age eight?"

Darcie dropped her gaze to the floor. "Well, I—"

"Speaking of reading, I've brought along my copy of the *Incunabulae Ferrum*." Darcie's head immediately came back up, but Greaves had already turned to Simon.

"Mr. Hayes. Our unexpected find."

Not everyone had received Denizen's recent wealth of family revelations. Knightly fire ran in Simon's veins, but where Abigail could relate her family history back to the Crusades, and the proof of Denizen's lineage was glaringly present—literally—Simon's parentage was still a mystery. Sometimes revelations cut out just when you needed them.

"Despite our best efforts," Greaves said, "sometimes a bloodline goes missing. The *Incunabulae* have a record of every Knight, going back centuries. If we can, we'll find your family together."

Simon's voice was a little hoarse. "Oh. OK."

Greaves smiled at him a moment longer and then turned to Denizen. His dark eyes gleamed. "And you must be Denizen Hardwick."

I must be, Denizen thought. *I wouldn't wish it on anyone else.*

"Yes," he said, and let his own small hand be engulfed. "It's—"

"Business, I'm afraid," Greaves finished for him. "Shall we?"

9

The Secret Life of Librarians

"It was a very pretty letter," Greaves began, "but I don't give skin for the promises of monsters."

Murmurs of approval rang out round the conference room—though *conference room* was a terribly boring name for a chamber so opulent. From furniture to fixtures, it felt like the kind of place where sultans had conferences, if sultans had conferences. Denizen didn't think they did, but until this morning he hadn't thought Knights had conferences, so what did he—

"Good morning."

Greaves clasped both sides of his lectern, his gaze sweeping the seated Knights. Denizen had been trying not to stare, but he had never seen such a diverse group of people in one place.

The only requirements for the war against the Tenebrous was fire and the will to use it. Breaches happened everywhere in the world, and so everywhere warriors had risen to fight them. Each sect, coven, and cult had sent representatives, many traveling thousands of miles. All here. All for this.

Denizen swallowed. *That's how important this is.*

"It has been too long since all those touched by iron have stood under the same roof," the Palatine said in warm tones. "The Knights of the Borrowed Dark, the Choir of Candles, the Burning Mirror, PenumbraCorp—"

"Cool," came a voice. "Hi. What do we know?"

Greaves's smile was faint. "The Palatine acknowledges Agent Strap of PenumbraCorp. Good to have you, Agent. It's been a while."

"Well," Strap said, thumbing his nose, "I hate the food."

Skinny limbs in a too-big shirt—the American might only have been a few years older than Darcie, but he wore exhaustion like another decade. There was a shiny bruise on his cheek.

"So what," he repeated, "do we know?"

It *was* a little fascinating to see so many different Knights in one place, but it had also begun to remind Denizen uncomfortably of the food chain. There had been a deceptively cheery graph in his schoolbook about it. The diagram explained that it took fifty antelopes to keep one lion fed. Predators needed space. They needed freedom. They weren't meant to all sit in one room.

The air hummed with the promise of violence.

"We will be met by three of the Forever Court and Mercy herself," Greaves said. "A Concilium of the worlds. It will be held in Retreat"— there were murmurings at that—"and I have secured undertakings from Mercy that should promote . . . trust."

He didn't look like he believed it either.

"We'll keep it short. Get in, get out. They want to honor the boy who saved the world from war."

Denizen tried very hard not to check whether people were staring at him.

"What kind of honor?"

This from a tall man leaning against the far wall. Iron had crept up his face like dark ivy, cracking and creasing his skin. He wore more of the Cost than any Knight Denizen had seen—even Vivian or Jack.

Denizen suddenly wondered what happened when the Cost was no longer something you could hide. His palms itched beneath his gloves.

"The Palatine acknowledges Singer Xi Che of the Choir." Greaves inclined his head. "And . . . we haven't been told."

"Why not?"

Vivian's voice cut through the tension like a garrotte. Every head turned. Sitting beside her, Denizen suddenly tried to make himself much smaller than he was.

Greaves's smile was sharp. It was clear this was an interruption he had been anticipating.

"Vivian?"

"Why *don't* we know what this honor is? Isn't it entirely possible that *honor* is their word for bloodbath?"

The conference room was silent. The Knights, Denizen realized, were hanging on Vivian's every word. She didn't seem to notice. Her words were for Greaves alone.

"In short, Palatine, how do we know this isn't a trap?"

"We don't," Greaves said shortly. "But what would you have me do?"

The question hung in the air, along with the busy silence of twenty very scary people considering the unknown. That was the heart of the matter. Had one of the Forever Court called this Concilium, it might have been dismissed as a trick. There was little known about the Court, but it all followed a certain blood-soaked theme.

Mercy was something else entirely.

Until her kidnapping had nearly plunged the worlds into war, no one had even known the Endless King had a daughter, and now, with the unpredictability that was so central to their race, she wanted to thank a human for saving her life.

"There's a lot we don't know about Mercy. What she wants, what she's capable of," Greaves said, meeting Vivian's eyes impassively. "But what we do know is what *we're* capable of. There's firepower amassed here the likes of which has not been seen in centuries. Should the Court for a *second* show their teeth . . . we'll set 'em alight."

He smiled brightly.

"Now, if you'll turn to page four of your briefing document . . ."

Denizen looked down at his empty hands. He had not been given a briefing document. He didn't even know there were briefing documents. The room crackled with the sound of rustling paper, and Denizen sank deeper into his chair, trying to look attentive while not actually having anything to look at.

The attentive look lasted all the way through Warrior Placement (pages 8–11). It began to falter around Watch Rosters (11–16). By the time Greaves started going through the Door-by-Door Fail-Safe Analysis, Denizen's mind had unhooked and was drifting through memory.

Her smile had been lit by starlight. There had been burning fingerprints on the books that she had read.

"I DON'T LIKE THIS."

Vivian tossed the briefing document at Denizen as they left the conference room. Maybe she already had it memorized. Maybe she just didn't bother with such things. But Greaves had finished his run-through by summoning Denizen, and now the two Hardwicks were striding up the corridor toward his office.

"What are you worried about?" Denizen said. There was an itch in the back of his head where a pair of Cants felt too close together. He'd spent the closing minutes of the meeting fighting the urge to just *say* them and be done with it.

Bad idea.

Though the Goshawk probably did have fire insurance . . .

Stop it.

"He probably just wants to ask me about Mercy, that's all." There was a tiny, ugly part of Denizen that quite enjoyed how Vivian's eyes narrowed when he said that. The thought that he'd be so open with someone she *clearly* disliked obviously bothered her. "I should probably tell him. He *is* the Palatine—"

Suddenly Denizen's back was against the wall, a pair of gray eyes staring down at him from a face of scars and fury. As always, Denizen was shocked and not shocked by just how fast Vivian was. How often had that narrowing of eyes been the last thing a Tenebrous saw?

She hadn't *touched* him. There were a good few centimeters between them. She'd just . . . *Vivianed.* And now Denizen's shoulder blades were trying to dig through the wallpaper.

"Tell him," she whispered. "*Tell him?* You have no idea how serious this is, do you?"

It was a scared little frown Denizen summoned

(Number Not Yet Categorized), but a frown nonetheless.

"What do you—"

Vivian's words bulldozed his. "You meet this *thing*, this creature, and suddenly you, a thirteen-year-old Neophyte, have seventy-eight Cants in your head. Perfect and fully formed. You speak them better than I do, you realize that? But I *earned* the twenty-four I use, and I feel the ache each of them cost me, and you *don't*, because a shiny little monster handed them to you and said *set me free*. I don't know why it did that. And you don't know why it did that. *And Greaves doesn't know it did that at all.*"

Denizen's eyes went wide. "What—"

"He would smile," Vivian hissed. "He would grin, and he would make jokes, and he *would take you away*—"

"Vivian?"

She froze. So did Denizen. Their heads turned in unison to see Greaves leaning against the wall, buffing his knuckles against his suit.

He smiled.

"You don't still hit kids in this country, do you?"

"No," Vivian said, and straightened immediately. "Mother–son discussion. You know how it is."

"Not even remotely," Greaves said. "Me and my mother get on fine." He indicated a door down the hall. "Now if you don't mind?"

The words weren't an order. Denizen suspected

Greaves rarely gave orders at all. Nevertheless, Vivian nodded curtly and stalked away up the hall.

The office was decorated in the same shades as the foyer below, the walls hung with paintings of undulating shapes. Greaves slid behind a desk of slick black wood.

They stared at each other in silence. Finally, the Palatine spoke.

"You're wondering why I called you here."

That wasn't what Denizen was wondering. Denizen, currently sitting uncomfortably on what had to be the most comfortable chair he'd ever sat on, was still reeling from Vivian's words.

Take you away . . .

Up close, the Palatine's air of command was even more potent. The office was just a rented one. Hundreds of people had sat behind that desk. Hundreds more would when Greaves was gone. But that no longer mattered: it was *his* office now, as surely as if he'd purchased every drop of paint.

Denizen kept his tone polite. "I assume it's to do with Mercy."

He was trying to separate his own impressions of Greaves from Vivian's obvious disdain. It was difficult—her personality tended to drive others along in front of it, like a tsunami. Greaves seemed to have a little of that too, but with a far more charming delivery system.

Denizen didn't like charming people. As someone who possessed little or no charm himself, he immediately distrusted it. The skeptical part of him saw the edges and aims of that easy familiarity. It had only taken Greaves half a second to exploit the cardinal route to each of his friends' hearts, as elegantly as D'Aubigny in a swordfight.

Darcie's love of books, Abigail's pride in her family, and Simon's lack of one. One. Two. Three.

It was the latter that was really bothering him. People's pasts weren't tools to be used against them. And now Denizen sat, wary of what Greaves's opening move would be.

"It is about Mercy, obviously," Greaves said. His accent was interesting. Consonants kept disappearing and then returning to ambush Denizen in odd places. "But we'll get to that later. First, I . . ."

His fingers drummed rhythmically on the desktop.

"I'm sorry about Grey."

Denizen went cold. There was a place in the back of his head so remote and silent that even the fire of the Tenebrae flickered out before it could reach it. He imagined it sometimes as an oubliette lined with steel boxes—feelings left to starve and be forgotten. It was where he had pushed his thoughts about Vivian when there had been a world to save. There were boxes marked CROSSCAPER and CORINNE.

There was one marked GREY.

Wars killed people. That was the point. When the Clockwork Three had prosecuted their tiny and vicious war against the cadre of Seraphim Row, there had been casualties, people that Denizen had only just begun to care about properly before they were taken away.

It seemed horribly selfish to mourn Grey more when D'Aubigny had died, but Grey had been Denizen's mentor, his first friend in this new and scary life. The Three had gotten inside Grey's head and made him do terrible things, and when they had no more use for him, they had thrown him away—a hollow, damaged wreck.

"We were friends," Greaves continued, his voice solemn. "Still are, in fact. He's recovering. We don't leave people behind. I wouldn't . . . I wouldn't leave him behind. I don't know if you'd want to . . ."

He adjusted the silver sword pin on his black silk tie. Grey had worn one just like it.

Denizen couldn't help himself. "Want to what?"

"Visit him. He asks about you."

For a moment, Denizen couldn't trust himself to speak.

"I'd like that," he said in a small voice.

Edifice Greaves nodded. "Not now, of course. Bit of a full plate at the minute." His fingers paused on the desktop. "I know your mother doesn't like me."

Denizen opened his mouth to speak, but Greaves shook his head.

"No. It's fine. We're very different people."

Greaves's hammer stood against the wall near the door, still wrapped in its sheath of silk. Denizen was trying not to look at it. There was a sense of danger about the Palatine—he had his fair share of scars and you didn't rise high in the Order on charm alone—but Vivian would never have left her hammer out of reach.

"I know."

If Greaves detected anything but the requisite politeness in Denizen's tone, he didn't show it. "With all respect to her—and I do respect her, believe me—Vivian Hardwick is a blunt instrument." He shrugged. "That isn't an insult. The Order is built on warriors like her: indefatigable, unstoppable, and unshakable in their dedication to the cause."

A slow heat was winding its way through Denizen's stomach, kindled by rising anger and the Palatine's friendly demeanor.

It wasn't that he disagreed—far from it. Vivian thought she was always right. She displayed as much empathy as a morning-star mace. Her earlier warning had been typical Vivian: aggressive, standoffish, only telling him things when he absolutely *needed* to know them . . .

She didn't give. She didn't compromise. She didn't trust; she gave orders and expected them to be followed, emotion be damned. Greaves had just elegantly summed up exactly why Denizen hadn't been able to bring himself to open up to his mother.

So then why was fire stalking the edges of his mind?

"I, on the other hand, take a longer view." Greaves thumbed his beard, a gesture that would have seemed thoughtful and unconscious had it not looked so rehearsed. "And the Order needs people like me too. People who look beyond the battle at hand. Soldiers, not warriors."

Turn to page four of your briefing document . . .

The corner of Denizen's mouth twitched. It was a struggle to deny the hot light seething up his spine. Forcing the power down had been difficult enough when all he had known was a single Cant. Now there were seventy-eight swooping like hawks in his head. It was a challenge not to breathe just *one*, to take that sourceless anger and *roar*.

"I didn't mean to cause offense, Denizen. I just wanted to let you know that . . ."

Denizen jumped a little in his seat. Had he slipped? Had Greaves seen the fire mounting beneath his skin?

"Know what?" Denizen said too quickly.

Ice. Waterfalls. Control. Cold, cold thoughts.

The power receded slowly, leaving behind scorched feelings of doubt and frustration.

"That Vivian's way isn't the only way," Greaves continued. "There are many opportunities to serve the

Order. Grey knew that. And I'm sure you know it too."

Denizen recognized that tone. Cheerful but brittle, like thin ice cracked by the passage of something beneath.

"Now tell me about Mercy."

He would take you away. . . .

Denizen wasn't sure what made him do it. It wasn't that he trusted Vivian (though, that was the horrible thing—he *did,* in this, a matter of war), but he told Greaves only the bare bones of the truth: Grey had been enthralled, but he'd let Denizen escape at great personal cost; Denizen had doubled back to Crosscaper and found Mercy, who told him Vivian's hammer would shatter her prison; Vivian had shattered her prison and rescued Grey.

The end.

"I see," Greaves said. "And Vivian did all that. By herself."

"Pretty much," Denizen said.

Greaves lifted an eyebrow.

"With a bullet wound?"

The handy thing about having an inferno lodged beneath your chest was that it made nervous sweats easy to explain. "*Umm* . . . She's pretty tough."

"That she is," Greaves said, after a searching look at Denizen's face. "Well. I'm glad we had this chat. The first of many, I'm sure."

"Um. Cool."

Greaves leaned forward.

"You're the future of the Order, Denizen. You, Darcie, Abigail, Simon—you deserve to be at the center of things. Not out here, in a border town, unable to see beyond the head of a hammer."

They stared at each other for a long moment.

"OK," Denizen said. He wasn't sure what else to say. "Are we . . . done?"

Greaves nodded, his smile folded away for his next appointment.

"For now."

10

Currency

"That's what they call it," Simon said, wriggling his bare toes in the carpet. *"Being a political animal."*

At the Goshawk, even the bedrooms given to half-trained Neophytes and troublesome world-savers were impressive. Vivian obviously had no intention of accepting Greaves's hospitality, but he'd gone ahead and booked them rooms anyway, and, for lack of a better place to wait for her, they'd been dumped there.

Dumped was the wrong word. The beds were vast meadows of white-and-black silk, like snowfields somehow warm to the touch. The air was filled with the subtle scent of flowers, as if whole forests were hidden behind the walls. You couldn't be *dumped* here; you'd bounce.

"This is ridiculous," Denizen said, settling on the corner of a bed. "I feel like I'm in a painting."

"Oh, we're far too scruffy to be in this sort of painting," Simon said, peeling a sock off and flinging it on the floor, where it sat like a sad little inkblot. "We're like the coffee stain where the artist put their mug down."

"Speak for yourself," Abigail said. She had insisted on trying out the shower and was now lost in one of the Goshawk's oversized, overfluffed bathrobes. She looked like a princess stuck halfway down the gullet of a polar bear. "I could get used to this."

She punctuated her words by flicking heavy black menus at Denizen, Darcie, and Simon. Denizen's stomach growled a thanks. What with all this talk of blunt instruments, heroism, and certain death, no one so far had had the decency to offer him a sandwich.

"Political animal," Abigail murmured, lost somewhere in the appetizers. "What like a walrus in a tie?"

"Thank you for that image, Abigail," Simon said. "No. Greaves is a—hang on. Why a walrus?"

"Dunno."

"Are walruses more political than other animals?"

"Well, bees are a monarchy."

"True. A parliament of walruses. Nope, doesn't sound right."

For two people who had met on a night of blood and malice, Simon Hayes and Abigail Falx had a shared talent for popping the screws of any serious conversation and cheerfully riding it downhill. It was a gift, Denizen often thought, and he loved them for it.

On any given day, Denizen Hardwick had about

thirty-seven thousand thoughts about whether what he was doing was good, whether it was bad, if it was going to harm somebody, was it *supposed* to harm somebody, was he standing funny when he did it—and overthinking wasn't the cool and interesting superpower that fiction made it out to be. It was just a bit awful all the time. With Simon, Darcie, and Abigail, he didn't have to think. They liked him. He liked them.

It was . . . automatic.

"You're thinking of owls," Denizen said. "A parliament of owls. I don't know what you call a lot of walruses. A mess, probably."

"And if they wore clothes they'd have monocles," Darcie finished.

"Exactly," Denizen said. "But guys, you didn't see Vivian. She was so *angry*. She said that if Greaves knew that Mercy had taught me the Cants, he'd take me away."

"I had been wondering about that," Darcie said in a quiet voice.

Denizen frowned. "What do you mean?"

"I didn't want to say earlier. I don't even really want to say it now. We have enough to be worrying about." She picked at the hem of her sleeve. "Have any of you not wondered why the Dublin cadre hasn't been reinforced?"

No one said anything.

"Garrisons shouldn't be left understaffed," Darcie

continued. "It's dangerous. And since D'Aubigny . . . and Grey . . . we've received no replacements."

In the back of Denizen's head, a steel box shifted, lid trembling. With a quiet breath, he clamped it shut.

"Vivian spends half her time on the road," Darcie said. "Surely you must have noticed."

Denizen had, as it happened, but with a dawning sense of shame he realized he had assumed it had been to avoid him.

"It might just be that the Order is spread thin. It's the nature of our work. But, if I were to be uncharitable, I'd ask whether Edifice Greaves might have a reason to be putting us under pressure."

"Because Vivian hasn't told him about what happened at Crosscaper?" Simon said incredulously. "Surely he wouldn't—"

"I don't know," Denizen said. "Everything he said was . . . calculated. Like a test, or something. Or he was feeling me out to see if I was like Vivian." He paused. "I think he likes pushing people's buttons. Getting them to do what he wants. As if he views everything we've been through as *currency*."

Darcie shook her head. Denizen had only ever heard her angry a couple of times, but it was in her voice now, deep and dark and cold. "That's what all this is about."

Denizen frowned. "What do you mean?"

"Everyone's here because you saved Mercy. And Greaves likes being popular, or else they'd all be staying on cots in Seraphim Row. So you're his new best friend. Or he'd like you to be. It looks good. Political currency.

"And, since this is all based on your connection to Mercy, he wants to know what that connection is. Plus . . . he has a history with Vivian."

Frown No. 11—Do I Actually Want to Know This?

"What do you mean, a history?"

"Nothing like that," Darcie said, her eyes going wide. "Or I don't think so anyway. But D'Aubigny told me once that while Greaves is *good* at being the Palatine, he wasn't everyone's first choice. When the last Palatine died, all the Mallei convened in Daybreak, the Order's ancestral headquarters. Edifice Greaves was chosen. Eventually."

Abigail leaned forward. "My dad said something similar. Vivian could have been Palatine. She was called to attend. But she . . ."

"She what?" Denizen asked.

"She didn't show up," Darcie finished. "She didn't even acknowledge the summons. Then suddenly, years later, her secret son appears and, three weeks into his training, defeats the Clockwork Three, saves the world, and ends up being owed a favor by the *Endless King*?"

"That's not what—"

"Yes, it is," Darcie said, in a voice both stern and kind. "Whether it was luck or coincidence or you being modest doesn't matter anymore. What happens next *does*."

"You're right," Denizen said. "I guess. And I'm not trying to be modest."

"OK," Darcie said.

He glanced over at Abigail. "What do you think?"

"I think I'm going to get the duck in pomegranate *jus* with the serrano ham and the hibiscus salsa," she said without looking up, "and the Goshawk didn't put prices beside its dishes, so I can't be expected to know better."

She sighed and closed the menu.

"I also think that Edifice Greaves wears a nice suit, and probably—*probably*—hasn't swung his hammer in anger in a while. But he is a Knight. No—he *was* a Knight, and then he was a Malleus, and then he became Palatine of the Order of the Borrowed Dark. Our leader."

Her voice sharpened. "First rule of combat is that you don't go in blind against a potential threat. That's why"—and she gave Darcie a respectful nod—"the *Luxes* are so important. Last winter, Knights all over the world were fighting for their lives against a threat they didn't understand, and then suddenly, in a quiet little corner of Ireland, that threat was ended. By you.

"They must have felt very helpless.

"And now we have a new situation, and you're in the middle of it again. There's a threat here, and maybe an opportunity, but nobody knows what's going to happen. Of course he needs to get the measure of you.

"Unknown quantities, Denizen. That's what kills you."

They all stared at her.

"Sorry," she said. "I'm hungry."

THAT EVENING THEY ATE like it was their last night on earth. Denizen had never stayed anywhere that put taste before functionality. Crosscaper had believed in three square meals a day—and then halving those meals to save money. Vivian cooked a stew that was the equivalent of high-octane engine fuel, and had the same taste and consistency.

The Goshawk didn't have cooks. It had *architects*, or possibly sorcerers.

"I can't," Abigail said, staring morosely at a vol-au-vent. "I won't. I refuse."

"Yield not," Denizen tried to say round a mouthful of mashed potato. It came out as *eehmf hmot*.

Simon and Darcie were flat on their backs. Neither had made a noise in some time.

When the knock came, it took Denizen a minute to process it through the gravy-fugue. With some effort, he glanced over at Abigail.

"Did you—"

"I did not," she said. "I'm never eating again."

It took two tries for Denizen to haul himself upright before padding over to the door and opening it to reveal his mother. Everyone immediately sat up—Darcie nudging Simon awake—and the Malleus eyed the graveyard of cleaned plates on the floor with what might have been amusement.

"I see you've been availing yourselves of the Palatine's generosity."

The Goshawk gave its receipts in tiny black boxes. So far no one had possessed the courage to open them.

"We've finished running through the preparations." She sniffed. "After a lot of chatting. We're ready to go to Retreat. This . . . whatever it is . . . is at sunset. Darcie, can you take Simon and Abigail back home?"

She nodded, though Abigail didn't look happy about it.

Vivian gestured at the door. "May I have the room for a moment?"

Despite their carbohydrate-induced comas, the other three Neophytes were gone before Vivian's words had vanished from the air. Denizen sat straighter, ignoring the protestations of his stomach.

"So." Vivian looked uncomfortable. "A bit different than what we're used to."

"Hah," Denizen said. "Yep."

"Mmm," she said.

Denizen was staring very carefully at a wall sconce half a meter to Vivian's left. He couldn't be sure, without sacrificing his very important perusal of the sconce, but he thought *she* might be giving serious eyeballs to the headboard in the corner.

"Did you talk to Greaves?"

"Not really," Denizen said. "I mean, I didn't . . . What did you mean when you said he'd take me away?"

Now that the immediate threat of Greaves's interrogation had passed, Vivian's walls seemed to be up again. Her gaze skipped across everything in the room that wasn't Denizen before she managed to speak.

"It doesn't matter. I'm taking care of it. Just do . . . do what you've been doing. Don't say anything to anyone about Mercy. I'll handle the rest."

"The *rest* of what?" Denizen said. Frustration was building again, that urge to just lash out and . . . and . . .

There was sweat on his brow once more.

"Denizen."

Reading Vivian's face was like trying to discern individual notes on a piano from several rooms away. Everything was hidden behind two layers of scowl. But this time he thought she looked . . . disappointed.

"You just have to trust me," she said softly. "And I . . ." She lifted her bag from her shoulder. "I have something for you."

It was a slim package wrapped in paper. Denizen took it, surprised at how heavy it was, and unwrapped it to find a knife nearly as long as his forearm in a plain black sheath.

"Draw it," she said. There was a strange tone in her voice.

The dry scrape of stone against leather filled the room. It was all one piece—blade, hilt, and rounded pommel—and curved slightly, like the talon of a great cat. Its knapped edge didn't gleam, though Denizen could *feel* the sharpness radiating from it like a whispered threat. There would never be more than the faintest shine from this weapon, and the leather that wrapped its grip was a dull gray.

Mica swarmed blackly in the stone knife's depths.

"Do you remember the shard I used to kill the Three?"

An ancient Malleus's hammer had once been buried in the chest of the Endless King's Emissary, before Denizen had shattered it against Mercy's prison. Vivian had used the largest shard to kill the Three, and it was that piece he now held, its imperfections planed away to leave a sliver of polished, murderous stone.

"You did this?" he asked. There was nothing fancy about the blade, no carvings, no flourishes. Jack was—or had been—Seraphim Row's weaponsmith, and he had always found some way to incorporate a touch of beauty to the killing edge. With this knife, the killing edge *was* its beauty. It was a perfectly simple piece of technology—just a hard line in the air, a border no monster would cross.

"I like working with my hands," Vivian said. She looked awkward. "It . . . helps me relax."

"Wow," Denizen said. "That's . . . I don't know what to say."

"It may not retain the hammer's potency," Vivian said, as if she hadn't heard him. "And you'll want something a bit bigger when you get older, but I thought for now it'd be a useful last-ditch weapon, a holdout when . . ."

She launched into a lecture, weighing the merits of knife-work versus swordplay, but Denizen wasn't listening.

He was watching her instead.

Vivian hadn't looked at him yet. She hadn't taken a seat. Now that he thought about it, he rarely saw her sit down at all. She paced, or stood with feet spread, so that even at rest she looked ready to throw a punch.

Denizen knew that should the floorboards so much as creak outside she'd have the knife out of his hands and into hers in a heartbeat. She always stood with her back to a wall. She smiled perhaps once a month. In a good month. And she was utterly fearless on the field of war.

And she couldn't look at him.

"Listen," he said. "I—"

The Malleus abruptly shoved both hands in her pockets and started toward the door as if she'd suddenly remembered she had eight other places to be. "Yes. Well. I'm glad you—yes."

Pulling the door open, Vivian glanced back at him, her face once more a calm, unshakable mask.

"Keep it close."

Whatever Denizen was going to say—and he wasn't really sure himself—went unsaid. She was already gone.

11

Where We Put Our Broken Things

An hour before sunset, the Knights deployed.

They drove a hush through the Goshawk's foyer, like static electricity before a storm. Waiters stopped in their tracks; guests paused with architecturally complex cakes mere centimeters from their lips.

First came Palatine Edifice Greaves and, though his title was a secret, he wore it like a crown. The menace in his grin was mirrored by the prowling of the men and women behind him—no two alike in appearance, but each possessed of that same dark purpose.

Tomoe Gozen, who slew Carcharadon after a day and a half of chasing the fiend through the understreets of Tokyo. Pierre Renaud, as deadly with one arm as most Knights were with two, and his duelist daughter, Camille. Eloise Cassidy and Nathaniel Gayle and Rowan, whom they called Head-Taker, and Malleus Vivian Hardwick herself.

They all wore gloves. They walked like wolves.

Behind them followed Denizen Hardwick—thirteen, worried, with a toothpaste stain on his shirt. The Knights stalked out to the waiting black jeeps as though nothing existed but their destination, and Denizen did the same, though for very different reasons.

He was thinking about monsters.

That's what the Tenebrous were, whichever way you looked at them. They were nothing but hunger and shadow until the reality of this world forced them to claw together a form. Even the ones who hadn't personally tried to eviscerate him had done a great job of scaring the hell out of him, cloaked as they were in a shroud of world-bending distortion and dread.

The jeeps were big and black and as blocky as tanks. Vivian sat across from him, her gray eyes fixed on something far away. They left the redbrick heart of Drumcondra, slipping through streets already darkening in anticipation of night.

The bad-dream angel. The eel-of-tweed. The Emissary and Pick-Up-the-Pieces and a dozen other Tenebrous Denizen had . . . encountered over the last six months.

The Clockwork Three.

The Endless King, so great and terrible that even his name made the shadows grow long.

Mercy.

I will trust you. And she had.

Vivian had once said the Endless King had his own sense of honor. He had certainly displayed a sharp understanding of justice. When Mercy had gone missing, he had reacted as any normal parent would—or so Denizen assumed. He wasn't by any means an expert.

There was no denying the fact that the Tenebrous didn't belong in this realm. The world itself flexed around them, as if trying to throw them off. But did that make them evil? *All* of them?

He ran a finger along the black iron of his palm. *This world doesn't like us either.*

Denizen had grown up on fantasy books, and plenty of them featured races who were simply *evil,* because that's what they *were.* He hadn't questioned it. When you were a kid, black robes and jagged armor made you evil. That was how you told good from bad.

Unfortunately, that idea fell apart as soon as you poked it, even if you weren't as skeptical as Denizen. Bad people—even the phrase sounded childish—could do good, and good people did bad things all too often.

Evil wasn't a cliff you fell from. It was a staircase you climbed.

But that was in books, and monsters were real, and they were going to meet some right now. It was hard to argue with empirical evidence. With bodies on the ground.

But that smile... Denizen swallowed. Monsters shouldn't have smiles like that.

* * *

Trinity College dominated the center of Dublin like a stone dragon curled on a hill—cobble-scaled and stern, its walls folded around itself like great wings. Passing through the front arch hushed the city outside until you could almost believe you'd traveled in time as well as space.

The jeeps pulled to a stop, half the Knights disembarking with Vivian and Denizen. The others drove away into the thickness of the traffic without a word.

As usual for a warm summer evening, the university's gates were clogged with packs of giggling international students, but they parted unconsciously before the Knights like flesh before a knife.

Denizen had to wonder what observers might think the Knights were. They didn't look like a tour group, unless assassin schools did day release. They certainly didn't look like students or lecturers. And then there was Denizen—a scrawny teenager sidling uncomfortably after them like a duck somehow adopted by a pack of wolves.

They wove through the campus, newer buildings clinging to the old like ticks, precarious and ready to be shaken off. A massive sculpture swept bladed limbs before it in Fellows' Square, looking uncomfortably like the war form of a Tenebrous. Students dotted the green, trying to soak up the fading sun, and the last tour groups of the evening lined up alongside the doors.

"The Long Room," Vivian murmured at Denizen's shoulder. "It—"

"—was built between 1712 and 1732," Denizen interrupted. "Extended by 1860 because they're allowed a copy of every book published in Ireland and the UK and they needed the space."

Vivian blinked.

"Sorry," Denizen said. "Books."

The electronic ticket gates had been disengaged and the group wasn't stopped by security, though the burly guard at the door eyed each Knight as if he were daring them to cause trouble. Denizen wasn't sure if that was brave or naïve.

Evidently, their visit had been prearranged. Even as they entered, Denizen noted another security guard ushering the other tour groups toward an exit, clearing the place the way you would for a visiting dignitary.

Which I guess Greaves . . . is?

Denizen jumped when the Palatine spoke right by his ear:

"This used to be a monastery, where some of our Order were brought if the trials of war became too much. A place of quiet, secrecy, and reflection. When this university was started, our garrison . . . adapted. We've lived in the cracks of this college for a long time—the shadows in its walls, the secret between its lines."

The rest of the Knights were waiting at the top of the stairs. Jack was there, and he and five others dragged massive black metal cases behind them, each one marked with the sigil of the Order—the hand-and-hammers.

Greaves nodded at each and then turned to Denizen.

"There are more discreet entrances . . . but I thought you'd appreciate this one."

Denizen followed his outswept arm and stared into the Long Room of Trinity College.

It resembled a library in the same way a mountain resembled a pebble—the same shape, but on a far more massive scale. Busts stared grimly from plinths—Newton, Goldsmith, Swift—their blank marble eyes burning into Denizen's, the walls carved deep with Latin. It had the reverent silence of a cathedral or a forest—that same sense of something ancient and powerful just a hair's breadth away. Knowledge prowled here, like a tiger in grass.

"Oh," Denizen said, the word immediately stolen away to be filed. The doors closed behind them with a muted click, leaving the security guards on the other side.

"Do they know?" Denizen asked.

"Certain people know certain things," Greaves said. "And other people know other things." He paused at an alcove marked MYTH, running his fingers lightly along the books like a pianist preparing to play.

Denizen frowned. "Are . . ."

There had been something in the Palatine's face.

"Are you enjoying this?"

Greaves's fingers stopped on a book and pulled.

"Not at all."

The bookshelf *moved.*

It slid aside on secret gears, folding to allow access to a spiral staircase. The effect was so absurdly conventional—libraries, book switches, and secret stairs—that for a second Denizen felt a shadow of Greaves's anticipation.

One by one, they descended the shaft, the staircase weaving downward like a coil of DNA. The whole tunnel couldn't have been more than a meter across—Denizen was the smallest of them by far and even he was cramped. He had no idea how Jack must have felt.

To take his mind off it, Denizen tried to calculate how far underground they were, before realizing he had no idea how to do that and concentrated on not slipping instead. When the bookcase closed again, the shaft became completely silent but for the sound of footsteps and slow exhalations of breath.

The tunnel was unlit, but darkness was no barrier to a Knight's eyes. The frosty glow of the *Intueor Lucidum* painted the world in lines of subtle silver—not banishing the dark but simply making it irrelevant. In the six months since Denizen's Dawning, he'd almost forgotten what the absence of light looked like.

The staircase eventually came to an end, metal

trembling as each warrior stepped from it. Denizen had been wondering whether it went on forever, a drill sunk deep into the earth. The air was bitterly cold.

How far down were they?

One of Greaves's men opened a thick steel door set into the wall and beckoned them all forward. Vivian's jaw was clenched. She looked even more annoyed than usual, which was saying a lot.

"What is it?" Denizen said quietly so that Greaves couldn't hear.

She simply shook her head. "You'll see."

The chamber beyond was low and long and made of stone, and it was entirely covered in carvings of Knights at war. Tiny figures crusaded across the ceiling or marched in regiments along the floor, crashing in great waves against the rows of doorways beyond.

Denizen was kneeling. He didn't even remember doing it. He just wanted to *see*. The detail of the Knights was excruciatingly fine. Some of the carved flagstones looked newly laid, the mortar still bright and fresh. Others looked like they had been there for centuries. He could make out the markings on their armor, the hand-and-hammers on every flag; he could make out the fragments of iron carefully crafted to represent the Cost they'd paid. . . .

They looked determined. They looked unafraid.

"When a Knight is . . ." For the first time since they'd

met, Greaves looked like he wasn't sure of the right words to use, though Denizen knew enough of him at this point to wonder whether it was an actual pause or a pause . . . for effect.

"Knights are powerful people. I don't just mean the Cants. No one is forced to enter the Order; they join because they are people of singular will and bravery, possessed of a rare kind of determination. A conviction. A courage."

He stared at each Knight in turn. "We are made of a different metal."

The first of the cases was being brought in, the Knights pausing as they heard Greaves's voice. Denizen watched their backs straighten at his words.

"The Order takes that metal and reforges it. We clothe that will in training, in strategy. Knights are taught to fight impossible battles against impossible odds, working in secret, unseen, undetected, and alone. That makes us dangerous."

"And then there are the Cants," Denizen said.

"And then there are the Cants," Greaves repeated. "That will, and that training, and the power to break the world with words of fire. Knights are human weapons . . . but, for all that, we are still human. And weapons break. And humans fail."

A thousand details that had been simmering just below Denizen's consciousness finally surfaced. Realization crept up on him slowly, like the taste of bile.

That was why this place disgusted Vivian. That was why it was called Retreat, not *The* Retreat. Each of the doorways had a thick steel door, with a shuttered slot at head height.

All the locks were on the outside.

"You kept them here," Denizen said, and there was horror in his tone. "You kept them here if they lost themselves."

"*Retreat,*" Greaves said. "When a Knight goes wrong, we're lucky if all they do is run." To his credit, the revulsion on his face looked entirely real. "This place is a necessary evil."

As most Tenebrous lacked hearts, brains, and other easily stabbable places, the Order's weapons had been forged with the same fire that infused their wielders. *Spoken steel.* The same etchings that characterized a spoken-steel blade marked these doors as well.

Greaves read the realization on his face and nodded. "You could roar every Cant you possessed and not make a scratch."

Shapes purred in Denizen's head, but he ignored them as best he could. *Not the time.* Or the place.

"The most secure location on three continents," Jack said. "We could hold it against half the Tenebrae."

"Is that what we're going to be doing?" Vivian said. She sounded far more comfortable with that than the idea of talking to them.

"No," Greaves said. "This is diplomacy." He drew his

hammer. "And that diplomacy comes with a price."

Vivian's eyes widened. "*That's* the promise you made?"

"Twelve Knights," Greaves said. "No hammers. They were very clear."

Mallei hammers were the most potent weapons the Order possessed. They were the only thing that could truly destroy an ancient Tenebrous instead of merely driving it back to the Tenebrae. Denizen could count on one hand the number of times he had seen Vivian without hers.

His hand immediately went to his bag, where the stone blade waited. Did it still retain any of the potency of a full hammer? Did Greaves know he had it? Should he say something?

Vivian's glare shut Denizen's mouth for him, and his hand dropped to his side.

"It's all right," Greaves said. His smile had returned, as if they weren't standing in an underground asylum about to meet monster nobility. "I didn't come empty-handed."

At his nod, the lids of the six cases were thrown wide. Inside each, packed in dark foam, was a suit of disassembled armor.

Denizen leaned forward. Each piece was ink-black, so dark even the silvered shades of the *Lucidum* seemed to slip from its surface. They were massive too—Denizen had spent plenty of time polishing Vivian's armor, and he had a beginner's knowledge of sizes and weights. Maybe Jack could have moved and fought beneath the massive plates of iron, but very few others.

"Hephaestus Warplate," Vivian whispered, an unfamiliar note in her voice. It was awe, plain and simple. "I've never seen it before."

"Well, we only get dressed up for special occasions," Greaves said wryly. "I figured this qualified." The humor vanished from his voice as he glanced at Denizen. "You asked me earlier if I was enjoying this."

Denizen colored.

"I take my joy where I can find it," the Palatine said. "We have lived this war for so long. If what happens here today has even the *chance* of ending it . . . For that, I'll make any promise. For that, I'll do anything. And so will you. Do you understand?"

Denizen did.

"Good," Greaves said. "Now let's go meet your public."

12

The Forever Court

They didn't have long to wait.

One by one, the hairs on Denizen's neck rose, the Tenebrae breathing along the shocked and upright strands. At first, it was a quiet wrongness—the familiar becoming unfamiliar, like a beloved song played slightly out of key.

Those with a Knight's blood were naturally more sensitive, and since his first Breach, Denizen's senses had been sharpened for strangeness. When normal people felt another world intrude on theirs, they got as far away as they could, making awkward jokes about it at home later, when surrounded by loved ones and bright lights.

I wish my friends were here.

Even as he had the thought, Denizen knew he wasn't alone. Around him, twelve Knights drew their weapons with a thoroughly reassuring rasp of steel.

"Hold," Greaves said. "They said sunset. We have a few minutes." He was half into a suit of Hephaestus Warplate, being helped by a small female Knight with a thundercloud of black-and-silver hair.

The armor was ludicrously large. Only one Knight—Nathaniel Gayle—had fully donned his, and he no longer looked like a person at all but a fortress come to life. Vanes rose above the armor's shoulders like smokestacks. The helmet was a blunt, eyeless fist of steel.

How can he fight if he can't see? Denizen couldn't imagine walking in the armor, let alone fighting in it—unless the Court were considerate enough to line up so he could just fall on them.

Denizen was staring at the Knight so intently that he flinched when sudden fire gleamed from the black armor's surface. Incandescence ran from joint to joint like magma worming its way through stone. Lines of light crisscrossed and split across each plate, diving in shafts of gold down chest and legs, coiling through pauldron and helmet.

The vanes emitted a purr of superheated air.

Eyes opened along secret seams—the red-gold of banked embers. Denizen knew that fire. It danced through his bones as well.

With a rumble akin to some great hidden forge, the Knight took a grinding step forward, shrugging massive shoulders into a brawler's stance.

He doesn't need a weapon, Denizen thought, staring at those huge, spiked fists. *He* is *a weapon.*

Vivian was looking at the armor with undisguised hunger. "Beautiful, isn't it?"

And it was, for sheer destructive potential. More of the Knights had donned the warplate, and now each was two and a half meters tall, spines barbed and flaring like the threatening hood of a cobra. Every breath they took was a rattling growl of metal.

Comforting. It was comforting. The chamber was filling with the corroded reek of the Tenebrae, and nausea was already fluttering in Denizen's throat, but as each Hephaestus Knight took their stand it was hard to imagine *anything* breaking that colossal line.

"In that armor, a Knight can punch through stone," Vivian murmured. "They were forged in the first days of the Order, in more . . . uncivilized times."

"Smiths gave their lives to forge each suit," Jack said. "The Cost was judged sufficient for weapons of such power. They're priceless, only unveiled in direst need."

People gave their lives to build those?

That made a horrible kind of sense—presumably, if there were more, they'd all be wearing one. Denizen had only been a Neophyte for six months, but he had always thought his clash with the Three had given him a crash course in just how bad the war against the Tenebrae could be. But to live in a time when Knights would give their life in one gasp just to forge a weapon for another? How desperate had things been? And, despite everything, a tiny part of Denizen couldn't help but imagine what it would be like to be sheathed in that power, to feel unearthly metal support your blows. . . .

Armored, but with his helmet at his side, Greaves glanced at Denizen as if he knew exactly what he was thinking. Denizen flushed and looked away.

Knights had spread out, all facing the simple wooden door at the far end of the chamber. Crossbows were prepped with spoken-steel bolts. The Penumbra-Corp agent, Strap, drew a bulky handgun from underneath his long coat. Mallei gave up their hammers for spoken-steel swords and axes, Vivian scowling as she parted with hers.

Denizen was suddenly struck by how few of the assembly's names he actually knew. No one had stopped for introductions. It didn't help that all their gazes were so intense that Denizen tended to immediately drop his eyes to the floor.

He didn't know their names.

A sick feeling bloomed in his stomach at that, a disquiet that was nothing to do with the Tenebrae.

They were here because of him. This was all happening because of him.

Denizen didn't like to think of himself dying. That was, he thought, pretty standard for a normal person. But what was generally a low-level dread had been kicked into overdrive by the idea of being pushed into the spotlight before the Forever Court. Denizen had been very busy worrying about himself.

He hadn't, for a second, thought about how other people might end up dying.

That's what Knights do. Denizen had his own experience of that choice. It was what had made him believe he wanted—no, *needed*—to be a Knight, to add his voice and fire to theirs. Knights died to keep the world safe from Tenebrous.

But now they might die for *him*.

The woman who had helped Greaves into his armor was standing directly in front of Denizen, her eyes pale and wide, her face a raw-boned collection of angles dusted by freckles. Black-and-silver curls bobbed to her shoulders. She might have been Jack's age. She might have been much younger.

The Tenebrae breathed through the room—and Denizen didn't know her name.

Beyond her there was a man as slender and lithe as a jaguar, muscles shifting beneath a mat of dense tattoos. He held a spear in one hand, its blade long and delicately curved—and Denizen didn't know his name.

This fear, this dread, it's the Tenebrae. Ignore it. It's just the bow wave of a Breach. It's—

It's the truth. Every drop of blood, every scrap of skin fed today to the cold hunger of the Cost—that was on him. If he said the wrong thing to Mercy—and suddenly *that* hit him—

She's going to be here soon and, oh God—

Denizen was filled with competing types of fear, and through it all came the dentist-drill whine of the rising Tenebrae. Air moved in ways it shouldn't. Watches vied with each other as to which could tick backward the fastest. A room of closed doors was suddenly filled with a fetid, creeping wind.

The walls shifted in Denizen's peripheral vision—closer, then farther away. He had the sickening thought that maybe the soil beyond had turned to liquid, an endless, hungry sea, and they were all adrift on it in a sinking chamber of stone.

The wooden door rattled on its hinges.

Blades rose, a forest of glinting steel. Hephaestus Knights squared their titanic shoulders, fire spitting from their joints.

"Steady," Greaves said.

Denizen slipped his hand into his bag, wrapping his fingers round the cool hilt that lay there.

The door rattled again. A screw popped free to bounce from the floor.

Maybe she doesn't want this meeting at all. Denizen's stomach had officially caved in on itself. *Maybe it's her dad. Dads are supposed to be overprotective, aren't they? Even giant god-father-monster things. Maybe this isn't diplomacy. Maybe this is about getting me to hold still so I can be swatted. . . .*

"Um," he said. "Sorry."

Not one of the Knights turned round.

Denizen's voice was a squeak. "Maybe we should—"

The door exploded.

Shards and splinters rode a wave of black liquid, the nightstuff of the Tenebrae. It seethed outward from the doorway, tendrils latching on to the wood like blind fingers seeking purchase. Great torrents heaved themselves out with soundless splashes, as if an ocean lay beyond the simple wooden doorframe. Denizen staggered as the whole chamber shook.

What had come before—the nausea, the intangible wrongness—was nothing compared to what hit them now. It felt like the world was ending, and all Denizen could think of was whether Darcie was clutching her head at home, whether Knights a thousand miles away felt the world flinch at such a grievous injury.

The wrongness gave another heave, punching the air from Denizen's chest, and what he drew in to replace it was pestilence so vile it made him gag.

And it spoke. It spoke in the tones of a prince.

Introducing . . .

How sly, that voice. How amused.

Liquid still flowed from the doorway, but before it could wash up against the boots of the Knights it *paused,* rolling back on itself as though meeting an invisible wall. Denizen watched the Knights carved into the floor drown beneath it.

The Herald of the Court, the Fatale Monstrum, the Smile Kuchisake . . .

A hand slid from the murk, followed by an arm with too many joints, and a bladed shoulder behind. Denizen's eyes slid from it like water from feathers. All he could see was a long slice of shine, like the monomolecular edge of a diamond. More of it passed through the blackness—long, gleaming limbs, a sharp teardrop of a head. He could only tell its shape from the distorted reflections painting the chamber a thousand hues, like the inside of a haunted kaleidoscope.

Mocked-By-a-Husband!

Its grin split the air in half.

To the left of Mocked-By-a-Husband, the nightstuff rippled like a pond suddenly hammered by stones. The ripples spread *in,* however, and from them burst the shapes of birds, a cacophony white as virgin snow.

Badb, the Covet Congress, What-Men-Called-Muinnin . . .

Pale crows spun and fluttered, slamming off floor and ceiling before coming together in a clot of wing and eye. The chamber rang with the sound of cawing, the scrape of talon and feather. The mass shifted, and twitched, and rose—a murder of birds in an approximate human shape.

Malebranche!

Two dozen sets of eyes blinked. Beaks long and sharp gleamed among feathers.

There was a third Tenebrous. Denizen hadn't even seen it appear. It was a man, or the shape of a man. He could barely see it behind the towering Hephaestus Knights, but in scattered glimpses he could see that it was sleek in the way sharks were sleek, and beautiful in the way spiders were beautiful.

It smiled at him. Denizen flinched so violently his shoulders hurt.

Even the disembodied voice seemed afraid.

Rout.

Was the voice coming from the blackness? Was it one of the Court speaking? Mocked-By-a-Husband didn't seem to have a mouth. Malebranche had too many. Rout—*no*. Denizen did not want to think about that smile again.

The voice paused, and each of the Court stood taller, resplendent in their shroud of unreality.

Attend upon the Forever Court!

Not one of the Knights moved. Denizen watched them because it was easier than looking at the monsters in front of them. Not one weapon shook or dipped.

How are they so calm?

Denizen suddenly understood Vivian's complete opposition to this meeting. Not just because it could be a trap, but because it was *unnatural* to be standing here and not lashing out with every weapon they had.

It was the first lesson humanity learned. Put a fire between you and the dark.

Power itched through Denizen's guts. He could already see the patterns the flames would make in the air. Rout first. That smile needed to be burned away. The Hephaestus Knights would follow his lead, he was sure of it. They'd take Mocked-By-a-Husband and then Denizen could—

A new light bloomed.

Attend upon Her . . .

If a Knight's fire was a searing summer heat, then her light was that of a faraway star. It fell like cool water upon Denizen's skin. Somehow, through the massive bulk of the Hephaestus Knights, it reached him. Maybe they had moved out of the way. Maybe it had just shone through them.

As if it were meant for him.

Mercy.

She wore a shawl of witchlight that shimmered with every step she took, becoming a longcoat, chain mail, a half-murk of cloud. Her limbs flashed with blue and lilac, the bright soft purple of an unworldly sunset.

The color of royalty.

The disembodied voice spoke again, but Denizen wasn't listening. He wasn't even afraid anymore, not really. There was only so much room in his head, and right now he was full of awe.

She was bent light and blizzard in the shape of a girl, features changing moment to moment, her eyes gleaming polar white. Purling threads of lightning lit her translucent skin from within. Denizen remembered the taste of that lightning on his lips, and blushed so hard it could have been considered an act of war.

"Hi," Denizen said. Syllables were suddenly very difficult. "Um. Hello."

Now a couple of the Knights looked at him, faces taut with surprise.

Wait. Am I not supposed to be—oh.

Greaves cleared his throat.

"The Order of the Borrowed Dark, and I, its Palatine and Malleus Primus, formally . . ." He paused, as if even he could not believe the words he was about to say. "Formally *welcome* you to the freehold of Dublin, and Ireland, and to the mortal plane. The words we speak are words of greeting. Not fire."

Mocked-By-a-Husband inclined its bladed head.

Wise, little meat.

Denizen felt rather than saw the Knights around him stiffen. The temperature of the room jumped twenty degrees, light streaking beneath skin.

Mercy didn't say anything. She just looked at each face in turn, as though committing them to memory. It was an effort for Denizen to drag his eyes from hers.

Forgive Mocked-By-a-Husband, Malebranche said in

twelve voices at once. The sound made Denizen want to throw up. *My dear comrade is out of practice speaking to any but itself. Allow me to caw in more civilized tones. Thank you, Palatine. This is . . . a strange meeting. We all know the truth of that.* Feathers rustled as birds settled into new positions. *But we of the Tenebrae are no strangers to change.*

Greaves's smile had never looked so forced. "Indeed."

Denizen had never considered before how *alien* birds were—all edges and hollow bones, switchblades sheathed in flesh. One by one, Malebranche's heads snapped forward to stare at him. He felt the weight of their glare like a physical blow.

And this is the boy.

"Let me guess," Greaves said drily, "you thought he'd be taller."

Its black eyes glimmered. *You all look the same to me.*

Idiocy, Mocked-By-a-Husband snapped, the syllables bouncing round the room like sharpened coins. Blades came up as the Court-creature took a step forward, shining limbs slicing the air. Even Malebranche jerked sideways in surprise. *Why do we bother? These things are paltry, short-lived. . . . What thanks do we owe them?*

Denizen could see them all reflected in her depths, tiny and pale and afraid. This Tenebrous *stank* of power. The air shimmered around her in a way Denizen had never seen before—not in the Three, not in Pick-Up-the-Pieces, not even in the Emissary itself.

What is to stop us cutting through these frail beasts and gorging ourselves on the city above—

"Do you know what a Claymore is?"

Mocked-By-a-Husband froze. Evidently, it was not used to being interrupted.

"Not the sword," Greaves continued calmly, "though thematically that's quite good. The M18 Claymore mine—a pretty simple contraption. Fires a whole mess of tiny spoken-steel balls at a very unfriendly velocity. One word from me and you'll have to be separated from each other with a sieve."

As one, the Court's heads bent to stare at the line of freshly laid flagstones on the floor.

Mocked-By-a-Husband purred again, but this time there was a note of uncertainty in its tone.

You would also die.

There was nothing forced about Greaves's smile now.

"We are Knights."

Now that we have all shown sufficient teeth . . .

Mercy's voice was a cascade of rain, each syllable soft and delicate.

Your precautions are . . . unnecessary, Palatine, but understood. Know, though, that my father is a King of his word. We are here under the colors of peace.

Greaves nodded. "The Order has always held the Endless King in respect."

It wasn't a lie. They had, the same way you respected forest fires and meteor strikes.

We are here to thank Denizen Hardwick. He saved me when I was struck low by villains within our own ranks. An act of bravery crossing two worlds. A human helping a Tenebrous. Her smile gleamed. ***A most unlikely thing.***

A heartbeat passed, and then—

But what if it wasn't?

The chamber was suddenly so quiet that Denizen heard Greaves blink in surprise. The Palatine's voice was careful.

"Excuse me?"

What if humans and Tenebrous coming together was not the event of a millennium, the unique consequence of a vicious crime, but instead a chance to talk of peace?

Shock rippled round the chamber at the word. Not one of the Knights took their eyes from Mercy, but Denizen saw shoulders tense and blades tremble. Even Greaves looked taken aback. It was harder to tell with the Court—alien bodies, alien reactions—but both Malebranche and Mocked-By-a-Husband swung round to stare at the daughter of their King.

Mercy's smile was innocent.

We will return here, on the last day of the moon's dark,

with a gift. Something to show our resolve toward a new path. She waved a hand. And, of course, our gratitude.

She didn't look at Denizen. She didn't even *glance* at him.

Would you meet us, Palatine? Would you listen to us, if we had words of peace to share?

To his credit, Greaves recovered magnificently.

"Such words would be very welcome," he said. "Here? The last day of the lunar cycle? And all accords and rules the same?"

Agreed.

Mocked-By-a-Husband growled low in its throat. ***You hardly think we will come back to this place, with your—your snares, your trap-things in the floor?***

Greaves shrugged with a clatter of armor. "That's the deal. That's *diplomacy*."

The darkness behind the Court began to recede, a tidal wave in reverse. Malebranche shook itself apart in a storm of glossy white wings. Mocked-By-a-Husband turned away, but not before baring her shard-teeth one last time. Mercy inclined her head. Perfectly demure, like the queen-in-waiting she was.

I keep my promises.

The shining form of Mocked-By-a-Husband turned sideways into the retreating murk and vanished, raw hostility rising off it like steam. Malebranche was a diminishing ripple in black liquid. Rout had already gone. Denizen had never seen it move.

Mercy bowed—once, low—and then came apart in a thousand curlicues of light. The doorway behind her no longer led to an ocean of black, but to another long corridor of stone. It was as if the Tenebrous had never stood there at all.

Except that where before thousands of carved knights had stood and marched, now there was only smooth stone, like a spoon licked clean.

"OK," Greaves said, when the eddying dread had faded. "*What?*"

13

The Trial of Ambrel Croit

"Know that it is not I who judge you," Grandfather said, each word a frozen nail, "for we have already been judged."

Panic. Uriel fought to push some measure of Croit dignity into his spine, but the shakes came all the same. He was surrounded by his Family in the midst of their stronghold. Their Redemptress hung above them, a spider-sprawl of wires topped by the most beautiful face he had ever seen.

This was his home. This was Her Shrine. This should have been the place where Uriel felt safest in all the world.

But Ambrel looked so *small*.

"We were judged long ago," the old man continued. He had traded his customary stiff black suit for a robe of unblemished Judging White, billowing sleeves hiding his right hand and his empty left. The other Croits, arrayed in a silent circle, wore the same.

Tabitha wore Accusers' Red and Ambrel knelt in Failure's Gray, her eyes downcast, her heartbeat pounding in Uriel's chest.

He had refused to wear the White. *Let them punish me for that. Let them do whatever they want, as long as they don't . . .*

"We were judged, and found wanting, and we wear that black Transgression on our skin. It is unavoidable, as we train for our War. But it is *only* in Her service that we use Her Favor, and *only* in the ways She provides."

Uriel didn't even have to look. Meredel would be fingering the splotch of iron on his cheek. Hagar's left eye wept constantly since one side of her face had turned fully to iron, and the silence was filled with the soft clicks of her blinking. Roch, Osprey, Adauctus . . . even Uriel, thumb relentlessly rubbing the cold spot in the center of his palm.

Every Croit dreamt of the day when their Transgression would flake from them like rust, and the fire of their Favor could spill out without fear.

"Accuse her," Grandfather said.

It was a good story, Uriel thought numbly, and Tabitha told it well—though in Uriel's memory neither of them had been quite so incompetent. To hear their aunt, the twins wouldn't have managed to cross the necropolis had only the crows stood against them. The part about the sword she told true. Why exaggerate when the truth was damning enough?

Ambrel's shoulders had slumped. She looked drained. Broken.

The little color in Grandfather's face had leached away by the time Tabitha finished. She took her place behind him once again, but not before Uriel saw a smile of cold triumph dart across her face.

It would have been a lie to say that Uriel had never contemplated violence against his Family, because siblings fought and Tabitha existed, but Croits were raised on violence. It was a natural part of life: *us* and *them*, and always, *always*, those two were on a terminal trajectory.

This was the first time, however, that he'd felt his Family was on the other side.

A Croit must always be ready to judge the unworthy.

But she isn't. She's my sister, and she believes.

"Have you anything to say in your defense?"

Slowly, slowly, Ambrel raised her head.

"Everything I have ever done," she said, "has been in service to the Redemptress. My every heartbeat has been for Her. Had our—*my* birthday proved me unFavored . . . I would have died. I would not have been able to live had She turned Her face from me."

She stared at the Redemptress with tears in her eyes.

"But She Favored me. Whatever happened in the

Garden of the Waiting, it was a mistake. Grandfather—you always told us never to surrender, never to accept defeat. That's all I was doing. I was desperate and I *reached*—"

She took a deep and ragged breath.

"I defended Uriel when I was assigned to hunt him with Tabitha. That was wrong, and I will do whatever Penance you require. But as for drawing his sword . . ."

Uriel had never been so terrified, nor so proud. Ambrel's voice cracked with sorrow and, yes, rage—the rage that boiled under the skin of every Croit, only needing the smallest of excuses to be set free.

"I didn't even know I could do it! How can it be wrong if I didn't even *know*?"

"Because I say so!"

Grandfather's words cut the Shrine to silence. Ambrel flinched. Meredel's hand went still on his cheek. The sneer disappeared from Tabitha's face. Echoes crashed round the chamber, sliced to pieces by the wires, until the syllables fell around them like rain.

A surge of nausea climbed in Uriel's stomach. The noise didn't stop. The echoes didn't die away. Croits were looking around bewilderedly, pressing hands against ears. Even Grandfather had the most disconcerting look of confusion on his face, and it took Uriel far too long to see the cause.

The wires were trembling.

Fat cables throbbed their vibrations against the

stone. Hair-thin filaments fluttered, separating from themselves in sine waves of absolute black. The walls shook as their secret tendons contracted, dust sloughing down in sheets of choking gray.

SNAP.

An iron statue fell as the wires pinning it to the wall retracted, curling back on themselves like sliced sinews. Uriel ducked away from their waspish hum. None of the Croits were standing now—none but Grandfather, prowling back and forth, seemingly mindless of the razor chords playing the air, and Ambrel, staring up with painfully wide eyes.

What is She—

The air was suddenly shocking cold. Motes of dust paused in their orbits and then fell as if turned to lead. A feeling of crushing, vicious *wrong* howled through the chamber, like nothing Uriel had ever felt before. It poisoned the air, painting him instantly in a layer of oily, freezing sweat. He barely noticed.

The Redemptress was screaming, and it sounded like the end of the world.

Stone shattered as Her wires flexed. The sound was everywhere—a retching, hive-hum drawl—and She clutched Her head with wire claws, back arched as though trying to tear Herself apart. Dust drizzled from the gaps in Her chest.

Ambrel was screaming too—cowering on her knees, a child before Her gigantic shadow. Such panic in her voice. Uriel barely recognized the words.

"I'MSORRYI'MSORRYI'MSORRYI'MSORRY—"

Osprey cowered. Magnus wept. Tabitha had fled, her robe a smear of red on the ground. Another moment, another second, and the castle would come down. Uriel almost welcomed the thought. At least then the howl might end.

"MAJESTY!"

Everything stopped. The wires froze in the air, a forest of beckoning fingers. Dust still fell from the ceiling, but the creak of abused masonry faded. Grandfather's voice echoed, and the universe held its breath.

I . . .

Darkness writhed in the cavern of Her skull. Tendrils wound and unwound, and Her empty gaze fell on the terrified faces of Her Favored.

I heard a door open.

Her voice was tiny.

It opened and I woke.

Each word a lost little thing.

Are you there?

Uriel had never seen Grandfather so gentle.

"My Redemptress, I . . ."

WHERE ARE YOU?

Suddenly She spun, wires thrashing, mouth twisted in a desperate snarl. Pillars came apart in slick-cut shards. She lifted the Adversary's iron bodies and stared into their faces before flinging them aside.

Ambrel. Uriel tried to inch forward, but a tendril scored the stone in front of him and he froze. *Ambrel, where are you?*

"He survived, Majesty!"

The Redemptress froze.

Soft light bled from the skin of Ambrel Croit. She got to her feet, heedless of the slicing strands, and stared up into the face of her goddess.

"The First Croit survived, Majesty. He survived, and we are what is left of him. We are his promise to serve You. To avenge You. We are Your Family and You will lead us to the War That Will Come."

Glacier-slow, the Redemptress frowned.

War? I don't . . . She looked around. ***This was our home.*** Her eyes traced the ruined stones. ***We were going to be happy here.***

Ambrel opened her mouth to speak again, but Grandfather cut her off.

"There was a battle, Majesty. The Adversary came and the castle fell. You slept. The First Croit couldn't wake you. But his Family waited. We waited for so long."

I slept. . . . I think I dreamt. . . .

Her voice was soft.

Am I the only one there is?

"We waited *so long,* My Lady," Grandfather repeated. There was a horrible, aching yearning to his voice that Uriel had never heard before. "But You've returned. I will call them—all the Croits, all Your servants. We are scattered, but for You . . . for You they will return."

Croits.

Uriel had never heard his name said like that before. Tasted. Weighed. As if the word were not simply enough.

Yes.

She stared down at each of them in turn. Uriel felt himself wither beneath that gaze, those twin points of shimmering black.

How many?

"Enough," Grandfather said. "I promise you."

Her voice was sharp.

There will never be enough to serve me.

The words were stilted, as though She were quoting. Wires skittered through the dark, and it was all Uriel could do to stop the fire rising up through him. It *recognized* Her. Osprey's hands were dug into his temples the way they always were when he was fighting for control. Meredel's fists were white by his sides.

Of course the Favor knows Her, a part of Uriel protested. *It's Hers.*

Rivulets of scarlet climbed his bones and it was only with the greatest of effort that he pushed them down again. Eager. That was it. They felt eager.

And angry.

The Adversary . . .

The Redemptress's eyes were wide. She descended

gracefully, pivoting as though on hidden joints. Black oil beaded on Her wires as She stared into Ambrel's eyes.

I remember that light, She whispered. ***We stole it. We stole it together.*** Her voice trembled. ***But all this . . . these words. This war . . . I don't, I DON'T REMEMBER—***

The trembles became a shudder, then a fit. Once more the chamber shook, and the Croits ducked for cover.

All but Ambrel. She stood tall and reached out to take the Redemptress's hand.

Grandfather stared. Uriel stared. They could do nothing else.

"That's all right," Ambrel said. Her smile was saintly. "We remembered it for You."

14

The Right Place to See

Vivian was right that the visiting Knights could have stayed in Seraphim Row. The mansion was so vast that Denizen's desire to explore the echoing, whispering darkness of the house had run out long before the corridors had.

Seraphim Row was *ample*. It was *commodious*. Had the Neophytes wanted a room, or a suite, or even a whole wing to themselves, the manor would have grimly obliged.

Ow.

Denizen reached down to massage his knee where he had banged it against the edge of Simon's bed. The other boy didn't notice, sleepily rearranging his blankets back over his head. Through unspoken agreement, Simon had not staked out his own room. He had just dragged a bed into Denizen's.

The Clockwork Three had taken their toll on

everyone. Simon claimed to have put those dark weeks trapped in Crosscaper behind him, but Denizen spent long nights listening to his friend tossing and turning, lost in bad dreams.

Now, however, possibly due to the excitement of meeting Edifice Greaves and consuming half of the Goshawk's larders, he was quietly snoring to himself. Denizen was another matter. He couldn't sit still, let alone sleep. He'd managed to ding himself off every piece of furniture in his room, despite having perfect night vision. His head felt full of fireflies and jittery lightning.

Surely that can't have been it.

Not that things hadn't happened. They had *definitely* happened. Mercy had just casually walked in—or floated in, Denizen supposed—and dropped the biggest metaphorical bombshell in the history of the Order.

Peace.

Not a single Knight had spoken on their way out of Retreat. Vivian had dropped Denizen home and turned on her heel to go right back out of the door again. Nobody had bothered to inform him as to what it might mean—*at least that's consistent,* he thought sourly—but he could guess.

Peace. Even the chance of it, even the chance of a conversation about it . . .

But that wasn't why Denizen was pacing. Peace was a huge thing. Crucial. Imperative. World-changing, even.

She didn't even look at me.

But why would she? Denizen wasn't an idiot. He *knew* it wasn't like they were just going to *hang out*. He'd read enough fantasy books to know that diplomacy didn't mean honesty and conversation. It meant fancy dinners, watching betrayal flash behind people's eyes, and not trusting Grand Viziers.

Some of that wasn't transferable to the real world; Denizen had actually been betrayed six months ago and that person had just looked terrified and nauseous. Betrayal hadn't *moved behind their eyes*, or peeked out from their ears or anything.

Denizen made a mental note to find out if Mercy had any Grand Viziers, and then a further mental note to tell her to get rid of them if she did.

That's if I get to talk to her at all.

Denizen's window caved in.

The glass took an age to come apart, each splinter twinkling sharp and limned with an eldritch blue glow. The light made something beautiful out of each shard—a snowflake, a sapphire—and for a second Denizen just stared, which was exactly the wrong thing to do when fragments of glass were hurtling toward your face.

And then he blinked, and saw it didn't matter.

Cradled in cerulean light, each sliver spun slow and lazy through the air, saving Denizen from a lifetime of eye patches and facial scars. He stepped carefully round the mist of particles still sluggishly breathing across the room and looked out the window.

Mercy glimmered on the far side of the street.

He couldn't use the front door—Vivian had come back earlier and might still be prowling around. That left . . .

A really *terrible* idea.

The Art of Apertura wasn't so much a set of syllables as it was the suck of a gale through a broken window. It was a Cant designed to wound the universe, ripping a hole between *here* and *there* with a fall through the freezing, numbing black water of the Tenebrae in between. As with most Higher Cants, it was as useful as it was dangerous. Knights only spoke it as a last resort.

Which means I really shouldn't use it as an elevator.

Skin crinkled and cooled as Denizen hooked his fingers before him and *pulled,* opening a yawn of shadow in the air. His fluency eased the Cost, but the universe's knee-jerk reaction to the insult of his power would not be defied, and Denizen still felt the prickle as his blood ran through veins suddenly stiff and cold. *You're getting used to that feeling,* a part of him whispered, but Denizen had already stepped forward before logic and rationality could fully catch up.

Eyes scrunched shut.

There are darknesses we're not meant to see through.

Breath held.

There are waters too cold to drink.

Cold like a slap, like a scalpel, like a hammer. A hard tug on the iron of his palms and then—

Denizen managed not to stumble as frigid water became hard tarmac, the clinging nightstuff of the Tenebrae hissing away from his limbs in streamers of black smoke. He had been immersed for less than a second, and yet it was a struggle not to draw on his fire to burn away the chill.

Impressive, Mercy murmured. She was barely a sketch in the air, just a sweep of lines in the shape of a girl. If anyone glanced at her from the wrong angle, they wouldn't see her at all.

The right angle, of course, being from his bedroom window.

"Hi," Denizen said. *Right, that's all I'm planning to say, is it?* He took a deep breath. "You broke my window." *Nailed it.*

I wanted to wake you, she said, and then suddenly dipped closer. ***I stopped the glass. Are you hurt?***

"No," Denizen said quickly. "No, I'm fine." He winced, glancing back to the window. "But Simon—"

Mercy crooked her hand, and Denizen saw blue light and glass shards puff outward from the window, their trajectory suddenly reversed. That would at least save Simon's feet in the case of a late-night run to the bathroom.

Although he'd probably have more questions about why I and the windowpane have both disappeared.

In fact, now that Denizen thought about it, he could suddenly think of all sorts of people who would question what exactly he and Mercy thought they were doing.

"This is a terrible idea," Denizen said, staring at Seraphim Row's great doors as if Vivian were about to burst through them with her hammer raised. "We should—"

Get out of here, Mercy finished. ***You're right.***

Seraphim Row masqueraded as the Embassy of Adumbral—a country barely larger than its own passport, the home of Daybreak, the Order's ancestral keep—hidden among other, real embassies with flags and gold plaques on the doors.

Denizen sometimes wondered if some of them were fronts as well, and whether other societies lurked behind an air of respectability. The Knights could hardly be Dublin's only secret.

What he was mostly worrying about was someone stumbling into a thirteen-year-old boy walking alongside a shimmering blueprint, a tracery-girl, the shape of the street behind her bent and warped like something seen through water.

Denizen pointed at a blocky town house.

"Most of the embassies close at five . . . ?"

A wrought-iron gate led to its backyard, held shut with a padlock. Excellent protection against trespassers, no doubt. *Unless they're me,* Denizen thought, a trifle smugly, until Mercy passed an ephemeral hand through the padlock and it clicked open to fall to the ground. She shot him a look that was half admonishing, half amused.

I'm a visiting dignitary, Denizen Hardwick. I can't be leaving property damage in my wake.

She had a point. Someone was going to come to unlock this gate in the morning, and that would be difficult if it had been melted in half.

Mercy drifted into the garden beyond, Denizen following sheepishly. When they were hidden from the street, she let out a sigh as faint as the parting of clouds and her luminescence grew. Miniature starbursts climbed her spine, a nuclear crescendo that painted the overhanging trees and grass a rich silver. Denizen's breath plumed in the sudden wintry air, an echo of the cold that had gripped Crosscaper the first time they met.

That's better, she murmured. ***Keeping myself hidden, keeping myself subtle . . . that's an effort.***

An effort she had obviously relaxed. As the light exhaled from her form, so did the alien feel of the Tenebrae. Softer than the raw assault of the Forever Court, the air still thrummed with her power.

Mercy glitched and blurred in Denizen's vision. He tasted snow, then tin, then something that might have been flowers. The rustle of the wind bent into a thousand whispers, speaking a language that, if he strained, he felt he could almost understand. . . .

He shook his head.

This is better, she said. ***We can speak here.***

"Yes," said Denizen. "Yep. Mmm."

Silence eddied the grass.

How could somebody have spent their entire life reading books and then, at a moment this crucial, have absolutely no words in their head? Denizen had weighed a thousand times the handful of sentences they'd shared. He'd barely managed to get out of that conversation alive—figuratively and literally—so no wonder he was terrified to start another one.

Just stare at the ground.

How have you–

"I looked for you," he said suddenly, and winced as his voice chose precisely *that* moment to crack. "I mean, in books."

She nodded. ***Did you find anything?***

"No," Denizen said. "And then I . . . I stopped looking. It felt weird. Like I wouldn't be learning about you from you? I'd be getting whatever the writer thought." He gave an awkward shrug. "It didn't feel right."

He looked up. Mercy had a hand over her mouth.

"What?" he said, flushing.

Nothing, she said. ***It's just . . . you're very sweet.***

"*Marmph,*" Denizen said, blushing so hard his vocal cords fused.

My father has kept me a secret for a very long time, she said, half to herself. *Even his closest servants were bound only to refer to me in half-truths. The mercy, as if I were a hidden trinket.* She shook her head. *He is . . . overprotective.*

"Yeah," Denizen said without thinking. "We noticed."

It took a second for his brain to catch up with his mouth. He began to stammer an apology, but by then she was already laughing, great peals that washed up like ice water against the garden's walls.

Denizen couldn't help it. He started laughing too—thin shoulders shaking, hand clasped over his mouth so the sound didn't escape.

It was the wrong place to be laughing. It was the wrong time to be laughing and the wrong thing to be laughing about. The Clockwork Three were dead, but their evil remained—the people they had hurt, the lives they had ruined. The Three fed on misery. What they had caused in the months since their destruction would have kept them sated for a long time.

But just for a moment . . . it felt good to laugh.

"I'm sorry," he said, after a final snigger. "We shouldn't . . ."

No, she said. *But laughter is too scarce in my father's Court.*

"Is he . . ." Denizen wasn't exactly sure how to phrase it.

Is he as terrible as all the stories say?

Denizen nodded.

Her smile was sad. ***He is the King.***

She didn't seem willing to say anything more, staring up instead at the cloud-buried sky.

The last place I saw you there were stars, she said. ***I've only ever seen them from the Tenebrae. It was lovely to stand underneath them, feel their light on my light.*** She frowned. ***Once I'd gotten out of the basement.***

"Oh yeah," Denizen said. "Sorry about that."

It wasn't your fault, she said. ***Do you miss them?***

"The stars?" Denizen said. "I do, actually. They're the only thing I really miss from Crosscaper. I'd already read all the books. And Simon came with me, so . . ."

Simon?

"My friend," Denizen said. "He was in Crosscaper when you were there, hiding from the Three."

Is he all right?

There was such simple concern in her voice. He smiled weakly. "Yeah, I think so. We're all a bit . . . I think he's doing OK."

He must be strong, she said. ***I saw what the place had become.***

Frost had made the grass stiff and brittle, weighing down the leaves above.

The Three had nested. I knew only the limits of my cage, Mercy said, and there was remembered pain in her voice. ***But my jailer walked the corridors for me. He told***

me stories even as he trapped me, and he brought me books when I wept.

Grey. The Three had made a thrall of him, but even as they took away his will he had still been fighting, bringing kindness into the dark.

Denizen swallowed, but the swallowing wasn't enough, and he caught himself before he hiccuped for breath.

"Sorry," he said. "Could you—"

Had he really been *laughing* a second ago? When people had laid down their lives for him? When Grey would be *fine* if the Three hadn't come after—

Mercy still continued blithely, even as her words made splinters of Denizen's heart.

I think he wanted someone to talk to. What they had done to him, the horror . . .

"Could you not—"

Jack swaying in a puddle of candlelight, holding something small in his arms.

Grey's hand a malformed claw of clockwork.

The unfamiliar look of terror on Abigail's face.

. . . must have felt so alone—

"Stop," Denizen said, and the grass crisped beneath his feet. His skin flashed gold, like the sun slipping through clouds, and Mercy darted away from its heat. Unearthly frost melted in a heartbeat to fall between them as rain.

"Sorry," Denizen said in a haunted voice. "Sorry, I—"

He felt sick. *Of course you do,* a voice whispered. *That's what they do to the world.*

Mercy looked at him as if she could read the thoughts in his head. Her light folded in on itself once more, until she was just a drift of lines in the air, a shape he wasn't at the right angle to see.

Then she wasn't there at all.

15

SHALLOWS

ONE THING SIMON HAYES had become very good at over the last six months was falling. His limbs curled protectively round himself like tumbleweed, and he didn't so much hit the ground as bounce off it into a standing position once again.

"Good," Darcie called, sitting cross-legged on the grass. "Both of you. Denizen—great punch."

"Yeah, Denizen," Simon said wryly. "I've always thought my nose would look slightly better to the left."

"Sorry," Denizen said. His fist ached. All of him ached, actually, the bone-weary throb of worry and fatigue. "I guess I'm just a little distracted."

"When I'm distracted, I tend to miss," Simon said, but his smile robbed the words of any sharpness. "You OK?"

Haven't slept. Hate everything. She just disappeared. But why wouldn't she? Stupid me getting feelings everywhere . . .

Denizen shrugged as nonchalantly as his tense shoulders would allow. "I'm fine. Definitely. Want to go again?"

"Nope," Simon said. "Abigail?"

Abigail was staring at the back door.

"Is Vivian coming?" she said. "Sorry, Darcie. I just—"

"Not at all," the *Lux* said. Simon and Denizen were novices to physical combat, but Abigail was anything but, and it took Vivian to push her beyond her limits. "She's been gone since this morning. I guess maybe with the—"

"Circus in town?"

Edifice Greaves stood in the back doorway. For someone who liked to make a grand entrance, he knew how to move quietly. Vivian would have disapproved of the Neophytes' inattention, but, considering who was doing the sneaking around, that disapproval would probably have had to join the line.

The Palatine grinned.

"Sorry. I let myself in." He held up a set of keys the size of Denizen's head. "Access all areas." A deep breath strained the stripes of his expensive shirt, as if he'd never tasted fresh air before. "Every time I get buried under a mountain of paperwork—requisitions, *budgets*—I like to get out. Be hands-on. Remind myself what we're actually doing."

As if on cue, something in his suit pocket buzzed. With the flourish of a magician releasing a flock of doves, Greaves withdrew it, pressed a button, and deposited it back.

"That would be the people who don't like me doing that. Oh well. How are we all getting on?"

All those hours discussing the possible motives of Edifice Greaves suddenly paid off. The Neophytes closed ranks as neatly as a Roman phalanx.

"Fantastic," Simon said. "I think my concussions have bruises."

"I gave him those concussions," Abigail said proudly, and then frowned. "Should we have told someone about that?"

"About . . . what . . . ?"

"*Simon*. That's not funny."

"Children," Darcie said patiently. "It's an honor, Palatine. I daresay you could favor us with some solid advice."

And he did.

"Simon, I've been the same height since I was nine. You know what you need? Tae kwon do. All about the reach."

For hours.

"You've heard the one about the parakeet and the spinster? No? Well, I'll be stripped of all titles if I tell it to you, but . . . Also, when you start laughing, that's when I'm going to hit you, so be ready."

It was Darcie's skepticism that went first. Abigail was so focused on trying to slip a fist or a foot past

Greaves's defenses that it wasn't clear whether she was actually listening to anyone. And though Denizen held out for as long as he could, and Simon did the same out of solidarity . . .

Greaves was an *extremely* charming human.

"My family? Always Knights. And always on the front lines too. There are lots of ways to serve the Order, but we went for the dirtiest fights, the last-ditch battles."

They sat on the grass. Denizen could *hear* the tremoring ache of his muscles, but it was a good, clean exhaustion—a world away from the dulling fatigue of a sleepless night. He'd even managed to keep a lid on the Cants while they trained, and he didn't have the energy left to wonder whether that was down to Vivian's warnings or because Greaves had a knack for teaching that his mother didn't.

Greaves looked around at Seraphim Row. "I always think of the barrier between worlds as a river, not a wall. In some places, the river is thin and shallow, and Tenebrous are able to ford it easily. In others, it's too wide and deep."

The Palatine was plucking blades of grass and laying them one by one on the knee of his black suit. He hadn't mentioned the Concilium. He hadn't mentioned Mercy. He hadn't spoken to them like children or held back any information. Nothing calculated. Nothing *political.*

Which one's the real Greaves? Is it as simple as that?

Why isn't anything simple?

"We always waded into the shallows," Greaves said. Abigail and Darcie were rapt. "It's practically a family tradition. I was a Knight Peregrine—traveling the world, reinforcing cadres when they needed it. That's where I met Grey."

With everything else going on in his head, Denizen hadn't thought it was possible to tense further, but tense further he did. *Now* the Cants were awake, stretching through him in yawns of molten gold.

Greaves held up his hands.

"Sorry. I know the last time I brought him up I crossed a line. I didn't mean to. I just—you all knew him as well. I guess I just wanted to understand what happened from someone who was there."

"I told you what happened," Denizen said stonily.

Greaves looked pained. "I'm not going to press you further about that night, Denizen. You were honest with me and I respect that."

Denizen squirmed at the earnestness in his voice.

"But in all our studies of the Tenebrous, all our research into what they can or cannot do, we never anticipated the Three." The pained look on his face turned to anger. "*Thralldom*. That's what Grey calls it, on the days that he can . . ."

Abruptly, he stood.

"I should be going."

"What?" Abigail and Darcie said together. "Why?"

He brushed grass from his knees. "They'll be sending out search parties by now. Thank you for this afternoon. It's good to get out of the office, even one as fancy as—"

"No," Denizen interrupted. Anger was spiking through him, anger at being manipulated by mention of Grey, and anger at not knowing if it was manipulation at all. The vault of boxes in his head shivered, flames lapping at its sides. Denizen could almost smell the burning of thousands of labels, thousands of names. "Say it."

When Edifice Greaves next spoke, it didn't sound like he was talking to them at all. His eyes fixed on something beyond the garden, and he spoke as if reassuring himself of one of many possible truths.

"Some days it's like nothing happened at all. There's always work to do around Daybreak that doesn't require combat. Some days I think he's almost . . . happy to be out of it."

Darcie's voice was soft.

"And other days?"

Greaves looked at her for a long moment, and then took out his phone. It was that, more than anything he could have said, that told the Neophytes this particular conversation was over.

"I have been a student of war my entire life," the

Palatine said, "and you would think that fighting the same war for centuries would mean we know our enemy. But time changes truth, and every new battle brings a horrible surprise. That's why I'm entertaining this second meeting.

"Half the Knights I've brought think we should be on our guard for a trap, and the other half think we should be planning one. Being a member of the Forever Court isn't an empty honor. Each of those creatures fulfills a role, has their own vassals—a chain of loyalty from the lowest beast all the way to the King himself. They're *important*. Mocked-By-a-Husband is a herald, Malebranche a spymaster."

Denizen swallowed. "And . . . the other one? Rout?"

"Executioner," Greaves said grimly. "Those creatures represent a significant portion of the Endless King's strength. And then there's Mercy, who we know nothing about."

Denizen could already see the mantle of Palatine settle back over Greaves, hiding the real—*had it been real?*—man from view.

"Half their leadership in one room . . . it's a great opportunity." Something dark passed over his face, just as it had when he'd spoken of Grey. "And I want to believe a Tenebrous is being honest with us. But it'd be a first."

He shrugged. "Then again, humans aren't great at opening up either, are we?"

The Neophytes left the garden soon after Greaves did, each one lost in thought. A part of Denizen wanted to talk to them, analyze the Palatine's every expression, every kind word . . . but what right did he have to try and instill doubt in them?

Denizen wasn't even sure how he felt himself.

16

SCAR TISSUE

SIMON SNORED.

That had never bothered Denizen. It didn't bother him now. It meant his friend had to be asleep. Those were the kinds of noises you could only fake with a miniature brass band. He eased the covers off himself slowly, counting the honks from the other bed as though they were the timer on a half-defused bomb.

Careful. Clothes folded under his pillow (so as not to open the closet), a note set on his covers (where it could easily be seen):

CAN'T SLEEP
GOING TO THE LIBRARY

He'd written it earlier (so as not to wince at the loudness of pens) and anyone would agree that it was a very Denizen note to leave.

He'd swiped *A Record of the Pursuivants* that morning and slipped it into a coat pocket so, if Simon *did* come down looking for him, his story would hold up.

Denizen had basically thought of everything.

What if she doesn't—?

Shut. Up.

Greaves had left Denizen with a lot to think about. His response had been to not think about it at all, and instead consider every angle of this midnight excursion.

He'd timed it perfectly. It was exactly the hour his window had imploded the night before.

If I'm wrong . . . if I scared her off . . .

He could just go back to sleep.

It was a thought that followed him as he crept out onto the roof and fell momentarily through the frigid black of another world. It was why he'd planned every action so meticulously, taking into account every single variable, every single contingency.

Because the one thing he *couldn't* plan for was if she didn't show up.

As he'd now been to the other embassy's back garden, he could picture it and so travel there directly. Denizen wasn't sure what happened if you tried to use the Art of Apertura to go somewhere you hadn't been, but he really did *not* want to find out.

Darkness thrilled away from his limbs as he stepped out of the shadow. His heart clattered unmusically in his chest and, perversely, a part of him wanted Simon's voice to ring out. It meant he'd have to turn back. He wouldn't have to talk. He wouldn't have to expose himself. It was a battle he wouldn't have to fight.

"Hello?"

The garden seemed unchanged from the night before. There was a little plot of flowers at the back, and some folded chairs where some employees had obviously set them out to enjoy the sunshine.

And . . .

If he focused, if he really concentrated, Denizen could feel the slightest hint of the Tenebrae. Something in the gleam of the streetlights. A tremble in the petals of the flowers.

Open and honest.

"I'm sorry," Denizen said to the empty air. "Last night you talked about Grey and I . . . I lost it. Ever since they took him away, every time I think about him, I get so . . . I get angry. And guilty. Because the Three were hunting my family, and I got him hurt.

"And I . . ." His voice broke. "I got D'Aubigny killed. And sometimes I miss Grey more, because I knew him better, and that makes me feel *terrible.* And *she* just seems to be unchanged, and when I'm around her my skin feels two sizes too tight, and either I snap at her or she snaps at me."

Denizen took a deep breath. "My anger is changing me. It's making me something I don't think I want to be.

"And the fire helps. And that's dangerous, because it's so hard to control, and . . . and sometimes I'm angry at you too. Because you made it harder. And then you left."

He trailed off. "So, yeah. Um. Again. Sorry."

No.

Her voice was soft as she unfolded against the dark of the garden, but she held Denizen's eyes with a gaze so strong he couldn't look away.

It is I who should apologize. We were burdened with a desperate moment, and I was not thinking of what would happen when the moment had passed. You find it hard.

"Yes," Denizen said.

It was absurd that he'd never admitted it before—not to Simon, not to Abigail, not to Darcie. Not to Vivian—though she had tried to warn him.

Well. She'd given him a knife. And an unhelpfully cryptic denouncement of their Order's leader. Her trying had sort of given him a headache.

"The Cants want to be used," Denizen said. *I'm not changing the subject. I'm not.* "I can feel them. My head is *full* with them. Ever since that night I can tell exactly what each one will do, but there's . . . there's more to them, isn't there? I feel like we're using them *wrong*, like if I just fitted them together in the right way . . ."

The fire in his stomach crackled and climbed, and it was an effort to stop him *showing* her what he meant, letting the Scintilla Scythe bleed into the Anathema

Bend, into the Staccato Gap and the Art of Apertura—letting them wind and whip and *build* . . .

No. Denizen raised cold walls in between him and its eagerness, and finally the flames fell away.

They're not for this world, Denizen, Mercy said. ***You see what it does to you.***

"We call it the Cost—scar tissue," Denizen said, staring down at the iron that stained his hands. "The price we pay for changing the world in a way it wasn't meant to change."

Your world's response to a fire it was never meant to feel. She drifted closer. ***Though not everything is the worse for being scarred, Denizen. Not always.***

She cast a glance at Seraphim Row.

I've always thought you Knights brave.

"What *are* the Cants?" Denizen asked. "It's so *frustrating*. I know what they do, but so little else . . . and I can't ask or . . ." *Or they'll ask me about you.* "What were they in your world?"

Her expression flickered, not in the human sense of muscles and sinews, but like a winter sun obscured by cloud. ***What do you know about the Tenebrae?***

Of all the ways Denizen had thought and hoped this conversation would go, he hadn't expected an exam.

"It's another world next to ours. You come here, you build a body from whatever's around, and you're—"

Wrong. That was the word he had been about to use, and he felt ashamed for it, even as the leaves behind

Mercy rustled and shifted, though there was no breeze to move them. Light fell from her to drizzle the grass with unburning flame.

"You're different," he finished lamely. "You don't fit here."

No, she said, *we really don't.* She raised a hand, and they both watched threads of lightning spark between her fingers. *But as to the rest . . .*

The Tenebrae is not a world, Denizen. Not as you would think of it. It is the space BETWEEN worlds–the yawn between realms, a sea that washes on many strange shores.

She said it so casually, like the existence of other universes was something she took for granted. The look on his face made her laugh.

I'm sorry. I shouldn't be surprised. You can't see them from here, can you? You brush up against the Tenebrae, and you think that's all there is. Oh, there are so MANY, Denizen. They crowd our sky, shine at us from every angle. The things you can SEE if you're brave enough to swim close to the edge.

Denizen couldn't help himself. "Like what?" he said excitedly.

She eyed him slyly. *Well . . .*

Frown No. 6—Insistent, which was probably improper to use on a visiting dignitary. "Oh, come on. You have to tell me!"

Fine, she said, mock-scowling. *Imagine reality after reality, laid upon each other like a great spinal column of*

broken glass. There are baby realms, just cold and stars and hope. Her own voice was hushed now, as if awed by the immensity of what she described. ***There are old and haughty places where great minds spin, wearing planets like the scales of snakes. There are galaxies spun from music, a single shimmering chord.***

Denizen was rapt.

I could show you someday, if you liked. A thoughtful frown crossed her face. ***You breathe . . . oxygen, right?***

She laughed again, a sound like raindrops, if raindrops knew how to dance. Denizen shivered at the sound.

With so many universes, the light of so many stars beating along our skin . . . We are changelings, Denizen—never bound to one shape, but finding many. Her face darkened. ***Or having them found for us.***

"Wait," Denizen said. He desperately wanted to get back to the bit where she smiled again. "What do you mean, 'found for us'?"

The air turned dead and cold. The Tenebrae rode the air like a thousand mingled scents, at once faint and strong enough to fur the throat.

Nothing about us is set, Denizen, she said. ***Not like this world, with its rigidity. We are border things, and what we see changes us. What we do and what is done to us. You met the Opening Boy?***

The weakest of the Three—it had *helped* Denizen,

desperate to die after the cruelties inflicted by its masters.

He might have been something different, before the Man in the Waistcoat closed his claws on him. So too the Woman in White. Those two had run together so long they had become dual aspects of the same creature. And Father sent Pick-Up-the-Pieces, didn't he? When I was missing?

"Yes," Denizen said. He was still wrapping his head round what she was saying, but it did make sense. *Sort of. A bit.* He'd already known the Tenebrous were able to slough their shapes, and the older they were, the better they were at it . . . "Grey and D'Aubigny fought it—um . . . him."

He was much diminished by that battle, she said. ***What did he look like, when he fought?***

"Cats," Denizen said. "Sort of."

Ah, she said with a strange tone of fondness. ***A hunting form.*** She saw the look on Denizen's face. ***But that is what I mean. Our purpose, our surroundings, a given name . . . they can influence us. Make us change. Our obsessions remake us.***

Denizen frowned. "What do you mean, our obsessions?"

Her voice came hesitant then. Almost . . . nervous, for the first time since they had met.

Nothing. I do not wish to . . .

"No," Denizen said. "What?"

She didn't look at him, her words instead directed up and into the clouded sky.

In a certain light, your mother and the Woman in White look very much alike.

Sudden revulsion gripped Denizen's throat. *Do they?* He tried picturing the Woman's gaunt, lupine features, but all that came to mind were scalpel limbs and a face of clicking, hungry gears.

I do not know whether that was the Woman's choice, or simply a response to a thought that ruled her mind. We are . . . terribly impermanent things.

She glanced at him once again.

And so we come to the fire.

"It's so bright," Denizen said, desperately relieved that the topic of conversation had changed. "And I've been in the Tenebrae. It's so dark and cold . . . They don't make sense together."

They never did, she said. ***But it warmed us for a time. We live in the shadow of stars but are not touched by their heat, and their light is so far away that it simply reminds us just how much in the dark we are.***

It was our sun, Denizen.

Light beat against the thin cage of Denizen's chest, as though it recognized her words. As soon as she said it, he *knew* it was true. A fire that fed on itself, that burned eager and clean and smokeless, hotter and brighter than the world could take. It made sense. No wonder the Tenebrae was so frozen and empty. He had their sun inside him, the whole Order did, and its passage scorched them black.

Mercy was looking up, her face thoughtful. Denizen wondered if she could see the stars through the sky's caul of cloud.

Sun is your word, she said, and something in her voice had changed. Her light changed too—sharper and colder, her features running like ice-flecked water. Denizen's stomach lurched, and he was reminded of the first time he had seen her, the artillery roar of her rage.

For us, it was the light we crowded round, the glow that warmed us. And then . . . it was stolen, Denizen. It was taken. And without it . . .

Her eyes *flared.*

What could we become in the dark but monsters?

17

FATAL FAMILY TRADITIONS

"SHE'S *WHAT*?"

Abucad Croit settled his hundred-dollar tie against his thousand-dollar shirt, gazing up at Eloquence with a pinched look of disdain. It was the only expression Uriel had ever seen his uncle wear. Years of focused displeasure at the world had solidified Abucad's features into a permanent grimace.

Perhaps that was understandable, considering the path his life had taken.

"She's speaking, Uncle."

The path to the castle gates was littered with shrapnel from Eloquence's descent, jutting from the dust like ragged teeth in a rotting jaw. Uriel had been perched on a shard for hours, watching the sun rise over the valley mouth. He was the only one who'd volunteered to meet the new arrivals.

All the others had stayed inside. With Her.

"This is why the old man called me out here?"

Disdain sharpened to disgust. Abucad looked even more like Grandfather now—the same dagger cheekbones and cadaverous frame. *Their statues would be identical,* Uriel thought, *should that honor be given.* Saying that Abucad Croit did not get on with his father would have been a laughable understatement, had either man ever smiled.

Grandfather's resemblance to Abucad made the young man at his side even more disconcerting. Uriel didn't know his name. Strange in itself—Uriel knew everyone's name, everyone that mattered—but the stranger resembled Grandfather as well, though softened by youth and fat. His eyes were fixed on the ruptured battlements, like he'd suddenly realized he'd taken the wrong turn in a fairy tale and had no idea how to get back.

"What did you bring *him* for?" Uriel bared his teeth at the stranger, and was rewarded by a flinch. *Pathetic.* If this was what Outside did to people, you could keep it.

Abucad sighed. "Because, unfortunately, this place still has a hold over some of our Family's more . . . traditional members, and I thought my son should be aware of it."

"Daniel," the unFavored son said, stepping past Abucad and sticking out a flabby hand. Uriel stared at it until he put it away.

"Don't bother," Abucad murmured, fixing Uriel

with his cold gaze once again. "So She's speaking, is She? And tell me, nephew, when She *speaks*, does everyone hear it? Or just Father?"

Daniel smiled ruefully. Uriel did not.

"Scratch that," Abucad continued thoughtfully. "I think you'd all hear it if he did. That's how far things have gone." He shook his head. "Uriel, you might not understand what I'm about to say, but I want you to listen."

He gestured at the barren hills, the white gleam of the Garden, and the black bulk of Eloquence, and when he looked back at Uriel there was something unexpected in his eyes.

Pity.

"This is not everything there is," he said. "I know that might seem difficult to believe, but there's *so much* out there, beyond this . . . tomb. Had I my way, I'd sell this island to whatever idiot would buy it, and forget it ever existed."

Uriel's eyes widened at such blasphemy, but Abucad wasn't finished.

"I recognize that our Family is . . . *different*, but for too long there's been a core of madness in the heart of the Croits, and I don't know if I can stand by and ignore it anymore. I didn't come here to kneel. I came here to see if any of you could be salvaged."

Uriel swallowed, bile burning his throat. The taste had been a constant since Her awakening—pervasive and cloying, as if the air itself had soured. Sunlight took away some of the sting, which was why Uriel had spent the morning out here, relishing the open space, trying to identify the rankness on his tongue.

Madness. That was what it tasted like. It tasted like madness.

"Big brother," a voice interrupted. Tabitha was stalking down the slope toward them, her ragged dress stained with dust. Ambrel walked with her, hair shimmering colorless in the sun.

Uriel felt a rush of shameful relief. Abucad's words had shaken him. He didn't know why, but they had. But now that Ambrel was here . . .

Since the Redemptress had awoken, there had been a sizzling, bright vitality to Uriel's sister. Not just the fire beneath her skin—a change Uriel understood all too well—but as if some other light shone through her, making her somehow bigger and more real than she had been before.

Let her talk to Abucad; meet his dry contempt with the fire of her belief. Uriel could hide in her shade. Ambrel took her customary place beside him, and immediately he felt stronger, one piece of a whole.

And yet a voice in his head . . .

Why is she with Tabitha?

Daniel had taken two steps backward. You didn't need a childhood in Eloquence to see the dangerous purpose in their advance.

"Tabitha. Ambrel," Abucad said warily. It hadn't escaped him either. It was ever this way with the Favored—as if fire knew fire. Two Croits together was an argument. Three was a tinderbox.

Tabitha's voice was cold.

"You bring unFavored *here*?"

Abucad's eyes narrowed. "He is my son, and every bit your relation as well." A strange expression crossed his face, as though he'd thought of smiling and then immediately reconsidered. "Sister, this is—"

"I don't care," Tabitha said flatly, and Abucad's eyes narrowed. She didn't seem to notice, fixing her brother with a slow, mad grin. "But it's good to see you, Abucad. How long has it been?"

"Someone has to run our ventures Outside, Tabitha," Abucad said, his voice guarded. He even said the word *Outside* differently, like it was familiar, a known thing. "Spending your whole life in one place is . . . unhealthy."

"I remember." Tabitha's voice was dark with mirth. "Father's rage was incandescent." She practically purred the word. "*Your. Little. Rebellion.* Spending time Outside is a necessary evil, but you've made a *life* out there, haven't you?"

"A lot of us have," Abucad said stonily. "You should try it."

"Why?" she said. "Everything is here. The time has come, Abucad. The Favored must return home, and when next we visit Outside it will be to storm it with fire." She sighed. "Only someone as utterly rigid as you, Abucad, could *know* that magic exists, and yet view it as an unnecessary complication."

"Tabitha, you're a lunatic," Abucad said, and there was only weariness in his tone. "You've always been a lunatic. And this lunatics' garden is where you belong."

He turned to the twins, Tabitha so thoroughly dismissed that for a moment Uriel couldn't help but admire him.

"I stood where you stand now," Abucad said, his eyes fixed on Ambrel and Uriel. "My sister speaks as if I didn't, but I did. I heard the old man's words, I knelt before Her, and I have been carrying Her Favor for twice as long as you've been alive. I was just as ready for our great rise, the War we would fight . . . and then I realized, as you will, that we're waiting for nothing."

He had never looked more like Grandfather than he did at that moment. Their clash had been legendary—long before Uriel and Ambrel's time, but the Family spoke of it in hushed tones all the same. The story went that Grandfather had been *outmaneuvered*, that Abucad had argued with such passion that, just for a moment, *he* had seemed to know what She wanted more than Grandfather himself.

"Whatever we are, *children*, whatever our power is—curse or genetic quirk or malady—there is no future in it. No purpose. We can do things. Yes, amazing, unbelievable things . . . but, every time we do, it uses us up. Even the old man knows that. You could marshal every Croit out there, every branch of our twisted Family tree, and all we'd amount to is a pack of thugs with a neat trick each.

"We're not *chosen*: we're shackled to this place and its old stories. We could be better than that. We should be better than that. Our money, our influence . . . we could *build* things."

He glared at Eloquence's broken husk.

"All your Grandfather wants to do is burn things down."

"You're *wrong*," Ambrel hissed, and there was the crackling of fire in her voice. Daniel was staring at her, his eyes wide. Had he never seen the Favor unleashed before? "We are chosen. We're different. And She will show us what we're meant to do."

"Or *you* could choose," Abucad said. "You don't have to stay here. Nothing grows in this valley. There's so much else you could do with your life."

Uriel didn't say anything.

"Your parents miss you," Abucad said. His voice was soft. "They tried to hide you from Father because they didn't want you to end up like him. Trapped in the past, praying to a goddess that doesn't . . ."

His voice trailed off, his eyes fixed on the castle. Daniel's shocked exclamation was drowned out by shifting rubble.

Wires were rising through the corpse of Eloquence. Like vines seeking the sun, they twisted upward, growing and growing and winding and weaving until the Redemptress swayed ten meters above the castle's remains—a jagged, skeletal flower atop a black metal stalk.

The nausea in Uriel's stomach doubled as she raised one slim arm. Beckoning or accusing, it was difficult to tell. Tabitha knelt, and a sudden smile split Ambrel's face, like the sun coming out on a cloudy day.

"Get back to the dock," Abucad whispered to his son.

"But—"

"*Now.*"

Daniel began to back away, down the slope, even as Abucad started to scale it. Tabitha and Ambrel didn't spare a glance for the unFavored. It was like he'd never existed.

"You came," Tabitha called. "Remember that, brother. You didn't have to, but you did."

Abucad didn't reply. When Uriel finally dragged his gaze away, Tabitha was staring at him.

"What?" he snapped. The Redemptress still swayed in his peripheral vision, like the scaffolding of a tower that had not yet been raised. She didn't look right in the sun—it bounced off Her in odd ways, and when it did, the edges of that sunlight were greasy and headache-bright.

"We've been attending Her for days," Tabitha said. "Teaching Her of our rituals and the War That Will Come."

There's so much else you could do with your life. Abucad's words were still echoing through Uriel. *There's so much out there, beyond this . . . tomb.*

"Get to the point, Tabitha," he said flatly. "Stop circling whatever insult you've prepared."

"No insult," Tabitha purred. "Just a question. Where were you?"

Uriel went cold.

"What?"

"Where were you?" his aunt said, with that wheedling sweetness that usually meant she was about to come at you with terminal velocity. Uriel turned away from her searching gaze and saw that the Redemptress had unraveled, slinking back into the stone and taking the icy knot in his stomach with Her.

It was scant comfort.

"Had to greet Abucad," Uriel said. "That's all."

"Is it?" Tabitha said, her fleshy lips parting in a smile. "This is a time of great change, Uriel. No one would blame you for . . . wavering. For letting the rust in. Maybe that's why you wanted to meet Abucad. Maybe you hoped he would take you with him when he left."

She'd stepped closer now. Uriel felt the sword in his heart waiting to be drawn.

"There's nothing wrong with *doubt,* Uriel. . . ."

Yes. There was. And Tabitha would cheerfully betray every word Uriel said to Grandfather for one more moment in Her presence. All the Croits were encouraged to do so.

It is all our responsibility to make sure the faith is kept.

Was there doubt in him? He had sat for hours, asking himself that same question.

Ambrel's terror at being judged for something that wasn't a sin.

The cold smile on Tabitha's face as Family sat in judgment of Family.

The lost, confused look in the Redemptress's eyes.

She hadn't risen like an avenging angel, full of burning Croit certainty. She'd been a frightened little girl calling for Her lost love. Even the times when She did speak like a conqueror seemed somehow false, like a mask She was forced to wear.

Thoughts were spiraling in Uriel like mayflies, born and dying in heartbeats, and no answers had been found. *Except one.* Rust was everywhere. It sought to sneak in through doubt and through fear. It was a disease.

And Uriel felt sick to his core.

"Tabitha."

Uriel had never heard Ambrel's voice so calm, so cold.

"We each serve Her in our own way. It is not your place to question that."

She sounded like Grandfather.

"Go."

Without a word, Tabitha bowed and stalked back up the slope. *No arguing, no insults* . . . She just left. Uriel stared at her retreating back in shock.

"Yeah, I don't know what that's about either," Ambrel said. "But I'm finding it very useful."

A sudden image burned its way into Uriel's head—the Redemptress and Ambrel eye to eye, his sister soothing the terror of a deity.

"I think I do," he said. "You have a way with Her."

Ambrel blushed. Uriel didn't think he'd ever seen her do that before. "Well. I just want Her to know how much I love Her. How much we love Her, I mean." Her voice turned sly. "Though it is nice watching everyone scramble around, pretending they haven't been horrible to us all these years. I walked right up to Tabitha holding her Accusers' Red robe and said, *You dropped this*. You should have *seen* her face."

She cackled. Uriel forced a smile.

"And have they . . . said anything about the trial?"

Just for a second, Uriel was back there, watching tears roll down his sister's face. The memory was so strong that he had to turn away.

"Not a word," said Ambrel. "But this is a time of—hey, what's wrong?"

"Nothing," Uriel said, a little too quickly. "I'm fine."

"That's what I told Tabitha," Ambrel said, and

frowned. "I don't know what she thinks she's doing. You're fine. Of course you're fine."

The simple belief in her voice made Uriel's chest ache. "Really?" he said, forcing some levity into his tone. "How do you know?"

She pushed her hair back from her face. "Remember the first time Grandfather told us about the Favor? And I cried because I was afraid at the thought of all that fire inside me?"

"I . . . yes."

"And you told me that it would be all right because it was one fire, and that all Croits shared it, and if it got too much you'd become that little bit stronger, just for me."

"Is that what I said?"

It was. He remembered it perfectly—Ambrel's hiccuping sobs, the patterns the lone candle had made on the wall. Uriel had been just as frightened as her for exactly the same reason, but he had said the first thing he could think of to make it OK.

That was how being a sibling worked. If Uriel was worried, Ambrel became more confident. If Ambrel faltered, it was Uriel's strength she drew on to pick herself back up. Abucad had thought to provoke some sort of reaction from the twins by mentioning their parents, as if either he or Ambrel had ever wasted a thought on a pair of unFavored who had sought to keep them from their destiny.

They didn't need parents. They had each other.

"That's how I know you're OK," she said. "If you weren't, you'd tell me."

She slipped her hand in his, and for a moment they just stood in silence, their grins mirrors of each other. She was right. What *was* he fretting about? Ambrel wasn't worried. She seemed to have forgotten the trial already, as if it had happened to an entirely different girl.

Maybe that's how I should look at it too. Tabitha was right: this was a time of great change. *Yes.* Even his nausea had disappeared now, leaving only the warm glow of the Favor in his chest. It felt good. It felt right.

Being out in the fresh air helped. Darkness held no fear for a Croit, not with the Luster, but it was easier to think, even if the wind did sound like . . .

Screaming.

Uriel's fear folded in a heartbeat, a sun's fire waking in his heart. He was moving before he knew it, tearing his sword from its sheath, running so fast he flew.

Ambrel was running with him. Of course she was. Underlying everything Uriel had been taught—the history, the scripture, the bladework—was a simple rule. The simplest.

Family was Family. You fought to protect that.

Us and them.

He didn't even notice the shiver that spun through him as he passed into the darkness of Eloquence. It didn't matter. He had brought light with him.

And the tiny little voice in his head—*Why does this feel so right?*

He leapt over massive blocks, slid down collapsed pillars, scraped his way between piles of rockfall. A tight, crazed smile danced across his face, and suddenly he held two swords—divine fire and mundane steel.

Ambrel's voice rang out behind him.

"Uriel, what are you—"

And a wire, bare centimeters from his eye.

Only his reflexes saved him. Uriel stopped dead, his chest still heaving, his sword of fire disappearing in a slash of smoke. The other clattered against the broken flagstones at his feet.

The wire swayed like a cobra. Uriel felt assessed, weighed, *judged,* the point gleaming, though there was no light to reflect from it. The Luster touched everything but its slim length, its blackness total and complete.

"Uriel."

Ambrel caught up to him, her eyes wild, but whatever she was about to say went unspoken.

The Shrine was full. Every Croit that lived in Eloquence was there. A sea of white, tired faces, all turned toward the Redemptress's rightful spot above them in Her web of strands.

Grandfather stood in Her shadow, frost-pale eyes fixed on his son. An ugly smile lurked around the tombstone slant of his jaw, and, once again, he glowed in Judging White.

"For too long, Abucad, you have concerned yourself with Outside."

"Yes I have," he said, in a voice quiet with defeat. "Because—"

"Stop it," Grandfather snapped. "Your reasons, your disobedience . . . irrelevant. Everything is different now."

That was why Abucad looked so lost. He'd spent his entire life fighting a different war from the one they had been promised—a war to move his Family into the light. He'd defied the old man in order to get a few Croits out into the world. Just a few, but maybe he'd hoped one day to have them all—living among real people, their Favor and Transgression hidden, the Redemptress a forgotten mystery time was never going to solve.

But none of that mattered anymore, because Grandfather had been right and Abucad had been wrong.

The Redemptress was real. Everything they had been taught was true.

We wanted to be safe. We took it to be safe.

The Redemptress's voice was half a howl. It had been *She* who'd screamed—wretched and inhuman, disobeying every law of sound. The entire Shrine went silent, hanging on every syllable that fell from those wirework lips.

Was that so . . . was that so wrong?

She looked around wildly for a moment, strands singing against each other, and then suddenly froze with the jump-start stillness of a spider. Her eyes found Abucad, and when She spoke, it was in the voice Uriel had always imagined the Redemptress to have: not tremulous and afraid but strident and powerful.

The voice of an empress.

Bring all who hold the fire. I have Favored you, and so you will serve.

"And if I don't?"

Abucad's challenge wasn't a roar or a shout but a whisper that hitched on every breath. It was still the bravest thing that Uriel had ever heard.

In response, Grandfather twitched the emptiness of his left sleeve. The watching Croits parted, and a figure stumbled forward, half led, half dragged by the wire round its neck.

"Father!"

What little color Abucad possessed fled.

"Bring them *back*," Grandfather growled. "Every Croit you've rusted with this poisonous regard for Outside. Tell them to abandon their lives and come here to gaze upon our glorious truth. Our War begins, Abucad. The faith must be kept. And if you are not strong enough to keep it . . ."

Daniel screamed as the wire dug deeper, black against the flesh of his neck. The Redemptress watched him the way a snake watches a mouse, and, if his grandson's struggles bothered the old man a jot, he gave no sign. Uriel was suddenly reminded of another scene, just a few days ago, when it was his sister there, kneeling and afraid.

He's unFavored. He's not Family. Not really. He's not . . .

Doubt was a poison.

We will keep it for you.

18

Don't Mention the War

"I NEED TO BUY a shirt."

With the grim dignity of two continents coming together, Vivian Hardwick's eyebrows knitted. "I'm sorry?"

Around them, waiters ghosted gracefully through the mechanics of lunch. The foyer of the Goshawk was scattered with Knights, most perusing briefing documents (*Forever Court Profiles [updated]*), others just staring off into space.

The Concilium was supposed to have been a one-off. No one had expected a second meeting but now, with peace on the table, everyone was staying put. Technically, you could call an extended trip to Dublin a holiday, but, as superb as Knights were at dealing out death and fire, Denizen had never met one yet who was any good at relaxing.

"A shirt," he said, shifting awkwardly from foot to foot. "Like to . . . wear."

Vivian carefully laid down the book she had been reading and regarded him evenly. Mercy's words skulked through his head—

In a certain light, your mother and the Woman in White . . .

—but for once Denizen didn't savor the unearthly sound of her voice. *No,* he thought, staring down at his mother. Even if there was some sort of twisted mimicry on the part of the Woman in White, the two could not have been more different. There was a chill sort of nobility to Vivian's weathered features, and there had been nothing noble about the Woman at all.

"I am familiar with the purpose of shirts," Vivian said. "I have in fact bought shirts myself." Her expression never changed. "Are you asking me for money to buy a shirt?"

When do we do that bit of our training? Denizen wondered. *When do we learn to act cool?*

"Yes," Denizen said. "Um. I don't have any myself." And this was true. Money was still a slightly foreign concept to Denizen. Since he was very young, food had been an institutional experience, arriving before 250 mouths at once. A similar system existed at Seraphim Row. Essentials like meals and his five or so different sets of workout clothes were just . . . *provided.*

"I already have to replace a window on your behalf," she said.

"I know," said Denizen. He'd passed it off as late-night knife-throwing practice gone awry and was still getting chewed out over it, but much less than he would have been if he'd told the truth. Much, *much* less. "Sorry."

Vivian nodded slowly, her gaze shifting to a nearby Knight who was trying and absolutely failing not to stand at attention. The blocky young man suddenly stood up even straighter and approached.

"Yes, Mal—*madam*?"

Denizen felt a little sorry for him. The Knights had all been instructed to be . . . discreet, but not addressing Vivian by her title looked to be causing him physical pain. She withdrew banknotes from a pocket and handed them to Denizen.

"I imagine Simon will be going with you?" she asked.

"And Abigail," Denizen said.

"Good." She transferred her granite gaze to the young Knight, now practically floating off the ground. Maybe he hadn't gotten to his *cool* training either. "My son is going to buy a shirt. Make sure nothing kills him. Understood?"

Even his nod looked military.

"Off you go, then," Vivian said, and returned to her book.

It was only long afterward, when Abigail was pestering the Knight for war stories, and he and Simon were trying to figure out what the difference was between blue and . . . other blues, that Denizen realized that asking Vivian for money was the most mother-and-son thing they'd ever done.

It took him much longer to realize that she'd been messing with him the whole time.

"Is he all right?"

"I don't know. What do you think he's doing in there?"

"Could be anything. Do you want to check?"

"God, no."

Denizen shot the bathroom door a look that should have crisped the paint. *I've only been in here ten minutes.* Twelve at the most, and four of those had been in the shower, and therefore there was *absolutely* no need for the theatrically loud voices coming from outside.

"Maybe he's dead."

"Maybe he's fallen in."

"Maybe he used a Higher Cant and knocked himself out again."

"Do you *mind?*" Denizen snapped. "I'll be out in a second. I'm just . . ."

He was poking his bangs. That's what he had been reduced to—poking his bangs and trying to figure out why they refused to stay in any shape except *haystack tuft.*

Oh, they *moved.* They had no problem *moving.* So

far, they had gone through *top of pineapple* and *haystack (in high wind),* and now they had firmly settled in *pillow factory mid-explosion.* They couldn't even be called *tufts* anymore. *Tufts* implied a sort of cohesion. They were *flufts,* and they irritated him greatly.

Denizen fought the urge to bang his head off the mirror. He could do magic. Actual magic. Why couldn't he get this small thing right? He could whip the fire of an unworldly sun from one hand and fuse air into an unbreakable shield with the other. He could slit a hole in reality itself and bring down these fragile walls. Seventy-eight ways he could burn the world—

He flinched back from the mirror. His eyes had been glowing, the pupils lit from within by twin points of fire. Sweat was suddenly on his brow. *Where had that come from?* All he'd been doing was staring at his hair, and then it felt as if the whole world were fuel, like his thoughts weren't his own . . .

Vivian's words came back to him. *With knowledge comes desire.* No wonder most Knights only learned a handful of Cants. There was so much aching *potential* in all seventy-eight. So much he could do. So much he was finding it difficult *not* to do.

That bleak thought followed him out of the bathroom to where Simon and Abigail were waiting in the guttering light of the candlewards. Abigail's bright blue eyes caught Denizen's and then traveled up to the top of his head.

"Did you . . . Were you doing something to your . . ."

Denizen shrugged awkwardly. "I was just trying to see what my . . ." He struggled for an answer that wouldn't make him sound like an idiot. "What my hair might do."

Good job.

"Right," Abigail said, still staring. "And how did that work out?"

Simon was staring at him shrewdly. Denizen's best friend wasn't an idiot. There was a very obvious reason why Denizen suddenly had an interest in new shirts and hair that pointed in just the one direction.

He didn't say anything, though, and for that Denizen was incredibly grateful and incredibly ashamed. Simon wasn't saying anything, because he thought it was a harmless, ridiculous crush. But if he knew that the kernels of a plan were forming in Denizen's head, resolutely against any kind of common sense whatsoever . . .

Bleak thoughts. Bleak, bleak thoughts.

"Do you guys ever think about meeting somebody?"

They had set up shop in the kitchen, a huge tome spread out on each trestle table, the pages the size of Denizen's torso. It had taken all their combined strength to lift and open each one.

Gold script on black leather, the words sharp and bright as if they had been embossed yesterday.

"I think I might be in love already," Darcie said, running her fingers down the crisp white vellum. "Every bloodline, every Knight. All contained in these pages. Fifteen hundred years of history. Our history. It's beautiful."

She was right. The Order of the Borrowed Dark usually didn't have time for artistry. When one of Greaves's Knights delivered the *Incunabulae*, Denizen had expected a dry list of names and dates. What he had gotten instead was a map—swooping lines, delicate curves, waterfalls of black, red, and gold ink that didn't just record each family's path through time but illustrated it in glorious detail. Names, battles, even careful drawings of Tenebrous adorned each page, the colors bright and fresh as if newly drawn.

"I was expecting dusty scrolls," Simon said. "All worm-eaten and stuff."

"There are plenty of those at Daybreak," Darcie said. "But they don't travel well. There have been far too many times in history when the Order has lost its records, or had them destroyed. These are the Palatine's personal copy. It's a great honor to be shown them at all."

"So let's get started," Simon said. There was a barely concealed hint of eagerness in his voice. "We'll work from the past forward while Greaves's team work back. He said it might be better if . . . if they looked into the accident instead of me. The only clue I have is a smushed silver fountain pen."

It was Simon's only possession from the car crash that had claimed his parents. With a thrill of shame, Denizen remembered envying Simon that one small relic.

They set to work.

Initially, the work was fascinating. So many Knights, so many battles, thousands of lives tantalizingly hinted at in ink. Desperate last stands, daring raids, terrifying monsters—it would have read like the most interesting fantasy book ever had it not immediately struck home with Denizen that these were real people. People who had fought the same battles he was fighting.

No wonder *peace* was such a powerful word. All the Order had ever known was war.

"So, meeting somebody," Abigail said idly, after about an hour of quiet note-taking. "What do you mean?"

"I don't know," Denizen said. Worry had wound his spine so tight that the back of his skull felt spring-loaded. "Like a boy," he added lamely. "Or a girl."

Simon was engrossed in his book, but Denizen *felt* his ears prick up.

"I'm not sure when I'd get the chance," Darcie said. "Though . . . that American agent. Strap, wasn't it?"

"Seriously?" Denizen said. "But he—"

"Looked like he'd been kicked through a hedge," Darcie finished. "He did, didn't he?"

She was smiling faintly. *Why is she smiling?*

It was reassuring—and a little disconcerting that Darcie was still smiling—to know that at least the *thought* of dating had occurred to his friends. But that was normal, wasn't it? Fancying people was normal.

Fancying *people*.

"I assume I'll just meet someone in the Order," Abigail said, scribbling a note on her little pad.

"A Knight?" Simon asked.

"Well, yeah," Abigail said. "I mean . . . can you imagine explaining all this to a civilian? What we do? Who we are?"

Denizen felt guilty contemplating his own heritage when they were supposed to be tracing Simon's, but he couldn't help thinking about Soren Hardwick. Denizen's father hadn't been a Knight. He hadn't had a thousand years of Hardwick history forging his life into a certain shape. Denizen didn't even really know Vivian, but Soren was a complete mystery. His favorite food, what music he liked, whether his lip had a strange freckle on it . . .

I don't even know what he looks like.

Vivian had no photos, or if she did, she had never volunteered to show them. All Denizen knew was that the Clockwork Three had murdered his father, and grief had turned his widow into an engine of war.

It was as if all his father had been was a dead man.

"It's hard," Darcie mused. "The cadres are spread out. You spend your second year of training at Daybreak, and there'll be Neophytes there, obviously." She frowned. "Not that they leave you a whole lot of time for courting."

"Courting," Simon and Abigail said together, and started to giggle. Darcie picked up a tea towel and threw it at them.

"What?" the *Lux* said, fighting chuckles herself. "I read a lot of old books. It just creeps in sometimes—stop it!"

Denizen watched them mess about with each other, his mind far away. He'd never really considered the fact there'd be other Neophytes at Daybreak. It had been six busy, complicated months since Denizen had had to deal with the fact there were other teenagers in the world at all.

Oh, he knew there *were*, but growing up in an orphanage had already made Denizen view normal, parented, school-attending teenagers as an entirely different breed, and now there was a cold black reminder in his palms to bring that divide home.

And since Mercy and the Cants . . .

It felt sometimes like he had very few people to talk to at all.

"So do we get to meet any of these Neophytes?" Simon asked, trying to wrest the tea towel from Abigail and getting absolutely nowhere. "You know, before they hand us a bunch of weapons and get us to try to kill each other?"

Darcie shook her head. "The Order has strict rules against gathering too many Neophytes in one place. For obvious reasons."

"Oh, of course," Simon said. "Well. No. Not of course. Why not?"

Darcie's smile faded. "Because they'd be too much of a target. One strike and you could cripple the Order for a generation."

The mirth drained away from the kitchen like someone had pulled a plug. Abigail's hands darted to her knives, leaving Simon holding the end of the towel forlornly. He looked at it as if he wished it were something a bit more useful as a weapon.

"That's why you're all trained at Daybreak," Darcie continued. "It's the safest place in the world. Something like the Concilium is unprecedented. They don't like gathering too many Knights together in case something happens and . . ."

Half their leadership in one room . . . it's a great opportunity.

Edifice Greaves spoke as precisely as other Knights

fought. There wasn't a single word, a single thoughtful beard-rub that wasn't calculated. He was the kind of person who would *happily* talk about peace . . . so long as the walls were wired with explosives and he was holding the trigger.

Vivian had worried about the Court setting a trap. But what if the Palatine were planning one instead?

It could happen so easily. So innocently. All it would take was one bad decision to turn that cramped chamber into a war zone and, though the King might retaliate, it would be missing half his strength.

I have to warn—

No. There was a right word and a wrong word for every situation, and in this one Denizen was very clear on the difference. Even if Greaves *was* planning to double-cross Mercy, telling her wouldn't be *warning*.

It would be treason.

"Denizen?" Darcie was looking at him with concern. "You've gone a bit—"

Denizen's mind worked furiously. He had to wa— *let Mercy know* what might happen without betraying his Order and his species. Maybe, if they hung out together long enough, an opportunity would present itself. And to give that opportunity time to arise, they should probably hang out *a lot*. He would be totally doing the right thing. Absolutely and completely. The entire fate of the world depended on him.

Again. Probably. If you thought about it *really*

specifically, and ignored the far more likely scenario that there was going to be a gigantic war, and he was going to get feelings all over it.

"I'm fine," he told Darcie. "Everything's going to be fine."

19

A Little Farther

You have no imagination!

"I don't need imagination," Denizen said, his eyes scrunched closed. "I don't have time for imagination. There's imagination, and then the real world, and the real world is always worse."

Silence, out there in the darkness beyond his eyelids, and then a voice, soft and musical.

All of it?

Don't blush. "No. OK. Not all of it."

Good. Now open your eyes.

Denizen did.

She smiled at him. "How do I look?"

Mercy stood in front of him. *Stood.* On *feet.* Feet that were attached to legs that sat under a torso that had two arms and a head crowned by a tangle of curls. All real. All human.

Her eyes were the color of sunlight on steel, her

skin amber in the streetlight's distant glow. The curls avalanching down her shoulders were silver, the color of freshly stamped moonlight.

"Well?" she said, a tad impatiently. "How did I do?"

Simon had been wrong. It wasn't that Denizen hadn't ever fancied people. He had seen movies and advertisements where everyone was floppy-haired and symmetrical, and it wasn't that Mercy looked like a movie star, or a model, or anything like that. She didn't. It was simply that Denizen knew nobody in the history of the world had ever looked like her before, and nobody would ever look like her again.

She wasn't pretty. She was poetry.

"Good," Denizen croaked. "You look very, very good." He glanced down. "Though you are wearing the exact same clothes as me."

"I needed a template," she said. *Said,* in a voice that played Denizen's spine like a piano. "Clothes are difficult. You have to do different textures and colors, not just loose folds of skin." She paused. "That's not acceptable, right?"

"No," Denizen said in as heartfelt a tone as he could muster without actually picturing it. "No it isn't."

"You're tricky," she said. "Lot of moving parts. I didn't do the organs. Nobody does the organs. Too hard to keep going. But the surface works, and that's what matters, right?"

"Umm . . ." Denizen said. "In this situation, I guess. How do you feel?"

Mercy had extended her arms, slowly moving each joint—fingers, wrists, elbows—before stretching up on her toes like a dancer. "Good," she said. "I think. Make faces at me?"

"What?" Denizen said, blushing.

"Make faces at me," she said. "I need to make sure I'm—wait, which one's that?"

"Confusion," he said. "And now amusement."

She scowled. "Am I scowling at you?"

"Yes."

"Good."

She pulled on a lock of her hair and watched it spring back into shape. "Flesh isn't difficult to spin; it's just . . . complicated. Especially if you want to pass among humans. You need to concentrate, make sure you're not slipping anywhere, and the longer you're here, the harder it becomes. That's why a lot of Tenebrous choose metal or stone. You can just let it set and focus on movement. Me, I like light."

"Light?" Denizen said, and she nodded, the briefest shine of white behind her teeth.

"I don't like the idea of just being one thing. Light's very difficult . . . but that's why I like it. A particle and a wave—constantly moving, never one thing or the other. I don't want to be *stuck*, you know?"

Denizen nodded, though he wasn't sure if he did. He had been nodding a lot lately—Mercy just *talked*, and he didn't want to stop her flow just because she had delved into subjects he couldn't possibly know about.

There were things they had in common—***frightening parents,*** as Mercy had once said—and things that seemed to be true for every teenager, whichever universe you were from. A lot of what she said only made sense if you were a Tenebrous, things that she had to search for a human term for. *That* frustrated her, but Denizen was content to let her find her own words instead of suggesting his own. There was something so fragile and gossamer about the friendship they were building that he was afraid that if he stopped her it would break.

And that was before . . .

Hey. This is fun. Like really *fun. But I think my superiors might be planning to assassinate you. But maybe not. Or maybe by accident on purpose. And I'm not sure your underlings aren't planning to do the same to us.*

Denizen ground his toes into the grass of their—of *the* garden—trying to find the words, *any* words to say.

"Where are we going?" She made eagerly for the wrought-iron gate and then blinked as he stepped in front of her.

"Wait," Denizen said. "Not that I don't think you've done a really good job with . . ." He swallowed. "Everything. But we can't go *outside.* It's too dangerous."

"Don't worry," she said brightly. "I'll protect you."

"It's not that," Denizen said. "What happens if you lose your human shape? If you get distracted, or if

your . . ." He waved his hands to indicate the reality-distorting aura each Tenebrous carried with them.

"Umbra," she said. "That's what I call it."

"OK," Denizen said. "If your umbra makes things go haywire . . . There are a *lot* of people in Dublin. With cameras. And phones that are cameras. And phones that are cameras that can phone people with cameras."

"What exactly are you worried about?" she said, eyes narrowing like she was contemplating going *through* him instead.

"Gardaí," Denizen said promptly. "Small children. Security cameras. Traffic stopping. The Knights. The Palatine. The Forever Court noticing you're gone and deciding to come looking for you. My *mother*. So many things."

She sighed. "I like children. Cameras are not fond of our kind. I will follow relevant traffic laws. The Knights and the Palatine are either in bed or trying to figure out what to do if things turn sour, which they *won't* because the Court have been as quiet as mice since my father decreed they must follow me. And I don't know what Gardaí are."

"Police," Denizen said. "It's what Irish people call police."

"Ah."

"You left one out," Denizen said. "The great and terrible Vivian Hardwick."

Mercy gave a passable approximation of Frown No. 12—Here Is Some Sympathy I Am Not Sure You Deserve. They had spent a long, giggly hour with him giving her a tour of 1 to 27. "You're angry with her."

"It's . . . it's not as simple as that," Denizen said, one hundred percent afraid that it was. "She's so . . . compartmentalized. She let me in once, and that was only because I didn't give her a choice. When I'm around her, she'll talk about everything but what happened with my dad, but then she expects me to be honest with her about . . ."

"About me?" Mercy said softly.

He squirmed a little. "We're strangers to each other, and I just can't bring myself to let her in when she won't do the same."

"I understand," Mercy said, toying with an argent curl. "My mother was only ever a story to me."

Silence then, until she took a breath and broke into a grin at the taste of air. "But, so far, all I've seen of your world has been two basements and a mountainside." The wicked look she gave him nearly stopped his heart. "You're being a terrible host. Come *on*. Show me a city."

THEY AMBLED, AND THEY talked.

He was still getting over that. This was the eighth night they had met up, and Denizen was operating on roughly an hour's sleep, but that didn't matter, because every time he left her it was hard not to just float back to his room.

They *talked.* They actually talked. Denizen had lost track of how many words they had exchanged. The luxury of that astounded him. To be able to *not* value every word that they shared, every expression, every shift of light . . .

They had been walking for nearly an hour before Denizen realized he'd totally forgotten to worry about Tenebraic ambushes or running into Greaves and Vivian out for a bag of chips.

Maybe I don't have anything to worry about. Maybe I'm imagining things. This is . . . this is fine.

Cars passed them without veering off the road in panic. The occasional pedestrian gave them no more of a glance than you would give a pair of normal teenagers—one with astonishingly bright hair, one with a haystack mess.

Besides, it was hard to worry when you were being asked so many questions.

"What period are those buildings from?"

"Georgian. Um. I think."

"So they came *after* those ones we passed before?"

"Think so. The city just kind of spread over the centuries. We built all the new bits on the old bits. It's sort of . . . patchwork."

"Interesting."

The path they took was as meandering as their conversations. Mercy was easily distracted, and all it took was one red traffic light—she was scrupulously adhering to each—for her to change direction.

She seemed extremely curious as to what thirteen-year-olds in Dublin actually *did,* something that was right up there with architecture as a subject Denizen was singularly unqualified to discuss.

"I don't know what real teenagers do," he said. "At Seraphim Row we train a lot. Running. Weapons—I'm not very good at weapons—and hand-to-hand stuff. And the Cants, obviously, though I don't have to work as hard . . ."

Except at controlling them.

Mercy looked thoughtful. "How do they feel in your head?"

Denizen shrugged. "Honestly? They feel alive. Sometimes they move in sync and I can almost see a shape. Like they're components of something bigger. You taught me how to use them, but I don't know if I *understand* them. Does that make sense?"

No, he thought, just as Mercy nodded.

"I don't know if Father quite understands them either," she said. "I think he once had dreams of commanding the fire himself, but we're not . . . solid enough to wield it."

"Sometimes it feels like we're not either," Denizen said, tracing a finger over the cold iron in his palms.

"That's what the Cants were for," she said. "A language of control, of manipulation, crafted to shape the fire like a blacksmith's mold. He never got them to work, though—for him anyway." She glanced at Denizen. "Do they make having the fire easier?"

Denizen shrugged. "Sort of. It's strange. They make it easier and safer—much safer—to channel the fire, but making it easier also makes it harder not to do it." What she had said at their second meeting hadn't left Denizen's head. "You said the fire came from the Tenebrae."

She frowned. "You don't know? The Order, I mean. It isn't something you were taught?"

"No," Denizen said. "We kind of just get the basics."

Like how to kill you, mostly. That thought led him right back to worrying about Greaves, and the false sense of peace he had been feeling began to drain away.

But he couldn't say anything. He didn't even know if his fears were justified. Maybe Greaves really did want peace. And, if Denizen told Mercy he suspected the Palatine might not be *entirely* trustworthy, would the Court spring a preemptive trap of their own? Plus, Denizen was learning valuable information about where the Cants came from. That was good, right? *Right?*

"I see," Mercy said. If she noticed Denizen's sudden tension, she gave no sign. There was a phrase Denizen had heard in an old TV show the orphanage director had liked—*Don't mention the war*. It loomed over everything they said, reflected in the sodium of the streetlights and the shineless black of Denizen's palms . . . but then she smiled, and they could just have been two kids out for a walk, having the weirdest conversation ever.

They were coming to the city center now. The streets were bright with taxis, crowded with adults laughing and chatting outside pubs.

"I don't know where the fire came from originally," Mercy said. She had spent the last five minutes trying to coax an alley cat from under a trash can, and now they ambled down a side street, the shops dark and shuttered for the night.

"Father sometimes speaks of his travels before he took his crown, the things he brought back." Something like a smile touched her face. "I think he stole the fire. Which, perhaps, makes it right that it was stolen from him."

It sounded like a myth, a thing so lost in time that any truth in it had been obscured, like layers of pearl coating a grain of sand. But it wasn't a myth, was it? Denizen rarely stopped to think about how his life had changed, because usually bits of it were trying to kill him, but this was the world he lived in now—thieves flitting between universes, inhuman kings guarding the hearts of suns. . . .

When she talked about it, the danger became almost beautiful.

"Who took it?" he asked. Denizen had a bit of a soft spot for the stories where the hero was a thief. They usually weren't three meters tall and lantern-jawed; they were small and quick and, if they saved the day, it was usually while they were just trying to get out alive.

Heroism by accident. Denizen could relate.

She smiled coyly. "We're a little special, Denizen Hardwick. Did you know that?"

"*Guh*," said Denizen. "Ahem. I mean—what?"

"It's a rare thing, a human and a Tenebrous working together. Almost unheard of. Your kind and mine were never meant to share the same universe. Every time it's happened, it's ended in pain and death. Until us."

The world was ending, Denizen wanted to say. *I wasn't being noble or anything, I was just extremely stressed. I should really be telling you about a possible assassination attempt, but if I do, this moment might end. And I really, really don't want this moment to end.*

"Oh," he said, instead of all that. "Cool."

"Come on," she said. "Let's go a little farther."

THE MAN BEHIND THE counter of the corner shop looked older than Seraphim Row. His heavy-lidded eyes flicked to Mercy, as she peered at the magazines in the rack, and then to Denizen, who was trying to make himself look as unsuspicious as he possibly could.

Mercy had been watching the displays in clothes shops like a hawk, and her copy of Denizen's outfit had been upgraded several times. Now she was wearing a silk blouse and trousers under a black, high-collared coat marked with gold and silver curlicues. Her hair—now a bob—gleamed silver in the beige of the lights overhead.

She tapped a plum-painted fingernail—she'd seen a scarf that color and liked it immensely—against her lip, moving to examine the rainbow spread of sweets in their displays.

"Just pick one," Denizen said from the doorway. It was as far as he'd wanted to come into the shop. "*Seriously*."

"I'm *looking*," she said, shooting him the most perfect annoyed glance Denizen had ever seen. "I don't know which one I want yet."

Overhead, the hum of the fluorescent light deepened to a tinny snarl. One of the fridges let out a coughing burble. The shopkeeper looked up in surprise.

"*Sorryaboutthatthereyougothanks*," Mercy said in one long breath, dropping a packet of sweets and a coin on the counter. It landed on its edge and didn't roll away.

"*Mercy*."

The man swept up his coin and favored Mercy with a wide smile—that turned into a frown when he looked at Denizen.

Why am I getting frowned at?

"No manners," the shopkeeper muttered, and winked. "Don't know what you see in him."

"Tell me about it," Mercy said, with exaggerated slowness. "Breaks my heart."

She tossed the sweets at Denizen, beaming widely.

"See?" she whispered as they stepped back onto the street. "I can totally be human."

Every light in the shop went out with a crackling *bang*. Each fridge coughed to a halt, and the cash register flew open so violently the shopkeeper fell off his chair.

Mercy and Denizen were already running.

THEY BARELY STOPPED UNTIL they came back to the garden. Denizen's chest was heaving, despite his training. Mercy wasn't out of breath at all, though the same flush that permeated Denizen's cheeks colored hers.

"That was ridiculous," he said, gasping.

"I know," she said, and their eyes met. Suddenly all Denizen's postponed awkwardness returned in full force.

"I . . . I should get back," he said. *Tell her. Say something.* It had turned out there was no good time to be a species traitor. And possible assassination just wasn't the kind of thing that came up in conversation—even theirs.

Even as that thought went through Denizen's head, he knew it was a lie. He wasn't not telling her out of loyalty to the Order, or Greaves, or to the human race. He wasn't telling her because he didn't want her to stop talking to him.

"I, um . . ."

"Denizen," she said, looking down so that her hair fell

across her face in an unearthly cascade. Her voice was quiet, and he found himself leaning close to hear her.

To hear her. Yep.

A trace of luminescence moved behind her eyes, spilling the faintest curls of blue and white down her cheeks. Denizen's stomach churned, and, as always, he couldn't tell whether it was down to the reality-warping umbra of a Tenebrous or . . . because he really, really liked her.

Denizen knew there were words to say. There absolutely were, but they retreated every time he tried to grasp them.

"*Mmrmph?*" he managed, and suddenly realized Mercy was standing directly in front of him. Light danced behind her pupils. He felt the chill of it on his face. Her voice was soft.

"I've heard about kissing."

"Oh," Denizen said, in a sort of strangled whisper. There wasn't room between them for anything else.

They had been this close once before, in Crosscaper, when Denizen had broken the circle holding Mercy and she had swept him up in her storm. He felt that same sort of weightlessness now.

"What's it like?" she whispered.

Denizen couldn't lie. "I have absolutely no idea."

He closed his eyes—

"DENIZEN HARDWICK!"

20

MONSTER

MERCY EXPLODED.

Light speared through Denizen's eyelids as he was flung backward in a wash of pressure, displaced air, and gritty, painful heat. He hit the grass with every part of his body at once.

Denizen would really have liked to lie there, cataloging his aches, but his training screamed that when attacked you did not *stay still*. Staying still was death.

Flames filled his body. He managed a sort of wobbling jump, that at least put him back on his feet, and saw that Mercy had shed her human form, becoming once more a shifting sculpture of light.

She was staring at the entrance to the garden. She was staring at—

"Oh *no*."

The words slipped, cartoonish, from Denizen's mouth before he even realized he'd said them aloud.

Then his brain shut down. His mouth stopped working. Even the fire in his stomach fled.

Vivian Hardwick stood at the gate to the garden, the streetlight stretching her shadow ogre-large. Her fists were clenched. Her eyes were narrow slits.

"What. Are. You. *Doing?*"

"Oh no," Denizen said again, and then clamped his hands over his mouth. His vocabulary was deserting him, like rats leaving a sinking ship.

Say something. Say something. SAY SOMETHING. He just needed a word. A justification. A reason why he had been about to kiss the princess of a race of extradimensional predators his mother had spent her entire life fighting.

Any minute now . . .

Malleus Hardwick, Mercy said, in the same smooth, diplomatic tone with which she had juggled a room full of voracious Tenebrous and adrenaline-jacked Knights. Her glow was fading as though she was trying to appear less unworldly. ***It is a pleasure to see you again.***

Vivian was actually vibrating with rage.

I know this looks . . . Mercy drifted forward. ***We can talk about this.***

All Denizen could do was nod fervently.

Vivian's voice was gravel thrown into a furnace. *"I fear you would not enjoy my choice of words."*

Denizen's voice finally kicked in, atonal with panic. "Hang on—"

Mercy cut him off. Now her eyes were narrowed too. ***Was that a threat?***

"No, no, of course not—" Denizen began, but Mercy's luminescence had already sharpened, glaciers of deeper blue slipping down her arms like armor, her eyes polar stars. Her voice had the deceptive calm of ice about to crack.

You forget yourself. I am not some runt starveling or lower beast. I am royalty.

"Listen, seriously—"

"Really?" Denizen's mother purred through her clenched teeth. "Shall we see if my hammer knows the difference?"

"Listen!" Denizen half shouted, and enough fire laced the words that Mallcus and Tenebrous turned to stare at him. "Could we all just *calm down?*"

I am very calm, Mercy hissed.

There was a muscle twitching in Vivian's cheek. Perhaps it was trying to flee.

"Fine," she said eventually, taking a deep and ragged breath. "Come with me, Denizen. *Now.*"

Denizen wasn't sure where he found it, but some single drop of defiance made him turn to Mercy and force a smile onto his face.

"Thank you for a lovely evening."

He turned to the gate, carefully keeping himself directly between Mercy and his mother to deliberately block Vivian from unleashing a Cant. Not for the first time since they'd met, Denizen assessed the odds that she might just do it anyway.

Denizen, Mercy called. She was already fading, strange echoes weighing her voice as if it were coming from farther and farther away. ***I will see you–***

"No," Vivian snapped. Mercy solidified briefly, nailed to the world by her tone. "I tolerated you trading vague promises with him before, and *long* have I regretted the reprieve your father and my exhaustion granted you that night. But no more. Do you understand me?"

I didn't realize you spoke for the Palatine, Mercy retorted icily. ***Perhaps the decision to snub my Concilium is not yours to make.***

Vivian cackled, a sound so hard and harsh that Denizen flinched. Mercy guttered like a candle half blown out.

"Is that what all this is about?" The bloodless grin on her face was far more threatening than a scowl. "All this? Just an excuse to prey on my son?"

"That's not—" Denizen began, before Vivian cut him off as with every other sentence he'd tried to finish in the last three minutes.

"Do as you wish, *Your Highness.* Complete your Concilium. Lead that pack of abominations you call a Court. Pretend to civility. To humanity."

Sudden fire haunted her eyes.

"But you will never speak to my son alone again."

Mercy's blue light faded before Vivian's red, and Denizen and his mother were alone.

She is going to *kill me.*

Denizen had read about bad dreams where the corridors lengthened, dimensions twisting out of true until you were trapped in the same spot no matter how hard you ran.

He would give anything to be in one of those dreams now.

Seraphim Row had never seemed as small as it did when Vivian marched him to his room. Through the foyer's sea of candles, up the sweeping staircase and its population of gravely horrified Mallei—Darcie passed them in the fluffy length of a stolen Goshawk robe, and the look on his face made her drop her book.

Well, maybe not the look on *his* face. He was angry, but it was a paltry thing—a weak, *I'm wrong* anger—nothing like the incandescent rage that beat against the back of his neck like a solar wind.

Vivian's footsteps rang on the flagstones, and to Denizen they sounded like the applause of an audience ready and waiting for the first good guillotining of the day. Or, worse, the ticking of a hard and horrible clock counting down his final moments.

Denizen hated clocks. He had nightmares about them. Nothing but him and a great and terrible darkness, his only company an endless *tick*—

And then they were in his room, and his time was at hand.

"Sit."

Denizen sat. Simon's bed was empty, blankets kicked back. That was good. A minimum safe distance was required. They should evacuate the street.

His room was uncomfortably warm, despite the draft from the window. That was Vivian's fault, or maybe his: when a Knight's emotions ran hot, they did too. His own fire was a guttering ember in his stomach, and Denizen wondered just how hard Vivian's was straining at the leash.

"Listen, Vivian, I—"

"We'll get you help," she said, and suddenly her fingers were on his cheeks, cold iron gripping him painfully. Her eyes bored into his. "Whatever she's done, whatever hold she's gained . . . we'll break it. I promise you."

Denizen blinked. "What are you talking about?"

She abruptly let go, turning away to stare at the paper taped over the window. Denizen could still feel the imprint of her fingertips on his cheekbones.

"Greaves will call it off," she growled to herself. "He'll have to. The whole Concilium is balanced on a knife-edge already; he'll never allow it, knowing that one of us is compromised. . . ."

"Compromised?" Denizen said indignantly. "What do you mean—"

Whatever he was going to say vanished from his mind when her eyes met his.

Vivian was crying.

Not a single muscle had moved on her face. She wore the same grim expression she always did, but tears rolled down her cheeks all the same. She didn't acknowledge them. Perhaps she didn't even know they were there.

"We'll get her out of your head, Denizen," she said, her gaze transfixing him like a crossbow bolt. "I promise."

Everything she had been saying finally clicked.

"You . . ." He couldn't believe it. "You think she's made me a thrall."

"I should have guessed," she said. "When she infected you with that knowledge, I knew there was more to it than just trying to save her own skin." Her fingers drummed against her thigh. "I missed the signs in him and I will *never* forgive myself for that . . . but I watched you so carefully. How could I have—"

Him. Grey.

"As if a Tenebrous would ever help a human," she snarled, and now her fingers clenched into fists. "A *child*." Her eyes wandered blindly across the room. *Looking for something to hit*. That was where Vivian's comfort lay—in violence and in rage.

"But what's her endgame? And how *dare* she—"

"*Stop*."

Denizen nearly shouted the word. Vivian froze mid-rant.

"Why does it have to be that?" he asked. "Why does it have to be thralldom or something gross and horrible? What—do you think she got captured by the Three just to get at me? It nearly killed her. Grey had turned; you were . . . *shot*—"

Not that you were being particularly helpful before that either, a cruel voice added.

"I needed help," Denizen said with slow and deliberate anger, "and *she* helped me. That's it. That's all." But it wasn't all, and the words weren't stopping. "Besides, I was only meeting up with her because . . . because . . ."

Vivian scowled. "Because what?"

Turns out there really is no good time to say this, no matter who I'm talking to, Denizen thought. *Oh well.*

"BecauseIthinkGreavesisplanninganassassinationmaybe possiblyIdon'tknow," Denizen blurted out all in one breath.

Vivian just stared at him. "Excuse me?" she said eventually.

"Greaves came to watch us train," Denizen said, and winced as her frown sharpened. *Probably should have mentioned that earlier.* "And he said something about the Court. How having half their leadership in one room was a great opportunity."

A gasp. An exclamation. Possibly a dead faint. Of all the reactions Denizen had imagined, exasperation was low on the list, but Vivian let out an exasperated sigh all the same.

"What?" he said, a bit stung that the revelation hadn't gone down as explosively as expected.

"You think," Vivian said acidly, "that the Palatine of the Order of the Borrowed Dark shared his top-secret plan for provoking interdimensional war with a group of *teenagers*?"

"Well, it wasn't exactly what he said," Denizen muttered. "It was . . ." He cringed a little at the following words. "It was the way he said it."

Vivian did not look impressed. Denizen considered mentioning that Greaves had rubbed his beard as well, but decided against it.

"I tried to warn you before," she said. "Greaves isn't to be trusted. He—"

"You didn't *warn* me," Denizen retorted. "You just snarled something cryptic and moved on. Like you *always* do. How am I supposed to know what to do if you won't tell me?"

"Fine," she snapped. "You want answers? Greaves has been on my back ever since that night at Crosscaper because before then we didn't know a Tenebrous could enthrall a Knight. Suddenly, as well as everything else, there's the danger that our own could be turned against us . . . and then there's you, a teenager who survived a brush with the King's daughter, a creature both incredibly powerful and previously unknown. We're just lucky Grey either doesn't remember or hasn't spoken of your new gifts. If he had, the Palatine wouldn't be bothering with subtle traps."

"What do you mean, traps?"

Vivian's eyes bored into his. "There are Knights watching the house."

And suddenly Denizen understood. *That's why he said it. To see what I'd do.* How better to figure out whether someone is a traitor than to leak sensitive information and see what they do with it? And the first thing a thrall-spy would do is run to the other side.

It was also the first thing Denizen had done . . . but that was different. Wasn't it?

Denizen flushed, but embarrassment quickly blanched to terror.

"What—what are we going to do? Did they see me?"

Vivian shook her head. "Precautions were taken. I've been waiting for Greaves to try something like this for a while. And you've been using the Art of Apertura to leave the building, haven't you? The *recklessness* of it. Even I wouldn't have known unless—"

Unless what? And what precautions? Denizen only had a moment to consider those questions before they were drowned in a rising wave of anger.

Anger at being caught. Anger at everyone playing games. *So far, the only person who's been straight with me is Mercy.*

"I am so *sick*," Denizen snarled, "of everybody

meaning five things at once. I am so sick of *mysteries.* I'm not a thrall. I'm not a spy. She's just . . . we're . . . Why can't it just be what it is? Why can't it just be that she . . . that she . . ."

"That she what?"

"That she likes me."

His voice cracked shamefully on the words.

"Denizen . . . Are you telling me that . . . ?" There had been less horror in Vivian's voice when she was talking about thralldom. "That you have some sort of . . ."

Vivian looked like he'd hit her with the business end of her own hammer.

"I suspected something," she said. "The new shirt. The strange way you've been acting. The God-awful amount of deodorant."

Denizen went bright red.

"But I thought it was Darcie. Not . . . not . . ."

Vivian Hardwick had a limited range of emotions. It took a moment for Denizen to identify the one frosting her voice now.

It was disgust.

"You don't know her," he snapped. "You don't know the first thing about her."

"It," Vivian countered, and her shock had given way to anger again too. "Not *her. It.* I cannot believe I have to explain this to you. You see a pretty face and a cute name and you think that's the *truth*? She's a *shape-shifter,* Denizen. Black oil and a mind so alien that the very world rejects it. *It,* Denizen. Not a *she,* not a girl. A thing. A monster."

"Well, can't she be both?"

For a moment, Vivian stared at him as if he'd just questioned the color of the sky. When she did speak, each word was as hard as a blow.

"Your father asked me that once."

Denizen went cold.

"Have you ever tried talking to them?" There was the slightest lilt to her voice, and Denizen realized with a shiver that Vivian had unconsciously slipped into Soren's accent. *"Have you ever tried greeting them without a sword in your hand?* As with a lot of things your father said, I wasn't sure if he was joking or not."

It was the first time she'd spoken about his father since the night she'd told Denizen how he'd died.

"The next week, a *thing* called the Mask of Prospero put half a hand of claw into my stomach. He never asked me that question again. Three years later he was dead."

She shook her head.

"How can you think they're people after meeting the Clockwork Three?"

That snapped something in Denizen. His spine lit up in red and gold. How dare she compare Mercy to the Three? They were *animals,* hunger wearing a human shape. Their only aim to breed misery, their every word a wound.

Not like her. Not like Mercy. There wasn't a trace of darkness in her.

Or . . . a part of him hissed, born of nausea and treachery, *maybe she's hidden it so completely you don't even know it's there.*

Some Tenebrous hunted. Others laid traps.

The Three had wormed their way into Grey's head without him knowing they were there. Could Mercy have done the same?

No, Denizen told himself. *Impossible.* It hadn't been a plan. It hadn't been a trick.

It couldn't be.

"I met her by chance," Denizen said coldly. "And she gave me the Cants because it was the only way to beat the Three. She saved us that night, even as we were saving her."

He stood. "I think you've been fighting them so long it's made you paranoid. She wants to end this war peacefully and you'd rather kill them all instead."

"Yes," Vivian said simply. "I would. And if you weren't a lovesick little boy, you would too."

"Well, I'm very sorry," Denizen retorted. "Perhaps I should try to be more like you. Someone cold. Someone who runs from love. Someone who only mentions *my dead father* when they need to win an argument."

Denizen knew as soon as he'd said it that he'd gone too far. Vivian didn't shout or scowl or snarl. Instead, she just . . . retreated. If the Cost had claimed her totally in that moment, she could not have been more still.

"Vivian," he said, when the silence had become unbearable, "I'm sorry. I didn't mean—"

"Whatever abilities you have, Denizen, whatever gift you think she's given you . . . it will not save you." Her voice wasn't angry, just tired. "The Order does not suffer traitors. Stop this madness or they will come for you . . . and I will not be able to stop them."

Let them try. I have the Art of Apertura. I have a sun inside me. Ground me, guard me, take away my freedom. I will find it again, in fire if I must. THEY CANNOT STOP ME.

The words ran through Denizen's head and then died, a flame without fuel. He wouldn't say them. He'd said enough already.

Vivian closed the door behind her. Denizen crossed the room to the window and peeled back the paper, lifting his face to the cool wind. *If only we were at the Goshawk.* Surely room service wouldn't bat an eyelid if he asked for an ice bath. He knew as sure as iron that the ice would melt before his anger did.

"Denizen?"

He had forgotten how quiet Simon could be, even before he'd developed his gift for invisibility. The taller boy slipped through the door and closed it gently behind him.

"How much did you hear?" Denizen asked tonelessly.

"Enough," Simon responded. He took a deep breath. "It was me who told her you were gone."

"What?" Denizen's hands had curled into fists. Thoughts of ice baths turned to steam in his head. He didn't know if his eyes were glowing or not, but Simon met them all the same.

"Finally found your note. Cute, but I knew it wasn't true. I knew what you were doing, who you were sneaking out to meet. Not where, but when I told Vivian she said she'd find your trail." He hesitated. "She said she had a long history of hunting monsters."

"Well, thanks for that," Denizen said bitterly. "It's not going to score you any points with Greaves, though, so maybe you should think the next time you throw your best friend under a bus—"

"What?" Simon repeated, and now *he* sounded angry. Denizen couldn't remember hearing that before. "You're skipping merrily into the night to hang out with a Tenebrous. And not just any Tenebrous but the daughter of the Endless King. Do you want me to count the ways you're being stupid?"

"Mercy's not a monster," Denizen snapped. "We were *fine*. She'd taken human form and we were just . . . just walking. And I can handle myself. Better than you. Better than most Knights, actually. I know the Cants. I know the Cost—"

Simon cut him off. It seemed to be the night for it.

"I'm not talking about the Cost, Denizen. I'm talking about the *danger*. Do the Court know what you're doing? What she's doing?"

Frown No. 1. "I don't understand."

"Yeah," Simon said. "Neither do I. But what happens if the Court find out she's meeting you? What happens if her *father* finds out? Or the Order, if they haven't already? Don't you think you might be putting her in danger? Apart from putting us all at risk because you *don't* know what Mercy wants and you *don't* know what might make her lose her temper."

Frown No. 3—The Rising Wave of *You Might Have a Point*.

"I'm sorry I ratted you out," Simon said, sitting down heavily on his bed. "And I'm trying to get where you're coming from. But you have to understand that I don't sleep anymore. I lie there, and I make the noises because I know you're listening, and sometimes that turns into real sleep and sometimes it doesn't. Because when I feel my eyes start to close . . . I imagine being back in Crosscaper. Asleep. Forever. With the Three getting fat off my fear."

He sounded so *tired*.

"We've been looking for my family all week, Denizen. Scouring the *Incunabulae*. Sometimes bloodlines . . . sometimes *families* just disappear. Sometimes people are just orphans. And Mercy might not be a monster, but I know there are monsters out there, and you're taking chances with them."

Denizen stared at him for a very long time. Finally, he said, "I can't believe you. You're so selfish."

Simon's brows lifted.

"I can't even be mad at you now," Denizen continued.

He gave his best friend a quick, hard hug.

21

Two of a Kind

Uriel wasn't used to novelty. It wasn't a concept that had any place under the rotted eaves of Eloquence. But the Redemptress's waking had created a new world, and each Croit had to find their place in it. There were different things required of them now and, while resisting change had previously been a valued trait in the Family, now it was nothing less than a mortal sin.

"Strike!"

Five baleful roars, five overlapping dawns, and five patches of rubble turned to bubbling slag. The air stank of ozone and glass. Meredel had never sounded so valiant, so purposeful.

"Again!"

White-hot light pealed a second time, a menagerie of different Prayers. The Favored under Meredel's tutelage unleashed their fire and then stepped back—not in perfect unison, but far more competently than when they'd first arrived. Only one staggered, falling to his knees and coughing through a flame-seared throat.

None of the others went to help. That wasn't how training worked.

Beyond them, Grandfather lectured the most recent arrivals. Some had already donned tunics and shirts marked with the Crow and the Claw, but others still wore their clothes from Outside—strange fabrics, garishly bright. With an eye attuned for spotting weakness, Uriel identified those whose gaze was bright with fervor and those who stared forward blankly as if Eloquence were a bad dream they'd spent years trying to forget.

Meredel bid his students hold their fire as Uriel approached, but he still gave the newcomers a wide berth. After their long absence from Eloquence, it was hard to bring out the Favor in some, and harder to control it in others. There had already been . . . clashes.

Despite the cold, sweat streaked Uriel's cheeks. Once he had known every outcrop and pothole on this hillside. Now it had been rearranged by the violent worship of the Croits, pitted by sizzling craters and scars, and he had to pick his way across.

"Meredel," Uriel said.

His cousin nodded, eyes still fixed on his *newcomers*. A placeholder title—Uriel had a feeling Grandfather would devise a grander name for them based on something from the histories—

Suddenly what he had just thought caught up to him, the disrespectfulness of it, and he felt the burn of shame, even as his head jerked involuntarily toward Eloquence.

Nothing. She's not . . .

Uriel took a deep, shaky breath. *What's wrong with me?* "How . . . how are they?"

"Learning," Meredel said.

Farther down the slope, Adauctus Croit's lanky form led a sweat-lathered group in swordwork. More modern weapons were arriving, but such things took time—even with Croit money involved—and in the meantime every sword, ax, and halberd had been pressed into service.

Focus. That was what Grandfather wanted. Wielding the weapons was a secondary concern. The days of that kind of warfare were long gone, and the destructive potential of a Croit went far beyond the point of a sword. But the Favor was dangerous, bound only by the will of the Croit that spoke it. Any distraction, anything that took your mind from taming that white-hot fire . . .

"Have you seen Ambrel?" Uriel said. "I . . . um . . . haven't. Have you?"

"Don't know," Meredel said. "Ask the Afterwoken."

It was as good a name as any. Uriel stared down at them. He hadn't learned their names—it was still strange for Uriel to have people in his life whose names he *didn't* know—and the thought of them knowing something about Ambrel that he didn't made his stomach turn.

They're not Croits, Uriel thought. *Not really.* They hadn't grown up in the shadow of the castle, sleeping on cots, learning everything they knew of the world straight from Grandfather's mouth. Every Croit was brought to Grandfather to be tested at thirteen, but Uriel and Ambrel had spent their entire lives here, confiscated from their unFavored parents.

It was the only thing their parents had done right.

"No," Uriel said. "I'll find her myself."

Another new concept, one far more disconcerting than the newcomers. Before the Redemptress had awoken, Uriel could have counted the beats of Ambrel's heart simply by counting his own. There had never been more than half a second's gap between them.

And there isn't. There won't be. Ever.

She wasn't in the Armory, its walls now bare of all that sharpened steel. The new crowdedness of the corridors was unnerving—at certain points Uriel had to push *through* Afterwoken, though one look at his dark expression was enough for most to realize who he was and jump out of the way. He wasn't sure what was more annoying.

Scaling the battered rib cage of a tower, he gazed out over the Garden, but the only color darting between the white marble was Tabitha exercising her cruelty on a stumbling, screaming cohort of Afterwoken. Ambrel wasn't in the Weeping Gallery either, but neither was anyone else, so Uriel stood there for a long time, listening to the wind wheeze between broken stone.

There was only one place he hadn't looked. Nausea bored through Uriel's stomach, as it had every day since . . .

Why won't I go? That's where she is. That's where She is. Faces swam across his vision, the two most important faces in his life. His sister and his Redemptress. They blurred together and were one.

What's wrong with me?

Attend.

He was running before the first echo of that unearthly voice. So was everyone else. Frustration built in Uriel as the exodus slowed his pace, and he was half tempted to split away, try some of the secret gaps and passages he and Ambrel had spent their entire childhood exploring, but . . .

The castle's shadows hung differently now, as if the stones that cast them had been rearranged. Corridors didn't lead where Uriel remembered them leading. Old handholds gave way, and places that had once stood firm now teetered, ready to fall.

Everything was different. Everything was the same. He had lived here almost every day of his life, and yet, with these new faces and the bleak taste of nausea and a sister-shaped gap beside him that had never been there before . . .

He felt like an outsider.

The Redemptress towered over the entrance to Eloquence, hair hanging round Her cheeks like the grasping legs of a spider, too heavy to be moved by the breeze. She had been spending more and more time outside in the last few days, relearning the touch of the sun.

In front of Her stood thirty-six Favored Croits, and half-Croits, and quarter-Croits, and drop-of-Croits. Each one had knelt in front of Her at the moment of their thirteenth birthday and each one had a Prayer to Her in their heart. Some had been in Eloquence for every minute of Uriel's childhood. Some had just visited. Some were complete strangers . . . but their destiny had always lain here.

Uriel's eyes found Abucad's and then immediately looked away.

Pushing through the crowd, Uriel tried to surreptitiously search for Ambrel. He just wanted to *talk* to her. Wanted to know if she felt the same otherness he did, the otherness that had come with the opening of wire eyes. He wanted to know if she was afraid.

He wanted to look into her eyes and still see his reflection there.

Do you feel it? The Redemptress's head was tipped

toward the sky, as if awaiting the first drop of rain. *Can you feel it coming?*

Her voice was soft, neutral, but the Croits around him tensed all the same. Uriel understood perfectly. When She opened Her mouth, there was no telling which voice would speak—the ice-cold conqueror or the lover tortured by loss.

"What is it, Majesty?"

Uriel stiffened as Ambrel appeared, followed closely by Grandfather. He strained to catch her eye, but her gaze was turned upward.

Go to her, Uriel told himself, but his limbs wouldn't move. The turmoil in his stomach deepened to pain.

"Yes," Grandfather said, placing his hand on Ambrel's shoulder. "Tell us."

Come close, She said, looking down on them. *You must all come close. I thought I was the last. . . . I thought maybe there was no one left but . . .*

Her arms rose, gathering them all up like a mother with Her children.

Tell me what you are.

Grandfather raised his arms in imitation, right hand clasping his empty left sleeve. Light prowled under his skin, spilling from his open mouth.

"We are the faithful. We are the Favored. We are the descendants of the First Croit and we carry his sacred charge."

More lights bloomed in eyes and mouths, staining

the gray dust a rich and hungry gold. His brothers and sisters around him drew on their fire too, and, despite himself, Uriel felt his own Favor rise, flowing through his limbs in a wave of heat and burning his doubt away.

This was right. *This* was proper.

Thirty-six Croits together, each one with the Favor in their hearts. What could you do with that much fire? What would you *want* to do?

Two Croits together was an argument. Three was a tinderbox. This many . . .

This was a crusade.

"We are Croits!" Grandfather roared, and a yell swept the hillside. Uriel cried out too, caught up in the power and the fury, and above it all the Redemptress frowned as if She had never heard the word before.

No.

The light died in stages, in a sort of sullen shock. She was no longer looking at them all; Her gaze fixed upon the horizon. Beneath Her, Croits exchanged glances like chastened children. A slow rasp built in the silence, circling them like the sleepy drone of a wasp.

Wires were slipping from the rubble, twisting in the air like vines seeking sun. They braided, wrapping themselves round each other, pushing Croit against Croit. It was suddenly hard to see, to breathe; someone staggered into Uriel and he pushed back, the wires whispering to each other as they tightened.

The Redemptress gave them a bitter smile.

You are mine.

And deafening came the sound of wings.

The otherness prickling Uriel's skin redoubled, the sensation of wrongness suddenly so strong it was like a physical pain. He tasted blood, then tin. The lattice of wires twisted around them, and Croits shoved and pushed in sudden panic. The ground shook, and suddenly there were *birds,* bursting somehow from the ground, spiraling upward round the Redemptress in a tower a thousand strong.

Uriel's Favor hammered against his chest, crying out to be drawn. *No.* In this press, he'd hurt nothing but Family. The shrieking flood of birds hadn't stopped, and when they banked overhead, it was like the sun had gone dark.

Then, finally, it ended. A final shape dragged itself out of the dust and into the sky, and then the whole crazed flock descended upon one of Eloquence's ruined parapets, bird clinging to bird, the crag of stone invisible beneath a heaving mat of shapes.

They were crows. He could see that now—mirrors to the emblem on his tunic, though the embroidery did not do these creatures justice—white, fat things, long of beak and black of eye. Uriel's skin prickled at the thought of so many razor points.

Croits around him swayed. Uriel caught a brief glimpse of Hagar vomiting into the dirt. One or two had simply fainted, held by their cousins so they didn't pitch forward onto the gleaming fence of wires. The birds' eyes followed those the most, as though they knew weakness when they saw it.

Carrion-eaters, Uriel thought, and then they spoke.

It feels soooo goooood to streeeeetcccchhh!

The voice seeped from a thousand beaks. Uriel had never heard such a voice before, with its clicks and wet snarls, but all he could think of was that it sounded *familiar.*

It sounded like the Redemptress.

Not the words but the nature of the voice—how it echoed oddly, slid into your ears like needles.

That's the first time you've ever thought of Her as wrong, a voice whispered, but the blasphemy went unnoticed.

Back! the Redemptress snarled, Her voice like tearing steel. ***Mine!***

And I thought I kept a full larder, the birds sniggered. Something like a head rose from the shifting, heaving mass—a clot of eyes and beaks and wriggling tongues. Someone vomited against Uriel's back, but he didn't dare take his eyes from this beast that spoke and felt like the goddess they were supposed to serve.

That we do serve, a voice whispered, but Uriel wasn't listening to it anymore. He couldn't. There was too much horror in the air.

Where is Ambrel?

Slowly, shouldering through the press, Uriel began to move. Above him, wires wove and rewove, widening the Redemptress's shoulders, lifting Her higher, bulking out Her spindly frame. Spines rose along Her back—long knives of black. When She next spoke, it was in a new tone altogether, as if this *creature* had shocked Her lucid.

Malebranche. You live. You . . .

We all LIVE, dear. The monstrous thing seemed amused. ***It was you who was dead.***

Something of the confused child entered Her voice. ***I fell.***

Memory's a little shaky, is it? Feathers rasped against feathers. ***I'm not surprised. Too long in this world and we really do start coming apart. You didn't fall, Coronus. You were PUSHED.***

Uriel hadn't managed to move more than a meter or so through the crush. All he wanted to do was draw his sword and *cut* his way to his sister, and every word exchanged by these giants made that desire stronger. Was this thing, this Malebranche, a god as well? How many of them were there?

Why didn't we know?

The Redemptress was trembling, Her wires hissing together.

How did you find me?

A single caw broke the air. The clustered murder lurched upward into something almost human-shaped—limbs thatched from wings and tiny bodies—and caught a descending crow from the air. It shook in the creature's grasp, gray where the others were white, nuzzling as if glad to be with its brothers.

I never lost you, dear. I have eyes everywhere. And it's funny what humans remember.

The Crow and the Claw. Uriel suddenly fought the urge to tear the emblem from himself. This was the creature they had carried through the centuries. This was the lie they had worn.

Crows always have a place on the battlefield.

The creature stroked its wayward son gently, crooning.

So long out in this rigid, searing world . . . So long by itself . . . It's almost a real thing itself now, a little mind away from mine.

There was a *snap.*

There. Better.

Uriel watched as the limp body of the gray crow was subsumed into the rustling mass. The creature stretched with a multitude of croaks.

I wondered if our return would wake you, and what you would do if it did. Malebranche finally seemed to notice the Croits below it, huddling in their cradle of wires. ***Didn't you learn anything the last time? What is your fascination with these little children and their flashbulb souls?***

You don't understand. The Redemptress growled so low Uriel felt his diaphragm vibrate. ***You've never understood.***

No, the beast murmured. ***I never, ever have.*** It rolled forward on legs made of jabbering crows, leaving crushed bodies behind. The proximity of it was horrendous. Uriel wiped a thread of blood from his nose.

Ambrel.

He pushed harder, squeezing between his cousins, stepping over those who had fallen, and all he could think was—

They're connected. They feel the same, and they share a past.

Come home, the hideous creature said, and all the mockery had left its voice. ***Come home and forget this world. You've been away so long that perhaps the King will show . . . clemency.***

Ambrel was steps away, her gaze fixed on the Redemptress, her hands clenched into fists. Uriel was nearly beside her.

The dark isn't so bad, Coronus. We've adapted. As we've always done.

Its voice was raw.

There is nothing in the light for us.

And Ambrel turned toward her brother and took his hand. Gold spilled through her, turning her skin the shade of a summer sunrise. Uriel's own Favor rose to meet it, and suddenly everyone around them was lit in honeyed light. Uriel could see panicked eyes, shaking hands—they were terrified, but they stood, and light rose within them.

They are the faithful. They are the Favored. The Redemptress halted over each word. ***They are descendants of the First Croit, and they carry his sacred charge.***

We do.

And just for a moment, despite the wretched violation of Malebranche's presence and the doubts growing like black flowers in his chest, Uriel believed in Ambrel. And that was enough.

The wires thrummed with tension.

They are Croits. And they are all I have left of him.

Malebranche shook its great feather-maned head. ***So be it.***

Wait.

There was aching pain in the Redemptress's voice. ***I never . . . I never meant to cause . . .***

I know you didn't, the monster said quietly.

Birds opened their wings and the creature came apart in spiraling crows.

Maybe you have it right, dear, it called from a thousand throats. ***Maybe we should all be gathering our little human cults. The King still has his, after all. . . .***

The wires suddenly tightened a full meter inward. Uriel fell against his cousins, and his cousins fell on him. Ambrel's hand was jerked from his.

The Redemptress's voice was a hiss.

The Order lives?

Oh, you HAVE been sleeping, the birds cackled. *Oh yes, Coronus—they THRIVE now, with the blood of thousands of our kind on their hands, and yet we meet with them under a banner of peace. And all because the King's little girl has taken a shine to one of them. Wasn't that what made you such adversaries to begin with?*

You see, there's this BOY. . . .

22

ICEBERGS

WORDS WERE IMPORTANT.

Denizen had grown up on words. They were comfort and protection. In the absence of family, and occasionally food, Denizen had subsisted on nothing else. He'd understood the magic of them long before he had known of the existence of *actual* magic.

But it wasn't magic words that were the trouble.

Some words had their own magic. Small words with massive meanings—words like *love* and *family*. They had to be small because people were already so afraid of them. Denizen had read once that the simpler a question, the more complex the answer. Giant questions boil down to a single number, and questions like *How could you?* might never get answered at all.

Words had power. Unseen, terrible power. And right now Denizen's words had transported him into a whole other world.

There was a guard outside his bedroom door.

Denizen rubbed sleep from his eyes. He hadn't left his room in a day, hoping that since Vivian hadn't grounded him he might gain extra points by grounding himself. He didn't know if Abigail knew what he'd done. He didn't know if Darcie did. He just knew he couldn't hide anymore.

The plan was to get up criminally early and find Vivian before anyone else woke. Denizen had spent yesterday planning exactly what he'd say, down to the last full stop, interspersed with horrified speculation as to what Greaves might do to him.

Kicked out of the Order.

Forced to go back to Crosscaper.

Incarceration in Retreat until the firing squad. With actual fire.

Forced to go back to Crosscaper.

No. Everything was going to be fine. Vivian had nearly been elected Palatine herself, wasn't that what Darcie had said? Surely she'd have some plan, some favor to call in; all she had to do was forgive him herself first.

And there was a *guard*. Outside his *door*.

"Morning, Jack," Denizen said haltingly.

"Morning," the Knight replied. He leaned against the wall nonchalantly, as if being outside Denizen's bedroom was exactly where he always was at seven in the morning.

"Umm . . ."

Had he just been passing by? He couldn't have been. There wasn't anywhere he could have been on his way to. Had he been sent here to fetch Denizen for something?

"Sorry," said Denizen. "Is there somewhere I'm supposed to be?"

"No."

"Right," Denizen said slowly. "Is there somewhere *you're* supposed to be?"

"No," Jack repeated.

Did he know? Had Vivian told him? Had *Greaves* found out? All sorts of small, important words rose up through the panicked mush of Denizen's brain.

Words like *security risk*. Words like *traitor*. Words like—

"Breakfast?" Jack asked, beckoning him to follow.

He'd brought it from the Goshawk—*of course he had, a fancy meal for a condemned man*—sourdough bread topped with eggs from a species of bird Denizen had never heard of, with a single sprig of parsley balanced on top like a lady's parasol. It tasted like ash.

There was no one else in the kitchen. Denizen knew this because he was studiously avoiding Jack's gaze in order to not start a conversation. Though Jack probably wouldn't speak to him anyway. You didn't speak to prisoners. They might infect you with dangerous ideas.

Great. I'm going to go down in history as the first person to ever try and kiss a Tenebrous. There'll be pictures of me in Seraphim Row. Denizen Hardwick—the Never-Knighted. They'll name a chapter in the handbook after me. They'll call it "Pulling a Denizen." Except they won't. Because no one in the history of the Order has ever been that stupid before, and no one ever will be again.

He stared morosely at his breakfast.

I didn't even get to kiss her.

"How are you doing, lad?"

The table creaked under Jack's massive forearms.

"Fine," Denizen said sullenly.

"You sound it."

Denizen was suddenly stuck in the difficult position of wanting to know how much Jack knew, without letting him know what he was supposed to know about.

I'll just talk about normal things. The weather, or the Order's preferred method of execution . . .

"I know, by the way," Jack said, tapping some sugar into his coffee. "Do you want to talk about it?"

Oh. Denizen jammed a bit of bread in his mouth so he'd have an excuse not to talk for a moment. He stared straight ahead, waiting for Jack to be disgusted, to call him a fool or worse—

"I understand, Denizen."

Denizen gave him a sidelong look.

"Well," Jack said, stirring his coffee, the spoon absurdly tiny in his massive hands, "I don't, if I'm being honest. I understand . . . bits of it. Not you liking her, obviously. That I don't understand. No, I just . . . no. I mean—"

"Right," Denizen said. "I get it."

Jack winced. "Sorry. But I know what it's like to be young and in love with the wrong . . . person. You're probably feeling a little stupid."

"I am," Denizen said, poking his food round his plate.

"Like a bit of an idiot."

"Yep."

"A complete—"

"*Yes,*" Denizen said. "I get it. Thank you."

"Sorry," Jack said. "But the Order are worried sick. None of us knew a Knight could be turned. *Vivian* didn't know, and she'd fought the Three more than any Knight alive. What happened to Grey . . ."

There was no anger in Jack's voice when he said Grey's name. It spoke of the kind of strength the Three would break their teeth on.

Boxes rustled in the back of Denizen's head. *The kind of strength I wish I had.*

Jack thumbed a coil of iron on his neck. "Vivian was trying to protect you. She knew Greaves would be working hard, trying to find out what happened: not because he's a bad guy—because he's not—but because he has people to protect. We need to know what Tenebrous are capable of so we can defend against it."

Something about the way Jack defended both Greaves and Vivian made realization dawn.

"Precautions were taken," Denizen breathed. "That's what Vivian said. She meant you."

"The Order likes to move Knights around a lot," Jack said. "It helps us share experience." A guilty look flashed across his face. "So there's nothing strange about me wanting to relocate away from this garrison after . . . what happened. And of course Greaves would jump at the chance to take me on as part of his staff, considering I was right on scene when everything happened. To be honest, I don't think he can figure out why anyone would want to work with your mother in the first place."

"So all this time," Denizen said slowly, "Vivian's had *you* watching *him*?"

The ingenuity of it astonished him. It wasn't that he didn't think Vivian was smart, but it was completely at odds with the way she presented herself as, well, a blunt instrument. It was . . . it was . . .

It was very Edifice Greaves.

"You were watching the house," Denizen said. "So Vivian could control what Greaves actually knew."

"No, no," Jack said. "Not me. Greaves isn't an idiot. But I put together the surveillance detail for him. Who better to ask than someone who knows some of Vivian's tricks? And you'd be amazed how many owe Vivian Hardwick a favor. Had those Knights seen anything, it wouldn't have been Greaves they went to. Not that they did see anything, but, then again, who'd expect a thirteen-year-old to know the Art of Apertura? Or be stupid enough to use it?"

Denizen flushed, and not just because of Jack's expression. The sheer amount of effort Vivian—no, *everyone*—had gone to in order to protect Denizen was starting to weigh on his sense of being the wronged party.

"I'm *not* a thrall," Denizen said.

"How would you know?"

Yesterday had been a long twenty-four hours, and a good portion of it had been spent staring into the mirror, asking himself the same question. It had taken even longer to find an answer that wasn't: *Because I don't feel like one.*

"Because Grey was coming apart," Denizen said, and there was shameful pride in how he was able to say that sentence without his voice breaking. "The pressure of them in his head was killing him. And I feel fine."

Mortified, stressed, and angry, but fine.

"But, Denizen, that's—"

"I trust her," Denizen interrupted, and Jack fell silent. "That's all. I trust that she wouldn't do that to me. I trust that she has a sense of honor. And there's no point in talking about peace *at all* if we don't start by trusting just one of them."

Jack blinked. "You . . . actually have a point." He

sighed. "You really do, at that. But you've only been in this war for six months. And hatred and fear build like rust, Denizen, and they don't just disappear. We've had people taken from us. That's a debt that can't easily be paid."

D'Aubigny. Grey. My . . . my father.

"Look," Jack said, "we'll handle Greaves. You didn't do anything suspicious—that he knows about anyway. It might take a while, and you're always going to have to be careful, but eventually something else is going to come along to take his attention. Let's get through this Concilium first."

"Do you think he'd try and ambush Mercy?"

Jack frowned. "I know him a little now, and I don't think he has anything other than the safety of his Knights at heart. A war wouldn't do anything for anybody. But that's not what you should be thinking about."

"No?"

"No," Jack said firmly. "You need to fix things with Vivian. She's been the way she is for a long time. I don't know if she can meet you halfway, and I know that's hard to accept, but in the end it doesn't matter."

A trace of surliness entered Denizen's voice. "Why?"

Jack looked old then, for the first time since Denizen had known him.

"Because we live in a world of loss. You go through

life thinking you'll be able to say everything you want to say . . . but sometimes there are no second chances and no last words. None of us know how much time we're given, but I do know it's never, *ever* enough. . . ."

"I understand," Denizen said softly.

"Good," said Jack. "So do it."

"Jack?"

"Yeah?"

Denizen swallowed. "Is it my fault?"

The huge man looked surprised. "What?"

"Everything," Denizen said. "What happened with the Three. D'Aubigny. Grey. Is it my fault? Mine and Vivian's for drawing them to all of you?"

Jack sighed. "I was never much of a Knight, Denizen. I like making things. I'm not afraid of a fight, never have been, but I didn't cleave to the war the way Corinne did. She was a force of nature, my wife. And she knew the risks of what she did. Grey too. That's what being part of the Order means. You didn't bring doom down on our heads. We were already facing the darkness. It's just . . . sometimes it wins."

He sounded so calm.

"Do you not want . . . I don't know . . . revenge?"

Jack shrugged. "There's no point to revenge. You either don't get it, in which case the want grows until it collapses your world around you, or you do get it. And then you have it. Great. Show me something you can build from revenge that you can't build from acceptance."

"And have you? Accepted what happened?"

"I'm trying," he said. "And you and Vivian should try too. Now finish your breakfast."

"Thanks," Denizen said, and gave him an awkward smile. "I didn't know pep talks were part of your guard duties."

"Guard duties?" Jack repeated. "Hang on—did you think I was, what, keeping an eye on you so you couldn't sneak off?"

Denizen flushed. "Weren't you?"

"No, you fool," Jack said with a touch of exasperation. "I wanted to see if you were all right. You thought I was a jailer, did you?"

He shook his head ruefully.

"You Hardwicks are all alike."

23

Line of Sight

So that was it, then. Denizen was going to lay his vault bare. He was going to tell Vivian that they needed to talk, that all they had was each other. She'd stare at him for the longest moment and then her lip would tremble, just a fraction, and her scarred arms would open wide.

They'd hug. Actually hug. The apologies would come thick and fast, hers to him and his to her, and they would step into the light of a new day together, mother and son united, their dark past behind them.

All they had to do was survive this Concilium first.

Denizen shrugged on a loose shirt to hide the scabbard of his stone knife. Jack had rigged up a harness for him with buckles for a scabbard on each side, reasoning that, since Denizen had so far displayed absolutely no proficiency with any class of weapon, it couldn't hurt to double up.

Now the hilt of his stone blade protruded from under one armpit, the hilt of a long knife from the other. Denizen had practiced drawing both at the same time and surprisingly managed not to handcapitate himself, so he was actually feeling a little optimistic.

Providing Greaves *had* only been trying to test whether he'd been compromised and wasn't actually planning a surgical strike against the Tenebrae's nobility. And providing the Court weren't planning their own ambush against the Order. And providing his mother *actually* showed up so he could be the bigger person and apologize.

"Where's Vivian?" he asked.

She hadn't been at dinner the night before and she hadn't been at breakfast that morning.

I'm trying to forgive you. Show up so I can forgive you.

"Don't know," Jack said. "She's probably already at Retreat. The Mallei have been working day and night to sort out some kind of terms."

"And?" said Abigail, leaning forward interestedly in her chair. They had gathered in the foyer to see Denizen and Jack off, the dawn bright and crisp outside.

"I think they've gotten as far as *Stop eating us,*" Jack said wryly. "But I'm not a politician."

"It's a good enough place to start," Darcie said.

She and the other Neophytes were dressed in running gear. Vivian had left the same instructions she always did when she went on one of her unannounced jaunts—keep training. Denizen understood the sentiment, though. The world didn't stop just because this meeting was happening.

Unless it does.

Darcie gave Denizen a searching glance. "How are you feeling?"

"Me?" Denizen said. "What? I'm fine, I—"

He and Simon had tacitly agreed that there was absolutely no sense in telling the girls what had happened—or almost happened; Denizen was never going to get over that—as there wasn't going to be a repeat performance and it would do nobody any good if Denizen died of embarrassment.

The thing was, Denizen hadn't taken into consideration the fact that there was very little that Knights, even Neophytes, didn't notice, especially when it came to their comrades.

And Darcie was his friend.

"I'm OK," Denizen said. "A bit nervous. I'm not sure what I'm actually supposed to be doing."

"*Nothing,*" Jack and Simon said together. Abigail and Darcie exchanged confused glances.

"Ahem," said Simon.

"Er," said Jack. "I mean . . . you're to keep quiet and be formally thanked. Then we get you out of there and see if we can hash out some sort of peace deal."

"Get thanked. Go home. Fine." Denizen hated his voice when it sounded like that. As nerve-racking as the thoughts of the Concilium and patching things up with Vivian were, they were failing to distract him from the fact this might be the last time he ever saw Mercy.

It can't be. It just can't. It was an occupational hazard of being a bookworm. You stopped thinking in terms of reality and started thinking of nick-of-time rescues and the power of a dramatic speech. It couldn't be over because it shouldn't be over.

The universe was many things—including a *multiverse*, apparently—but surely . . . surely it couldn't be that unfair?

"All right," Jack said. "Time to go."

Simon gave Denizen a hug, conveying a wealth of instructions in a one-nanosecond glare. Abigail gave him a rib-creaking squeeze that sent a thrill of shame through him. He felt extremely bad about not telling the girls. There was a chance—a small chance—that Darcie might hear him out, but Falxes went back as far as Hardwicks when it came to killing Tenebrous, and Abigail's dad had been hurt last year, when the King's Pursuivants had been searching for Mercy, so Denizen honestly didn't know how she'd react.

Maybe today will *be the last time I ever see her, and I'll never have to tell Abigail at all.*

Running away again. Ironically, it seemed to be what Hardwicks did best.

"Be careful," she said, and punched him lightly on the arm.

"Ow," Denizen said. "And thanks."

"Ready?" Jack said, shrugging a battered old duffel bag onto his shoulder with a muted clatter of weaponry.

"Sure."

Darcie gave him a quick hug, but not before he noticed the tiredness in her eyes. "Are you OK?" he asked, concerned—and annoyed that he'd been so wrapped up in himself that he hadn't noticed.

"Yes," she said. "Just . . . bad dreams. That's all."

It was a lovely morning for a walk, which annoyed Denizen no end because it would have been the perfect time to have a lot of emotions at Vivian, had she bothered to show up.

Was it some sort of special power? One possessed not by Knights but by mothers—the ability to be exactly where you didn't want them to be but absent when you did? It very well might have been. Denizen had never had a mother before so he had no idea.

I should just try to kiss Mercy again, and then Vivian would magically materialize.

It was a full minute before he realized what he'd just thought.

No. Bad Denizen.

Avoiding confrontation—except the violent kind—was a particular skill of the Hardwick family. Jack had given Denizen a fervent desire to speak to Vivian, but as they approached Trinity College it felt like that fire was starving from lack of fuel.

They pushed their way past a meandering group of language students and crossed the cobbled main square, Denizen trying to get used to the motion of the knives in their scabbards. He kept checking his shirt buttons to make sure they didn't accidentally open and announce his stabby intentions to the entire populace.

A little part of him wondered again whether bringing the stone knife broke the Concilium rules, but they had said *no hammers,* hadn't they? And in the grand scheme of things, surely it was excusable compared to a surprise bunch of antipersonnel mines.

Well, it was too late now, and he needed all the points with Vivian he could get. People got annoyed if you acted ungrateful about their presents, and this wasn't an ill-fitting sweater or a book you'd already read: it was a one-of-a-kind magical knife with the power to—possibly—slay the unslayable. Besides, Denizen had an orphan's natural thrift: gifts were rare, and you kept them close.

A group of Knights was waiting outside the Long Room's entrance, and there was Vivian, a few meters away from everyone else, rigidly glaring off into space.

Denizen slowed as though the cobblestones under

his feet had turned to glue. Jack's presence was at his back like a friendly wind, but Vivian radiated *not now* like a cracked nuclear reactor. Of course, she always did that. Even her rare smiles had a certain bleak aspect to them, as if she always knew exactly how many she had left.

Now was probably not the time. Maybe there was never going to be a time. If only she'd give him some sort of sign that there was a human being under all that accreted annoyance—

A hand found his shoulder.

"Hey, kid," Edifice Greaves said. "Good to see you."

Frown No. 5—Don't Patronize Me, *Adult*. Otherwise known as the I See What You're Doing, the I Know What You're Up To, and the Don't Lie to Me and Pretend You're About to Trigger an Interdimensional War Just to See What I'll Do, You Smarmbucket.

Greaves wilted in the face of Denizen's new and improved No. 5. He actually looked a little hurt. A part of Denizen wavered—he didn't actually *know* Greaves had set him up. Did he? Jack thought he was a good guy, and Vivian tended to see the world less in terms of good and bad, and more in *my way* and *other*.

I want a form, Denizen thought. *I want everyone to have a form, and you have to fill out your intentions and list why you're doing what you're doing. And you're not allowed to lie.*

"Let's just do this," he said.

"Fair enough," Greaves replied in a neutral tone, and suddenly all the Knights were moving. Denizen immediately made a beeline for Vivian—not to talk but for some nod or glance that might fan the coals in him back to life.

It was no use. She was lost in the sudden flow of dangerous people, long legs keeping her one step ahead. Buffeted this way and that, Denizen tried to reassure himself that it was a coincidence that every time a space opened up between him and Vivian, it was immediately filled by a Knight.

It's just a cramped space. That's all.

All Denizen could do was stare impotently at the back of Vivian's head. People got out of *her* way. Was that a skill you learned eventually as well?

The gift shop was deserted but for a few tourists poring over printed maps. Sunlight slunk in through the high windows of the Long Room, trying and failing to bring a shine to the marble busts lining the alcoves. It was busier here—maybe half a dozen people, a tweed-clad professor who seemed to be spending far more time gawking at the arriving Knights than reading the book in his hands. Denizen fought the urge to frown at him as well. He'd had a hard time trusting tweed since the last time he was in a bookshop.

Greaves was looking around for a security guard to close the place up, but there were still people entering. A girl glared at the velvet rope holding her back from the older books, another boy reading from a pamphlet beside her.

Denizen's gaze skipped over them distractedly. Greaves *couldn't* be planning an ambush. And even if he were, he wouldn't bring a Neophyte into it, would he?

He put you in a room with a bunch of explosives, didn't he? And maybe he knows you have the extra Cants as well. Maybe this is another test.

No. This was going to be the first time a Tenebrous talked peace with a human. A step in the right direction after centuries of war. Everything was going to be fine.

Denizen glanced back at the last shards of sunlight hanging in the doorway to the Long Room for one last iota of reassurance—

And the lights went out.

It was nothing as natural as a power outage. Instead, the room seemed to disappear beneath a falling veil of electric black. Shadows unzipped themselves from under tables and beneath pillars—swallowing shelves, eating displays. It was as if the air had turned into the water of an ocean trench, so dark it was practically solid.

Half the lamps went dark with the dry snap of broken fuses. The others slid to crimson in a dozen bloody shades, their bulbs throbbing slow in heartbeat time.

Denizen had thought he knew the dimensions of the room, but now he felt he was adrift, drowned in dark and silence. He spun, and then spun again, which failed to achieve anything except making him extremely dizzy. All he could see was a shifting obsidian murk broken by red lights like distant, dying stars.

In that single, horrible instant, Denizen was suddenly reminded of every childhood fear he'd had of the dark. He'd forgotten what it was like. Knights didn't see it. He blinked, waiting for the *Lucidum* to kick in, but it didn't. Fear thrilled up his spine. Had darkness always been this black? This cold?

He'd forgotten how afraid it could make you. He'd forgotten how it attacked.

The Court. Were they attacking? There was no sickening lurch in his stomach of the kind that normally announced a Tenebrous. Denizen didn't understand—for them to do this, he'd be able to feel it, he'd have to—

And then a light bloomed. Relief burned through Denizen, though the darkness remained, clustering round the glow like a weight that could not be pushed away. It didn't matter. Denizen knew that rich shade of flickering gold.

The color of firelight and home.

A Knight. Denizen ran toward the figure—they'd know what to do. He squinted to try and make out who . . .

It was the girl from the other side of the room. The stranger. There was a sword in her hand. Smoke rose from her vicious smile.

"Burn for Her," she whispered.

24

Shadow Puppets

Denizen's world became roaring flame.

He'd been in enough life-or-death situations by now to know that time didn't actually slow down when you were being attacked. In reality, you were speeding up. Your brain realized before you did that every second was crucial—which was why Denizen had all the time in the world to watch the girl's mouth open, white-hot light erupting *through* her, borne on the wave of a warbling shriek.

That's not a Cant, he thought in the first third of a second as the fire ate the distance and the darkness between them, illuminating a staccato blurt of floor and shelf. He should know. He was carrying all seventy-eight of them in the back of his head.

She's just channeling the fire herself, came another thought, a third of a second after the first. *That's insane.*

And then another, this one far more urgent.

GET OUT OF THE WAY!

A desperate leap took him out of the path of the murderous tongue of flame, one side of his face immediately stinging with what Denizen could only accurately call sunburn.

Stone hissed and split. Afterimages turned Denizen's vision inside out, making the world a luminescent veinwork before his eyes adjusted to the gloom. They hadn't had to acclimatize to real darkness for six months, and they were hideously, nauseatingly out of practice.

Somewhere behind him came a hoarse, faraway boom, followed by a flash of fire that too briefly outlined a host of moving shapes—shadow puppets against the murk. Light crashed and gleamed through the dark, a storm somewhere out of sight.

No, Denizen thought, trying to feel his way in front of him, to find some kind of shelter or cover. *Not a storm. A barrage.*

The Knights were being attacked.

Denizen's frantic pawing finally found the edge of one of the huge shelves. The girl prowled closer, her light illuminating her and nothing else, and that was only one of an avalanche of things that did not make any sense.

She's a human. Why is she doing this?

How *is she doing this?*

Only once had Denizen used the fire within him

without the protective limitations of a Cant, and it had knocked him out for a day and a night. The Cants were—what was it Mercy had said?—a *language of control*. A mold to provide the inferno with direction and shape.

And this girl was using it free and unfettered, with only her will to guide it. The effort must have been incredible. The danger involved, the Cost . . . and she was using it against another human being. A human being that happened to be Denizen, actually, which he was going to process right after he got over the shock of betrayal. This didn't happen. It had never happened, not in all the battles the Knights had fought. It didn't—

Oh God, Denizen thought, *is she a thrall?*

The horrified notion had no time to bloom before another light appeared. Denizen was almost grateful for the interruption, had it not been the boy from earlier, eyes molten, the shifting light painting him as gaunt and deadly as a butterfly knife. A blade of pure fire shone in his hand like the sword of a fallen angel.

It was the push Denizen needed. Maybe it was his training finally kicking in. Maybe it was the fact he was now outnumbered two to one and neither stranger seemed ready to offer an explanation. It might even have been because Denizen was a Hardwick, and there were a thousand dead ancestors screaming that his family didn't take being attacked lying down.

Questions could wait. This was war.

The girl shrieked fire again, but Denizen ripped the universe open with a pass of his fingers and let the light disappear into the bottomless depths of the Tenebrae. The boy's eyes widened, and the Cants crackled like laughter in Denizen's head before he snarled the shape of the Qayyim Myriad.

A dozen tiny suns exploded into life, orbiting him once, twice—crisping the floor in wavering lines—before hurtling forward with eager wails. Fire beat against his chest, desperate to be used, but a Knight was supposed to be a strategist, and calculations were clicking in Denizen's head.

The girl shouted half the orbs down with a messy splatter of flame. The sword of fire licked out to detonate three more before they could impact, the boy ducking and weaving and somersaulting—*somersaulting*—in a move that would have done Corinne D'Aubigny proud. The remainder grounded themselves in the wall, exploding in sparks and soot.

Denizen didn't mind that particularly, just as he didn't register the pinch and tickle of his cooling skin. The Myriad had just filled in some of the running equation of how he was going to get out of this alive.

Most Knights learned twenty or so Cants. It was all you really needed, and the Cost was a great deterrent to showing off. Specializing simplified things while still allowing a Knight to change strategy on the fly, in case . . . well, in case of this exact situation.

The girl prepared herself to strike again. He could see it in the way she dug her toes to ward against recoil, in the reflexive way she licked her lips. Practiced movements, which meant *training*. For a Knight, the Cants did some of the heavy lifting when it came to shaping the fire, but these strangers were doing it all manually, which meant—

Helios Lance. Denizen flung a streaking arrow of light at the girl, and when the boy summoned his sword again to deflect it, Denizen knew that he was right.

They had one trick, one trick each. Denizen had no such limitation. Unfortunately, that brought him right up against the great towering limitation he *did* have.

They were trying to kill him. And he couldn't kill them.

Somewhere distant—or not distant; Denizen had no idea how large the library was anymore—explosions boomed, figures silhouetted before disappearing again, dreamlike and haunting. Sounds swam in and out of focus, and, if Greaves or the others were calling out orders, Denizen couldn't hear them. It was like they'd never existed, conjured away by this sorcerous gloom—just another power Denizen had never dreamt possible.

Who are these people?

His attackers were advancing now, and Denizen was running out of ideas. He wasn't even sure whether he felt right about unleashing his power on Tenebrous anymore, not after moonlight conversations and lightning-haunted lips. As pale and lupine as his assailants were, they were human. They were *kids*. And that meant Denizen couldn't burn them alive.

Fast on the heels of that thought came a second—*Why not?* Fear became anger, and anger became rage, the Cants swirling like kites in his head. That was the point of a Knight, wasn't it? To defend your comrades? By far the best thing, by far the *easiest* thing, would be to turn these *traitors* into char and identify them from their dental records.

Another howl turned the bookshelf Denizen was sheltering behind into a cliff of flame. Books fell around him, their pages ablaze. *Do something. Do something.* He'd feel like a right idiot if all this was happening and he died from smoke inhalation.

The pair were stalking toward him, movements perfectly in unison. This close, they were obviously brother and sister. Same angular features, same cave-fish-pale faces, his fingers reaching out every so often to brush hers—

Siblings. And suddenly there victory was, and Denizen wasn't sure if he should be proud or ashamed of the cruelty of it.

He lurched forward through oily smoke, marble shards slicing his cheek as Samuel Taylor Coleridge came apart under fire. Denizen barely noticed. *Closer. Have to get closer.* This was short-range stupidity.

Fire whirled through Denizen's mind—and the boy and girl disappeared.

Not to Denizen, because he was standing in front of them, but to each other—separated by a curtain of bent light. *The right place to see.* It was nowhere near as good as Simon's, but in this chaos of shadow and smoke it didn't need to be. Cants didn't just make people vanish either, but Denizen was wagering neither sibling knew that.

To them, it would look like the other had simply blinked out of existence.

Denizen had been hoping for a moment of confusion. What he got was a full-on meltdown. The girl's wail was earsplitting, her terrified gaze sweeping from Denizen to the empty space where her brother had stood. On the other side of the warping curtain, her brother did the same, staring with a mixture of horror and fury that lasted until Denizen's staggering charge bore him to the ground.

Punch him in the face, Denizen thought frantically, and then punched him in the face. He didn't think it was a good idea to wait and see whether one punch was enough, so he hit him again, skinning his knuckles on the teenager's sharp cheek, and when light began to gather in the boy's crazed eyes, Denizen hit him so hard he fell forward and banged his own head on the floor.

Ow, he thought, rolling onto his back with a gasp—giving him a really excellent view of the girl charging *through* the veil of light, steel sword in hand.

She looked extremely angry.

Had she just brought down her sword, Denizen would have died right there, but instead she took in a breath, her eyes blooming roses of gold. Denizen sympathized, for what it was worth—the fire was hard to ignore at the best of times. It didn't stop him from kicking her in the knee, though, and when she stumbled backward he hit her with an Anathema Bend that flung her onto her back.

She didn't move. A wisp of smoke curled from her lips.

Move, Denizen. She wasn't dead. He'd barely let it coalesce—it must have been like being clocked with a mattress. She could come round at any second. But the floor was very comfy all of a sudden, and if he used the prone body of her brother as a pillow . . .

MOVE!

He finally convinced himself to get up, staggering away from where the pair lay, the tidal shadows swallowing them completely in just three steps. Denizen's heart pounded harder with every vicious flash of light and every muffled roar. The world was so dark he felt he was running on the spot. Sometimes figures would dart past him, close enough to touch, then vanish as though they had never existed.

History books portrayed battles as geometric

lines—duels between minds, where the weapons were regiments and the casualties a footnote at the bottom of the page. That wasn't what they were at all.

They were chaos.

"There!"

The two men came out of nowhere, resolving from the darkness like ghosts. Fear burst through Denizen. *Were they centimeters away from me this whole time?* The fact that the men seemed just as panicked as him wasn't helping his nerves. Men that large weren't supposed to look afraid.

One of them held a syringe. The other clutched some rope.

Denizen scrabbled for his power, and a shape blew through the murk, limbs eddying smoke. The first man managed a pathetic yelp as hands and feet found his joints and persuaded them against themselves, and the second had barely turned before Vivian Hardwick folded him up along his seams as well.

She spun, panting, as they both hit the ground.

"Hi," Denizen said. "Um. What's going on?"

It felt weird to *speak* again. Vivian evidently felt the same—she swallowed, and then spoke in a low, dry rasp.

"Four warlocks, maybe a dozen other men. Mercenaries, by their training."

"Does your count include two kids?" Denizen asked.

In unspoken unison, they stood back to back, turning in slow circles.

"No," she said. "You—"

"They're unconscious by the door," Denizen said. "No idea for how long. Wait—*warlocks*?"

"It's as good a name as any," Vivian growled. "Until I get some answers."

That was when Denizen noticed the neat hole in the shoulder of her shirt.

"You've been *shot*," he said.

"What?" she responded distractedly. "Oh. Right. Yes. Ricocheted off the iron." She didn't even look down, and her next words were clearly not intended for anyone but herself. "At least Grey knew where to shoot."

Her hammer was still slung across her back. That more than anything underlined what was happening—the sheer impossibility of it. *We're under attack. By humans.* Suddenly the Order's fear of thralls seemed perfectly rational. The Knights had spent centuries training to fight a war against monsters. This was something else entirely.

"They're not using Cants," Denizen said. "I don't know what they're capable of."

Vivian indicated ahead. "This conjuration has been twisting sound, messing with direction. We're gathering everyone to organize a counterattack. Once we take out the source of this darkness, we'll have them."

Denizen tried to feel bad for whoever Vivian was

going to happen to next, but his head was full of fire and the gleam of a needle in the dark.

Let it out, a part of him snarled. *Banish this smoke with a scream. If it moves, burn it. You can worry about consequences later. Or never at all . . .*

"Lead the way," he whispered.

25

The War That Will Come

Uriel climbed to his feet, throat thick with the smell of burning books.

Pain radiated from his left cheekbone, and he'd bruised his back when the boy had slammed into him. He took a deep breath, dismissing the pain as a Croit was meant to do. He'd received worse in training.

Far worse, actually. Croits knew how to punch.

Tabitha's darkness still fogged the air, but Uriel could feel a trembling hesitancy to it. It was incredible that she'd been able to keep it going this long, but Uriel remembered the look on Tabitha's face when the Redemptress had laid Her cold black hand on her cheek. Tabitha would hold it forever if she could.

Ambrel. Uriel looked around wildly, calling his Prayer to hand, its golden light revealing . . . nothing. She wasn't there. Had the Adversary killed her? Burned her? Was she already ashes because he'd been *stupid enough to get knocked out*—

"No," he said. He said it aloud, because his voice sounded a little like hers and it reassured him. "No."

The boy—*Denizen Hardwick,* that was what Malebranche had called him—could have killed them. The power he had wielded was far beyond anything Uriel or Ambrel could do, so *versatile*—Uriel could still hear the unearthly syllables ringing in the air. *Words.* How could words be so powerful?

Just for a second, Uriel felt himself suddenly wanting to say those words himself. How had they sounded? If he just—

No. He drove the blasphemous thought down.

Uriel began to run through the darkness, letting his sword die away in his hand. It wouldn't do to reveal his position, and there was no telling whether he'd run into friend or foe first. He needed to find one of the Family or, failing that, some of the men Grandfather had hired for this raid. Bodyguards—mundane men with a mundane love of violence and money. Did they know what all this was? Were they afraid?

Fear was kindling in his own stomach, but Uriel drew on the Favor of his Redemptress to blot it out. This was the War That Will Come. This was what they had been promised. If they did well—if they served—then they would all be saved.

If . . .

"Stop it," he whispered to himself. "Stop it."

If they're telling you the truth.

The Adversary was supposed to be an army of cold iron statues, animated by a terrible mind, living avatars of Transgression and shame. They weren't supposed to be boys with names, and wide, frightened eyes, and power the same shade of gold as the Croits'. *It had been the Favor.* Uriel knew it as surely as he had felt the iron in Denizen's knuckles against his cheek—the iron that was supposed to be the Croits' alone.

If everything isn't a lie.

"STOP!"

The word didn't come from Uriel's mouth but from a woman in a floral-pattern dress carrying a broadsword. No—not a woman. *An Adversary.* Her black-and-silver curls bobbed as she launched a kick at Uriel's head, and he almost breathed a sigh of relief.

Finally something I understand.

Uriel ducked under the blow, which meant he was at exactly the right height to get punched as she turned the kick into a vicious pirouette. He rolled with it—his other cheekbone now alight with pain—and drove his foot into the pit of her stomach. She staggered, but flicked her blade at his eyes before he could take advantage of her momentary weakness.

It vibrated off the edge of Uriel's Prayer instead.

They both stared at each other—she at the bar of

rippling fire that protruded from Uriel's fist, he at the steel sword that had stopped it.

That's not how it's supposed to work, he thought dumbly. There were a whole host of ruined blades back at Eloquence to prove it.

She looked just as surprised as he did. There was light gleaming from her blade too, slender spirals of gold and red. It was beautiful. Uriel would have loved to look at it properly, were it not trembling a hair's breadth from his face.

And then, just as suddenly, the moment broke. A hazy glow pierced the darkness, a cloudy sunrise, then a blinding noon. The shock wave slapped both Uriel and the woman-Adversary from their feet, and the shadow above became the shadow of a shelf coming down.

It clipped him—just clipped, that was all—but he fell hard, head spinning. Books pelted deafeningly down. When he finally got to his feet, the woman was gone, and the ringing in his head had resolved to that of a bell—some kind of alarm. The fact that he could hear it clearly was a bad sign. Tabitha was losing her grip.

We don't have much time.

Uriel ran toward where the fires were brightest. That's where he'd find Ambrel. That's where he'd find the Adversary. *Shouldn't be hard,* a voice whispered cruelly in his head. *They look exactly like you.*

Uriel had been raised on stories of the army of the Adversary—the evil night to the Croits' virtuous day.

But they weren't. They weren't monsters of sin powered by one evil mind—they were people, people with the same gifts as him.

They may as well be Family . . .

The whole world was coming down around his ears, the roars of battle tolling the collapse of everything he knew. The contradiction of what had been drilled into him and the evidence of his own eyes felt like a knife driven between the two halves of his brain.

Uriel felt like he was coming apart. He felt like he was falling—and then something caught his foot, and he was falling for real. He had a second to twist, drawing his blade and slashing it back against whatever had grabbed him—

And Tabitha looked at him with eyes threaded with filaments of iron. The whites of her eyes were all that remained. Everything else was dull and black.

Uriel's reflexive strike had removed four of the fingers on her outstretched hand. Tabitha hadn't appeared to notice.

"Uriel . . ."

Even her voice was deeper—a leaden, heavy thing, like air pumped through rigid bellows. She struggled with every word, the iron curls of her hair clanking against the floor.

"Tell Her I'm sorry I'm not strong enough . . . Tell Her I . . ."

The darkness was wavering, tattering, fading, but Tabitha refused to fail her Redemptress, still clutching night as her Transgression swallowed her.

Tabitha died with Her name on her lips, and Uriel broke.

I have to find Ambrel. We have to get out of here. Forget the Redemptress. Forget Grandfather, and the War, and whoever these people are. This isn't safe. We aren't safe.

The only thing I believe in is us.

And then he looked up, and there Denizen Hardwick was. The target. The source of the Redemptress's hate.

He really was just a kid. Probably older than Uriel, but with a touch of that Outside softness that made him look younger. There was soot staining his shaggy red hair, a bruise darkening one side of his face, and a tremor in his left eye. Uriel knew that tremor. He fought it every time the Favor wanted to be free.

"Wait," Denizen said. Uriel flinched at the sound of his voice. "You don't have to . . . We can talk, OK? You don't have to do this."

Hollow understanding stole across Uriel, even as his expression went still and steady, so as not to give anything away.

"Yes," he said, staring past Denizen, "I do. She has my Family."

And Ambrel lunged.

Denizen had barely a moment to cry out before the needle plunged in deep. Fire gathered in his eyes, his mouth—and then faded as the drug took effect.

His eyes found Uriel's for a second and then rolled to white.

They moved in unison, Ambrel taking his legs, Uriel his shoulders. There were two knives in scabbards under his shirt. *He could have used them on me when I was down.* That's what a monster would have done. That's what a Croit would have done.

Uriel flung them from their sheaths. Without them, Denizen weighed barely anything at all. Darkness died around them in soft and falling shards, and Uriel and Ambrel picked up their Adversary and ran toward the light.

26

The Natural State of Denizen Hardwick

Denizen woke, but only halfway.

That was new. Usually waking up was immediate, even in those first weeks in Seraphim Row with all the running and jumping and Abigail kicking him through things. The process was simple and familiar: his eyes would open, body delivering its sleep-postponed communiqués to swiftly draw a mental map—legs, torso, head, and even the distant cold of his iron palms.

Now it felt like a gust of wind had scattered the letters. The post office was under siege, the messenger pigeons shot down in droves or plucked out of the air by cunningly trained hawks. The ones that did get through were bedraggled and surly, no help at all.

After a ridiculous amount of concentration, Denizen finally came to the conclusion that he had legs. He had definitely had legs before. Surely he'd remember losing them? Then again, it had been a battle. All sorts of horrible things happened in battle. But he still had legs, so that was a victory, wasn't it?

Good. Great! Two limbs down. Nearly halfway. Forty percent, maybe. How much are legs?

Denizen was being dragged. He could tell by the rat-a-tat bounce of his shoe tips off the ground, each impact shivering his body back to a dreamy awareness.

More appendages reported for duty. He obviously had a head, as something had to be doing his thinking for him, though at the minute it didn't seem to be doing a very good job. Someone had gone ahead—*haha, a head*—and packed it with clouds, his vision filled with drifting silver patches.

Perhaps whoever was dragging him could help? Denizen opened his mouth—it took a couple of tries: someone had coated the inside of it with hair and glue—and posed a friendly query to the pair of hands under his shoulders.

Unfortunately, due to all the hair and glue, the words came out as a sort of strangled "*auk*"—like someone strangling an auk. The hands did not reply. Perhaps *they* were missing their head. Perhaps the disappearance of body parts was going around, like a specific and gruesome winter cold.

Blearily, Denizen tried again, but when no words would come, a single thought dropped through his mind like the sweep of a guillotine.

I seem very relaxed about this.

Another thought.

I'm never relaxed about anything.

This wasn't normal. The fluffiness and drowning warmth *were* pleasant . . . but they weren't Denizen. This was someone else's design. The clouds clung and slowed each thought, but Denizen wielded his growing horror like a knife, slowly cutting his way to clarity.

Because someone doesn't want me to. That was what kept him going.

Someone wanted him silent.

Denizen didn't think he was claustrophobic, though he had avoided small spaces up until now precisely because he didn't want to find out. He had the sneaking suspicion he was home to a whole plethora of phobias he hadn't discovered, simply because he hadn't been exposed to them yet.

But now he felt trapped in his own body—weighed down by limbs he couldn't control, his mind fogged and indistinct, and worst of all . . . his *voice* had been taken from him, replaced by a weak mewl.

That's not what my voice is supposed to be.

"Is . . . awake?"

A voice drifted into his awareness. Denizen tried to make out the words, half to understand what was happening and half as some kind of comfort. They had voices. Maybe he would get his back.

"Tol– you not to let him –ake up!"

Denizen opened his mouth in a horrid yawn, as if trying to speak round the clot—

And the sharpness found his neck again.

". . . YOU HEAR ME?"

This time Denizen managed to wake up three-quarters of the way and, though he still felt packed in cotton wool, at least he knew immediately that the wool was an outside influence.

Someone was talking to him, and he was no longer being dragged anywhere. These, Denizen thought sluggishly, were definitely both improvements.

He lifted his head and the world swam back into view.

He was propped—no, *had been* propped, he definitely hadn't made it there himself—against a rough stone wall, cold enough to make him shiver through his shirt. From what he could muzzily make out, the rest of the room was just as medieval, the floor a canted slope of shattered flagstones and heaped debris. Denizen spent a long moment trying to figure out the patterns in the stone before dragging himself back to the present.

OK. May not be normal quite yet.

His thoughts felt slippery—flitting around like rain-wet birds, never staying still or gaining cohesion. He had to keep lunging for them and weighing them down.

I've been captured. This is bad.

When the hand struck him, both he and it rang with iron. Suns rose behind his eyes, not the ones he knew but dark things of purple and gray and blue.

". . . give him too much, did you?"

Denizen fought the urge to snigger. They were worried about him, apparently. Maybe they were right to be—the cotton wool packing his skull had turned to steel shavings with jagged sharp edges. He had a sneaking suspicion that there was a lot of pain on the horizon, and he would quite like not to be here when it arrived.

". . . him again."

This time the slap was almost soft.

Dizzily, Denizen regarded the two young men in front of him. They were disconcertingly alike—pale eyes burning fever-like from almost translucent faces, framed by shocks of graying hair. Great swaths of the left one's neck and hands had turned black and hard. Denizen recognized the Cost at once. *So much of it.*

The other was just bruised.

"You . . ." Denizen croaked. "I fought you. I . . ."

"Fetch Grandfather," the youth snapped. Gone was the uncertain boy Denizen had tried to reason with. Now he was chill and imperious, and the other boy practically ran.

"Yes," Denizen said, who was definitely not taking all this as seriously as he should be. "Grandfather. Good."

The boy looked like he would hit Denizen again, so Denizen very quickly shut up. However, as the minutes dragged and more and more pain started to make itself known, he began to think it wouldn't hurt—more than it did already—to talk. The way the boy had looked at him in the Long Room . . .

Denizen knew that look. He'd worn it himself, the night he'd found out that the world was a much darker and stranger place than he'd been led to believe. It was a frown of horrible revelation, and despite the awful circumstances he was currently in, a tiny part of him felt an even tinier pang of pity.

"So . . ." he said tentatively, "is this a castle? It looks like a castle."

After Denizen's eyes being gummed shut for so long, the boy's sword of fire was suddenly very bright. Its point wavered in front of Denizen's throat, the heat scorching some of his inner cobwebs away. Or maybe that was the adrenaline. Denizen wasn't sure.

All he knew was for the first time since somebody had jabbed a needle in his neck, Denizen Hardwick felt his fire return. It was weak, just an ember . . . but it was there, and shapes in the back of his head shuddered as if waking from hibernation.

Now all he had to do was survive until it came back in full.

"How did you know that?" the boy snarled. "I swear

to Her, if you're using your Adversary . . . witch . . . powers, I'll—"

The sword was *very* hot.

"I'm not doing anything!" Denizen said. "Just . . . it really looks like a castle." He thought about raising his hands in the traditional *means no harm* gesture, but reasoned that, when you could shoot fire out of your hands, the gesture might be meaningless. "Just making conversation, that's all."

There. Was that another ember kindling? Was that his power stretching out just a little bit more?

"Making conversation," the boy whispered. "We . . . we know what you are, *Adversary*. And we will not be tempted." His eyes flicked round the chamber as if he were concerned about being overheard. Denizen followed his gaze, mostly because it gave him something to look at other than the glowing sword in his face.

There was a wire coiled in the corner of the room. Denizen hadn't noticed it at first, because of the drugs and the sword and all the kidnappingness, but it was long and black and very out of place among all the medievalry. The boy was looking at every other part of the room *but* where the wire was, which to Denizen spoke volumes.

He was about to take advantage of the last of his chemically induced recklessness and ask some pointed questions, but then Grandfather stepped into the room, and Denizen became suddenly very lucid indeed.

"Uriel. This is the Adversary?"

His first impression of the warlock leader—and there was nobody else this person could be—was of weight. Not physical weight: every time Grandfather turned his head, Denizen thought his cheekbones would split his skin. No, it was a sort of *density*, as if lesser humans had been folded over and over again like a samurai sword, forging a man far more substantial than his size would suggest.

Not huge but *deep*.

The boy's—Uriel's—sword vanished in a waterfall of sparks and he bowed low to the floor.

"Yes, Grandfather."

Adversary.

That was the third time Denizen had heard that word, and it was starting to worry him. Grandfather hadn't called him *the boy*, or *the prisoner*, or the *innocent person we're definitely going to set free, possibly with a burger*. The word *adversary* was an iceberg word because it was so vague. It could mean anything—an ideology, a country, a whole way of life. Calling something an *adversary* meant you didn't have to think of it as a *person*.

Come on. The fire in his stomach was building slowly, as if bewildered at being gone in the first place. *Come on*.

"Denizen Hardwick," the old man hissed, pearl-gray gaze pinning Denizen to the wall. The syllables might have been different, but the sentiment was the same. *Enemy. Anathema. Wrong.*

Denizen would be the first person to admit he wasn't perfect. He could be stubborn, sullen, and uncooperative, and recently he seemed to have lost his grip on the inner dial that careered between *cowardly* and *reckless,* and they were only the things he could think of. But Denizen knew he had never done anything to deserve the way Grandfather looked at him.

It was hatred. Intimate and personal. You had to know someone your entire life to hate them like that. Denizen did not want Grandfather to strike him. He knew that if he did, the sheer gravity of the man's hate might crush him the way a black hole crushed a sun.

"Witness, Family," he said. Denizen couldn't look away from the bleached opalescence of the man's pupils, but he had the sense that there were a lot of people in the corridor beyond. Grandfather certainly spoke as if the whole world were listening. "It may look like a human. It may even resemble one of *us*. But it is not. It is a monster—a living insult to Her We Serve. But we have brought it low, despite its dread powers, and we—"

Still clawing his thoughts together, Denizen tried to follow what Grandfather was saying. They'd drugged him with some sort of chemical that made it almost impossible to gather the concentration needed to manipulate the Tenebrae's fire. Definitely impossible in their case—Denizen wouldn't have been able to re-create their manipulations of the fire even if they hadn't pumped him full of whatever-it-was.

But I don't have to. Because a Knight had the arcane language of the Cants to assist him, and Denizen had a borrowed fluency.

Come on. The fire twitched and spread. *I would really quite like to leave now.*

"Long have we waited for the War That Will Come," Grandfather orated, "and now it is upon us. The Adversary is loose in the world. Our Redemptress returns to lead us to glorious battle, and our salvation is at hand—"

"Hang on," Denizen said groggily, more to scrape the last of the fur from his throat than anything else. "You're not going to tell me about some sort of prophecy, are you?" That was what always happened in books. He'd been quietly dreading one since his thirteenth birthday.

Grandfather just spoke over him. "Our new crusade will be anointed with the blood of this monster, and—"

"Hang on," Denizen repeated. This seemed like a *very* bad conversational path to go down. "How much blood are we talking about here?"

"Wait, Grandfather."

The girl from the library pushed her way through

the watching warlocks. She had the same washed-out paleness they all had, which made her eyes blaze even fiercer—wild and green and full of something far more worrying than Uriel's fear or Grandfather's contempt.

Interest.

"Ambrel," the old man said, in the sort of indignant tone Vivian used when she had only just started getting her rant going before someone had the foolishness to interrupt. "Do not think—"

"You weren't *there,*" she said.

He blinked.

"His command of the Favor is like nothing I've ever seen," she continued. "And in the coming War we could use—"

"*It is not the Favor,*" Grandfather snarled.

Ambrel nodded. "Of course, Grandfather. But . . . would it not be advisable to learn everything we can from the prisoner—the *Adversary*? For the War That Will Come?"

"I think that's a great idea," Denizen said. Uriel, Grandfather, and Ambrel were standing over him. There were four others crowding the doorway. Outside that . . . Denizen didn't know. Fortunately, if all went well, he wouldn't have to find out.

Just a little more . . .

"Every bit of information about the Adversary is vital," Ambrel said. "And we can always kill him afterward."

“Less in agreement with that,” Denizen offered, but Grandfather wasn’t listening.

He was staring at Ambrel. So were the others. Her eyes were bright, wide, and innocent, and an annoying part of Denizen pointed out that part of her idea made more sense than anything anyone else had said so far. Unfortunately, the other half of her idea was him being murdered, and that seemed to be part of a package.

“I’m really enjoying all this,” he said, everyone turning to him with varying mixtures of anger, contempt, and fear. “And I’d be really glad to share. Firstly—”

Denizen lunged forward and reached for every single spark of power in his chest.

“*This* is the Art of Apertura.”

27

Gravity

Grandfather lurched backward as Denizen bent his fingers into claws and *pulled*, a yawn of deeper dark splitting the air in front of him . . . before promptly closing with a snap, flinging Denizen's head back with the worst and most immediate headache he'd ever had.

Oh no. After six months of unnatural fluency, Denizen had almost forgotten that, if you attempted a Cant you weren't ready for, it felt like vomiting wasps. Sharpened wasps. Holding toothpicks.

Ow. Ow ow ow. No Higher Cants. Higher Cants were bad.

Denizen wanted to do nothing more than curl up and press his skull into the cold stone floor, possibly until it fractured. However, the last conversation on everyone's lips had been about murdering him, and the gathered warlocks' shock was slowly hardening into anger.

Grandfather in particular looked incandescent, which focused Denizen immensely. *OK. Think small.*

The Anathema Bend—not a roar but a whisper, not a shield but a rake. Two lashes of fused air swept Grandfather and Uriel sideways, before Denizen hissed again and a third threw Ambrel *through* the warlocks filling the doorway.

Denizen was up and scrambling before any of them hit the floor. For the first two steps, his legs felt like wet rope, but fire and fear forced them straight and he ran—all those cold morning runs unleashed in a frantic blurt of speed. He leapt over downed bodies, smashed his shoulder against the side of the corridor, and was away.

Where he was going hadn't quite been decided yet, but Denizen had learned that in terms of life-and-death situations, it was the journey and not the destination that counted.

Behind him, shouts were rising. Denizen flicked the ghost of a Qayyim Myriad back at them. The orbs dug into the stone walls, sparking smoke and shards.

Think. Think. He pelted through crumpled archways, power itching through the channels of his brain. It *was* a castle—not that being right about that was a major comfort at the minute—and one that seemed to be in even worse shape than him.

Doors were crushed mouths with jagged teeth. The floor canted at odd angles or fell away entirely.

Twice Denizen wove an Anathema Bend just to cross a yawning chasm. There were no lights—of course there weren't—and the *Intueor Lucidum* painted everything a wan, hollow silver.

And they were chasing him. No, *stalking* him. Denizen could see shadowy shapes through gaps and hollows in the walls, white faces pressed up against cracks, darting away as he drew near.

Denizen wanted nothing more than to open an Apertura and get out of there. He wanted Simon and Abigail and Darcie and stupid conversation, not these pale things with their starving eyes.

His head swam, from both the pain of overreaching with the Art and the effort of maintaining his grip on his power. He ducked under a fallen archway, dizzy with the desire to just smash it aside. The Cants in his head were swirling, writhing. It was hard to find room to think between their jagged shapes. Maybe the pain hadn't been *that* bad. Maybe the Cost would be worth it . . .

He took turn after turn through deserted chambers, thoroughly and utterly lost. His pursuers had vanished, but Denizen still checked every corner before he turned it, heart in his mouth. Another left, another right, he ducked through a half-collapsed doorway . . .

And slowed when he saw the wire.

It crossed the chamber in a diagonal slash, stark black in the *Lucidum*. The way Uriel had looked at it . . .

A crawling sickness built in Denizen that had nothing to do with chemicals, a sickness that increased the closer he got to the wire.

A sickness that he knew.

There was a Tenebrous here. Everything that was happening—the strange cult, this ruined castle, Denizen's *massive* headache—the Tenebrae was worked through it all.

I need to get out of here. This was too big for him. The Concilium and Mercy and his relationship with Vivian . . . how was there *room* in the world for that complicated mess and whatever was going on here as well? How much was one person supposed to deal with at once?

As he watched, the wire suddenly snap-slithered away with a miniature avalanche of dust. Denizen approached cautiously. There were shouts echoing through the castle, far enough away that he couldn't make out what was being said, but close enough for him to be very aware of the sheer number of voices.

Burn them. Voices rumbled through the stonework, but the voice in Denizen's head was louder. *Eulice's Ram through the wall. And the next wall. And the next. Sear the rubble out of existence. Burn anyone in my way to ash and char, and if there is a Tenebrous here, make them understand what it means to trespass in our world.*

Denizen was shaking. It took him a full minute to realize he'd stopped walking and had both hands pressed to the side of his head. The sheer aching *potential* of what he could do and *he* was running? *They* should run! Everyone should!

How dare they attack him!

He spun to stare back the way he'd come, but nothing moved in the dusty labyrinth. Except . . .

Wires crossed the path he'd taken in a night-black lattice, glistening, slippery, and sharp. They hadn't been there a second ago, and as he watched, more extended from the dark stone of the walls, feeling their way blindly like roots in search of water.

Denizen ran.

A chamber littered with the tattered banners of long-dead wars led to a cramped passage that in a heartbeat was a thicket of wires. Backtrack, turn right—half run, half stumble down a sloping chute just in time to see strands strangle out a minuscule glint of sun. A cluster of figures at the end of a long hall; Denizen loosed a halfhearted Helios Lance and they scattered, but again the wires came down and hid them from view.

Trapping him. Funneling him. Directing him where they wanted him to go.

BURN THEM!

He wanted to. He *wanted* to. But if he started he might never stop so instead he ran, mind ablaze with pain. Wires closed over every path he found, bar one—down, down into the heart of the ruin. Denizen followed it. He had no choice.

Denizen descended, and around him wires hissed over stone. He'd been navigating by the *Lucidum* for so long he'd almost forgotten he was in the dark, but this was a special kind of night—a liquid, heavy thing that he could feel against his face. The nausea, the distortion—the familiar yet always unfamiliar jolt of the Tenebrae—became so strong that Denizen had to lean into it like a sailor would the wind.

Impressions washed over him—the musty smell of age, the faint odor of sweat. Thousands of dusty hand-prints overlaid each other until the walls were just muddy smears of fingers; the ghosts of sea anemones in the dark.

His stomach twisted from the Tenebraic chill seep-ing from every stone. His head screamed with the *need* to sweep all this away. The last few steps were a tor-ment and, as he staggered into a huge chamber, Deni-zen told himself it was *that*, all the myriad pains he had endured, that made him fall to his knees before Her.

The right place at the right time.

The great blade of Her spine flexed as the Tenebrous swooped to regard him, arms extended like an ice skater about to take that first, perfect leap. Her face flickered with emotions Denizen had no hope of reading.

That's all a hero is, Denizen Hardwick. That's all they ever are.

Figures were emerging. A *lot* of figures. Twenty . . .

thirty . . . ? Whoever these people were, they had only attacked Trinity with a fraction of their strength. It made Denizen wonder what the others had been doing.

They had traded tattered finery for robes of deepest, darkest red.

That's all HE was, before you and your cursed ilk came to destroy the love we had tried to build.

Don't recall ruining anything, Denizen wanted to say, but the flippancy had dried in his throat. Ever since that first step into the darkness at Seraphim Row, Denizen had felt the weight of the Order pressing down on him. It was as if history had a gravity, the Order some vast beast and Denizen tiny before it.

He felt that same sort of smallness now.

What had Grandfather called her? *The Redemptress.* She bared wire teeth in Her black wire skull. Denizen had only met a few Tenebrous, but he was starting to understand that, in the same way each human voice was a unique map of emotion and personality, the warping influence of a Tenebrous had its own flavors and resonance.

There was something of the Court to Her—that twisted, sickening nobility—but as he stared he could see Mercy as well. They could have been sisters, with the same hauntingly beautiful features, the same sense of great power and strange grace.

The King didn't need to do what he did, She murmured,

and inwardly Denizen wondered when he had started thinking of Her with a capital letter. ***All we wanted was to be free. To start a new life. We shouldn't have stolen it, but we needed to be SAFE, and my beloved . . . he said it would be best to be armed . . . to be powerful . . .***

She seemed to have forgotten Denizen was there, eyes tracking round the chamber as if watching prey scuttle and flee. Denizen blanched as he noticed the pile of iron limbs and staring heads tossed in the corner like so much debris. Arms rigid, legs bent at stiff angles—it would have been almost comical had he not known that here were people claimed by the Cost and the fire inside.

The fire inside. There was something about the Redemptress's words. Something familiar.

Grandfather watched him with steely hate from under Her shadow, Uriel and Ambrel behind. The others spread out to surround him, staring with a mixture of fascination and fear.

"Know that it is not I who judge you," Grandfather intoned, "for we have already been judged."

His thin lips twisted in a sneer.

"We were judged and found wanting, and we wear that black Transgression on our skin. It is unavoidable, as we train for our War against the Adversary—monsters led by a monster, the things that cast down Eloquence and the First Croit, long ago. They would have killed him, if they could. And then none of us would exist. Our ways forgotten. Our Redemptress abandoned. *That is what this thing wants.*"

Denizen's fearful gaze went from face to face. There was no pity there. No mercy. *Are they all thralls?* They had to be.

The alternative was far, far worse.

"Accuse him," Grandfather said.

Black liquid beaded on wire. ***How could you turn on us? What had we done? What had HE done? You were all born close to the dark. You were all . . . you were all Family.***

The huge woman made of wires was taking up a great deal of Denizen's focus, but out of the corner of his eye he could see Her words send a ripple of confusion through the gathered Croits. It didn't make him feel much better.

And then the King offers you the Cants and you TURN on us. All we wanted was to be left alone—

Denizen had a flashback to the arcane terminology of Greaves's briefing document, and the pathetic relief he'd felt when he'd come across a recognizable phrase. *The King.* This creature was a Tenebrous. There was only one King She could be talking about.

It was a bad sign when you were so out of your depth that you started thinking of the Endless King as a lifeline. Pieces were clicking together in Denizen's head, but too many were still missing, and it was extremely hard to concentrate when there were thirty-odd crazy people staring at you and a Tenebrous pounding insanity into the world.

And you are TOLERATED. You and his little girl. Talking about PEACE. Why should you have peace?

Wires were flexing. The walls were trembling. The beads of black in the corners of Her eyes looked like tears.

When we were given none?

Ambrel's voice was soft.

"Majesty?"

The Redemptress had begun to sob, Her head buried in Her hands. The girl stepped forward—past a surprised Uriel and an angry-looking Grandfather—and gazed up at Her with what Denizen felt was an extremely creepy look of devotion.

The Redemptress's shoulders were shaking.

"Majesty, would you feel better if we killed him?"

Denizen had never heard his own murder pitched in so gentle a tone.

"Would that be revenge? Would that be enough?"

The shaking stilled.

There will never be enough, the Redemptress growled. Her hands were growing, wire weaving on wire until each claw was a cluster of short swords, shoulders jagged battlements of spikes. Denizen was so focused on the nightmare spectacle before him that he didn't notice the filament until it snaked round his neck.

He flinched back. The noose moved with him. He could feel it, slippery and supple, delicate yet stronger than steel.

Don't move. Don't move.

The Redemptress reared.

It is not your fire. It is his. It is mine. Touch it, even THINK about it . . .

Denizen *felt* the wire sharpen, keen and murderous against his throat.

I will think on your fate, Denizen Hardwick. In the meantime . . . let her worry. Let her wait. Let her know what loss feels like.

Her voice was ragged with anger and sorrow.

As I do.

28

What a Croit Believes

Breathe.

This is what I believe.

Feet pounding on the cracked dirt.

We are chosen. We are special. The Redemptress stole fire from a dark and distant place and She Favored us, Her Family, with it.

Sweat stinging his eyes.

But we failed Her in a great battle against the Adversary—creatures of iron animated by a single terrible mind—and so we were cursed with the creeping black of our Transgression.

Far enough away from Eloquence that Uriel could smell the salt of the sea, far enough that his legs were pillars of pain, and still he could *feel* Her, an itch between his shoulder blades.

And so we waited for the day She would return and lead us in the War That Will Come, so that we may be redeemed.

Breathe.

This is what we believe. This is what a Croit believes.

This is what we've been led to believe—

"Uriel?"

He slowed, letting out an involuntary hiss as his exertions caught up with him in a chorus of aches. Through the Garden of the Waiting . . .

All of them, they waited, and . . . and for what?

. . . up the steep incline of the valley wall, through hill and dried-out thicket to here, where cliffs fell to a turbulent sea.

It had not been far enough.

"You're crying," Ambrel said. "Are you all right?"

"The wind," he said tonelessly, scrubbing a hand over his eyes. "That's all."

She stared at him a moment longer before turning away to look at the vastness of the ocean. It must have an Outside name. They'd probably have to learn it. If the Croits were to rule the world, then they'd need to know the names for things.

Unless we start renaming everything, Uriel thought. A whole world, named for the ramblings of a grieving goddess. Would the sickening pall of Her presence infuse everything then? Would there be anywhere you could go to escape it?

This was the first time the twins had been alone since the raid. Always *something,* some sermon or training session, keeping them apart. Uriel would have thought it by design had he not known the truth—he could spend all the time in the world with Ambrel if he were willing to spend all his time with Her.

"So what did you think?" Ambrel said.

Uriel was momentarily caught off guard.

"Of what?"

"Of *Dublin*, you goose," she said. "Did you ever imagine something so huge? I mean, I've seen pictures of cities in books, but I never imagined so many people, so many colors and buildings and strange devices. . . . It was *amazing*, wasn't it?"

He couldn't help but smile back, a real smile, the first one in what felt like forever. He could lose himself in books and the histories, but when *she* found something that she loved it was infectious. Inspiring.

"When did *you* read a book?"

She clipped him across the ear.

"Over your shoulder at some point, probably. But, *seriously*, that place was magical. Just . . . magical." Her grin turned dreamy. "And it'll be ours."

A chill went through Uriel. "What?"

Ambrel hadn't heard him. "I mean, maybe not ours specifically, but I'm sure we could ask Grandfather. There are much bigger cities. And then *you* could live in that library—we'd rebuild it, obviously—and I could try out a skyscraper, and we could go for runs in the parks and visit the others, and—why are you looking at me like that?"

"Ambrel . . ." *Say it. Be honest with her.* For a while, it had almost been a novelty to have a secret from his twin. There had never been a reason to have one before. Would she listen to him? Would she report him to Grandf—*No.* She wouldn't. He trusted her.

But the childish hope in her voice . . .

"Ambrel, do you really believe that?"

Her smile disappeared. "Believe what?"

Everything. Of the two of them, Uriel had always been the more diligent student. He was good at details. And the Redemptress had awoken, and since then every single tenet of his Family's beliefs had been proved a lie.

That She had fallen along with Eloquence in a great battle was true enough. It was all She seemed to be able to remember. But they had been promised a savior, not a creature of crazed anger and grief. There had never been a mention of Malebranche, and so far there had been no talk of the Croits' salvation at all.

And then there was Denizen Hardwick. A living, breathing Adversary, who wasn't a creature of Transgression but a boy who seemed very confused as to what was going on. A boy with the same gifts as them, but far more versatile . . . almost as though he hadn't been taught that a person could have only one Prayer.

Was that a sin? Was that what made him an Adversary?

Wasn't that why they had put Ambrel on trial?

Uriel couldn't get the words out. It was so open out here that he could imagine sky and dirt and sea as all there was to the world, so desolate and stark that he could see all the way back through time—the winding path of his Family shaped by a thousand thousand lies.

But there still wasn't space for what he wanted to say.

"Ambrel, there were so many *people.*"

Stalling. Stalling while he tried to navigate the path between what he wanted to say and what he thought she could handle. Grandfather had been very clear on what would happen if anyone was overheard sharing weak thoughts, but that wasn't Uriel's worry at all.

"So?" she said, fixing him with her stark green stare.

"What do you mean, *so?*" he responded. "You saw how many people lived in that city. How many must there be in Ireland? In the world? How are *we* supposed to take that over? All we've been told—"

Don't. Not yet. Draw it back.

He coughed. "I just . . . surely you can't believe that we're just going to . . . get all we were promised? Just like that?"

"Of course I do," she said simply. "Don't you?"

He turned away before that gaze could draw the truth out of him, but staring out into the sea gave him no comfort because he knew that beyond the waves was Outside, and War. A War they had been promised they would win.

What good are promises now?

"I do believe," he lied. "But I just can't see the *how*, you know? I can't see from *here* to *there*. I don't know what we're going to lose on the way."

"Victory's about loss, Uriel," Ambrel said, and her voice was gentle. "The Redemptress has lost more than any of us."

"Tell that to Tabitha," he said bitterly, folding his arms around himself.

Ambrel frowned. "Uriel . . . you hated Tabitha."

Uriel scowled back. "Everyone hated Tabitha. That's not the point. I'm just . . . I'm just scared, that's all." *Yes.* Better to admit his own weakness, here, to her, when it was safe, rather than point out the cracks spreading in everything else. His weakness she could handle, but the weakness of the truth . . .

"Oh, Uriel," Ambrel said, throwing her thin arms round his neck. "Is that all?"

"*Gack*," he said, stumbling back in surprise. She didn't let go, instead grabbing him by the scruff of the neck so he had no choice but to look at her.

"Uriel," she said. "I'm terrified." He struggled against her, but she held him fast. "I'm always terrified. I have been since She woke. Sometimes it's all I can do to keep going. Sometimes I just feel *sick*—"

A terrible kind of hope—*She feels it too?*

"But then I remember," she said. "All our lives we've been told that we're special. That we're better than everyone else. That we are *chosen*. And it's only now, after looking upon Her, after everything that's happened, that I realize . . .

"They were right. It's us, Uriel. This is our time. We were promised, and we will be redeemed."

Redemption. No more Transgression, their fire flowing free without the crawling cold that came after it. And then . . . what? More war? Sending fire down those crowded streets Ambrel had loved so much? A thousand wire nooses around the necks of those who wouldn't comply?

And her eyes were so wide, and her smile was so bright, and Uriel could not for the life of him figure out when the half second between him and his sister had become so long.

"And the boy? Denizen?"

His voice was tired. It didn't matter what he said, or how he said it. She wasn't going to listen. Her mind had been made up centuries ago by the First Croit and the first lie.

She was certain.

Ambrel's eyes were bright. "He can teach us. With that power and Her at our head, we'll be unstoppable."

For a horrible moment, Uriel wished she were right. The only hope, the *only* hope, for Uriel's Family against the Adversary and the uncounted millions of Outside was that Uriel was wrong and the Redemptress was right.

Unless . . .

"You're right," Uriel said quickly. "It's just fear. I have to trust that the truth is bigger than I understand, and that the path set for me is the right one. Right?"

Ambrel squeezed his shoulder. "Set for us, brother. We're going to walk it together. Into the light of a new truth."

She started to lope back toward Eloquence, and so Uriel's final words were lost to the wind and the sea.

"I don't want a new world. I was happy with the one I had."

THERE WAS NO GUARD on the chamber when Uriel approached. Why would there be? They'd put Denizen far away from any Croit-occupied rooms—to avoid corruption, obviously—and this part of the castle was silent but for the whispers of settling stone.

The boy looked up as Uriel approached.

"OK," Uriel said, "convert me."

29

Revelation

It didn't take very long. Denizen had initially been suspicious, but there was no strategic advantage in Uriel's questions. He just wanted to know about the Tenebrous. About the iron in both their palms. Denizen talked until his throat was hoarse and Uriel's reluctant interest turned to horror, and then . . . they just sat in silence.

Finally, Uriel spoke.

"I've never been afraid of the dark. Not even before my thirteenth birthday. Not being able to see doesn't matter when you know other people have seen already."

A tear rolled slowly down his dust-stained cheek.

"Night comes and shadow falls and fear takes root in lesser hearts . . . but not ours. Not Croits. We can always see the path ahead."

"Intueor Lucidum," Denizen said. "The Shining Gaze."

"We call it the Luster," Uriel replied forlornly.

"Oh," Denizen said. "That's actually much better." His next words were tentative. "So . . . so do you believe me? That I'm not your Adversary?" *And don't need to be sacrificed or used as crusade-paint?* That was sort of the important bit for him.

"It's not that I believe you," Uriel said hollowly. "It's that it makes so much *sense*. I've never seen the holes before because I've never looked for them. And when *She* was asleep it was easy—we just did as we were told, and it all just seemed . . . far away."

"A story," Denizen said.

"Yes," Uriel responded, "a story that all of us were living . . . But it's not true. It's all wrong. Everything is *wrong*, and I'm the only . . . the only . . ."

He looked like he was about to be sick, and Denizen suddenly realized that was why Uriel had come down here by himself. This wasn't some officially extended hand of friendship—Uriel's doubts were his and his alone. Which meant the whole vital-fluids anointing was still on the table. *Great.*

Denizen's bitter flippancy disappeared as Uriel brought a fist to the side of his own head with a dull smack. Sweat was running down his face, despite the chill of the cell, his breathing a thready gasp of fear.

"It's all a lie. All of it. She's just one great lie—"

Denizen flinched as Uriel hit himself again, his eyes tracking wildly across the broken flagstone floor.

"Everything has been a lie . . . all of it, all of us, Grandfather, his *arm*, oh no, oh no, oh no . . ."

The Croit boy was coming apart and Denizen couldn't blame him. What did you say to someone who had been lied to for this long?

Actually, now that he thought about it . . .

"I know you're angry," Denizen said. It was funny, in a twisted sort of way—he'd spent so long picturing these words, but he never thought he'd be the one saying them. "I know that once one thing turns out to be a lie, you start questioning everything you've ever been told. Even yourself. I know it destroys trust. And I don't know if that can be fixed, and it shouldn't be you doing the fixing. I know this isn't fair."

Uriel was staring at him, eyes wild, fist paused shaking at his temple. Denizen took that as a positive sign and plowed ahead. He was about to launch into the second part of Vivian's imagined apology speech—it was a really good bit too, full of clever symmetry and heart-rending honesty—but the words wouldn't come.

It was like the way the Cants sometimes twisted into their own patterns, as if they knew better than him what shape they had to be. What Denizen wanted to say . . . what he had wanted to hear . . . was gone.

In its place was cold, hard truth.

"But this is war."

Uriel's trembling stopped.

"You might be hurting, and that hurt might be justified, but all that matters is the fight in front of you. All there is now is keeping people safe. They're depending on you, even if they don't know it, even if they *never* know it, and if your scars are the price you pay for their lives, then you pay it. Being hurt . . . being *human*, can wait. We have a duty."

Oh, Vivian. He'd been an idiot. He understood. He finally understood, bone-deep and nerve-sharp. He couldn't blame her for the choice she'd made any more than he could blame the world for being what it was. She'd done what she had to do to keep him safe, and whether she'd been right or wrong . . .

Life was too short to keep punishing her for it.

"So," he said, "what are you going to do about it?"

Certainty replaced panic in glass-gray eyes. "I'm going to save my Family."

"Right," Denizen said. "Good. Ummm . . . how?"

Frown No. 27—I Am Facing Impossible Odds. Denizen knew that one when he saw it.

"It's Her," Uriel said finally. "Before She awoke, there wasn't this unity, this fear. Now all of them live and die by Her word."

"OK," Denizen said, very aware that, though Uriel appeared to be calmer, only a moment ago he had seemed to be trying to rearrange his thoughts from the outside. The last thing Denizen wanted to do was push too hard, too soon. *Let him say it himself.* "So what do we do?"

Uriel's voice wavered. "The Order. Your people. Would they help us? I can't fight Her on my own. Or any of the rest of the Family." He thought for a second. "Well. A few of them. But not all. If She was gone, I could maybe try and talk Ambrel round, and some of the others . . ."

"Uriel."

"What?"

Denizen's words were careful. "You know what the Knights will do if they come here. Your family . . . if there's any way not to hurt them, the Order will find it, but . . . I can't promise the same about her."

He wasn't sure if he was saying it to Uriel or himself. Denizen couldn't kid himself about what a rescue mission would mean. The Order had spent centuries fighting Tenebrous, and Denizen couldn't get out of his head the phrase *When all you have is a hammer, everything starts to look like a nail.*

What had Mercy said?

Your kind and mine were never meant to share the same universe. Every time it's happened, it's ended in pain and death. Until us.

And the Redemptress's words, redolent with madness and misery.

Why should you have peace? When we were given none?

Pieces. Pieces assembling in Denizen's head. He swallowed. "First, we need to get you in touch with the Order. Where actually are we?"

"It's Eloquence. The seat of our Family since . . . well, since forever."

"OK. What country?"

Uriel looked blank. "It's . . . Eloquence. We're on an island, if that helps?"

"Not particularly," Denizen said. "How did you get to Trinity?"

"The Family have bodyguards, people we hire for . . . things," Uriel said. "They had a plane waiting, and then a truck."

Denizen frowned. "How long was the plane ride? Did you see any street signs?"

Uriel shook his head. "We were told not to concentrate on the trappings of Outside. So I . . . I meditated. I think the plane ride was a few hours."

Too long to walk or drive, basically. That was as accurate as it was going to get.

"How do you . . ." He didn't want to antagonize Uriel, but frustration and fear were making his head ache. "How do you not know where this place is?"

"We learn what is useful for the War That Will Come," Uriel said. "Weapons training, our Prayers, our history, relevant Outside technologies. We don't need to know anything else."

"And how much does Grandfather know?" Uriel had

latched on to removing the Redemptress as the means of salvation for his family, but Denizen had looked into the old man's eyes and there had been a vicious kind of madness staring back.

"Stop it," Uriel snapped. "He couldn't know—he's as misguided as the rest of them. It's *Her*. That's who we need to stop."

"I completely agree," Denizen lied. However tangled the web between him and Vivian, he had the firm impression that it was *nothing* compared to the trials of Uriel's childhood. "What about—"

Rage twisted Uriel's features. "What would *you* know about us? It's Her fault. My Family are innocent. The bird-thing says you're just slaves as well and—"

"I didn't mean to . . . Wait." Uriel looked indignant at being interrupted, but Denizen didn't care. "A bird-thing?"

"Yes. It was a . . . a Tenebrous. I think. It felt wrong, like—"

"Like a wound in the world," Denizen finished. "Was it a *group* of bird-things? Like a flock all moving at once?"

Uriel nodded. "How did you know?"

Malebranche.

Denizen honestly hadn't thought there was any more room for urgency in his head. All that worry about whether Greaves was planning an ambush, and a traitor in Mercy's own ranks had been preparing one all along. It made total sense: if there were Knights who didn't want peace, why not Tenebrous?

"You need to get to the Order," he said. "They need to know about the . . . bird-thing. And you have to make them tell Mercy as well." He was momentarily so distracted by wondering whether Malebranche counted as a Grand Vizier that he didn't notice Uriel staring at him. "What?"

"Mercy," Uriel said. "Is that *your* Tenebrous?"

"Excuse me?" Denizen said. "What are you—? Listen. She's not *my* Tenebrous." *If anything, I'm probably her human,* he thought, and then immediately tossed those feelings in a box until later. "Look . . . the Order doesn't want to fight your family. We already have a war on our hands." *Think. Think.* "What about phones or computers?"

"Grandfather has a phone," Uriel said. "No one else. Maybe on the next raid I could . . ."

Denizen fought the urge to bang his head off the stone behind him. "We can't wait that long. Has anyone said what they plan to do with me?"

Uriel shook his head. "My sister wants you to teach us what you can do. These . . . Cants."

"Oh." Well, that was going to be a problem. Denizen had no idea if he *could* teach the Cants. Technically, he hadn't learned them at all. Mercy had just poured them into his head. Before that, he'd only known Sunrise, and that was more from overhearing Grey use it than any actual teaching. That was the problem with Higher Cants—they weren't particularly difficult to say; it was just about knowing *where* and *when*. . . .

"Uriel," he said suddenly. "Do you remember when we fought in the library? And when I tried to escape from here? Do you remember what I did?"

"Yes, why?"

"Do you remember when Ambrel screamed at me, and I opened a hole in the air to swallow her fire? And when I spoke to Grandfather about the Art of Apertura?"

"Yes," Uriel said. "You made a funny face and sort of half fell over."

Denizen scowled. "Well—yeah, but do you remember the *sound*? That was a Cant. It lets you use the Tenebrae as a shortcut from one place to another. You've been to Trinity—you could get back there and tell the Order where you are. It's practically instant: your family wouldn't even notice you've gone."

If it works, his skepticism added.

And if you survive, whispered everything else. There was a kernel of a plan forming in Denizen's mind, but that involved only risking his own life. Risking someone else's was something different entirely.

His guilt redoubled when he saw the raw hope on Uriel's face.

"So they might never know," Uriel whispered. "Ambrel might never know."

"She might not. But it's dangerous. *Really dangerous.*"

"I don't care," Uriel said, his voice trembling with fervor. Denizen suddenly felt even worse. "But . . ." Uriel's smile vanished. "I'm not sure if I remember it. It was the strangest thing I'd ever heard. Barely like sound at all."

"I know," Denizen said. He could feel the Art of Apertura at the back of his head, wide awake and eager. He had to choose his words carefully because he knew that if his concentration broke, it might bolt for his mouth. "But sometimes they want to be said. I wish I could say it for you, but the Cants *draw* the fire through you and . . ."

The wire trembled at his neck.

"I've trained for years to speak my Prayer," Uriel said. "Focusing my mind into the shape of a sword. What if I can't—"

"That's all the Cants are," Denizen said. "Just a way to channel the fire." He tried to keep desperation out of his tone. "We just have to try. Reach back, think of how it sounded, how it made you feel. You have to *remember*—"

His next words were cut off by the wire jolting at his neck, tugging him toward the door of his cell. Uriel leapt backward, eyes wide with sudden fear.

"Listen," Denizen said. "Picture where you want to go. Picture it on the other side of a dark corridor, as a painting behind a painting, and lift your fingers like

you're tearing your way through. You'll fall through dark water. Don't open your eyes, don't—"

The wire *yanked.* Denizen half came to his feet with it. *Just a second,* he thought, *just one second more.*

"Don't open your eyes. The iron will drag you. There are *things* in the—"

No more words would fit around the pressure in his throat. The message of the Redemptress was clear.

Come.

30

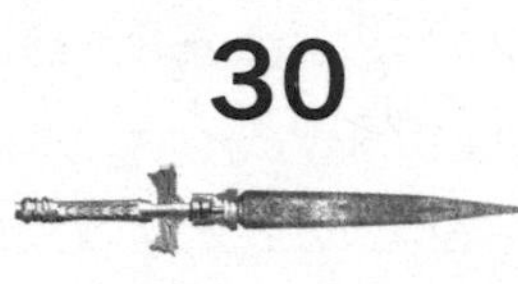

The Pull of the Wire

The castle might once have been massive, but its fall had fractured its innards into a maddening maze. There were any number of paths through Eloquence, and Uriel knew them all.

The second Denizen surrendered to the wire's pull, Uriel was up and running. Grandfather had told them all as children that the Redemptress could see sinful thoughts in their heads, and there was a child's terror in his heart. *Did She know?*

She can't. If She could, Uriel would have been long exposed. Grandfather's warnings were lies. Just like everything else.

It's not his fault. Uriel scrambled up a half-collapsed wall, squeezing between the two crumbling pillars separating the Abyssal Gate and the crushed tunnel network that had once been the East Tower. Grandfather had been lied to as well, lies told and retold from the moment Eloquence fell, from the First Croit to the last.

It all stemmed from Her.

Finally, his running slowed, and he lost himself in a crowd of Croits. There was Abucad, haggard and drawn, and Osprey, and Magnus. Uriel hadn't seen the latter since Tabitha died. Tears had cut a path through the dust on his cheeks.

Uriel fell into step with Abucad. His uncle had lost weight, and there was a bruise under his left eye. No one knew better than Uriel and Ambrel that it was common for those who were low in Grandfather's favor to suffer at the hands of those who enjoyed it, and these days you couldn't get much lower than Abucad. Being seen with him was only marginally better than being caught talking to Denizen, but Uriel had a sudden desperate need to actually *talk* to someone and not just hear Her words parroted back.

"Uriel," the older man said. "Have you recovered from the battle?"

"Yes," Uriel said. "I think so. I . . . I'm sorry about Tabitha."

"It's the way she would have wanted to go."

He said it like a curse.

They descended deeper and deeper into the ruin. Uriel looked around before he spoke again, his voice meant for Abucad alone. "Do you . . . do you think Grandfather knew what these . . . what the Adversary was capable of?"

Do you think he knows what they really are?

Abucad's voice was grim. "Did he say he didn't?"

"Yes."

"Then he didn't."

Uriel opened his mouth to ask again, but Abucad threw him a furious look.

"Stop, Uriel. I . . . the time for this has passed. I'm sorry." He swallowed. "I have a son."

I'm Family too, Uriel wanted to say. *We're all Family.* But that was it, wasn't it? Abucad would do whatever the Redemptress wanted, because he cared about what happened to those who shared his blood. And the worst thing was—so did the Order. The Croits would slaughter every Knight they could in return for a salvation that would never come . . . but the Order wouldn't do the same. Uriel had seen this truth, even before he'd talked to Denizen. There was a *reluctance* to the Knights when they had fought the Croits.

The Order had looked genuinely surprised that human would attack human.

Nausea flexed like a fist in the pit of Uriel's stomach. He couldn't think. Nothing seemed permanent—not the stone around him, nor the familiar faces of his Family as they entered the Shrine one by one.

Not even Her.

In slow and terrible increments, She turned to regard them, black eyes flicking from face to face. The piled iron statues of the long-dead Adversaries just stared at Uriel, hands reaching out at strange angles to grab at the air.

Uriel tore his gaze away from them. It gave him a now-familiar ache to see that Ambrel was standing beside Grandfather. They used to wait for each other at the entrance. When had that stopped?

Denizen Hardwick.

The crowd parted as Denizen half walked, half stumbled into the chamber, wire noose around his neck. At a sharp look from Grandfather, two cousins came forward and draped him in black. A pang of fear went through Uriel. He had never seen a robe of that color before.

Another new and terrible thing.

The Judging White of Grandfather's robe was nearly Failure's Gray after long weeks of wear. He looked like he hadn't slept since the Redemptress had awakened.

"We have thought long and hard about the fate of this Adversary, and—"

Do you know them? the Redemptress said in the chill voice of an empress. *The Cants. Do you know them?*

She twitched, quick as thought, and when the wires stilled, Her voice was that of a frightened girl.

The fire, it marks you. If I had known, I wouldn't have . . . I would never have let you . . .

Twitch, and the voice was cold again.

The weapons of the enemy will be our weapons. You will teach us the Cants that the King would not, and here we will

forge an army and storm the dark itself. He will pay for what he did. For what he would not do.

"No."

He looked tiny before Her, just a scrawny little boy with no weapons and a razor leash around his neck, but his voice didn't shake.

"I'm not going to give you weapons to hurt the people I care about. I don't even know if I can, to be honest. I didn't really learn them in the . . . conventional way. But I don't think you're going to kill me, because then you won't have a prisoner at all. And you don't want to kill me . . ."

He took a breath.

"Because you know what grief is like—"

"Do not speak to Her like that!" Grandfather snarled, but the Redemptress held up a hand and the old man's mouth shut with a *clack*.

For a long moment, She was silent. *He silenced Her.* Her face was unreadable, and, as the quiet stretched, Uriel wondered who was going to speak from that woven-wire mouth. Would it be the grief-stricken widow? Or the ruler, the warrior, the queen of revenge?

His answer was not long coming. With a rasp of slashed air, wires spun and writhed from the body of the Redemptress. They snaked through the crowd, alive and seeking, before whipping outward to tumble Croits to the ground. One was left—standing, shaking, alone in the middle of the floor.

What was her name? Uriel didn't know. So many had come in the last few weeks . . . She had the pale skin and graying hair of a Croit, but her eyes were bright blue—she was some lesser cousin, barely in her twenties, a girl who'd trained at Grandfather's feet and then gone off into the world.

You're right, the Redemptress said, as wires plunged down like sharp-tipped rain, ***I want you alive.***

Uriel *had* seen that girl before. He just hadn't recognized her without the look of rapture she'd worn ever since coming home. The same look they all wore since a goddess had awoken and told them they were special.

Now she just looked terrified.

The wires froze centimeters from the girl's pale skin, tracking the passage of tears down her cheeks like a scorpion's hovering tail.

I'll kill one of them instead.

"You . . . you *monster.*"

The words seemed to echo round the chamber for far longer than they should have. Maybe it was the silence that always followed Her words, or how Her radiating aura of wrongness twisted sound . . . but Uriel had a sinking feeling that it was the words themselves.

It took him a moment longer to realize that he was the one who'd spoken them.

Thirty-odd pairs of eyes stared at him. There was a quiet shuffling as the Croits closest to him tried to subtly inch away.

"What did you say?" Grandfather's voice made everyone flinch. "How dare you—"

"We're supposed to be Her Favored!" Uriel retorted. He couldn't help himself. All his anger and frustration and loneliness boiled to the surface. He'd tried *so hard.* Every time the Family had shamed him for his parents' betrayal, every time training had felt impossible, or Ambrel had been afraid—he had held on. He had *believed.*

Family. That was what was important. And all this thing saw them as was *leverage.*

"Surely you can't go along with this?" he shouted desperately at the gathered Croits. Not one of them would meet his gaze. "This isn't *right.*"

Meredel was staring at the floor, lips moving silently to himself. Osprey, Adauctus, the Afterwoken . . . all of them turned their eyes away.

The only people who didn't were Grandfather, Denizen—who looked extremely annoyed—and the Croit girl the Redemptress intended to kill.

He looked at all of them, because he knew, eventually, he'd have to face her.

"Ambrel . . ." It was nearly a plea. "Ambrel, you *can't* think this is right."

No hint of emotion crossed her face. Uriel was so used to being able to read every minute detail of her features that to see nothing there at all scared him more than the Redemptress. Finally, she spoke.

"It was my idea."

His heart stopped. For a moment, all there was in his chest was a lump of cold iron, sluggishly pushing horror through his veins. "What?"

"Victory is loss, Uriel," she whispered. "Nothing is a sacrifice if we do it for Her."

He staggered backward, away from that gaze. *How . . . How can she . . .*

"You will do as you're *told,* Uriel Croit," Grandfather said, advancing. "You will do what you were raised for. What we were all raised for. That's what Family means."

Uriel didn't look at Ambrel again, because he knew if he did his heart would break.

"That. Thing. Isn't. Family."

The words had barely left his mouth before Grandfather's left sleeve *cracked* through the air and spun him off his feet. Uriel felt a rib give way, like a hinge he didn't know he had, and pain followed him all the way to the ground.

It took him a long time to raise his head.

Grandfather stood over him, flanked by the Family, and in slow, measured jerks he pushed up his sleeve.

A Croit chose their Prayer from the histories, and yet what Grandfather had done was a singular devotion. Uriel had always assumed that it was from some tome or codex he didn't know . . . because, now that he thought about it, Uriel had always just assumed that

Grandfather knew more than he did about everything.

But if the Redemptress was just a Tenebrous, just a *thing,* and all their histories were lies, then maybe Grandfather had simply done it because it was the kind of thing he thought should be done, the kind of thing that *looked right,* and maybe everything the Croits had ever believed was just a madman raving in the dark.

It began at the bend of the old man's elbow, the skin long lost to black. The iron had been *carved*—the marbled strata of muscle and bone exposed in varying dark shades, down to the wrist, the palm, and a single finger terminating in a razor-sharp point.

It was a promise. A declaration. No gloves, no makeup, and no masks. Grandfather would never pretend he was anything else than a weapon for an inhuman hand.

"You have no knowledge of what I have done," the old man hissed, "and of how willingly I have done it. My entire life. The lives of every Croit before me. Every moment a promise. Every choice a battle."

Fire leaked from the bones of his sharpened hand. Uriel began to honestly worry that he might die.

"You were supposed to be a continuation of that. The sum total of everything this Family is supposed to be, sharpened down to you.

"And you *question*. How dare you? All I have done. All I will do. It means something." The light in Grandfather's eyes dimmed, just a fraction. "It has to."

"Stop."

Denizen had come as close as the wire noose would allow. "Just stop. If you leave him alone, if you let him live . . . I'll do it. I'll teach you."

Good, the Redemptress said, as if the last few moments hadn't happened. ***We begin tomorrow. The King will be slain with his own Cants. My love will be avenged.***

Denizen was dragged away. Uriel didn't know why She even thought the noose was necessary. She had a far more effective one now anyway. Denizen Hardwick wouldn't let others die for him.

What monster would?

Slowly, painfully, Uriel got to his feet. Grandfather was already striding away. No one would look at him.

"Ambrel, I . . ."

She stared at him like he was a stranger.

"Don't talk to me," she whispered. "Just . . . just don't."

She walked after Grandfather, and at the entrance they both turned to look at him. Uriel had seen that look before, but never directed at him.

"Get out of my sight," Grandfather said. "And think on your sins."

"Yes, Grandfather," Uriel murmured. *I will.*

31

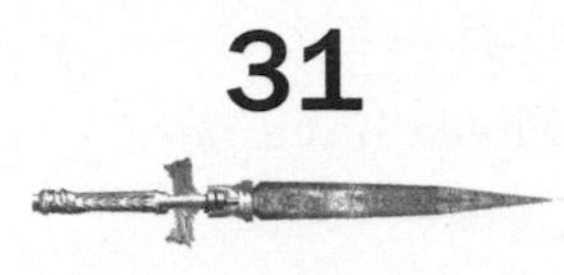

SIMPLICITY

WELL, THAT HAD BEEN a disaster.

Denizen stumbled along the corridor, halfway between an awkward run and a prolonged collapse. If he moved too slowly, the wire would start to draw tight round his neck; and if he moved too fast, the knot banged painfully off his Adam's apple. He had no idea what would happen if he tripped, but he'd rather not find out.

He hadn't seen where Uriel had gone after his outburst, but silently he hoped it was as far away as he could, Art or no Art.

They passed through atriums punctured by fallen pillars, through wrong-angled staircases and broken doorways, before finally reaching the lower depths and Denizen's cell. If Simon were here, he would've been able to extrapolate information about the guard from his clothing and mannerisms. Abigail would already have produced a hidden knife to cut herself free. Darcie would have taken one sniff of the air and deduced the castle's exact location.

Vivian would never have been captured in the first place.

All Denizen could do was stand in the middle of the cell and wait for the wire to relax enough for him to sit down. The Croit guard gave him one last look of disgust and left him alone with his doubt and exhaustion.

And his magic.

It started slowly. Denizen had been trying to stay calm, carefully experimenting with the give of the wire, when the fire unfurled itself like a cat stretching in sunlight. Denizen froze. Usually, the power of the Tenebrae came when it was called, or responded to strong emotions like anger or fear.

This was the first time it had simply presented itself, like a sword being unsheathed, ready for his hand.

A bead of sweat slid down Denizen's forehead. The urge to lash out at the Redemptress every time he was in Her presence had been almost overpowering, even though his brain *knew* that it was suicide. That had scared him almost more than She had. Had he done it, he would have died, and yet he still wanted to do it anyway.

The fire sat there, in the pit of his stomach, a reservoir of power so pure and clean and eager that Denizen at once felt tiny before it and the mightiest human in the world. It was ready, willing; he could almost see the patterns of light overlaid across his cell, every place the fire would touch.

His control wavered. It was all well and good, Denizen thought, when you were training in the safety of Seraphim Row, or in battle, where you could immediately clamp it back down when you no longer needed it.

But here . . .

The fire came with danger. It came when it tasted the Tenebrae in the air. It came when its wielder was angry, and it came when they were afraid.

No wonder the Croits were insane. This place hungered to be burned.

How far would he get? How far would the Cants take him if he really, *really* cut loose? Denizen could feel them perched on his nerve endings, waiting to be called. *It'd have to be something big*, he thought. In his head, the Cants rearranged themselves, and Denizen felt the fire tremble at each new path it could take.

The cold of the castle seemed very distant now. Denizen knew that the second his skin began to heat, the wire would contract, but maybe if he drew on as much power as he could . . . maybe if he drank it all in and became a sun himself, a walking solar flare . . . then maybe the wire would burn instead of cut, and he'd be free to burn with it.

Denizen.

The Cants could be combined. Knights did it all

the time. Words became phrases became sentences, each syllable changing the one before. That was what language was. Cants moved in his head like soldiers marching in step. Ten, fifteen, twenty—how much skin would he have to give to speak all of them?

Would there even be a Denizen left?

Stop.

The fire lapped at the bottom of his heart, above it circled the Cants, and in between was Denizen—just a knot of thoughts and worry and frowns, and if he let the three meet, he'd cease to exist. Wouldn't that be better? Just let them have one another and ride the updraft of his own immolation.

"Adversary."

Denizen opened eyes he didn't remember closing. For a moment, his brain heard his name and rejected it as unimportant. You couldn't set fire to anything with *those* syllables. Curlicues of fire danced across his vision, begging to be made a reality, outlining the walls, the floor, and the girl holding something sharp.

Wait. Go back.

"What did you do to my brother?" she hissed.

Denizen suddenly realized he had no idea how long Ambrel had been standing there—how long *he'd* been standing there, swaying on his feet, listening to the music of seventy-eight stars. Even in the *Lucidum*'s washed-out shades, he could tell her eyes were sore from crying, her hair a tangle down to her shoulders as if she'd been tearing at it.

Her grip on the knife was rock-steady.

This must be what having an office is like, Denizen thought distantly. *People just drop in to see you.* Admittedly, everyone so far had pulled some kind of weapon on him, but that was apparently just his life now. *That's* why the Knights were so calm all the time. You ended up just navigating the sharp edges on autopilot.

"What did you do to him?" she snapped again, each word punctuated with a jab of the knife. Denizen tried to focus. Autopilot or not, that was an extremely sharp knife. No, not a knife. Something sharp with the same shape.

Focus.

"I didn't do anything," he said carefully. "And I thought the plan was to not kill me?"

Ambrel paced back and forth. "I don't have to kill you," she said.

"Oh," he replied. "Good?"

Suddenly her fingers were tangled in his hair, yanking his head back to expose his throat. Denizen's hands rose to grab her—then stopped as she nestled the point of the blade right in the hollow of his throat.

They both stood there, very still, and Denizen realized that he was in fact in no way used to life-or-death situations at all.

"What did you *do?*" she whispered. "There's something *wrong* with him and I don't . . . I don't know how to fix it . . ."

A drop of blood made its slow progress down Denizen's neck. Adrenaline pounded through his system, speeding his thoughts, urging him to act.

No. Denizen might have had an unparalleled understanding of the Cants, but he still needed a working throat to use them. And, in the unlikely event he managed to take down Ambrel before she cut his throat, he still had the Redemptress's noose to worry about.

So instead Denizen stayed very still and hoped human words would be enough. "Ambrel."

He was one hundred percent sure that speaking had widened the wound at his throat, but he continued anyway.

"I didn't do anything to your brother. Honestly. I'm just a *kid.*"

His voice broke on the last word and he swallowed it back. He was, wasn't he? In the last six months, he had been flipped, kicked, punched, and exhausted by his training, but he'd endured because a secret part of him had known that the Cants gave him a get-out-of-jail-free card. Mess up a kick? *Grand.* He had half a dozen Cants that could do far more damage. Miss a target for the thirtieth time? *Fine.* He could obliterate it and half the wall behind with a thought.

But take that away and he was just a boy. A tired

boy whose life could be snuffed out without anyone breaking a sweat.

"I'm just like you. We grew up different, that's all. I don't have some special power or anything. Well—except for the magic. And I didn't corrupt Uriel. He just . . ."

Ambrel withdrew the weapon far enough that Denizen no longer grazed it with each swallow, but not far enough that for a second he felt safe.

"He just what?" she said.

This was the second Croit he was giving emotional counseling to in less than twenty-four hours. He wasn't even surprised. Who else would they talk to? *They're just kids too.*

"He's afraid for you," Denizen said. "That's all. I could see it in that chamber." *Because we definitely haven't been plotting his escape behind your back.* "I know what that means. So does Uriel. You're family. *That's* what's important."

Ambrel stared at him for a long moment and then nodded slowly.

"It is," she said. "You're right." She abruptly let Denizen go. By the time he managed to look up, she was gone.

32

Us and Them

How long do I have? Who will they send?

The questions distracted Uriel from the grinding pain of his broken rib as he leapt between the spires and slabs of his Family's dead. The two were inextricably linked, after all. Each run of the Garden had been preceded by an analysis of his brethren's abilities. Not just their Prayers but the strategies of their hearts.

Uriel knew exactly how long it took Adauctus to screw up the strength to be violent, how vicious Clothilde was when cornered. Even the Afterwoken—the only thing Uriel hadn't bothered learning about them was their names.

He had bolted for the Garden as soon as Denizen had been dragged away. No order had been given to stop him, but it wouldn't be long coming. He was *insurance* now, for Denizen's good behavior.

Uriel kicked off from a slanting tower of marble,

twisting in midair, measuring how much the rib pulled him up short. He'd need to know that too. Better now than if it came to blades.

The twins had never really been tolerated by the Family. Grandfather trained them twice as hard to make up for their parents' mistake, and that same mistake had made them a target. Even being Favored hadn't brought them any peace—though those that *had* attacked them afterward had very swiftly learned to regret it.

And then *She'd* woken, and everything changed. He'd been part of something—or Ambrel had and, as always, that meant he had too, a mere half second behind.

And now that precarious prestige was gone.

Uriel scaled his grandmother's spire, practice compensating for the grace his injury stole, and counted the figures walking from Eloquence's gates.

One. Castabel, a nasty piece of work. He was mostly a stranger—Grandfather used him to assassinate anyone who threatened Croit holdings out in the world.

Two. Hagar. *Hagar? Ungrateful* . . . What about the time Uriel had caught her using her Prayer on the beach alone? *Practicing*, she had said, as if it wasn't obvious that she was simply giving in to the temptation of the flame. Uriel hadn't said anything to Grandfather and yet here she was.

Two, then. Two wasn't a problem, even if one

was Castabel. Hagar was useless if you came at her head-on, and Castabel enjoyed himself far too much. Uriel would frustrate him by striking at her and then Ambrel could—

Oh. He wasn't used to thinking of himself in the singular. Getting used to a broken rib had been the easy part.

Uriel clamped down on the tremors before they started, digging his nails into the iron-streaked meat of his palms. *Don't think about it.* He had to do this. The Redemptress would use them without a thought—leave them like Tabitha. She didn't *care.*

But Uriel did.

He swung himself higher, careful to use the spire to hide the outline of his slender form. It was strange: only now, on the cusp of betraying them, did he truly understand what serving the Croits meant.

They wouldn't forgive him. None of them. If what he did became known—and it would; he was done with lies, even to himself—Uriel would be a traitor. Maybe Denizen's people would offer him some kind of asylum, but not as a Croit. He'd be disowned. Nameless.

It didn't matter. A Croit was required to sacrifice everything to keep the Family safe.

Even the Family itself.

What about—

Uriel strangled the thought before it could grow. He stabbed it with a blade of fire, chopped it to pieces, and buried them in the deepest dark. Ambrel would understand. And, even if she didn't, she would be alive. Even if she hated him forever, she'd be alive.

Uriel took one last glance at the gates of Eloquence, wondering whether it was the last time he'd ever see them, and then paled as far as his Croit countenance would allow.

Dozens of figures were walking from the gates, holding hands up to guard against the setting sun. No, not dozens. Thirty-three. Precisely the number of Favored Croits now resident in Eloquence, minus Grandfather, Ambrel, and himself.

Not Ambrel. The slightest spark of hope kindled in Uriel's chest. He didn't dare acknowledge it, in case it went out.

Run, Uriel. The words came in her voice, so comforting he found himself blinking back tears. *Run.*

He ran.

Down pathways, between monoliths, under dolmens, and over graves. One side of his chest was in agony, but he ignored it, scrabbling for alien syllables in his head.

Oh, the *Favor* was there. With a hateful kind of irony, the less he believed in the Redemptress, the harder it burned. But a sword was no good to him now.

They would be running too.

Through the Victorian Age with its army of marble mustaches, via a detour into the ruffs and rapiers of the Elizabethan, in case Osprey was in his favorite hiding spot between

DAVENTRY CROIT

~ DIED IN SERVICE ~

and

GOSSIFER CROIT

~ DIED INSANE ~

They would be entering the maze of the dead from all sides, choking off potential routes, running Uriel down like a dog. What would they do to him? He needed to be *alive* to ensure Denizen's cooperation, but that was all. What was the price for a Favored speaking out against the Redemptress? Was his blood still too precious to be spilled, or had he gone too far?

Think. It was Uriel's only chance to be merely hated, instead of dead. *Think.*

Picture where you want to go. Picture it on the other side of a dark corridor, as a painting behind a painting, and lift your fingers like you're tearing your way through.

Uriel focused on the splendor of the Long Room in Trinity, picturing the austere marble busts—not difficult, considering his surroundings—and polished wood floors. It was nearly a castle itself, not riven and destroyed like Eloquence but bright and safe and solid. A place that let the sun in.

Uriel imagined it at the end of a long tunnel. No—he put the salvation of his Family at the end of that tunnel; he put his heart and his soul into that mental image and reached out his hands to pull it home.

The Favor flickered and boiled, unsure what form to take. Uriel remembered the shape of Denizen's mouth as he had spoken, the raw and rushing shape of the sound . . .

Come on.

Fire was burning his throat.

Come on.

Was that the first syllable? It slipped and slithered like something alive, and Uriel fought to contain it, to say it . . .

Please.

He leapt—

Athelstan Croit—two and a half meters of muscle, scars, and blind faith. He slapped his younger cousin out of the air with no trouble at all.

Agony. That was how much a broken rib was going to limit him. Uriel's tenuous grip on the Cant fled as he cracked against the roof of

KAELAN CROIT

~ DIED A MARTYR ~

He stifled his yell of pain half not to give away his location and half because the agony was just too great. It was hard to hear his thoughts around the shrieking in his chest.

Athelstan. Athelstan. His Prayer was something like . . .

The giant parted his hands, and twin curves of dripping fire burst from his palms, glowing like the noonday sun.

Yes, that was it.

By reflex, Uriel's mind slid into the particular mathematics of combat. He was wounded. He was alone. His opponent was fresh, uninjured, and guaranteed reinforcements, which would have been more than enough without him also being so large that his every step tremored the ground.

Uriel had only two points in his favor. The first was that Athelstan had been Outside for years, while Uriel knew this necropolis like the back of Ambrel's hand.

The other was that Athelstan still believed.

Uriel didn't bother parrying the first downward slash. It would have broken his arms. Instead, he dodged the sizzling blades, staggering backward as Athelstan rumbled toward him. A tiny, cruel part of him shook its head at his cousin's foolishness. You didn't need strength when your blades would cut through anything, so all the huge man's muscles really did was reduce his maneuverability.

Heaving his wounded body through the gaps in

Athelstan's reach, Uriel led the giant man toward the towering marble form of Kaelan Croit. Athelstan's features were twisted in the frustrated snarl of someone trying to stamp on a particularly irritating ant.

"Stay *still*!" he roared, and Uriel obliged, freezing just long enough for Athelstan to triumphantly bring both scythes of fire around in an incandescent, unstoppable arc. Had Uriel not ducked, it would have removed everything above his collarbones.

Instead, it turned Kaelan Croit's shins to a spray of marble shards.

The huge statue swept inexorably down, and Athelstan, frozen with horror at what he had done, would have been driven into the ground like a nail under a hammer had not Abucad tackled him out of the way. The two Croits tumbled to one side as the statue crashed to the grass.

Uriel didn't know why he hesitated, but for half a second Abucad's eyes met his.

"*Go*," he said. Athelstan had fallen badly, cracking his head on a plinth. Unconscious but uncrushed. Abucad's voice was low and fierce. "I'll draw them off. I don't know how much time I can give you but—"

"Thank you," Uriel said. "I—"

"Just *go*," Abucad said, "and, if you do have some sort of plan, remember Daniel. *Remember my son.*"

Uriel ran, and Abucad's shout rose behind him.

"NOTHING HERE! KEEP LOOKING!"

It might buy him a minute. Maybe two. He had to try the Cant again.

Uriel grasped for that first syllable, cursing as it slipped away. It felt like trying to grab mist.

He wasn't even sure what era he was in now. All the marble faces around him were blurring together—disapproving, cruel, reaching down for him with white, cold hands. It showed how desperate he was when seeing the familiar, Transgression-stained face of

ISKOR CROIT

~ DIED IN SHAME ~

was a comfort.

Think, Uriel. Think of escape. Think of—

"Brother!"

Such a simple word, but relief suddenly pounded through Uriel's chest like cool water. He turned, forgetting his pursuers, the danger, and the Redemptress.

She came. She came to help me.

Together we have a chance.

And then he saw her robe.

Ambrel jumped from the lip of Iskor's tomb to land lightly on the earth, limbs wreathed in Accusers' Red. The vivid hue bleached her skin and, with her hood up, she was just a skull, pale and staring, swimming in cloth the color of blood.

Back in the Shrine, she'd been wearing Judging White. They all had.

She changed for this.

"There's rust in you, Uriel."

With horror, Uriel realized Ambrel was holding a file.

"Ambrel," he whispered, and was immediately disgusted by how weak his voice sounded. "Ambrel, why do you have a—"

"It wouldn't be enough," she hissed. Golden light was crackling between her teeth. The file was an ugly, toothed thing, built to slice iron like soft fat from bone. "I could sharpen myself, show my devotion like Grandfather, and it still wouldn't be enough. Because it's not my weakness. It's yours. Just one more thing you don't want to share with me."

Every training session, every battle they had shared, and Uriel had never heard his sister in such pain.

"When were you going to tell me?" she said. "When did it happen—when you stopped believing?" Tears streamed down her cheeks. "What's *wrong* with you?"

"Nothing's wrong with—"

"*Stop lying,*" she snapped. Uriel couldn't take his eyes from the eager gleam of the file in her hand. "Grandfather's right. This is our time. The Redemptress has risen, and we have a chance to rise with Her. This is what we were made for. You've forgotten that."

"I haven't forgotten anything," Uriel retorted. Shouts were rising through the necropolis now. Seconds were ticking away. "I'm the only one who remembers. We were raised to look after our *Family,* Ambrel. To take care of each other. That's not what this is about. The Redemptress is just some monster who fed the First Croit pretty words, and we're so desperate for salvation that we're swallowing them whole. She's *insane.* So is Grandfather. That's why our parents wanted us to get away—"

"Our *parents.*" Ambrel laughed, the sound choked in bitterness and rage. "Two strangers whose only useful act was creating us. You're not going to sway me with them. They tried to keep us from our destiny. From Her."

She spat at his feet. "And so are you."

"I'm just trying to keep you *safe*—"

"I know," she whispered, and suddenly her voice was raw and soft, anger draining away like pus from a wound. "I know you are. That's the problem. We don't *matter,* Uriel. Nothing matters but the War. *That's* Family. The salvation of all, not just one. Tabitha was right about us. You and I have been dedicated to each other. And we've been wrong. That's why I have to do it."

Uriel went cold. "What?"

"I have to prove I'm worthy. I have to prove I'm Favored."

He took a step toward her. "Ambrel, what are you—"

She punched him in the jaw.

Uriel staggered backward and she followed, robes fluttering. He dodged her second blow and caught her third with his palm, but he was injured, and anger had given her a desperate strength. She'd always been faster than him. Always quicker to violence. Ambrel was a Croit to the core.

She jabbed the file at him like a blade.

"It was supposed to be *us,*" she snarled. "We were supposed to be strong together. Why did you have to let me down—"

Uriel's fist killed the rest of her sentence, and suddenly they were on the grass, his fists hammering her temples while her fingers found his throat. There were no more lies now. Every betrayal, every slight, every way in which they had ever failed each other—it all came out in a flurry of bone and muscle.

And Ambrel was winning.

This was the fight for which Croits had been made. Believer and unbeliever, one strong in their faith and one weak in their doubt. Uriel's vision clouded as Ambrel's iron fingers dug into the meat of his neck. Her voice was acid in his ears.

"Why couldn't you just *believe?*"

Because it's wrong.

Fire rose through the pain, spilling into half-numb

limbs. Ambrel's grip loosened, just for a second, and all Uriel wanted was the words to end this, to escape this place that they had come to—

And the Art of Apertura slipped out.

Uriel's shadow tore along a seam, and suddenly the tombs and the grass and the undimmed stars fell *up*. Ambrel went rigid against him, and black water closed over them both.

Don't open your eyes.

Cold.

Cold.

Cold.

It was several centuries before Uriel could think anything else. When he did, each thought came slow and stiff with ice. Denizen had warned him, but . . . the unworldliness of it, the immensity . . .

A humbling cold, one that told Uriel just how small and unimportant and alone he was.

Alone. Ambrel.

Uriel sluggishly became aware of hands still wrapped round his neck, the fingers frozen claws. A knee bumped against his stomach, robbed of any momentum by the water, and he lifted his arms to grab her, fighting the tug of Transgression-riddled hands that now weighed as much as planetary cores.

The iron will drag you.

Who had said that? Uriel dismissed the thought. Up

and down didn't matter anymore. His only direction was her.

He tried to tangle a hand in the brittle seaweed of her hair. They had lived their lives just a half-second apart, and if he could save all those half seconds, use them to talk to her, to make her see—

Something brushed against his back. It wasn't Ambrel; her hands were pulling free from his neck, her legs feebly beating against his. No, it moved too quickly, too confidently—

Like I used to, Uriel thought, dreamy with hypothermia.

There are things *in the . . .*

The Tenebrae. That's what this was. That's where *She* came from. Panic bloomed like frost in his head as Uriel imagined hundreds of Her, diving round them with hideous grace, trailing their tendrils for struggling prey . . .

Uriel's Transgression dragged him down, and he fought to hold Ambrel close even as she fought to kick away. *Stop it, please, stop—*

He'd explain it to her. He'd hold her. She'd be angry, so angry, but they were brother and sister, two people sharing a life. He just had to make her see. Numb, his fingers began to close—

A half second too slow.

Something snatched Ambrel from him so hard its

backwash hit him like a slap. Uriel screamed, and the cold that had gone before was *nothing* compared to the dark water in his mouth. It washed out the fire in his stomach, froze him solid from the heart outward. He felt teeth shatter in a scream—

Ambrel . . . Ambrel, NO—

His sins dragged him down, but Uriel fought against them—*his sister was gone, his sister was taken*; there was burning heat on his back and the aching chill of space on his cheek.

AMBREL!

And icy blackness became the smell of smoke. Uriel stepped out onto unexpectedly solid ground, and then his legs simply went, spilling him onto his face. His skin prickled as beaded black liquid left in a thousand tendrils of smoke, but inside him a lump remained, frozen solid—the space where a sister used to be.

People were shouting. His arms were grabbed and twisted behind him. Sunlight seared his freezing skin.

Uriel barely noticed.

There was a clump of hair in his hand. His fingers had finally closed.

33

ADVERSARY

"MOVE," THE GIRL SAID, her finger pressed to Uriel's temple, "and you burn."

Uriel just stared at her. Details drifted through his head—the amber cast of her skin, the strange clothes, and the pinned-up knot of black hair—but none found any purchase. None sank in. He was nothing but a message now. A message and half a heart.

"I need to speak to Edifice Greaves."

"We know," the boy snapped. "You said."

With Tabitha's darkness long dead, Uriel could see just how much damage the Long Room had sustained. The bookshelves were chewed skeletons of wood and char, the floor lacerated by broken glass, and various sections had been cordoned off with black tape.

It looked like Eloquence, and dimly Uriel wondered if this would be the world if the Croits were to win—just ruin and ash, stamped with the Crow and the Claw.

"Edifice Greaves," Uriel repeated hoarsely. "I need to speak to—"

"We *heard* you," the angry girl said, her finger pressing down painfully. *Simple yet effective,* came the dry and distant thought. All it would take was a word and Uriel's skull would be leaking smoke.

It hurt to talk. The inside of his mouth was cut to pieces from where teeth had cracked, his tongue like a frozen brick since he'd gotten a mouthful of . . . whatever it was between *here* and Eloquence. It wasn't water. Water didn't fight its way out of your mouth to become ribboning smoke. Water didn't deaden your thoughts as well as your skin.

The only thing it hadn't numbed was the pain.

She's gone. She's gone. She's gone.

Had Uriel any strength left, he would have spoken the Art of Apertura and flung himself back in, again and again, until he found her. But he didn't. There was nothing left. Fire guttered in him like a wet candle struggling to burn. Maybe it would return. Maybe it wouldn't.

He was surely out of Favor now.

Another girl stood farther off, a long blue coat folded over one arm, her eyes wide behind dark lenses.

"Where is Denizen?" the boy said. He could have been a Croit—pale and skinny—though Uriel's practiced eye could tell he didn't know one end of a sword from the other. "You took him. *Tell us where he is.*"

"Edifice Greaves," Uriel croaked. "I need to speak to—" The boy's eyes were shining with tears. Uriel could feel the girl's iron finger trembling against his skin. They were *afraid.* Not of him, though Croitly pride said it was.

They were afraid for their friend.

"He's alive," Uriel said. "He sent me here. He—"

The door at the far end of the hall opened and footsteps rang out. Uriel didn't turn, not wanting to spook the finger at his temple, instead watching relief mingle with frustration on his captors' faces. Finally, hands slid under Uriel's armpits and set him on his feet to face the leader of the Order, the Adversary he'd been raised his whole life to hate.

"Edifice Greaves," the man said. "And you are?"

He didn't look like a vast and terrible mind living in a host of iron bodies, but at this point that didn't surprise Uriel. There were five other Knights surrounding him, each radiating violence.

"You're in charge," Uriel said. It wasn't a question.

"It doesn't feel like it," Greaves said, and there was nothing pleasant in his smile. "I'm told you just fell out of the air."

"They're a lost bloodline," the boy snapped. "They have to be."

"Tanglearches," the girl with the blue coat said. "Or perhaps Kenns. We've been going through the *Incunabulae* since before the attack; we haven't *slept* since—"

"Of course they're a lost bloodline," Greaves said sharply. The teenagers abruptly shut up, their faces twisted in shock. He turned to one of the Knights beside him. "Get them out of here. Now."

"We're not going anywhere," the boy said. "You think *you* were our first call?"

The door's hinges hadn't been in the best shape after the battle, and the woman's entrance proved to be the last straw. She had crossed the room before it clattered to the floor, her movements as mechanically graceful as the unsheathing of a sword. Her short-cropped hair was silver against her skull, scars dribbling down the side of her neck. The glare she gave Uriel made his rib ache.

"You took my son," she said. Never in history had there been a clearer declaration of war.

"Yes," Uriel said. "Would you like him back?"

The boy abruptly sat down on the floor, his hands wrapped round himself like he was freezing. The girl with the blue coat put both arms round his shoulders and for a second they just stayed there, swaying back and forth.

Uncomfortable, Uriel looked away.

"And we're not a lost bloodline," he said. "You are.

All of you. We were the first. The First Croit met the Redemptress in the dark, and together they stole a great fire and brought it back to this world. An Adversary came, men and women of iron, and they flung our castle down. The Redemptress slept and we waited. For now. For this."

Even after all he'd been through, his throat still rebelled at the words he was about to say.

"But it's lies. She's not our Redemptress. She's a Tenebrous. A monster. And She has to be stopped."

Uriel wasn't sure what he expected. Shock, perhaps, or disbelief. Why *should* they believe him? They had no proof of anything but how his Family had attacked them.

"OK," Greaves said.

"OK?" Uriel repeated. Confusion finally dented the black miasma in his head enough for him to feel something. "Is that . . . it?"

The Knights separated with military precision, some slipping out of the door, others on phones talking quickly and quietly. The teenagers were caught between eyeing each other and staring at Uriel.

"*No,*" the woman growled. "Where is Denizen?"

"At Eloquence," Uriel replied. "He taught me how to get here. The uh . . . the Art of Apertura—that was what he called it. He said you'd help me."

The boy winced. Both girls' eyes went wide.

Denizen's mother's face was granite. Uriel had the sudden sense that everyone was pointedly trying not to look at Greaves.

"Did he?" the Order's leader said. "Interesting." He fingered the sword pin on his tie. "Well. You'll tell us everything you know about this Tenebrous. I want a profile on each of your family, location, defenses—"

"I'll tell you everything," Uriel said. "On one condition."

He didn't look at Greaves as he said it. Instead, he watched Denizen's mother and his friends. Strange as it sounded, Uriel understood their anger far better than he did Greaves. Retaliation was what Family was about.

Us and them.

"You have to save my Family."

Greaves's smile disappeared.

"I know what I'm asking. They won't go down without a fight. But we're like you and we don't deserve to die for being lied to. I want your promise that, if I give you what you need, you won't kill them. You'll help them."

"Strange sentiment," Greaves responded, "from someone willing to betray their family."

"I am not betraying my Family." The void in Uriel's head shivered, as if something underneath was trying to push its way out. "I am betraying Her."

"You realize, of course, that they'll be trying their best to kill us."

Uriel nodded. "Those are my terms."

"We could just make you tell us," Greaves said mildly. He didn't bother making more of a threat. He didn't have to—Denizen's mother was radiating menace enough. Just being in her presence was like being held over a precipice.

Uriel almost laughed, but the bitterness of it closed his throat. "No you couldn't."

Greaves's eyebrow lifted.

"Why not?"

"Because I'm a Croit."

It had been so long since he had felt the vicious certainty of his heritage, so long since he had seen it anywhere but in the eyes of his sister. It drove cold fury into his words. "We are raised to hate. We are trained to kill. You think this"—he jerked his head at the destroyed library—"was a battle? This was an opening salvo. A stretch of muscles long asleep. You don't remember where you came from, but my history has been beaten into me since the moment I drew breath. There are fifteen centuries of Croits behind me, fifteen centuries of praying for war against you, and, when we come, we will win, because you have rules and we do not.

"We are . . . we are fanatics."

His words silenced the room. Even Denizen's mother looked taken aback.

"And yet you're here," the angry girl said. "Why?"

The dead blackness in Uriel's head was cracking. His hands were trembling and he squeezed them into fists.

"I was trying to save my sister. My twin. I did all this for her, and I . . . I . . ."

Tears burned his eyes. He could barely force words past them.

"I lost her in the darkness."

Greaves and Vivian exchanged glances. Uriel felt like the cold had taken up permanent residence in his chest. His heart was missing every second beat. It took a while for Greaves's words to reach through that aching systolic gap.

". . . get Denizen out before the attack. It's the best way. If this boy can . . ."

"I can't do it," Uriel said, his voice still hitching. "None of them trust me. And, besides, the Redemptress—" Hate flooded through him as he said Her name. That was good. Hate was stronger than sorrow. It would keep him upright until this was done. "The Tenebrous is made of wire. She keeps one around Denizen's neck at all times."

There was an audible creak of iron as Vivian's hands clenched into fists. Uriel remembered Abucad's desperate words.

"And there is another prisoner too. An UnFavored . . . a normal person. I can't get close to them. Ambrel could but . . ."

Hold on to the hate. Uriel was still shaking, but now it was with rage. It was Her fault. It *was*.

Greaves was frowning. "It's a hostage situation. A perfect one. We can't charge them; they'll take us apart. We need some kind of an in."

"Umm . . ."

The tall, thin boy had raised a hand. Greaves's features twisted in annoyance, but Vivian's glare shut his mouth before he could speak, a fact that seemed to surprise even him.

"Simon?" she asked.

"I can't believe I'm saying this," he said, eyeing them nervously. "But I have an idea."

34

Blunt Instrument

This time, when Denizen was dragged into the Shrine, there was no one to greet him but the arachnoid geometry of the Tenebrous Herself. Denizen flinched as Her umbra washed over him, wringing sweat from his skin and tears from his eyes. It was bad everywhere in Eloquence. Here it was almost intolerable.

Her pin-thin pupils gleamed.

"You will be taught our ways. The true ways."

Denizen hadn't noticed Grandfather lurking between the shattered pillars. He swept by Denizen and, with no little care, propped something on the broken stone.

"And, in return, you will teach me. I will take on the burden of your dark knowledge and decide where it can be put to best use."

He'd set down a little blackboard on an easel. It was the saddest thing Denizen had ever seen.

"OK," Denizen said. "But where's Uriel?"

The old man's eyes narrowed.

Denizen forced some iron into his voice. "I told you I'd help you if you didn't hurt Uriel. Where is he? I want to see him before we start."

It had been a long and sleepless night for Denizen. He'd had ample time to think about what his conversations with the twins might have set in motion. The best-case scenario was that Ambrel had teamed up with Uriel and they'd used the Art of Apertura to escape. Unfortunately, there were a whole lot of other possible scenarios, and in quite a lot of them Denizen Hardwick was basically a murderer.

How could I have sent him?

"Grandfather!"

One of the other Croits—*Osprey?*—entered the Shrine, panting and sweat-streaked, and behind him came the rest, at least twenty, crowding the stone doors. Denizen's heart sank.

"Where's Ambrel?" the old man said. "She was supposed to—"

Osprey shook his head. "We searched the necropolis for hours. They're not—" He fixed his eyes on Denizen and stopped talking so abruptly it would have been comical had the situation not been what it was.

Not in front of the prisoner . . .

So it was bad news. Had Uriel escaped? Had Ambrel helped him?

No. Denizen had dabbled in hope before. Every orphan in Crosscaper had. *Maybe someone will come along and tell me it's all been a mistake, that I don't belong here—that there's a family and a home and love waiting for me outside these miserable walls.*

Hope was paralyzing. It encouraged you to put your determination aside and rely on somebody else's, when that energy would be much better spent being your own best chance for happiness, your own best plan for survival.

But someone did show up at Crosscaper.

Shut up.

I wish he were here now.

And then the crowd parted and any thought of hope fled. Ambrel Croit walked her brother into the Shrine, a knife at his throat. Both their eyes were wide and bright—his with fear, and hers with triumph.

"Here he is, Grandfather. Ready for judgment."

Oh no . . .

"Good," said the old man. "Are they all present?"

Ambrel nodded. "This should be witnessed by everyone." Even as she spoke, the last few Croits entered. The Redemptress's gaze swept over each, Her hands squeezing Her temples.

Echoes . . . she whispered. ***I see echoes . . .***

Ambrel shoved Uriel forward so he fell to his knees, and stalked to Denizen's side, sheathing her knife under her blood-red robes. She didn't spare him a second glance.

"Uriel Croit," Grandfather intoned. "Know that it is not I who judge you, for we have already been judged."

"No."

Uriel didn't rise to his feet. He didn't draw his sword or attempt to fight.

Instead, gasps circled the chamber as he did something only one Croit had ever done before.

He *argued.*

With *Grandfather.*

"It's all lies, Grandfather. Can you admit that to yourself? Or are you so committed that you'd kill me rather than face the truth?"

Grandfather's mouth opened and closed, pale eyes wide. Just for a second, the patriarch was nothing but an old man, not particularly tall, not particularly anything.

His robe was wrinkled. He looked like he hadn't had a good bath or a good sleep in a very long time. There were liver spots on the back of his one good hand, and while the other Croits huddled together in the constant background hum of the Redemptress's presence, he stood very much alone.

And then he scowled, and suddenly defying his will was as impossible as walking on the surface of the sun.

"I didn't think it would be you."

Uriel paled, an impressive feat for a Croit.

"There is always rust. It creeps in through the cold and the wet; it blooms in doubt and fear. It seeps in through blood. I knew that Ambrel had some of your parents' willfulness, but I'd taken you for someone stronger. I thought that, even after your parents' sins, you could be redeemed. There is no mind stronger than one that has passed through doubt."

He shook his head. "But you are rotten. You are rusted. And I do not know if even I can sharpen you to good use."

Do you hear that? For once in Denizen's experience of this madhouse, no one was paying attention to the Redemptress. ***Echoes, echoes, echoes . . .***

Uriel was shaking now. The other Croits exchanged glances as if they didn't know what to do. Ambrel had unsheathed a knife just enough that the blade gleamed from her pocket, her fingers shaking on the hilt.

"I'm sorry, Grandfather," Uriel said. "I'm sorry I can't just believe. I'm sorry I'm the wrong kind of strong."

Denizen stared at the blade, the slick length of it, the way it caught the light in a thousand swarming points. *Now* Ambrel met his gaze, her eyes green-white and incandescent.

"Uriel," Grandfather whispered.

Denizen knew that blade. He knew who had carved it.

"What have you done?"

Ambrel winked, and the world went mad.

The Tenebrae didn't flood into the chamber; it *stabbed,* a dozen points of yawning dark. Figures leapt from each, trailing molten light. Everything happened with the luxurious, deceptive slowness of a flame catching your hand, and Denizen could only stare as Ambrel's robes came apart, as pale cheeks turned paler and green eyes blued and burst to lightning.

Familiar lightning.

The Redemptress screamed. Grandfather roared. The wire around Denizen's neck pulled tight—

And Mercy cut him free.

Fire.

Denizen turned half a hundred wires to steam before they could touch his flesh. All the Cants he had imagined, all the suns he had been desperate to say, they spun from him like rain from a storm, and the Redemptress reared back as Her limbs flashed to flame.

Eloquence shook as Knight met Croit in open battle. A blurred *something* pounded across the chamber, and through his own personal inferno, Denizen saw that it was a Hephaestus Knight—charging knots of enemies and hurling them back. There was something terrifying about it, even though Denizen knew there was an ally inside. Nothing that big should move so fast.

Greaves was there, elegant in his suit, so much of Grey in his graceful strikes. Jack was his polar opposite—a siege engine catching bullets on his fists, his whole frame alight with golden flame.

And Vivian Hardwick dueled with Grandfather himself.

The man was ancient—his bones bundles of dried twigs, his head a crow's skull on a gaunt and bobbing neck—but he fought like a demon, great sweeps of his bladed arm followed by crushing blows with his right. His movements were stiff but unstoppable, and Denizen had a horrid image of iron spreading beneath the skin—hardening muscles, weighing down bone, spreading its rigid cancer through vein and sinew.

The old man's face was exultant. *This was it.* The battle he had wanted. The moment he had waited for.

The War That Will Come had come at last.

Vivian's face had no expression at all. Her white cloak billowed out behind her, her hammer a centrifuge spinning her one step ahead of Grandfather's jagged iron edge.

Denizen read it all with a single glance: the shouts and the roars, the violence, the air painted with shock and flame. It was the most he could spare, because the Redemptress of the Croits was coming after him with the power of a natural disaster and the viciousness of a broken heart.

Dust sheeted from the ceiling as wires rebuilt Her, no longer a beautiful and imperious statue but a raptor-witch of spines and claws, a living guillotine descending upon him. Her first blow broke Denizen's hastily summoned shield, sending splinters of iron through his fingers, Her arms thickening to jagged flails that *struck* and *struck* and *struck.*

Her face was a black nest of shrieking strands.

Denizen's world shrank to the half-second gap between each Cant. All that control, all that restraint . . . gone. He felt like laughing. Screaming. He was no longer a boy; he wasn't Crosscaper and books and Soren and sadness. He was a paper lantern with the heart of a star.

His vision popped and crackled as one of his pupils fractured to a crazed web of iron. The cut round his neck had already been cauterized in the heat. White was wreathing round him from where his sweat was turning to steam.

And it wasn't enough.

Denizen knew that, even as he flung himself sideways to avoid Her shrieking lunge. A razor-tipped tentacle whipped past his face and he burned it to cinders, but he was tiring, and tiring was bad, because the Cants didn't care if there was any of him left when they were done.

They just wanted to burn.

Let them. Let them burn. Isn't that what they're for? Isn't that how we've always used them? Killing Tenebrous is our calling. Our duty. Our right.

What could we become in the dark but monsters?

The sorrow in the Redemptress's eyes.

Your father asked me that once. Three years later he was dead. . . .

Denizen turned, the Cants calling, screaming, *shrieking* to be used—

Your kind and mine were never meant to share the same universe. Every time it's happened, it's ended in pain and death. Until us.

You're very sweet.

"STOP!"

She stopped. She actually stopped. The trembling blade of a wire hovered a few centimeters from his eye. There were more that had been aimed at other places. Denizen didn't dare look down.

The battle was still happening; he could hear it, but he didn't care.

He only had eyes for Her.

"You loved. You stole. And we knew fire." He spoke very quickly, because the wires were very close. "The fire of the Endless King. You stole it together."

It was his idea. Her eyes were wide. ***All I did was tell him about it. I thought it was just to keep us safe, but he said that there was so much he could do with it . . . And then the King took humans and made them Knights, arming them with great and powerful words. . . .***

"The Cants," Denizen said. "A better and safer way of channeling the fire and holding back the Cost. How . . . how much of it had taken the First Croit by the time they attacked?"

The Redemptress drew back in on Herself, the chamber shaking as wires retracted, and Denizen could see from the corner of his eye that those fighting nearest to him were turning to stare.

We didn't know . . . we didn't know what the fire would do. . . .

Her voice rose to a snarl.

We just wanted to be LEFT ALONE!

"Of course you did," Denizen said hurriedly. "And then they came, and the castle fell. . . . You were injured . . . you slept . . . and he survived. And he remembered You."

More Knights had stopped fighting now, mainly because the Croits had stopped fighting them.

The Redemptress's voice was small.

We were in love.

"That's what all this is," Denizen said. "That's why he called the iron Transgression. That's why he devoted his entire life to building a dynasty that would protect You."

He took a deep breath.

"Survivor's guilt. He loved You, and he lost You, and all this is the story he told himself to take that pain away. He thought it was his fault."

The Redemptress began to keen, clutching Her head with melted jags of hands.

IT WASN'T SUPPOSED TO BE LIKE THIS!

"No," Denizen said. "I know it wasn't." Tenebrous

were impermanent, malleable. How much of Her ambition, Her anger was the First Croit's?

And how much of his was the fire's?

Denizen felt it even now—battering against his rib cage, seeking freedom. She was so close. It could just burn Her and be done with all this. Burn all of them. Who would dare stop it? Who would dare stand in its way?

I would, Denizen thought, and clamped the inferno down. *Because I'm not a monster either.*

"It doesn't have to end like last time. You can just leave. You can be free. Isn't that what he would want?"

Everyone was staring at Denizen now as if he'd gone insane. Which he definitely had.

But he had to try.

"We've all lost people in this war. So it should stop. Please."

Light boiled in the vane-vents of the Hephaestus Knights. Eloquence was shaking, collapsing, but here in this chamber there was only silence and Denizen's words.

"We don't have to lose any more."

The Redemptress looked at him like a lost little girl. She opened Her mouth—

"No!"

And Uriel Croit's scream turned half Her head to flame.

Gold fire leapt from his jaws in a mirror of his sister's Prayer, tearing away scads of burning wire. When that light faded, the boy summoned his sword, flinging it like a spear again and again, scouring the humanity from the Redemptress's scream.

Suddenly more fire found Her—Edifice Greaves leading his Knights in volleys of red and gold. A Hephaestus Knight tangled its fist in a clot of strands and *pulled*, and She jerked to one side in a spray of sparks. Uriel never relented, and every second scream was his sister's name. Grandfather went down under Vivian's fists. Croits were running, screaming, falling. Abucad even turned his fire on the Redemptress Herself.

She didn't fight. Didn't run. She just sank to the floor, curling Her burning body around the shape of someone who wasn't there.

And Denizen stared into Her fire until he was sure his eyes were dry.

35

Flashbulb Souls

There are always those born closer to the light. A curious girl, who swam near the edge of things, who saw the shape of a boy outlined against the sun. His shadow fell across her—

There are always those born closer to the dark. A quiet boy, and sharp, a boy obsessed with edges, who saw the shape of a girl outlined at dusk. Her voice called out to him—

"Tell me your name?"

What are you?

She whispered to him through the skin of the world. She told him of the twilight in which she lived, and the King she was bound to marry, and how much she desired to walk under other skies.

He described the far-off stars to her. He told her of his desire to be a hero, of how darkness was no barrier to his sight, and he was glad of that. Because it brought him to her. She was the only family he'd ever need.

She shared things with him that she could not share with anyone else, because she craved the light.

He shared things with her that he could not share with anyone else, because he was not afraid of the dark.

They fell in love.

They'd run away together.

Nothing would keep them apart.

"If He comes after us, we'll be ready. There must be *something*. Some secret, some weakness to Him!"

He is the King. But there is one thing . . . a weapon. A fire. He stole it. We could . . . we could . . .

She just wanted to be free.

"A weapon . . ."

She led him into the half-twilight of her world.

He drank deep of the fire.

*And the Tene*brae went dark around them.

*The cold near*ly killed him.

And they ran.

There was a spot of iron in his palm.

The King's rage was terrible.

But more than that . . . it was SLY.

Why simply take revenge, when in taking revenge He could ensure that no human would trust a Tenebrous again? Why simply take revenge, when He could arm the humans, set them to guard their own borders so He did not have to?

This is how the mind of a King must work.

"We'll be safe here. Safe from everyone. The things I can do now. The *power.*"

Your . . . your hand. What's happening to you?

Once the fire entered the human realm, it grew in many hearts (there are always those born closer to the dark).

The King found His own warriors and armed them with Cants of His own design, to slow the spread of iron.

Maybe it was right what He had done.

Humans love fire.

And Tenebrous are easily changed.

Her lover had already filled her head with thoughts of rule.

She'd only ever wanted to be free.

Perhaps it was the right order to give.

"Please, my love. Run. I can't—"

I WON'T LEAVE YOU!

A castle fell.

A heart broke in darkness.

And a Family remembered.

She loved.

She stole.

And the world knew fire.

36

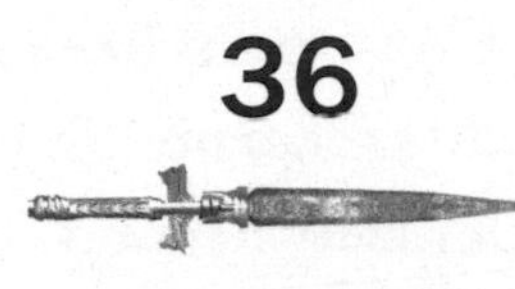

The Color of Royalty

Story finished, Mercy's voice trailed away, her light almost but not quite crafting shadow puppets on Retreat's carved walls. Behind her loomed the Court—the shining bulk of Mocked-By-a-Husband and the sleekly smiling Rout.

Beyond, a simple wooden doorframe once again led to a darker place.

The gathered Knights had not bothered to light torches. Instead, they stood solely in the wan unlight of the *Lucidum* and Mercy herself. The Tenebrous's light was not kind—it gleamed bright on bandages, deepened scars to brushstrokes of black.

Denizen Hardwick had never been so tired in his life. They had come straight to Retreat after a two-day journey back from Eloquence, which had turned out to be on a tiny island off the coast of Scotland. The First Croit and the Redemptress had chosen their hiding place well—it didn't appear on any maps, the water so full of rocks it was like the sea had teeth.

The Art of Apertura would have gotten them back in a heartbeat, but after learning what had happened to Ambrel Croit, Denizen had no desire ever to use that Cant again. Besides, everyone had given more than enough skin already.

For me. Shame had kept him from sleeping on the trip home; shame for those who had been injured, shame for a black shape in golden flames.

This is war, he told himself. It didn't make him feel any better. Despite Mercy's gifted fluency, Denizen had paid his own Cost in the battle. His hands were all iron now, cold and stiff, and his left pupil had fractured. Now he saw the world half in the colors of the real, and half in shifting grays and blues. It was why he was pointedly staring at Vivian's back instead of at the Court.

He was afraid of what he might see.

"You're telling us the Endless King founded the Order of the Borrowed Dark."

Greaves looked as tired as Denizen, but his back was straight, his voice as rich and commanding as ever. Maybe it was pride, maybe the simple logic of not looking weak in front of predators. But the first thing the Palatine had done after the battle was offer his phone to Denizen for a short, desperately relieved call to

Simon and the others, so he was prepared to give Greaves a pass either way.

Mercy continued.

The Redemptress—Coronus, as we called her—and her lover stole the fire, but such things have a life of their own. What it was in our world is not what it became in yours. Once in one human heart, it spread, blooming in those with a connection to the Tenebrae.

The King could not have his vassals coming to this world and starting their own petty empires, so he armed the Order with the Cants, and they cast Coronus and her lover down. They believed their duty complete . . . and so they found a new one.

"Protecting this world from Tenebrous," Greaves said. Knights at the back were murmuring. The Order's origins had been lost in mystery for centuries. After a certain point, history became story, and story became shadows on a cave wall. There had been too many battles to fight to wonder why they were being fought at all.

Just so.

"And would they?" Greaves said.

Would they what?

"Have started their own *petty* empire," the Palatine said, his tone innocent, his eyes cold. "Was the King really protecting us . . . or just using us to remove the star-crossed lovers who had insulted him so?"

Would you like to ask him yourself?

Denizen didn't know a lot about politics, but he could tell a veiled rebuke when he heard it. So could Greaves; the Palatine's gaze uneasily flicked to the darkness beyond the door.

The silence stretched, and Denizen placed a hand over his fractured eye to chance a look at Mercy. She had returned to her form of smoke and silver, the hand that had wielded Vivian's stone blade held across her chest as if it pained her. That blade—carved from a Malleus hammer—was anathema to a Tenebrous. Denizen wondered how much damage it had done her, wielding it to save him.

Mocked-By-a-Husband's teardrop head twisted to regard the Palatine.

What will happen to the Croits?

Greaves gave a humorless smile. "We'll look after them. They are our brothers and sisters, after all. The Order is strengthened by their contribution."

It was an optimistic reading of the situation. Some of the Croits had surrendered as soon as it looked like the Redemptress was losing. Others, led by Abucad, had begun helping the Knights as soon as the other hostages were freed.

A couple had escaped and some had fought on. Those were being . . . detained.

Good, Mercy said drily. *Which brings us to our final matter.*

Rout dipped a long arm in the seething darkness of the doorway, withdrawing a long roll of cloth, like a bundled-up carpet. Denizen would have called it black if it wasn't being held against the gap between realities themselves.

The Tenebrous laid down the roll of cloth on the floor at the point where miniature carved knights became featureless, eaten stone. It was hard to tell without looking at Rout properly, which Denizen absolutely did not want to do, but did it seem *uneasy*?

Denizen Hardwick.

Denizen swallowed and began to weave his way through the ranks of Knights. Jack was there, and he smiled grimly as Denizen passed. Vivian gave him the smallest nod and Denizen nodded back. Finally, one of the Hephaestus Knights moved aside, like a continental shelf detaching, and Denizen was suddenly standing beside Edifice Greaves with nothing between him and the Forever Court.

Mocked-By-a-Husband's jaws split open, revealing row after row of jagged glass teeth. Rout leered its oily leer, and two weeks ago Denizen might have cowered.

That was then. This was now.

He took his iron hand away from his iron eye and stared at them—the void-black skein lurking beneath their borrowed forms, animating crystal, flesh, and bone. What was it he had thought, back when he had met his first Tenebrous and Vivian asked him what he had seen?

Darkness. Living darkness.

And then Mercy was in front of him, bathing Denizen with her light.

For your services. For your help. For your valor and your heart . . .

Denizen flushed.

Thank you.

Do I . . . bow or something? Too late—he was already bowing, and far more gracefully than he believed himself capable. From the looks on some of the Knights' faces nearest him, they hadn't believed him capable either.

I can look cool.

Mercy indicated the roll of cloth and Denizen knelt, wobbling a little on his exhausted legs. He gripped one of the folds, half expecting something horrible to happen. *Snakes. Hidden Tenebrous. I don't know. Pins.* The cloth did feel slightly . . . slimy to the touch, as if it hadn't been woven but grown.

He threw back a hem and gasped.

Hammers. A dozen of them, unadorned and bleak, with long wooden hafts and thick iron heads. They weren't pretty or ornate—except for a dark patina of age, they looked as if they could have been picked up in a hardware shop down the road. But Denizen knew they couldn't.

Greaves knelt beside him with a growl of warplate, and then rose, hefting one in each hand. Mocked-By-a-Husband let out an immediate, involuntary hiss, like steam escaping a broken boiler. Mercy drifted backward on some unfelt current, and even Rout's eyes flicked to the doorway behind it.

"Where did you . . ." The Palatine's voice held an uncharacteristic hint of awe. The Order jealously guarded their store of ancient hammers, weapons forged in antiquity that could destroy even the most potent of Tenebrous. They were the reason Mallei weren't allowed to fight alone, and whole cadres had been deployed to retrieve these precious weapons when they were lost. One hammer was a priceless relic.

And here were twelve—simple, brutal, and inarguably, unstoppably *real*. It might have been Denizen's imagination, but he thought he felt the warping umbra of the Court flicker and diminish, just a little.

Your most potent weapons, Mercy said. ***Kept from you in times of war. This . . . incident may have shown us we have more work to do—on both sides—before true peace can be achieved, but let the return of these relics be a gesture of respect. Of understanding.***

Denizen was having trouble imagining the destructive potential of one of those hammers combined with the power of a suit of Hephaestus Warplate. By the looks on the Tenebrous's faces, they were considering the same. Behind him, Denizen could feel the sudden tension of each of the assembled Knights calculating just how quickly they could make it to the bundle on the floor.

We are not having another battle.

"Thank you," he said, stepping in between Greaves and Mercy. "For helping to rescue me. For everything."

Mercy inclined her head. ***You're welcome.*** She looked around. ***Uriel. He isn't . . .***

Denizen shook his head. He'd been filled in a little by Vivian on the way home. Grudgingly, she had admitted that not only had Mercy's disguise provided their way in to the Shrine, but she had also guided the Knights' use of the Art of Apertura to Eloquence without laying the burden of transporting them all on Uriel.

Another new thing.

It had proved scant comfort. Even Denizen was a little discomfited—although Mercy had shed her Ambrel-form as soon as she could, occasionally a slant of expression would cross that ever-shifting face and Denizen would be suddenly reminded of tears and a sharp point at his throat.

"He . . . declined the invitation," Denizen said. "But I'm sure he's grateful."

Then our business is concluded. For now.

"Is it?" Greaves was still weighing the hammers in his hands. "I don't see Malebranche. He told the Croits where to ambush us. The Endless King's spymaster, working against his daughter. What does that mean for us? For peace?"

Mercy nodded, light dancing beneath the shimmering curtain of her skin. *Malebranche . . . yes. Was it pity that made him help her? Or did he see opportunity? A chance to weaken the King, a chance to cultivate a secret, hidden blade in another world? It is no coincidence that the Croits have worn crows for centuries.*

I think, she said, *I would prefer to view him as someone who once saw two lovers separated, and desired purely to help.*

"You'll excuse me if I find that difficult, considering recent events," Greaves said.

We are not what we were, Mercy said quietly. *Either way, it no longer matters.*

"Doesn't it?" Greaves said.

Mercy lifted her good hand, and a single feather fell from her palm. It had been burned black.

Darkness coiled behind her smile. For the first time, Denizen could see it.

You mind your house, I'll mind mine.

37

The Wrong Kind of Strong

"You could stay, you know."

Denizen Hardwick and Uriel Croit sat on the curb outside Seraphim Row. Denizen had his head tilted back as far as it could go without dislocating something. The sun was warm on his skin, and he felt like he could sit there forever, reminding himself that there was such a thing as wind, and light, and growth.

His neck hurt. Accidental cauterization was an occupational hazard of being a Knight. He'd have a scar for the rest of his life, and there was the faintest trace of hoarseness in his voice now, as though he were constantly in need of clearing his throat.

"I can't," Uriel said. One of the Knights had used the Bellows Subventum, the Cant of healing, on his fractured rib. Every so often, he'd press his hand against it, as if surprised not to find pain. "Some of the Family want to be Knights. That's their choice. And it's been so long since any of us were given a choice at all. But it's not for me. Not yet."

Vivian and Greaves stood farther up the driveway, locked in quiet conversation. Without looking, Denizen knew that Vivian would have one eye on them. She hadn't moved more than six meters from him since they'd been reunited.

There were stranger families out there.

"Then what?" Denizen said.

"My uncle's going to help me track down the Croits that fled so we can help them," Uriel said. "Try and bring our Family properly into the world. But before that . . . I'm going to find my sister."

Denizen's eyebrows lifted. "I thought . . ."

Weary determination made Uriel look ten years older than he was. "There's a chance she's alive. A small chance, but still. The . . . Mercy said she would do whatever she could to locate her. And if she's in that world, or this world . . . I will do anything to bring her back."

He let out a long and ragged sigh.

"Even if it's just to bury her."

He rose to his feet. A black jeep was coming round the corner and, as it idled to a halt, Uriel picked up his bag and approached it.

Denizen frowned. "You're going with Greaves?"

"Just for a little while," Uriel said. "One thing I have to do before I leave."

"Listen," Denizen said. "If you ever need anything . . .

you know where we are." He stuck out his hand. Uriel stared for a moment, like he wasn't sure what it was for, and then shook it.

He paused, just for a moment.

"There is one thing you can do."

"What?"

"Before the battle, I had to spend an hour with . . . with Mercy. I had to describe Ambrel to her. We had to build a picture for her to imitate. It . . ." Uriel's voice shook a little before he straightened it out. "It hurt to see it. Copy after copy, and me standing there saying, *A little taller, nose a little longer*. And I don't know—maybe she picked up on it, or maybe she was thinking of the hate I had . . . have for the Redemptress, but that's when she told me Ambrel could still be alive and she might be able to help."

"But that's . . . good, isn't it?"

"Denizen—I saw what She did to my Family, what my Family did to themselves . . . all out of some warped sense of obligation. All out of debt. And now I'm right back where I started." The rage and loss in Uriel's face made Denizen's iron eye itch. "Be careful who you think you owe."

It was a long and thoughtful walk back up the driveway. When Denizen reached the others, Greaves was smiling, watching the sun in its slow climb over the gargoyles above.

"I've always liked Dublin," he said. "I don't visit enough."

Vivian had no expression on her face. Neither did Denizen.

It was an obscene hour in the morning. Denizen had no idea how long he'd been awake. Part of him wanted to go inside and rouse Simon and the others, but he knew they'd immediately want the whole story, and he wasn't ready for that.

Greaves held out his hand, and Denizen shook it, trying not to let Frown No. 5 twist his features *too* much.

"Well, nothing particularly went to plan," the Palatine said. "But Mercy seems to have a good head on her shoulders. I guess we'll see what tomorrow brings."

"What about the Long Room?" Denizen asked. "Surely people are going to wonder—"

Greaves waved a hand. "People wonder things all the time. There are currently eighteen theories doing the rounds in various media outlets, ranging from *publicity stunt* to *gas leak*. One blogger is very sure that it was aliens. We could go and deny things—Trinity certainly is—but you can't convince people that *nothing* happened. I generally find the best course of action is to convince them that *everything* happened. Several of the best theories were"—he cleared his throat—"suggested by us. None are even a tiny bit close to the truth."

"And the Croits?" Vivian asked. Distaste had turned her voice flat and cold.

"Oh, they're dying to get sworn in. Safer magic and a chance to strike back at the monsters that ruined their family? People want purpose, and you'd be astonished how easy it is to redirect fanaticism."

He said it so casually, as if more than a millennium of misery had turned out to be icing on the cake. Denizen couldn't help himself. "Things worked out pretty well for you, then?" he said, struggling to keep his tone neutral.

Greaves gave him a self-satisfied smile. "For us, Denizen. For the Order. Victories are opportunities. If I see a chance to achieve several things at once, why not take it?" His smile grew sharper. "And, speaking of victories, shall we have a discussion about the skills you displayed sending us young Uriel? And fighting the Redemptress?"

Denizen froze. It had taken every scrap of his fluency with the Cants to keep himself alive. He hadn't really had time to think about discretion.

"We don't need to talk about it now," Greaves said, turning to Vivian. "Not when I'm seconding Denizen to the Office of the Palatine so we can adequately and . . . honestly explore your relationship with the daughter of the Endless King."

DON'T BLUSH. DON'T BLUSH.

"Capital idea," Vivian said.

“What?” Greaves and Denizen said together.

“Office of the Palatine,” Vivian said. “Sounds great. When do I start?”

“What?”

Greaves was a master at controlling his expressions, but there was nothing controlled about the outrage on his face. Vivian didn’t seem to notice. Instead, she was staring off into space, ticking off items on her fingers, an uncharacteristically wide-eyed look of innocence on her face.

“Obviously, you’d have to be deposed first, but I’d wager the revelation that you diverted Order resources in a time of crisis to spying on a thirteen-year-old boy would raise a few eyebrows back at Daybreak. And the job has been offered to me before.”

“Vivian,” Greaves said, low and dangerous. “You wouldn’t.”

Vivian looked him dead in the eye, and there was more emotion on the battered facade of Seraphim Row.

“Edifice Greaves, you know exactly what I do to things that hurt my family.”

Greaves flinched, and then turned to Denizen, the path of least terrifyingness.

“And what about you, Denizen? You’re content to stay out here, fighting petty battles?”

“What can I say?” Denizen replied, giving Greaves his best Malleus face. “I guess I’m just a blunt instrument.”

Greaves scowled.

"This conversation isn't over." He began to stalk down the driveway. "You'll have new Knights in the next few weeks. Try to keep them alive this time."

Her eyes narrowed.

"And I'm reassigning Jack to you. I suspect he'd like to stay." His gaze held Denizen's for a moment. "And he'll give you Grey's address. If you still want to write to him."

"Oh," Denizen said. "Thank you."

The Palatine nodded. "Until next time."

"Yep," Denizen said.

"Mmm," Vivian added.

It was only when the jeep had disappeared round the corner that Denizen turned to his mother.

"I don't think he likes us very much."

Denizen had never heard Vivian snigger before. It was a terribly undignified snigger, and Denizen found himself suddenly quite fond of it.

"My heart bleeds," she said. "Tea?"

They went to make tea. The kitchen was deserted and, for a while, Denizen and his mother were lost in the simple ritual of getting cups and saucers and milk. The kettle shrilled and, as the water turned dark, Denizen said what he should have said the night they'd killed the Clockwork Three.

"I need your help."

Vivian put down the kettle.

"I'm afraid of what I'm able to do," he continued, watching steam waft from his tea. "The Cants aren't just words. It's like they're alive. I can feel them in my head. Pushing at me. Wanting to be used. There have been so many times where I've longed to just cut loose—"

Even as he spoke, he could feel movement in the back of his head. He had used them more in the last week than ever before, and they seemed to have been *strengthened* by this, coming closer and closer to the surface.

"Teach me better control. Help me find out what's happening to me. Because I can't do it myself, and I can't keep walling myself off from it forever. And I want . . ."

He sniffed. He felt very young, and very old, and very, very tired.

"And I want to be able to talk to you. Talk to you properly. About Dad. And about us."

Denizen had seen his mother angry, and he'd seen her . . . well, angry was the main one. He'd never seen her at a loss for words.

Eventually, she spoke. "Do you know why Jack left?"

"He told me you'd sent him as . . . a double agent, or something."

She sighed heavily. "He's very kind. I did, yes. But Greaves believed it was because I was too cold and unfeeling for Jack to follow and . . . he wasn't wrong. When Corinne died and Grey . . . fell, I knew I should have been there for him. For you too, all of you.

"Jack came to me to talk, after the Three. But his loss was too close to mine. So I did what I always do—I withdrew. I retreated. I've never been good at letting people in. Except your father, and that was so natural that I barely felt it happening. One day he was just . . . there."

She gave Denizen a half-smile. "Hardwicks aren't great with emotion. We're our own worst enemies, really." She paused. "Which, considering our vocation, is actually rather impressive."

Denizen's look was withering. "Are you . . . *proud* of that?"

Vivian shrugged, clasping her hands round her own cup.

"Perhaps we can . . ."

She hesitated.

"Perhaps we can help each other."

Denizen smiled hesitantly. "I'd like that."

"Maybe we'll be lucky," she continued ruefully, "and some good will come of the Concilium. Humans and Tenebrous *working* together—I never thought I'd see the day." She gave her son a sharp glance. "I told you to keep that blade close."

"I did," Denizen protested, before raising an eyebrow. "Would you really have deposed the Palatine of the Order of the Borrowed Dark for me?"

Vivian's cheeks had gone pink. "Well, I guess we'll never know now, will we?" She smiled to herself. "Let's concentrate on fixing this house first—"

"You mind your house, I'll mind mine," Denizen said suddenly. All the color had drained from his face.

"What?"

"That's what she said. Mercy. *You mind your house, I'll mind mine.*"

Vivian frowned. "And?"

"Not her father's house," Denizen whispered.

Mine.

EPILOGUE

FAMILY

URIEL CROIT STOOD JUST out of the reach of the street-light's glow.

The street was aggressively forgettable—just a row of identical redbrick houses adorned with wreaths of ivy like freshly dug graves. Despite its anonymity, he'd had no trouble finding it. The Family kept a very close eye on its unFavored. It was how Grandfather had caught Uriel's parents so quickly the first time.

He shifted uncomfortably in his Outside clothes. He'd have to get used to them. Eloquence was rubble now. The architecture of his childhood had collapsed without black wire to support it. Nothing had been saved.

Not yet.

The door was white. Uriel's knuckles rang against it.

I could go.

I could just go.

Just go.

He had half turned away when the door opened, painting him in warm yellow light.

"Uriel."

She had bright green eyes, her hair the patchwork gray and black of a Croit. He was older, shorter, chubby, and he clutched her waist with the kind of fussy protectiveness that made Uriel at once doubt their history and be certain of it. He knew that look. It was the look of someone who'd do anything they could to keep their family safe.

"Hello, Mother. Hello, Father."

He wasn't given room for anything else. A whirlwind of hugs, of affection, of contact. He had to hold himself back from fighting it. It wasn't the way he was used to being touched.

Their kitchen was bright and warm. Little notes to each other. Paintings. They'd built a life here. A life together.

Uriel's mother pressed a cup of tea into his hands.

"Where's Ambrel?" she asked.

He dropped the cup. The sound was very loud, and Uriel Croit stared at his fingers—trembling, unable to close. Too numb. Too cold.

Things so easily become a ruin.

A FURTHER SECRET ABOUT WRITERS . . .

. . . IS THAT EVERYTHING NEEDS a second draft. You miss details the first time round. Words are forgotten, or move, or the ending changes the beginning. (I'm looking at you, Ambrel Croit.) Though this book was a continuation of the same story, the telling of it became a very different beast, and I have new people to thank.

Firstly, always, my family for their constant championing of me and this nonsense job I do. Special thanks in particular to my dad, now the terror of many a rural bookshop. Thank you for carrying that newspaper clipping in your pocket.

To the wizard-seraph-rock-star-supernova agents of Darley Anderson—you are tireless and wise. Clare, Sheila, Mary, Emma, thank you for pens, penguins, advice, curries, Tenebris—everything, basically. Thank you for getting me here.

Ben, Caroline, Wendy—thank you for your patience and your guidance and your patience and also did I mention you're really patient? (They would have edited that sentence.) You guys are my *Intueor Lucidum*. Thank you for helping me to see in the dark. To my stellar publicity team—Tania, Claire, Jess, Vicky, Hannah, Emily, and Annabel—the Cants that shape the fire. Thank you for being magic.

This book would not be the dark, strange, sad thing it is without the friendship and tutelage of three of the most talented writers I've ever had the misfortune to read. Graham Tugwell, Deirdre Sullivan, and Sarah Maria Griff—heroes, monsters, Doomsburies. Let's be terrible forever.

A book never comes from a single place, but I owe a special debt to Dr. Sarah J. Nangle for the Croits. Thank you for your insight, your knowledge, your advice and support. I owe Siobhan for letting me skulk around the Long Room picturing the whole place on fire, Melissa for banning chats and burgers, Dearbháil for portraits, Shannon for awkward door-slams, Arvind for *more* sword fights, Roe for nonfiction, and Kerrie O'Brien for poetry.

Finally, thank you to honorary Mallei Vanessa O'Loughlin and Rick O'Shea, and to all those who keep letting me stand in front of a mic or a classroom—Elaina, Niamh, Aidan, William and Laura, Annie, Claire, and many, many more.

And *finally* finally, thank you for reading. We're very nearly there.

Two down . . .

One to go.